This was her o~~~ ... time she had every right to put her lips on this man, and she wasn't missing the opportunity.

The other people in the room vanished as she reached out and flattened her palms on Jonas's lapels. He leaned in and put one hand on her jaw, guiding it upward. His warmth bled through her skin, enlivening it, and then her brain ceased to function as his mouth touched hers.

Instantly, that wasn't enough and she pressed forward, seeking more of him. The kiss deepened as his lips aligned properly and, oh, yes, that was it.

Her crush exploded into a million little pieces as she tasted what it was like for Jonas to kiss her. That nice, safe attraction she had been so sure she could hide gained a whole lot of teeth, slicing through her midsection with sharp heat. The dimensions of sensation opened around her, giving her a tantalizing glimpse of how truly spectacular it would feel if he didn't stop.

But he did stop, stepping back so quickly that Viv almost toppled over, but he caught her forearms and held her steady... though he looked none too steady himself, his gaze enigmatic and heated in a way she'd never witnessed before.

* * *

Best Friend Bride

BEST FRIEND BRIDE

BY
KAT CANTRELL

First Published in Great Britain 2017
By Mills & Boon, an imprint of HarperCollins*Publishers*
1 London Bridge Street, London, SE1 9GF

© 2017 Kat Cantrell

ISBN: 978-0-263-92828-0

51-0717

Our policy is to use papers that are natural, renewable and recyclable products and made from wood grown in sustainable forests. The logging and manufacturing processes conform to the legal environmental regulations of the country of origin.

Printed and bound in Spain
by CPI, Barcelona

USA TODAY bestselling author **Kat Cantrell** read her first Mills & Boon novel in third grade and has been scribbling in notebooks since she learned to spell. She's a Harlequin So You Think You Can Write winner and a Romance Writers of America Golden Heart® Award finalist. Kat, her husband and their two boys live in north Texas.

One

Jonas Kim would typically describe himself as humble, but even he was impressed with the plan he'd conceived to outwit the smartest man he knew—his grandfather. Instead of marrying Sun, the nice woman from a prominent Korean family, a bride Grandfather had picked out, Jonas had proposed to Viviana Dawson. She was nice, too, but also his friend and, more importantly, someone he could trust not to contest the annulment when it came time to file it.

Not only was Viv amazing for agreeing to this ridiculous idea, she made excellent cupcakes. It was a win all the way around. Though he could have done without the bachelor party. So not his thing.

At least no strippers had shown up. Yet.

He and his two best buddies had flown to Vegas this morning and though Jonas had never been to the city of sin before, he was pretty sure it wouldn't take much to have naked women draped all over the suite. He could think of little he'd like less. Except for marrying Sun. That he would hate, and not only because she'd been selected on his behalf. Sun was a disaster waiting to happen that would happen to someone else because Jonas was marrying Viv tomorrow in what would go down as the greatest favor one friend had ever done for another.

"Sure you wanna do this?" Warren asked as he popped open the bottle of champagne.

Also a bachelor party staple that Jonas could have done without, but his friends would just laugh and make jokes about how Jonas needed to loosen up, despite being well aware that he had been raised in an ultra-conservative family. Grandfather had a lot of traditional ideas about how a CEO should act, and Jonas hadn't landed that job, not yet. Besides, there was nothing wrong with having a sense of propriety.

"Which part?" Jonas shot back. "The bachelor party or inviting you morons along?"

Hendrix, the other moron, grinned and took his glass of champagne from Warren. "You can't get married without a bachelor party. That would be sad."

"It's not a real wedding. Therefore, one would assume that the traditions don't really have to be observed."

Warren shook his head. "It is a real wedding. You're going to marry this woman simply to get out of having a different bride. Hence my question. Are you sure this is the only way? I don't get why you can't just tell your grandfather thanks but no thanks. Don't let him push you around."

They'd literally been having the exact same argument for two weeks. Grandfather still held the reins of the Kim empire closely to his chest. In Korea. If Jonas had any hope of Grandfather passing those reins to him so he could move the entire operation to North Carolina, he had to watch his step. Marrying a Korean woman from a powerful family would only solidify Jonas's ties to a country that he did not consider his home.

"I respect my elders," Jonas reminded Warren mildly. "And I also respect that Sun's grandfather and my grandfather are lifelong friends. I can't expose her or it might disrupt everything."

Sun had been thrilled with the idea of marrying Jonas; she had a secret—and highly unsuitable—lover she didn't want anyone to find out about and she'd pounced on the idea of a husband to mask her affair. Meanwhile, their grandfathers were cackling over their proposed business merger once the two families were united in marriage.

Jonas wanted no part of any of that. Better to solve the problem on his own terms. If he was already married, no one could expect him to honor his grandfather's agreement. And once the merger had gone through, he and Viv could annul their marriage and go on with Jonas's integrity intact.

It was brilliant. Viv was the most awesome person on the planet for saving his butt from being burned in this deal. Tomorrow, they'd say some words, sign a piece of paper and poof. No more problems.

"Can you guys just be happy that you got a trip to Vegas out of this and shut up?" Jonas asked, and clinked glasses with the two men he'd bonded with freshman year at Duke University.

Jonas Kim, Hendrix Harris and Warren Garinger had

become instant friends when they'd been assigned to the same project group along with Marcus Powell. The four teenagers had raised a lot of hell together—most of which Jonas had watched from the sidelines—and propped each other up through everything the college experience could throw at them. Until Marcus had fallen head over heels for a cheerleader who didn't return his love. The aftermath of that still affected the surviving three members of their quartet to this day.

"Can't. You said no strippers," Hendrix grumbled, and downed his champagne in one practiced swallow. "Really don't see the point of a bachelor party in Las Vegas if you're not going to take full advantage of what's readily available."

Jonas rolled his eyes. "Like you don't have a wide array of women back in Raleigh who would get naked for you on demand."

"Yeah, but I've already seen them," he argued with a wink. "There are thousands of women whose breasts I've yet to ogle and I've been on my best behavior at home. What happens in Vegas doesn't affect my mom's campaign, right?"

Hendrix's mom was running for governor of North Carolina and had made him swear on a stack of Bibles that he would not do anything to jeopardize her chances. For Hendrix, that meant a complete overhaul of his social life, and he was feeling the pinch. So far, his uncanny ability to get photographed with scantily clad women hadn't surfaced, but he'd just begun his vow of chastity, so there was plenty of opportunity to cause a scandal if he really put his mind to it.

"Maybe we could focus on the matter at hand?" Warren suggested, and ran his fingers through his wavy brown hair as he plopped down on the love seat near the floor-to-ceiling glass wall of the Sky Suite they'd booked at the Aria. The dizzying lights of Vegas spread out in a panoramic view sixty stories below.

"Which is?"

Warren pointed his glass at Jonas. "You're getting married. Despite the pact."

The pact.

After the cheerleader had thoroughly eviscerated Marcus, he'd faded further and further away until eventually, he'd opted to end his pain permanently. In the aftermath of his death, the three friends had sworn to never let love destroy them as it had Marcus. The reminder sobered them all.

"Hey, man. The pact is sacred," Jonas said with a scowl. "But we never vowed to remain single the rest of our lives. Just that we'd never let a woman take us down like that. Love is the problem, not marriage."

Once a year, the three of them dropped whatever they were doing and spent the evening honoring the memory of their late friend. It was part homage, part reiteration of the pact. The profoundly painful incident had affected them in different ways, but no one would argue that Warren had taken his roommate's suicide harder than anyone save Marcus's mother.

That was the only reason Jonas gave him a pass for the insult. Jonas had followed the pact to the letter, which was easier than he'd ever let on. First of all, a promise meant something to him.

Second, Jonas never got near a woman he could envision falling in love with. That kind of loss of control... the concept made his skin crawl. Jonas had too much to lose to let a woman destroy everything he'd worked for.

Warren didn't look convinced. "Marriage is the gateway, my friend. You can't put a ring on a woman's finger and expect that she won't start dreaming of romantic garbage."

"Ah, but I can," Jonas corrected as he let Hendrix top off his champagne. "That's why this plan is so great. Viv knows the score. We talked about exactly what was going to happen. She's got her cupcake business and has no room for a boyfriend, let alone a permanent husband. I wouldn't have asked her to do this for me if she wasn't a good friend."

A friend who wasn't interested in taking things deeper. That was the key and the only reason Jonas had continued their friendship for so long. If there was even a possibility of getting emotional about her, he'd have axed their association immediately, just like he had with every other woman who posed a threat to the tight rein he held on his heart.

Hendrix drank straight from the champagne bottle to get the last few drops, his nearly colorless hazel eyes narrowed in contemplation as he set the empty bottle on the coffee table. "If she's such a good friend, how come we haven't met her?"

"Really? It's confusing to you why I'd want to keep her away from the man voted most likely to corrupt a nun four years in a row?"

With a grin, Hendrix jerked his head at Warren. "So Straight and Narrow over there should get the thumbs-up. Yet she's not allowed to meet him either?"

Jonas shrugged. "I'll introduce you at the ceremony tomorrow."

When it would be unavoidable. How was he supposed to explain that Viv was special to a couple of knuckleheads like his friends? From the first moment he'd met her, he'd been drawn to her sunny smile and generosity.

The little bakery near the Kim Building called Cupcaked had come highly recommended by Jonas's admin, so he'd stopped in to pick up a thank-you for his staff. As he'd stood in the surprisingly long line to place his order, a pretty brown-haired woman had exited from the back. She'd have captured his interest regardless, but when she'd stepped outside to slip a cupcake to a kid on the street who'd been standing nose pressed to her window for the better part of fifteen minutes, Jonas couldn't resist talking to her.

He'd been dropping in to get her amazing lemon cupcakes for almost a year now. Sometimes Viv let him take her for coffee to someplace where she didn't have to jump behind the counter on the fly, and occasionally she dropped by the Kim Building to take Jonas to lunch.

It was an easy, no-pressure friendship that he valued because there was no danger of him falling in too deep when she so clearly wasn't interested in more. They weren't sleeping together, and that kind of relationship wouldn't compute to his friends.

Didn't matter. He was happy with the status quo. Viv was doing him a favor and in return, he'd make it up to her with free business consulting advice for the rest of her life. After all, Jonas had singlehandedly launched Kim Electronics in the American market and had grown revenue to the tune of $4.7 billion last year. She could do worse than to have his undivided attention on her balance sheet whenever she asked, which he'd gladly make time for.

All he had to do was get her name on a marriage

certificate and lie low until his grandfather's merger went through. Then Viv could go back to her single cupcake-baker status and Jonas could celebrate dodging the bullet.

Warren's point about marriage giving a girl ideas about love and romance was pure baloney. Jonas wasn't worried about sticking to the pact. Honor was his moral compass, as it was his grandfather's. Love represented a loss of control that other men might fall prey to, but not Jonas. He would never betray his friends or the memory of the one they'd lost.

All he had to do was marry a woman who had no romantic feelings for him.

Viviana Dawson had dreamed about her wedding day a bunch of times and not once had she imagined the swirl in her gut, which could only be described as a cocktail of nerves and *holy crap*.

Jonas was going to be her husband in a few short minutes and the anticipation of *what if* was killing her.

Jonas Kim had asked her to marry him. *Jonas*. The man who had kept Viv dateless for almost a year because who could measure up to perfection? Nobody.

Oh, sure, he'd framed it all as a favor and she'd accepted under the premise that they'd be filing for annulment ASAP. But still. She'd be Mrs. Kim for as long as it lasted.

Which might be short indeed if he figured out she had a huge crush on him.

He wasn't going to figure it out. Because *oh, my God*. If he did find out…

Well, he couldn't. It would ruin their friendship for one. And also? She had no business getting into a serious relationship, not until she figured out how to do and be whatever the opposite was of what she'd been doing and being with men thus far in her adult dating life.

Her sisters called it clingy. She called it committed. Men called it quits.

Jonas was the antidote to all that.

The cheesy chapel wasn't anything close to the venue of her fantasies, but she'd have married Jonas in a wastewater treatment plant if he'd asked her to. She pushed open the door, alone and not too happy about it. In retrospect, she should have insisted one of her sisters come to Vegas with her. Maybe to act as her maid of honor.

She could really use a hand to hold right about now, but no. She hadn't told any of her sisters she was getting married, not even Grace, who was closest to her in age and had always been her confidante. Well, until Grace had disappeared into her own family in much the same fashion as their other two sisters had done.

Viv was the cute pony in the Dawson family stable of Thoroughbreds. Which was the whole reason Viv hadn't mentioned her quickie Vegas wedding to a man who'd never so much as kissed her.

She squared her shoulders. A fake marriage was exactly what she wanted. Mostly.

Well, of course she wanted a real marriage eventually. But this one would get her into the secret club that the rest of the married Dawson sisters already belonged to. Plus, Jonas needed her. Total win across the board.

The chapel was hushed and far more sacrosanct than she'd have expected in what was essentially the drive-through lane of weddings. The quiet scuttled across her skin, turning it clammy. She was really doing this. It had all been conceptual before. Now it was real.

Could you have a nervous breakdown and recover in less than two minutes? She didn't want to miss a second of her wedding. But she might need to sit down first.

And then everything fell away as she saw Jonas in a slim-fitting dark suit that showcased his wiry frame. His energy swept out and engulfed her, as it always had from that first time she'd turned to see him standing outside her shop, his attention firmly on her instead of the sweet treats in the window.

Quick with a smile, quicker with a laugh, Jonas Kim's beautiful angular face had laced Viv's dreams many a night. He had a pretty rocking body, too. He kept in great shape playing racquetball with his friends, and she'd spent hours picturing him shirtless, his chest glistening as he swung a racket. In short, he was a truly gorgeous individual who she could never study long enough to sate herself.

Jonas's dark, expressive eyes lit up as he caught sight of her and he crossed the small vestibule to sweep her into a hug. Her arms came up around his waist automatically. How, she had no idea, when this was literally the first time he'd ever touched her.

He even smelled gorgeous.

And now would be a great time to unstick her tongue from the roof of her mouth. "Hey."

Wonderful. They'd had spirited debates on everything from the travesty of pairing red wine with fish to the merits of the beach over the mountains. Shakespeare, *The Simpsons*. But put her in the arms of the man she'd been salivating over for months and the power of speech deserted her.

He stepped back. Didn't help. And now she was cold.

"I'm so glad you're here," he said, his smooth voice

ruffling all her nerve endings in the most delicious way. Despite being born in North Carolina, he had almost no accent. Good thing. He was already devastating enough.

"Can't have a wedding with no bride," she informed him. Oh, thank God, she could still talk, Captain Obvious moment aside. "Am I dressed okay for a fake marriage?"

His intense eyes honed in on her. "You look amazing. I love that you bought a new dress for this."

Yeah, that was why she passed up the idiots who hit on her with lame lines like "Give me your number and I'll frost your cupcakes for you." Jonas paid attention to her and actually noticed things like what she wore. She'd picked out this yellow dress because he'd mentioned once that he liked the color.

Which made it all the more strange that he'd never clued in that she had a huge thing for him. She was either better at hiding it than she'd had a right to hope for, or he knew and mercifully hadn't mentioned it.

Her pulse sped out of control. He didn't know, she repeated silently. Maybe a little desperately.

There was no way he could know. He'd never have asked her to do this marriage favor otherwise.

She'd been faking it this long. No reason to panic.

"I wanted to look good," she told him. *For you.* "For the pictures."

He smiled. "Mission accomplished. I want you to meet Warren."

Jonas turned, absently putting his arm around her and oh, that was nice. They were a unit already, and it had seemed to come so naturally. Did he feel it, too?

That's when she realized there was another man in the vestibule. Funny, she hadn't even noticed him, though she supposed women must fawn all over him, with those cheekbones and that expensive haircut. She held out her hand to the friend Jonas had talked endlessly about. "Nice to meet you. Jonas speaks very highly of you."

"Likewise," Warren said with a cryptic glance at Jonas. "And I'm sure whatever he's told you is embellished."

Doubtful when she didn't need Jonas's help to know that the energy drink company his friend ran did very well. You couldn't escape the logo for Flying Squirrel no matter where you looked.

Jonas waved that off with a smirk. "Whatever, man. Where's Hendrix?"

"Not my turn to babysit him." Warren shrugged, pulling out his phone. "I'll text him. He'll be here."

Somehow, Jonas seemed to have forgotten his arm was still around Viv's waist and she wasn't about to remind him. But then he guided her toward the open double doors that led to the interior of the chapel with firm fingers. Well, if this almost-intimacy was part of the wedding package, she'd take it.

"I'm not waiting on his sorry ass," Jonas called over his shoulder. "There are a thousand more couples in line behind us and I'm not losing my spot."

Warren nodded and waved, still buried in his phone.

"Some friends," Jonas murmured to her with a laugh, his head bent close. He was still taller than her even when she wore heels, but it had never been as apparent as it was today, since she was still tucked against his side as if he never meant to let go. "This is an important day in my life and you see how they are."

"I'm here." For as long as he needed her.

Especially if he planned to put his arm around her a whole bunch more. His warm palm on her waist had oddly settled her nerves. And put a whole different kind of butterfly south of her stomach.

Wow, was it hot in here or what? She resisted the urge to fan herself as the spark zipped around in places that *could not* be so affected by this man's touch.

His smile widened. "Yes, you are. Have I mentioned lately how much I appreciate that? The slot for very best friend in the whole world has just become yours, since clearly you're the only one who deserves it."

As reminders went, it was both brutal and necessary. This was a favor. Not an excuse for a man to get handsy with her.

Fine. Good. She and Jonas were friends, which was perfect. She had a habit of pouring entirely too much of herself into a man who didn't return her level of commitment. Mark had stuck it out slightly longer than Zachary, and she didn't like to think about how quickly she'd shed Gary and Judd. A sad commentary on her twenties that she'd had fewer boyfriends than fingers on one hand.

A favor marriage was the best kind because she knew exactly how it would end. It was like reading the last page of the book ahead of time, and for someone who loved surprise flowers but hated surprise discussions that started with "we have to talk," the whole thing sounded really great.

No pressure. No reason to get clingy and drive Jonas away with her neediness. She could be independent and witty and build her confidence with this marriage. It was a practice run with all the best benefits. He'd already asked her to move into his penthouse on Boylan

Avenue. As long as she didn't mess up and let on how much she wanted to cling to every last inch of the man, it was all good.

Back on track, she smiled at the friend she was about to marry. They were friends with benefits that had nothing to do with sex. A point she definitely needed to keep in the forefront of her brain.

A lady in a puke-green suit approached them and verified they were the happy couple, then ran down the order of the ceremony. If this had been a real marriage, Viv might be a little disappointed in the lack of fanfare. In less than a minute, traditional organ music piped through the overhead speakers and the lady shoved a drooping bouquet at Viv. She clutched it to her chest, wondering if she'd get to keep it. One flower was enough. She'd press it into a book as a reminder of her wedding to a great man who treated her with nothing but kindness and respect.

Jonas walked her down the aisle, completely unruffled. Of course. Why would he be nervous? This was all his show and he'd always had a supreme amount of confidence no matter the situation.

His friend Warren stood next to an elderly man holding a Bible. Jonas halted where they'd been told to stand and glanced at her with a reassuring smile.

"Dearly beloved," the man began and was immediately interrupted by a commotion at the back. Viv and Jonas both turned to see green-suit lady grappling with the door as someone tried to get into the room.

"Sir, the ceremony has already started," she called out to no avail as the man who must be Hendrix Harris easily shoved his way inside and joined them at the front.

Yep. He looked just like the many, many pictures she'd seen of him strewn across the media, and not just because his mother was running for governor. Usually he had a gorgeous woman glued to his side and they were doing something overly sensual, like kissing as if no one was watching.

"Sorry," he muttered to Jonas. His eyes were bloodshot and he looked like he'd slept in his expensively tailored shirt and pants.

"Figured you'd find a way to make my wedding memorable," Jonas said without malice, because that's the kind of man he was. She'd have a hard time being so generous with someone who couldn't be bothered to show up on time.

The officiant started over, and in a few minutes, she and Jonas exchanged vows. All fake, she chanted to herself as she promised to love and cherish.

"You may kiss the bride," the officiant said with so little inflection that it took a minute for it to sink in that he meant *Jonas* could kiss *her*. Her pulse hit the roof.

Somehow, they hadn't established what would happen here. She glanced at Jonas and raised a brow. Jonas hesitated.

"This is the part where you kiss her, idiot," Hendrix muttered with a salacious grin.

This was her one chance, the only time she had every right to put her lips on this man, and she wasn't missing the opportunity. The other people in the room vanished as she flattened her palms on Jonas's lapels. He leaned in and put one hand on her jaw, guiding it upward. His warmth bled through her skin, enlivening it, and then her brain ceased to function as his mouth touched hers.

Instantly, that wasn't enough and she pressed forward, seeking more of him. The kiss deepened as his lips aligned properly and oh, yes, that was it.

Her crush exploded into a million little pieces as she tasted what it was like to kiss Jonas. That nice, safe attraction she had been so sure she could hide gained teeth, slicing through her midsection with sharp heat. The dimensions of sensation opened around her, giving her a tantalizing glimpse of how truly spectacular it would feel if he didn't stop.

But he did stop, stepping back so quickly that she almost toppled over. He caught her forearms and held her steady…though he looked none too steady himself, his gaze enigmatic and heated in a way she'd never witnessed before.

Clearly that experience had knocked them both for a loop. What did you say to someone you'd just kissed and who you wanted to kiss again, but really, that hadn't been part of the deal?

"That was nice," Jonas murmured. "Thanks."

Nice was not the word on her mind. So they were going to pretend that hadn't just happened, apparently.

Good. That was exactly what they should do. Treat it like a part of the ceremony and move on.

Except her lips still tingled, and how in the world was Jonas just standing there holding her hand like nothing momentous had occurred? She needed to learn the answer to that, stat. Especially if they were going to be under the same roof. Otherwise, their friendship—and this marriage—would be toast the second he clued in to how hot and bothered he got her. He'd specifically told her that he could trust her because they were *friends* and he needed her to be one.

"I now pronounce you husband and wife," the officiant intoned, completely oblivious to how the earth had just swelled beneath Viv's feet.

Jonas turned and led her back up the aisle, where they signed the marriage license. They ended up in the same vestibule they'd been in minutes before, but now they were married.

Her signature underneath Jonas's neat script made it official, but as she'd expected, it was just a piece of paper. The kiss, on the other hand? That had shaken her to the core.

How was she going to stop herself from angling for another one?

"Well," Hendrix said brightly. "I'd say this calls for a drink. I'll buy."

Two

Jonas had never thought of his six-thousand-square-foot penthouse condo as small. Until today. It was full of Viviana Dawson. Er, *Kim*. Viviana Kim. She'd officially changed her name at the Department of Motor Vehicles, and soon, she'd have a new driver's license that said she had the legal right to call herself that. By design. His sense of honor wouldn't permit him to outright lie about his relationship with Viv; therefore, she was Mrs. Kim in every sense of the word.

Except one.

The concept was surreal. As surreal as the idea that she was his wife and he could introduce her as such to anyone who asked.

Except for himself apparently because he was having a hard time thinking of her that way no matter how many times he repeated the word *wife* when he glimpsed her through the archway leading to the kitchen. Boxes upon boxes covered every inch of the granite countertops, and though she'd been working on unpacking them for an hour, it looked like she'd barely made a dent.

He should quit skulking around and get in there to help. But he hadn't because he couldn't figure out how to manage the weird vibe that had sprung up between them.

That *kiss*.

It had opened up a Pandora's box that he didn't know how to close. Before, he'd had a sort of objective understanding that Viv was a beautiful woman whose company he enjoyed.

Ever since the ceremony, no more. There was a thin veil of awareness that he couldn't shake. But he needed to. They were living together as *friends* because she'd agreed to a favor that didn't include backing her up against the counter so he could explore her lush mouth.

He liked Viv. Add a previously undiscovered attraction and she was exactly the kind of woman he'd studiously avoided for nearly a decade. The kind he could easily envision taking him deeper and deeper until he was emotionally overwhelmed enough to give up everything.

The problem of course being that he couldn't stop calling her, like he usually did with women who threatened his vow. He'd married this one.

He was being ridiculous. What was he, seventeen? He could handle a little spark between friends, right? Best way to manage that was to ignore it. And definitely not let on that he'd felt something other than friendly ever since kissing her.

All he and Viv had to do was live together until he could convince his grandfather to go through with the merger anyway. Once the two companies signed agreements, neither would back out and Jonas was home free. Since he was covering Viv's rent until then, she could move back into her apartment at that point.

This plan would work, and soon enough, he could look back on it smugly and pinpoint the exact moment when he'd outsmarted his grandfather.

Casually, he leaned on the exposed-brick column between the dining room and the kitchen and crossed his arms like everything was cool between them. It *would* be cool. "What can I do?"

Viv jerked and spun around to face him, eyes wide. "You scared me. Obviously."

Her nervous laugh ruffled his spine. So they were both feeling the weirdness, but it was clearly different weirdness on her side than on his. She was jumpy and nervous, not hot and bothered. He had not seen that coming. That was…not good. "Sorry. I didn't mean to. We've both been living alone for so long that I guess we have to get through an adjustment period."

Which was the opposite of what he'd expected. They'd always been so relaxed with each other. How could they get back to that?

She nodded. "Yes, that's what I've been telling myself."

Was it that bad? Her forlorn voice tripped something inside him and it was not okay that she was uncomfortable around him now. "Best way to adjust is to spend time together. Let me help you put away these…" He grabbed a square glass dish from the counter. "Pans?"

"Pyrex." She smiled and it seemed like it came easier. "I can't imagine you care anything about where I put my bakeware."

He waggled his brows. "That depends on whether that's something you use to make cupcakes or not."

Her cupcakes weren't like the store-bought ones in the hard plastic clamshells. Those tasted like sugared flour with oily frosting. Viv's lemon cupcakes—a flavor he'd never have said he'd like—had a clean, bright taste like she'd captured lemonade in cake form.

"It's not. Casseroles."

"Not a fan of those." He made a face before he thought better of it.

Maybe she loved casseroles and he was insulting her taste. And her cooking skills. But he'd never said one word about her whipping up dinner for him each night, nor did he expect her to. She knew that. Right?

They had so much to learn about each other, especially if they were going to make this marriage seem as real as possible to everyone, except select few people they could trust, like Warren and Hendrix. If word got back to his grandfather that something wasn't kosher, the charade would be over.

And he'd invested way too much in this marriage to let it fail now.

His phone beeped from his pocket, and since the CEO never slept, he handed over the glass dish to check the message.

Grandfather. At 6:00 a.m. Seoul time. Jonas tapped the message. All the blood drained from his head.

"Jonas, what's wrong?" Viv's palm came to rest on his forearm and he appreciated the small bit of comfort even as it stirred things it shouldn't.

"My grandfather. My dad told him that we got married." Because Jonas had asked him to. The whole point had been to circumvent his grandfather's arranged-marriage plan. But this—

"Oh, no. He's upset, isn't he?" Viv worried her lip with her teeth, distracting him for a moment.

"On the contrary," Jonas spit out hoarsely. "He's thrilled. He's so excited to meet you, he got on a plane last night. He's here. In Raleigh. Best part? He talked my dad into having a house party to welcome you into the family. This weekend."

It was a totally unforeseen move. Wily. He didn't believe for a second that his grandfather was thrilled with Jonas's quick marriage or that the CEO of one of the largest conglomerates in Korea had willingly walked away from his board meetings to fly seven thousand miles to meet his new granddaughter-in-law.

This was something else. A test. An "I'll believe it when I see it." Maybe Grandfather scented a whiff of the truth and all it would take was one slipup before he'd pounce. If pressed, Jonas would feel honor bound to be truthful about Viv's role. The marriage could be history before dark.

A healthy amount of caution leaped into Viv's expression. "This weekend? As in we have two days to figure out how to act like a married couple?"

"Now you're starting to see why my face looks like this." He swirled an index finger near his nose, unbelievably grateful that she had instantly realized the problem. "Viv, I'm sorry. I had no idea he was going to do this."

The logistics alone… How could he tell his mom to give them separate bedrooms when they were essentially still supposed to be in the honeymoon phase? He couldn't. It was ludicrous to even think in that direction when what he should be doing was making a list of all the ways this whole plan was about to fall apart. So he could mitigate each and every one.

"Hey."

Jonas glanced up as Viv laced her fingers with his as if she'd done it many times, when in fact she hadn't. She shouldn't. He liked it too much.

"I'm here," she said, an echo of her sentiment at the wedding ceremony. "I'm not going anywhere. My comment wasn't supposed to be taken as a 'holy cow how are we going to do this.' It was an 'oh, so we've got two days to figure this out.' We will."

There was literally no way to express how crappy that made him feel. Viv was such a trouper, diving into this marriage without any thought to herself and her own sense of comfort and propriety. He already owed her so much. He couldn't ask her to fake intimacy on top of everything else.

Neither did he like the instant heat that crowded into his belly at the thought of potential intimate details. *He* couldn't fake intimacy either. It would feel too much like lying.

The only way he could fathom acting like he and Viv were lovers would be if they were.

"You don't know my grandfather. He's probably already suspicious. This house party is intended to sniff out the truth."

"So?" She shrugged that off far too easily. "Let him sniff. What's he going to find out, that we're really legally married?"

"That the marriage is in name only."

To drive the point home, he reached out to cup Viv's

jaw and brought her head up until her gaze clashed with his, her mouth mere centimeters away from his in an almost-kiss that would be a real one with the slightest movement. She nearly jumped out of her skin and stumbled back a good foot until she hit the counter. And then she tried to keep going, eyes wide with…something.

"See?" he said. "I can't even touch you without all sorts of alarms going off. How are we going to survive a whole weekend?"

"Sorry. I wasn't—" She swallowed. "I wasn't expecting you to do that. So clearly the answer is that we need to practice."

"Practice what?" And then her meaning sank in. "Touching?"

"Kissing, too." Her chest rose and fell unevenly as if she couldn't quite catch her breath. "You said we would best get through the adjustment period by spending time together. Maybe we should do that the old-fashioned way. Take me on a date, Jonas."

Speechless, he stared at her, looking for the punch line, but her warm brown eyes held nothing but sincerity. The idea unwound in his gut with a long, liquid pull of anticipation that he didn't need any help interpreting.

A date with his wife. No, with Viv. And the whole goal would be to get her comfortable with his hands on her, to kiss her at random intervals until it was so natural, neither of them thought anything of it.

Crazy. And brilliant. Not to mention impossible.

"Will you wear a new dress?" That should not have been the next thing out of his mouth. *No* would be more advisable when he'd already identified a great big zone of danger surrounding his wife. But *yes* was the only answer if he wanted to pull off this plan.

She nodded, a smile stealing over her face. "The only caveat is no work. For either of us. Which means I get dessert that's not cupcakes."

Oddly, a date with Viv where kissing was expected felt like enough of a reward that he didn't mind that addendum so much, though giving up cupcakes seemed like a pretty big sacrifice. But as her brown eyes seared him thoroughly, the real sacrifice was going to be his sanity. Because he could get her comfortable with his hands on her, but there was no way to get *him* there.

The date would be nothing but torture—and an opportunity to practice making sure no one else realized that, an opportunity he could not pass up. Having an overdeveloped sense of ethics was very inconvenient sometimes.

"It's a deal. Pick you up at eight?"

That made her laugh for some reason. "My bedroom is next door to yours, silly. Are we going to have a secret knock?"

"Maybe." The vibe between them had loosened gradually to where they were almost back to normal, at least as far as she was concerned. Strange that the concept of taking Viv on a date should be the thing to do it. "What should it be?"

Rapping out a short-short-pause-short pattern, she raised her brows. "That means we're leaving in five minutes so get your butt in gear."

"And then that's my cue to hang out in the living room with a sporting event on TV because you're going to take an extra twenty?"

Tossing her head, she grinned. "You catch on fast. Now, I have to go get ready, which means you get to unload the rest of these boxes."

Though he groaned good-naturedly as she scampered out of the kitchen, he didn't mind taking over the chore. Actually, she should be sitting on the couch with a drink and a book while he slaved for hours to get the house exactly the way she liked it. He would have, too, simply because he owed her for this, but she'd insisted that she wanted to do it in order to learn where everything was. Looked like a date was enough to trump that concept.

As the faint sound of running water drifted through the walls, he found spots in his cavernous kitchen for the various pieces Viv had brought with her to this new, temporary life. Unpacking her boxes ended up being a more intimate task than he'd anticipated. She had an odd collection of things. He couldn't fathom the purpose of many of them, but they told him fascinating things about the woman he'd married. She made cupcakes for her business but she didn't have so much as one cupcake pan in her personal stash. Not only that, each item had a well-used sheen, random scrapes, dents, bent handles.

Either she'd spent hours in her kitchen trying to figure out what she liked to bake the most or she'd cleaned out an estate sale in one fell swoop. He couldn't wait to find out, because what better topic to broach on a date with a woman he needed to know inside and out before Friday night?

As he worked, he couldn't help but think of Viv on the other side of the walls, taking a shower. The ensuing images that slammed through his mind were not conducive to the task at hand and it got a little hard to breathe. He should not be picturing her "getting ready" when, in all honesty, he had no idea what that entailed. Odds were good she didn't lather herself up and spend extra time stroking the foam over her body like his brain seemed bent on imagining.

What was his *problem*? He never sat around and fantasized about a woman. He'd never felt strongly enough about one to do so. When was the last time he'd even gone on a date? He might stick Warren with the workaholic label but that could easily be turned back on Jonas. Running the entire American arm of a global company wasn't for wimps, and he had something to prove on top of that. Didn't leave a lot of room for dating, especially when the pact was first and foremost in his mind.

Of course the women he dated always made noises about not looking for anything serious and keeping their options open. And Jonas was always completely honest, but it didn't seem to matter if he flat-out said he wasn't ever going to fall in love. Mostly they took it as a challenge, and things got sticky fast, especially when said woman figured out he wasn't kidding.

Jonas was a champion at untangling himself before things went too far. Before *he* went too far. There were always warning signs that he was starting to like a woman too much. That's when he bailed.

So he had a lot of one-night stands that he'd never intended to be such. It made for stretches of lonely nights, which was perhaps the best side benefit of marriage. He didn't hate the idea of having someone to watch a movie with on a random Tuesday night, or drinking coffee with Viv in the morning before work. He hoped she liked that part of their marriage, too.

Especially since that was all they could ever have between them. It would be devastating to lose her friendship, which would surely happen if they took things to the next level. Once she found out about the pact, either she'd view it as a challenge or she'd immediately shut down. The latter was more likely. He'd hate either one.

At seven forty he stacked the empty boxes near the door so he could take them to the recycling center in the basement of the building later, then went to his room to change clothes for his date.

He rapped on Viv's door with the prescribed knock, grinning as he pictured her on the other side deliberately waiting for as long as she could to answer because they'd made a joke out of this new ritual. But she didn't follow the script and opened the door almost immediately.

Everything fled his mind but her as she filled the doorway, her fresh beauty heightened by the colors of her dress. She'd arranged her hair up on her head, leaving her neck bare. It was such a different look that he couldn't stop drinking her in, frozen by the small smile playing around her mouth.

"I didn't see much point in making you wait when I'm already ready," she commented. "Is it okay to tell you I'm a little nervous?"

He nodded, shocked his muscles still worked. "Yes. It's okay to tell me that. Not okay to be that way."

"I can't help it. I haven't been on a date in…" She bit her lip. "Well, it's been a little while. The shop is my life."

For some reason, that pleased him enormously. Though he shouldn't be so happy that they were cut from the same workaholic cloth. "For me, too. We'll be nervous together."

But then he already knew she had a lack in her social life since she'd readily agreed to this sham marriage, telling him she was too busy to date. Maybe together, they could find ways to work less. To put finer plea-sures first, just for the interim while they were living together. That could definitely be one of the benefits of their friendship.

She rolled her eyes. "You're not nervous. But you're sweet to say so."

Maybe not nervous. But something.

His palms itched and he knew good and well the only way to cure that was to put them on her bare arms so he could test out the feel of her skin. It looked soft.

Wasn't the point of the date to touch her? He had every reason to do exactly that. The urge to reach out grew bigger and rawer with each passing second.

"Maybe we could start the date right now?" she suggested, and all at once, the hallway outside her room got very small as she stepped closer, engulfing him in lavender that could only be her soap.

His body reacted accordingly, treating him to some more made-up images of her in the shower, and now that he had a scent to associate with it, the spike through his gut was that much more powerful. And that much more of a huge warning sign that things were spiraling out of control. He just couldn't see a good way to stop.

"Yeah?" he murmured, his throat raw with unful-filled need. "Which part?"

There was no mistaking what she had in mind when she reached out to graze her fingertips across his cheek. Nerve endings fired under her touch and he leaned into her palm, craving more of her.

"The only part that matters," she whispered back. "The part where you don't even think twice about get-ting close to me. Where it's no big thing if you put your arm around my waist or steal a kiss as I walk by."

If that was the goal, he was failing miserably because it was a big thing. A huge thing. And getting bigger as she leaned in, apparently oblivious to the way her lithe body brushed against his. His control snapped.

Before he came up with reasons why he shouldn't, he pulled her into his arms. Her mouth rose to meet his and, when it did, dropped them both into a long kiss. More than a kiss. An exploration.

With no witnesses this time, he had free rein to delve far deeper into the wonders of his wife than he had at the wedding ceremony.

Her enthusiastic response was killing him. *His* response was even worse. How had they been friends for so long without ever crossing this line? Well, he knew how—because if they had, he would have run in the other direction.

He groaned as her fingers threaded through his hair, sensitizing everything she touched. Then she iced that cake with a tentative push of her tongue that nearly put him on his knees. So unexpected and so very hot. Eagerly, he matched her sweet thrust with his own. Deeper and deeper they spiraled until he couldn't have said which way was up. Who was doing the giving and who was greedily lapping it up.

He wanted more and took it, easing her head back with firm fingers until he found the right angle to get more of her against his tongue. And now he wanted more of her against his body.

He slid a hand down the curve of her spine until he hit a spot that his palm fit into and pressed until her hips nestled against his erection. Amazing. Perfect.

The opposite of friendly.

That was enough to get his brain in gear again. This

was not how it should be between them, with all this raw need that he couldn't control.

He ended the kiss through some force of will he'd never understand and pulled back, but she tried to follow, nearly knocking herself off balance. Like she had at the ceremony. And in a similar fashion, he gripped her arms to keep her off the floor. It was dizzying how caught up she seemed to get. A rush he could get used to and shouldn't.

"Sorry," he said gruffly. "I got a little carried away."

"That's what was supposed to happen," she informed him breathlessly, "if we have any hope of your grandfather believing that we're deliriously happy together."

Yeah, that wasn't the problem he was most worried about at this moment. Viv's kiss-swollen lips were the color of raspberries and twice as tempting. All for show. He'd gotten caught up in the playacting far too easily, which wasn't fair to her. Or to his Viv-starved body that had suddenly found something it liked better than her cupcakes.

"I don't think anyone would question whether we spark, Viv," he muttered.

The real issue was that he needed to kill that spark and was pretty certain that would be impossible now.

Especially given the way she was gazing up at him with something a whole lot hotter than warmth in her brown eyes. She'd liked kissing him as much as he'd liked it. She might even be on board with taking things a step further. But they couldn't consummate this marriage or he could forget the annulment. Neither did he want to lead her on, which left him between a rock and an extremely hard place that felt like it would never be anything but hard for the rest of his life.

"In fact," he continued, "we should really keep things platonic behind closed doors. That's better for our friendship, don't you think?"

He'd kissed his wife and put his hands on her body because she'd told him to. And he was very much afraid he'd do it again whether it was for show or not unless he had some boundaries. Walking away from Viv wasn't an option. He had to do something that guaranteed he never got so sucked into a woman that she had power over his emotional center.

Thankfully, she nodded. "Whatever works best for you, Jonas. This is your fake marriage."

And how messed up was it that he was more than a little disappointed she'd agreed so readily?

Three

Viv hummed as she pulled the twenty-four-count pan from the oven and stuck the next batch of Confetti Surprise in its place. Customers thronged the showroom beyond the swinging door, but she kept an eye on things via the closed-circuit camera she'd had installed when she first started turning a profit.

Couldn't be too careful and besides, it made her happy to watch Camilla and Josie interact with the cupcake buyers while Viv did the dirty work in the back. She'd gotten so lucky to find the two college-aged girls who worked for her part-time. Both of them were eager students, and soon Viv would teach them the back-office stuff like bookkeeping and ordering. For now, it was great to have them running the register so Viv could focus on product.

Not that she was doing much focusing. Her mind

wandered constantly to the man who'd kissed her so passionately last night.

Jonas had been so into the moment, so into her, and it had been heady indeed. Score one for Viv to have landed in his arms due to her casual suggestion that they needed to "practice." Hopefully he'd never clue in that she jumped when he touched her because he zapped a shock of heat and awareness straight to her core every dang time, no matter how much she tried to control it.

Of course, he'd shut it all down, rightfully so. They were friends. If he'd been interested in more, he would have made a move long before now.

Didn't stop her from wishing for a repeat.

A stone settled into her stomach as three dressed-to-the-nines women breezed through the door of her shop. On the monitor, she watched her sisters approach the counter and speak to Josie, oblivious to the line of customers they'd just cut in front of. Likely they were cheerfully requesting to speak with Viv despite being told countless times that this wasn't a hobby. She ran a business, which meant she didn't have time to dash off with them for tea, something the three housewives she shared parentage with but little else didn't seem to fully grasp.

Except she couldn't avoid the conversation they were almost certainly here for. She'd finally broken down and called her mother to admit she'd gotten married without inviting anyone to the wedding. Of course that news had taken all of five minutes to blast its way to her sisters' ears.

Dusting off her hands, Viv set a timer on her phone and dropped it into her pocket. Those cupcakes in the oven would provide a handy out if things got a little intense, and knowing Hope, Joy and Grace, that was likely. She pushed open the swinging door and pasted a smile on her face.

"My favorite ladies," she called with a wave and crossed the room to hug first Grace, her next-oldest sister, then Joy and Hope last. More than a few heads turned to check out the additions to the showroom. Individually, they were beautiful women, but as a group, her sisters were impressive indeed, with style and elegance galore.

Viv had been a late-life accident, but her parents tried hard not to make her feel like one. Though it was obvious they'd expected to have three children when they couldn't come up with a fourth virtue to name their youngest daughter. She'd spent her childhood trying to fit in to her own family and nothing had changed.

Until today. Finally, Viviana Kim had a new last name and a husband. Thanks to Jonas and his fake marriage deal, she was part of the club that had excluded her thus far. Just one of many reasons she'd agreed.

"Mom told us," Hope murmured, her social polish in full force. She was nothing if not always mindful of propriety, and Viv appreciated it for once, as the roomful of customers didn't need to hear about Viv's love life. "She's hurt that you ran off to Vegas without telling anyone."

"Are you happy?" Grace butted in. She'd gotten married to the love of her life less than a year ago and saw hearts and flowers everywhere. "That's the important thing."

"Mom said you married Jonas Kim," Joy threw in before Viv could answer, not that she'd intended to interrupt before everyone had their say. That was a rookie mistake she'd learned to avoid years ago. "Surely his family would have been willing to make a discreet contribution to the ceremony. You could have had the wedding of the year."

Which was the real crime in Joy's mind—why spend *less* money when you could spend more, particularly when it belonged to someone else? Joy's own wedding had garnered a photo spread in *Bride* magazine five years ago, a feat no other Raleigh bride had scored since.

It had been a beautiful wedding and Joy had been a gorgeous bride. Of course, because she'd been so happy. All three of her sisters were married to handsome, successful men who treated them like royalty, which was great if you could find that. Viv had made do with what had been offered to her, but they didn't have to know that. In fact, she'd do everything in her power not to tip off her sisters that her marriage was anything but amazing. Was it so wrong to want them to believe she'd ended up exactly where she'd yearned to be for so long?

"Also, he's Korean," Hope added as if this might be news to Viv. "Mom is very concerned about how you'll handle the cultural differences. Have you discussed this with him?"

That was crossing a line. For several reasons. And Viv had had enough. "Jonas is American. He was born in the same hospital as you, so I'm pretty sure the cultural differences are minimal. Can you just be happy for me and stop with the third degree?"

All three women stared at her agape, even Grace, and Viv was ashamed at how good the speech had made her feel. She rarely stood up to the steamroller of her sisters, mostly because she really did love them. But she was married now, just like they were, and her choices deserved respect.

"Jonas does make me happy," she continued, shooting Grace a smile. "But there's nothing to be concerned about. We've known each other for about a year and our relationship recently grew closer. That's all there is to it."

Despite the fact that it was absolute truth, prickles swept across her cheeks at the memory of how *close* they'd gotten last night.

An unconvinced expression stole over Hope's face. As the oldest, she took her role as the protector seriously. "We still don't understand why the secrecy. None of us even remember you so much as mentioning his name before."

"Of course we know who he *is*," Joy clarified. "Everyone in Raleigh appreciates that he's brought a global company to this area. But we had no idea you'd caught his eye."

Viv could read between those lines easily enough. She didn't wear nine-thousand-dollar Alexander McQueen suits to brunch and attend the opera with a priceless antique diamond necklace decorating her cleavage. "He's been coming in to buy cupcakes for quite some time. We go to lunch. It's not that big of a mystery."

Did it seem like a mystery to others? A lick of panic curled through her stomach. She couldn't ruin this for Jonas. If other people got suspicious because she wasn't the type of woman a billionaire CEO should want to marry, then everything might fall apart.

Breathe. He'd made that decision. Not her. He'd picked Viv and anyone who thought she wasn't good enough for him could jump in a lake.

"But he married you." Grace clapped her hands, eyes twinkling. "Tell us how he proposed, what you wore at the wedding. Ooooh, show us pictures."

Since his proposal had begun with the line "This is going to sound crazy, but hear me out," Viv avoided that subject by holding out her left hand to dazzle her sisters with the huge diamond and then grabbing her phone to thumb up the shots Warren had taken at Jonas's request. The yellow of her dress popped next to Jonas's dark suit and they made an incredibly striking couple if she did say so herself. Mostly because she had the best-looking husband on the planet, so no one even noticed her.

"Is that Hendrix Harris in the shot?" Hope sniffed and the disapproval on her face spoke volumes against the man whose picture graced local gossip rags on a regular basis.

"Jonas and Hendrix are friends," Viv said mildly as she flipped through a few more pictures that mercifully did not include North Carolina's biggest scandalmonger. "They went to Duke together. I'll try not to let him corrupt me if we socialize."

As far as she could tell, Hendrix had scarcely noticed her at the wedding, and he'd seemed preoccupied at the cocktail lounge where they'd gone to have drinks after the ceremony. The man was pretty harmless.

"Just be careful," Hope implored her, smoothing an invisible wrinkle from her skirt. "You married Jonas so quickly and it appears as if he may have some unsavory associations. I say this with love, but you haven't demonstrated a great track record when it comes to the men you fall for."

That shouldn't have cut so deeply. It was true. But still.

"What Hope means is that you tend to leap before you look, Viv," Grace corrected, her eyes rolling in their sister's direction, but only Viv could see the show of support. It soothed the ragged places inside that Hope's comment had made. A little.

"It's not a crime to be passionate about someone." Hands on her hips, Viv surveyed the three women, none of whom seemed to remember what it was like to be single and alone. "But for your information, Jonas and I were friends first. We share common interests. He gives me advice about my business. We have a solid foundation to build on."

"Oh." Hope processed that. "I didn't realize you were being so practical about this. I'm impressed that you managed to marry a man without stars in your eyes. That's a relief."

Great. She'd gotten the seal of approval from Hope solely because she'd skirted the truth with a bland recitation of unromantic facts about her marriage. Her heart clenched. That was the opposite of what she wanted. But this was the marriage she had, the one she could handle. For now. Tomorrow, Jonas would take her to his father's house to meet his grandfather and she hoped to "practice" being married a whole lot more.

Thankfully, she'd kept Jonas in the dark about her feelings. If he could kiss her like he had last night and not figure out that she'd been this close to melting into a little puddle, she could easily snow his family with a few public displays of affection.

It was behind closed doors that she was worried about. That's where she feared she might forget that her marriage was fake. And as she'd just been unceremoniously reminded, she had a tendency to get serious way too fast, which in her experience was a stellar way to get a man to start looking for the exit.

That was the part that hurt the most. She wanted to care about someone, to let him know he was her whole world and have him say that in return. It wasn't neediness. She wasn't being clingy. That's what love looked like to her and she refused to believe otherwise.

But she'd yet to find a man who agreed with her, and Jonas was no exception. They had a deal and she would stick to it.

The house Jonas had grown up in lay on the outskirts of Raleigh in an upscale neighborhood that was homey and unpretentious. Jonas's father, who had changed his name to Brian when he became a legal US citizen upon marrying his American wife, hadn't gone into the family business, choosing to become a professor at Duke University instead.

That had left a hole in the Kim empire, one Jonas had gladly filled. He and Grandfather got along well, likely because they were so similar. They both had a drive to succeed, a natural professionalism and a sense of honor that harbored trust in others who did business with Kim Electronics.

Though they corresponded nearly every day in some electronic form, the time difference prevented them from speaking often, and an in-person visit was even rarer. The last time Jonas had seen Grandfather had been during a trip to Seoul for a board meeting about eighteen months ago. He'd invited his parents to come with him, as they hadn't visited Korea in several years.

"Are you nervous?" Jonas glanced over at Viv, who had clutched her hands together in her lap the second the car had hit Glenwood Avenue. Her knuckles couldn't get any whiter.

"Oh, God. You can tell," she wailed. "I was trying so hard to be cool."

He bit back a grin and passed a slow-moving minivan. "Viv, they're just people. I promise they will like you."

"I'm not worried about that. Everyone likes me, especially after I give them cupcakes," she informed him loftily.

There was a waxed paper box at her feet on the floorboard that she'd treated as carefully as a newborn baby. When he'd reached for it, she'd nearly taken his hand off at the wrist, telling him in no uncertain terms the cupcakes were for her new family. Jonas was welcome to come by Cupcaked next week and pick out whatever he wanted, but the contents of that box were off-limits.

He kind of liked Bossy Viv. Of course he liked Sweet Viv, Uncertain Viv, Eager-to-Help Viv. He'd seen plenty of new facets in the last week since they'd moved in together, more than he'd have expected given that they'd known each other so long. It was fascinating.

"What are you worried about then?" he asked.

"You know good and well." Without warning, she slid a hand over his thigh and squeezed. Fire rocketed up his leg and scored his groin, nearly doubling him over with the sudden and unexpected need.

Only his superior reflexes kept the Mercedes on the road. But he couldn't stop the curse that flew from his mouth.

"Sorry," he muttered but she didn't seem bothered by his language.

"See, you're just as bad as me." Her tone was laced with irony. "All that practice and we're even jumpier than we were before."

Because the practice had ended before he started peeling off her clothes. Ironic how his marriage of convenience meant his wife was right there in his house—conveniently located in the bedroom next to his. He could hear her moving around between the walls and sometimes, he lay awake at night listening for the slightest movement to indicate she was likewise awake, aching to try one of those kisses with a lot less fabric in the way.

That kind of need was so foreign to him that he wasn't handling it well.

"I'm not jumpy," he lied. "I'm just…"

Frustrated.

There was no good way to finish that sentence without opening up a conversation about changing their relationship into something that it wasn't supposed to be. An annulment was so much less sticky than a divorce, though he'd finally accepted that he was using that as an excuse.

The last thing he could afford to do was give in to the simmering awareness between them. Jonas had convinced himself it was easy to honor the pact because he really didn't feel much when it came to relationships. Sure, he enjoyed sex, but it had always been easy to walk away when the woman pushed for more.

With Viv, the spiral of heat and need was dizzyingly strong. He felt too much, and Marcus's experience was like a big neon sign, reminding him that it was better never to go down that path. What was he supposed to do, stop being friends with Viv if things went haywire between them? Neither was there a good way to end their relationship before the merger.

So he was stuck. He couldn't act on his sudden and fierce longing to pull this car over into a shadowy bower of oak trees and find out if all of Viv tasted like sugar and spice and everything nice.

"Maybe we shouldn't touch each other," he suggested.

That was a good solution. Except for the part where they were married. Married people touched each other. He bit back the nasty word that had sprung to his lips. Barely.

"Oh." She nodded. "If you think that won't cause problems, sure."

Of course it was going to cause problems. He nearly groaned. But the problems had nothing to do with what she assumed. "Stop being so reasonable. I'm pulling you away from your life with very little compensation in return. You should be demanding and difficult."

Brilliant. He'd managed to make it sound like touching her was one of the compensation methods. He really needed to get out of this car now that he had a hyper-awareness of how easily she could—and would—reach out to slide a hand full of questing fingers into his lap.

Viv grinned and crossed her arms, removing that possibility. "In that case, I'm feeling very bereft in the jewelry department, Mr. Kim. As your wife, I should be draped in gems, don't you think?"

"Absolutely." What did it say about how messed up he was that the way *Mr. Kim* rolled off her tongue turned him on? "Total oversight on my part. Which I will rectify immediately."

The fourteen-carat diamond on her finger was on loan from a guy Jonas knew in the business, though the hefty fee he'd paid to procure it could have bought enough bling to blind her. Regardless, if Viv wanted jewelry, that's what she'd get.

They drove into his parents' neighborhood right on time and he parked in the long drive that led to the house. "Ready?"

She nodded. "All that talk about jewelry got me over my nerves. Thanks."

That made one of them.

His mom opened the door before they'd even hit the stone steps at the entryway, likely because she'd been watching for the car. But instead of engulfing Jonas in the first of what would be many hugs, she ignored her only child in favor of her new daughter-in-law.

"You must be Viviana," his mother gushed, and swept Viv up in an embrace that was part friendly and part *Thank you, God, I finally have a daughter.* "I'm so happy to meet you."

Viv took it in stride. "Hi, Mrs. Kim. I'm happy to meet you, too. Please call me Viv."

Of course she wasn't ruffled. There was so little that seemed to trip her up—except when Jonas touched her. All practicing had done was create surprisingly acute sexual tension that even a casual observer would recognize as smoldering awareness.

He was currently pretending it didn't exist. Because that would make it not so, right?

"Hi, Mom," he threw in blithely since she hadn't even glanced in his direction.

"Your grandfather is inside. He'd like to talk to you while I get to know Viviana. Tell me everything," she said to her new daughter-in-law as she accepted the box of cupcakes with a smile. "Have you started thinking about kids yet?"

Jonas barely bit back another curse. "Mom, please. We just got here. Viv doesn't need the third degree about personal stuff."

Right out of the gate with the baby questions? Really? He'd expected a little decorum from his mom. In vain, obviously, and a mistake because he hadn't had a chance to go over that with Viv. Should they say they didn't want children? That she couldn't have any?

He and Viv clearly should have spent less time "practicing" and more in deep conversation about all aspects of potential questions that might come up this weekend. Which they'd have to rectify tonight before going to bed. In the same room.

His mother shot him a glare. "Grandchildren are not personal. The hope of one day getting some is the only reason I keep you around, after all."

That made Viv laugh, which delighted his mother, so really, there was nothing left to do but throw up his hands and go seek out Grandfather for his own version of the third degree.

Grandfather held court in the Kim living room, talking to his son. The older Jonas's dad got, the more he resembled Grandfather, but the similarities ended there. Where Brian Kim had adopted an American name to match his new homeland, Kim Jung-Su wore his Korean heritage like the badge of honor it was.

Kim Electronics had been born after the war, during a boom in Korean capitalism that only a select few had wisely taken advantage of. Jonas loved his dad, but Grandfather had been his mentor, his partner as Jonas had taken what Jung-Su had built and expanded it into the critical US market. They'd created a chaebol, a family-run conglomerate, where none had existed, and they'd done it together.

And he was about to lie to his grandfather's face solely to avoid marrying a disaster of a woman who might cause the Kim family shame.

It was a terrible paradox and not for the first time he heard Warren's voice of reason in his head asking why he couldn't just tell Grandfather the truth. But then he remembered that Sun's grandfather and Jonas's grandfather had fought in the war together and were closer than brothers. Jonas refused to out Sun and her unsuitable lover strictly for his own benefit. No, this way was easier.

And it wasn't a lie. He and Viv were married. That was all anyone needed to know.

Grandfather greeted Jonas in Korean and then switched to English as a courtesy since he was in an English-speaking house. "You are looking well."

"As are you." Jonas bowed to show his respect and then hugged his dad, settling in next to him on the couch. "It's a pleasure to see you."

Grandfather arched a thick brow. "An unexpected pleasure I assume? I wanted to meet your new wife personally. To welcome her into the family."

"She is very honored. Mom waylaid her or she'd be here to meet you, as well."

"I asked your mother to. I wanted to speak with you privately."

As if it had been some prearranged signal, Jonas's

dad excused himself and the laser sights of Jung-Su had zero distractions. The temperature of the room shot up about a thousand degrees. One misstep and the whole plan would come crashing down. And Jonas suddenly hated the idea of losing this tenuous link with Viv, no matter how precarious that link was.

"Now, then." Grandfather steepled his hands together and smiled. "I'm very pleased you have decided to marry. It is a big step that will bring you many years of happiness. Belated congratulations."

Jonas swallowed his surprise. What was the wily old man up to? He'd expected a cross-examination designed to uncover the plot that Grandfather surely suspected. "Thank you. Your approval means a lot to me."

"As a wedding gift, I'd like to give you the Kim ancestral home."

"What? I mean, that's a very generous gesture, Grandfather." And crafty, as the property in question lay outside of Seoul, seven thousand miles away from North Carolina. Jonas couldn't refuse or Grandfather would be insulted. But there was an angle here that Jonas couldn't quite work out.

"Of course I'd hoped you'd live in it with Sun Park, but I understand that you cannot curb the impulses of the heart."

Jonas stared at his grandfather as if he'd suddenly started speaking Klingon. The impulses of the heart? That was the exact opposite of the impression he'd wanted to convey. Sure, he'd hoped to convince everyone that they were a couple, but only so that no one's suspicions were aroused. Solid and unbreakable would be more to his liking when describing his marriage, not *impulsive* and certainly not because he'd fallen madly in love.

This was the worst sort of twist. Never would he have thought he'd be expected to sell his marriage as a love match. Was that something that he and Viv were going to have to practice, too? His stomach twisted itself inside out. How the hell was he supposed to know what love looked like?

Regardless of the curveball, it was the confirmation Jonas had been looking for. Grandfather was on board with Viv, and Jonas had cleared the first hurdle after receiving that ominous text message the other day. "I'm glad you understand. I've been seeing Viv for almost a year and I simply couldn't imagine marrying anyone else."

That much at least was true, albeit a careful hedge about the nature of his intentions toward Viv during that year. And thankfully they'd become good enough friends that he felt comfortable asking her to help him avoid exactly what he'd suspected Grandfather had in mind. Apparently throwing Sun in his path *had* been an attempt to get Jonas to Korea more often, if not permanently. It was counter to Jonas's long-term strategy, the one he still hadn't brought to Grandfather because the merger hadn't happened yet. Once Park Industries and Kim Electronics became one, they could leverage the foothold Jonas had already built in America by moving the headquarters to North Carolina, yet keep manufacturing in Korea under the Park branch.

It was also the opportune time to pass the reins, naming Jonas the CEO of the entire operation. The dominoes were in much better position now, thanks to the huge bullet Viv had helped him dodge without upsetting anyone. It was…everything.

Grandfather chatted for a few more minutes about his plans while in the US, including a request for a tour of the Kim Building, and then asked Jonas to introduce him to Viv.

He found her in the kitchen writing down her cupcake recipe for his mother.

"You got her secret recipe already, Mom?" Jonas asked with a laugh. "I guess I don't have to ask whether everyone is getting along."

His mother patted his arm. "You obviously underestimate how much your wife cares for you. I didn't even have to ask twice."

Viv blushed and it was so pretty on her, he couldn't tear his gaze from her face all at once, even though he was speaking to his mom. "On the contrary, I'm quite aware of how incredibly lucky I am that Viv married me."

"You didn't have to ask me *that* twice either," Viv pointed out. "Apparently I lack the ability to say no to anyone with the name Kim."

An excellent point that he really wished she hadn't brought up on the heels of his discovery of how much he enjoyed it when she called him Mr. Kim. All at once, a dozen suggestions designed to get her to say yes over and over sprang to his lips. But with his mom's keen-eyed gaze cutting between the two of them, he needed to get himself under control immediately.

"Come and say hi to my grandfather," he said instead, and she nodded eagerly.

She was far too good to him. For the first time, it bothered him. What was she getting out of this farce?

Some advice about how to run her business? That had seemed inadequate before they'd gotten married. Now? It was nearly insulting how little he was doing for her.

She had to have another reason for being here. And all at once, he wanted to know what it was.

Four

Ten minutes into dinner, Jonas figured out his grandfather's angle. The wily old man was trying to drive him insane with doubt about pulling off this ruse, especially now that he had *impulses of the heart* echoing through his head. Jonas was almost dizzy from trying to track all the verbal land mines that might or might not be strewn through random conversational openers.

Even "pass the butter" had implications. Grandfather hated butter.

And if Grandfather failed at putting Jonas in the loony bin, Viv was doing her part to finish the job, sitting next to him looking fresh and beautiful as she reminded him on a second-by-second basis that she was well within touching distance. Not just easily accessible. But *available* to be touched. It was *expected*. Would a loving husband sling his arm across the back of her chair? Seemed reasonable.

But the moment he did it as he waited for his mom to serve the kimchi stew she'd made in honor of Grandfather's visit, Viv settled into the crook of his elbow, which had not been his intent at all. She fit so well, he couldn't help but let his arm relax so that it fully embraced her and somehow his fingers ended up doing this little dance down her bare arm, testing whether the silkiness felt as good all the way down as it did near her shoulder.

It did.

"...don't you think, Jonas?"

Blinking, Jonas tore his attention away from his wife's skin and focused on his dad. "Sure. I definitely think so."

"That's great," Brian said with a nod and a wink. "It wasn't a stretch to think you'd be on board."

Fantastic. What in the world had he just agreed to that had his father winking, of all things? Jonas pulled his arm from around Viv's shoulders. At this point, it seemed like everyone was convinced they were a couple and all the touching had done nothing but distract him.

Viv leaned in, her hand resting on his thigh. It was dangerously close to being in his lap. One small shift would do it, and his muscles strained to repeat the experience. But before he could sort her intention, she murmured in his ear, "We're playing Uno later. As a team. You'll have to teach me."

Card games with a hard-on. That sounded like the opposite of fun. But at least he knew what he'd absently agreed to, and shot Viv a grateful smile. Her return smile did all sorts of things that it shouldn't have, not the least of which was give him the sense that they were coconspirators. They were in this farce together and he appreciated that more than he could say. At least they could laugh about this later. Or something.

Grandfather was watching him closely as he spooned up a bite of stew, and Jonas braced for the next round of insanity. Sure enough, Grandfather cleared his throat.

"Will you and your bride be starting a family soon?"

Not this again and from his grandfather, too? Obviously Jonas's mother had a vested interest in the answer strictly because she wanted babies to spoil, but Grandfather wasn't asking for anything close to that reason. It was all part of the test.

"Not soon," he hedged because family was important to the Kims. It was a source of frustration for both his parents and his grandparents that they'd only had one child apiece, and Jonas imagined they'd all be thrilled if he said Viv wanted a dozen. "Viv owns a bakery and it's doing very well. She'd like to focus on her career for a while."

Yes. That was the reason they weren't having kids right away. Why had he been racking his brain over that? Except now he was thinking about the conversation where he had to tell everyone that while he cared about Viv, they were better as friends, so the marriage was over. While it soothed his sense of honor that it was the truth, he'd never considered that the annulment would upset his family.

"We're having her cupcakes for dessert," his mother threw in with a beaming smile. "They look scrumptious."

Perfect segue and took some heat off a subject that Jonas suddenly did not want to contemplate. "The lemon are my favorite. One bite and that was when I decided I couldn't let Viv get away."

The adoring glance she shot him thumped him in the gut. The little secret smile playing about her lips worked in tandem, spreading tendrils of heat through him in ways that should be uncomfortable at a table full of Kims who were all watching him closely. But the sensation was too enjoyable to squelch.

"Honestly, that was when I knew he was special," Viv admitted, and Jonas nearly did a double take at the wistful note in her voice. "He appreciates my cupcakes in a way regular customers don't. A lot goes into the recipes and I don't just mean my time. It's a labor of love, born out of a desire to make people happy, and I can see on his face that I've done that. Most customers just devour the thing without stopping to breathe, but Jonas always takes one bite and immediately stops to savor it. Then he tells me how great it is before taking another bite."

Well, yeah, because he could taste the sunshine in it, as if she'd somehow condensed a few rays and woven them through the ingredients. How could he not take his time to fully appreciate the unique experience of a Viviana Dawson cupcake?

Jonas blinked, dragging his lids down over his suddenly dry eyes. He didn't do that *every* time, not the way she was describing it, as if a cupcake held all that meaning.

He glanced at his mom, who looked a little misty.

"That sounds like a magical courtship," she said.

"Oh, it was," Viv agreed enthusiastically. "It was like one of those movies where the hero pretends he only wants the cupcakes when he comes into the shop, but it's really to see the baker. But I always knew from the first that the way to his heart was through my frosting."

His mother laughed and Jonas checked his eye roll because the whole point was to sell this nonsense. Everyone was eating it up, no pun intended, so why mess with the ridiculous story Viv was spinning?

Except the whole thing made him uncomfortable.

Surely his grandfather wouldn't appreciate hearing his successor described with such romanticism. If anything, Viv could help Jonas's case by telling everyone how hard he worked and how difficult it was to pry him away from his cell phone when they went to lunch.

He sighed. She couldn't say that. It would be a big, fat lie. When he did anything with Viv, he always switched his phone to do not disturb. He loved listening to stories about her sisters, or a new recipe she was working through. But it didn't mean he was gaga over her like a besotted fool.

Yet…that's what he needed his grandfather to buy, as difficult as it was to envision. Grandfather hadn't accepted Jonas's marriage to Viv because she'd helped him increase profits or created an advantageous business alliance. Viv was an *impulse of the heart*.

How had he gotten caught in the middle of trying to prove to his grandfather that Jonas was a committed, solid CEO candidate, while also attempting to convince him that he and Viv had fallen in love? And Jonas had no illusions about the necessity of maintaining the current vibe, not after his grandfather smiled over Viv's enthusiastic retelling of what would probably forever be called the Cupcake Courtship. It was madness.

"Will you bring your wife to Seoul to visit the Kim ancestral home?" Grandfather asked in the lull. "It's yours now. Perhaps you'll want to redecorate?"

Jonas nearly groaned. He hadn't had four seconds

to mention the gift to Viv. Her eyebrows lifted in silent question and he blessed her discretion.

"We're actually looking for a house together in Raleigh," Jonas improvised much more smoothly than he would have guessed he could. Viv's eyebrows did another reach-for-the-sky move as he rushed on. "So probably we won't make it to Korea anytime soon. But we do both appreciate the gift."

Nothing like a good reminder that Jonas's home was in America. The future of the company lay here, not in Seoul. The more he could root himself in North Carolina, the better. Of course the answer was to buy a property here. With Viv. A new ancestral home in North Carolina. Then his statement to his grandfather wouldn't be a lie.

"Yes, thank you so much, Mr. Kim," Viv said sweetly. "We'll discuss our work schedules and find a mutual time we can travel. I would be honored to see your ancestral home. Mrs. Kim, perhaps you'd advise me on whether the decor needs refurbishing?"

Jonas's mom smiled so widely that it was a wonder she didn't crack her face. "That's a lovely idea. I would be thrilled to go to lunch and discuss the house, as I've always loved the locale."

Speechless, Jonas watched the exchange with a very real sense of his life sliding out of control and no way to put on the brakes. In the last two minutes, he'd managed to rope himself into shopping for a house in Raleigh, then traveling to Korea so Viv could visit Seoul with the express intent of redecorating a house neither of them wanted…with his mom. What next?

"While you're in Korea," Grandfather said, and his tone was so leading that everyone's head turned toward him, "we should discuss taking next steps toward increasing your responsibilities at Kim Electronics. The board will look very favorably on how you've matured, Jonas. Your accomplishments with the American market are impressive. I would be happy to recommend you as the next CEO when I retire."

The crazy train screeched to a halt in the dead center of Are You Kidding Me Station. *Say something. Tell him you're honored.*

But Jonas's throat froze as his brain tried to sort through his grandfather's loaded statements.

Everything he'd worked for had just been handed to him on a silver platter—that Viv was holding in her delicate fingers. The implications were staggering. Grandfather liked that Jonas was married. It was a huge wrinkle he had never seen coming.

Now he couldn't annul the marriage or he'd risk losing Grandfather's approval with the board. How was he supposed to tell Viv that the favor he'd asked of her had just been extended by about a year?

And what did it mean that his insides were doing a secret dance of happiness at getting to keep Viv longer than planned?

The spare bedroom lay at the end of a quiet hall and had its own en suite bathroom. Nice. Viv wasn't too keen on the idea of wandering around in her bathrobe. At least not outside the bedroom. Inside was another story.

Because Jonas was on this side of the closed door. Time to ramp it up.

If she hoped to build her confidence with a man, there was no better scenario to play that out than this one, especially since she already knew they were attracted to each other And headed for a divorce. None of this was real, so she could practice without fear.

She shivered as her gorgeous husband loosened his tie and threw himself onto the bed with a groan. *Shivered.* What was that but a commentary on this whole situation?

"Bad day, sweetie?" she deadpanned, carefully keeping her voice light. But holy cow, Jonas was so sexy with his shirtsleeves rolled up and his bare feet crossed at the ankle as he tossed an elbow over his eyes.

"That was one of the most difficult dinners I've ever endured," he confessed, as if there was nothing odd about being in a bedroom together with the door closed, while he lounged on the bed looking like a commercial for something sensual and expensive.

"Your family is great." She eased onto the bed because she wanted to and she could. It wasn't like there were a ton of other seats in the cute little bedroom. Well, except for the matching chairs near the bay window that flanked an inlaid end table. But she didn't want to sit way over there when the centerpiece of the room lay on the bed.

As the mattress shifted under her weight, he peeked out from beneath his elbow, his dark eyes seeking hers. "You're only saying that to be nice. You should stage a fight and go home. It would serve me right to have to stay here and field questions about the stability of our marriage."

As if she'd ever do that when the best part of this fake marriage had just started. She was sharing a bedroom with Jonas Kim and he was her husband and the night was rife with possibilities.

There came the shiver again and it was delicious.
Careful.

This was the part where she always messed up with men by seeming too eager. Messing up with Jonas was not happening. There was no do-over.

Of course, scoring with Jonas had its issues, too. Like the fact that she couldn't keep him. This was just practice, she reminded herself. That was the only way she could get it together.

"I'm not staging a fight." She shook her head and risked reaching out to stroke Jonas's hair in a totally casual gesture meant to soothe him, because after all, he did seem pretty stressed. "What would we fight about? Money?"

"I don't know. No." The elbow came off his face and he let his eyes drift closed as she ran her fingers over his temples. "That feels nice. You don't have to do that."

Oh, yes. She did. This was her chance to touch Jonas in a totally innocuous way and study her husband's body while he wasn't aware.

"It's possible for me to do something because I want to instead of out of a sense of obligation, you know."

He chuckled. "Point taken. I'm entirely too sensitive to how big a favor this is and how difficult navigating my family can be."

Stroking his hair might go down as one of the greatest pleasures of her life. It was soft and silky and thick. The inky strands slid across her fingertips as she buried them deep and rubbed lightly against his scalp, which earned her a groan that was amazingly sexy.

"Relax," she murmured, and was only half talking to herself as her insides contracted. "I don't find your family difficult. Your mom is great and I don't know if you know this or not, but your grandfather does not in fact breathe fire."

"He gave us a house." His eyes popped open and he glanced over at her, shrinking the slight distance between them. "There are all sorts of underlying expectations associated with that, not the least of which is how upset he's going to be when I have to give it back."

She shrugged, pretending like it wasn't difficult to get air into her lungs when he focused on her so intently. "Don't give it back. Keep it and we'll go visit, like we promised."

"Viv." He sat up, taking his beautiful body out of reach, which was a shame. "You're being entirely too accommodating. Were you not listening to the conversation at dinner? This is only going to get more complicated the longer we drag it out. And we *are* going to be dragging it out apparently."

Normally, this would be where she threw herself prostrate at a man's feet and wept with joy over the fact that he wasn't calling things off. But she wasn't clingy anymore. Newly Minted Independent Viv needed to play this a whole different way if she wanted to get to a place where she had a man slavishly devoted to her. And she would not apologize for wishing for a man who loved her so much that he would never dream of calling the duration of their marriage "dragging it out."

"You say that like being married to me is a chore," she scolded lightly. "I was listening at dinner. I heard the words *CEO* and *Jonas* in the same sentence. Did you? Because that sounded good to me."

"It is good. For me. Not you. I'm now essentially in the position of using you to further my career goals for an extended period of time. Not just until the merger happens. But until my grandfather retires and fully transitions the role of CEO to me. That could take months. A year."

Oh, God. A whole year of living with Jonas in his amazing loft and being his wife? That was a lot of practicing for something that would never be real. How could she possibly hide her feelings for Jonas that long? Worse, they'd probably grow stronger the longer she stayed in his orbit. How fair was it to keep torturing herself like this?

On the flip side, she'd promised to do this for Jonas as a favor. As a *friend*. He wasn't interested in more or he'd have told her. Practice was all she could reasonably expect from this experience. It had to be enough.

"That's a significant development, no doubt. But I don't feel used. And I'm not going anywhere."

Jonas scowled instead of overflowing with gratitude. "I can't figure out what you're getting out of this. It was already a huge sacrifice, even when it was only for a few weeks until my grandfather got his deal going with Park. Now this. Are you dying of cancer or something?"

She forced a laugh but there was nothing funny about his assumptions. Or the fact that she didn't have a good answer for why she didn't hate the idea of sticking around as long as Jonas would have her. Maybe there was something wrong with that, but it was her business, not his. "What, like I'm trying to check off everything on my bucket list before I die and being married to Jonas Kim was in the top three? That's a little arrogant, don't you think?"

When he flinched, she almost took it back, but that's how Newly Minted Viv rolled. The last thing he needed to hear was that being married to him occupied the top spot on all her lists. And on that note, it was definitely time to put a few more logs on the pile before she set it on fire.

"Running a cupcake business is hard," she told him firmly. "You've built Kim Electronics from the ground up. You should know how it is. You work seventy hours a week and barely make a dent. Who has time for a relationship? But I get lonely, same as anyone. This deal is perfect for me because we can hang out with no pressure. I like you. Is that so hard to believe?"

Good. Deflect. Give him just enough truth to make it plausible.

His face relaxed into an easy grin. "Only a little. I owe you so much. Not sure my scintillating personality makes up for being stuck sharing a bedroom with me."

"Yeah, that part sucks, all right," she murmured, and let her gaze trail down his body. What better way to "practice" being less clingy than to get good and needy and then force herself to walk away? "We should use this opportunity to get a little more comfortable with each other."

The atmosphere got intense as his expression darkened, and she could tell the idea intrigued him.

"What? Why? We've already sold the coupledom story to my family. It's a done deal and went way better than I was expecting. We don't have to do the thing where we touch each other anymore."

Well, that stung. She'd had the distinct impression he liked touching her.

"Oh, I wish that was true." She stuck an extra tinge of dismay into her tone, just to be sure it was really clear that she wasn't panting after him. Even though she was lying through her teeth. "But we still have all of tomorrow with your family. And you're planning to meet mine, right? We have to sell that we're hopelessly in love all over again. I'm really concerned about tongues wagging. After all, Joy's husband knows everyone who's anyone. The business world is small."

Jonas's eyes went a little wide. "We just have to sell being married. No one said anything about love."

"But that's why people get married, Jonas." Something flickered through his expression that looked a lot like panic. And it set a bunch of gears in motion in her head. Maybe they should be using this time to get matters straight instead of doing a lot of touching. Because all at once, she was really curious about an important aspect of this deal that she'd thus far failed to question. "Don't you think so?"

"That people should only get married if they're in love? I don't know." But he shifted his gaze away so quickly that it was obvious he had something going on inside. "I've never been married before."

That was a careful way to answer the question. Did that mean he had been in love but not enough to marry the girl? Or he'd never been in love? Maybe he was nursing a serious broken heart and it was too painful to discuss. "Your parents are married. Aren't they in love?"

"Sure. It's just not something I've given a lot of thought to."

"So think about it." She was pushing him, plain and simple, but this was important compatibility stuff that she'd never questioned. Everyone believed in love. Right? "I'm just wondering now why you needed a fake wife. Maybe you should have been looking for someone to fall in love with this whole time instead of taking me to lunch for a year."

He hadn't been dating anyone, this she knew for a fact because she'd asked. Multiple times. Her curiosity on the matter might even be described as morbid.

"Viv." His voice had gone quiet and she liked the way he said her name with so much texture. "If I'd wanted to spend time with someone other than you over the last year, I would have. I like you. Is that so hard to believe?"

Her mouth curved up before she could catch it. But why should she? Jonas made her smile, even when he was deflecting her question. Probably because he didn't think about her "that way" no matter how hot the kiss outside her bedroom had been. One-sided then. They were friends. Period. And she should definitely not be sad about that. He was a wonderful, kind man who made not thinking wicked thoughts impossible the longer they sat on a bed together behind closed doors.

Yeah, she could pretend she was practicing for a relationship with some other man all she wanted. Didn't change the fact that deep in her heart Viv wished she could be the person Jonas would fall madly in love with.

But she knew she couldn't keep Jonas. At least she was in the right place to fix her relationship pitfalls.

Now, how did one go about seducing a man while giving him the distinct impression she could take him or leave him?

Five

The bed in Jonas's mother's guest room must have razor blades sewn into the comforter. It was the only explanation for why his skin felt like it was on fire as he forced himself to lie there chatting with Viv as if they really were a real married couple having a debrief after his family's third degree.

They *were* a real married couple having a chat.

If only she hadn't brought up the *L* word. The one concept he had zero desire to talk about when it came to marriage. Surely Viv knew real married couples who didn't love each other. It couldn't be that huge of a departure, otherwise the divorce rate would be a lot lower.

But they were a married couple, albeit not a traditional one behind closed doors. If they were a traditional married couple, Jonas would be sliding his fingers across the mattress and taking hold of Viv's thigh so he could brace her for the exploration to come. His lips would fit so well in the hollow near her throat. So far, she hadn't seemed to clue in that every muscle beneath his skin strained toward her, and he had no idea how she wasn't as affected by the sizzling awareness as he was.

They were on a bed. They were married. The door was closed. What did that equal? Easy math—and it was killing him that they were getting it so wrong. Why wasn't he rolling his wife beneath him and getting frisky with breathless anticipation as they shushed each other before someone heard them through the walls?

"Since we like each other so much, maybe we should talk about the actual sleeping arrangements," she suggested. "There's not really a good way to avoid sharing the bed and we're keeping things platonic when no one's around."

Oh, right, because this was an exercise in insanity, just like dinner. He really shouldn't be picturing Viv sliding between cool sheets, naked of course, and peeking up at him from under her lashes as she clutched the pale blue fabric to her breasts.

"I can sleep on the floor," he croaked. She cocked a brow, eyeing him as if she could see right through his zipper to the hard-on he wasn't hiding very well. "I insist. You're doing me a favor. It's the least I can do."

"I wasn't expecting anyone to sleep on the floor. We're friends. We can sleep in the same bed and keep our hands off each other. Right?" Then she blinked and something happened to her eyes. Her gaze deepened, elongating the moment, and heat teased along the edges of his nerve endings. "Unless you think it would be too much of a temptation."

He swallowed. Was she a mind reader now? How had she figured out that he had less than pure thoughts about sharing a bed with his wife? How easy it would be to reach out in the middle of the night, half-asleep, and pull her closer for a midnight kiss that wouldn't have any daylight consequences because nothing counted in the dark.

Except everything with Viv counted. That was the problem. They had a friendship he didn't want to lose and he had taken a vow with Warren and Hendrix that he couldn't violate.

"No, of course not," he blurted out without checking his emphatic delivery. "I mean, definitely it'll be hard—" *Dear God.* "Nothing will be hard! Everything will be…" *Not easy. Don't say easy.* "I have to go check on…something."

Before he could fully internalize how much of an ass he was making of himself, he bolted from the bed and fled the room, calling over his shoulder, "Feel free to use the bathroom. I'll wait my turn."

Which was a shame because what he really needed was a cold shower. Prowling around the house like a cat burglar because he didn't want to alert anyone he'd just kicked himself out of his own newlywed bedroom, Jonas poked around in his dad's study but felt like he was intruding in the hallowed halls of academia.

He and his dad were night and day. They loved each other, but Brian Kim wasn't a businessman in any way, shape or form. It was like the entrepreneurial gene had skipped a generation. Put Brian in a lecture hall and he was in his element. In truth, the only reason Jonas had gone to Duke was because his father was on faculty and his parents had gotten a discount on tuition. They'd refused to take a dime of Grandfather's money since Brian hadn't filled a position at Kim Electronics.

If his dad had taken a job at any other university, Jonas never would have met Warren, Hendrix and Marcus. His friendship with those guys had shaped his twenties, more so than he'd ever realized, until now.

The funeral had been brutal. So hard to believe his friend was inside that casket. His mom had held his hand the entire time and even as a twenty-one-year-old junior in college who desperately wanted to be hip, he hadn't let go once. Marcus had been down in the dumps for weeks, but they'd all shrugged it off. Typical male pride and bruised feelings. Who hadn't been the victim of a woman's fickle tastes?

But Marcus had been spiraling down and none of them had seen it. That was the problem with love. It made you do crazy, out-of-character things. Like suicide.

Jonas slid into his dad's chair and swiveled it to face the window, letting the memory claw through his gut as he stared blindly at the koi pond outside in the garden. There was no shame in having missed the signs. Everyone had. But that reassurance rang as hollow today as it had ten years ago. What could he have done? Talked sense into the guy? Obviously the pain had been too great, and the lesson for Jonas was clear: don't let a woman get her hooks into you.

That was why he couldn't touch Viv anymore. The temptation wasn't just too much. It was deadly. Besides, she was his friend. He'd already crossed a bunch of lines in the name of ensuring his family bought into the marriage, but it was all just an excuse to have his cake and eat Viv, too.

Bad, bad thing to be thinking about. There was a part of him that couldn't believe Viv would be dangerous to his mental state. But the risks were too great, especially to their friendship. They'd gone a whole year without being tempted. What was different now? Proximity? Awareness? The fact that he'd already kissed her and couldn't undo the effect on his body every time he got within touching distance of her?

That one.

Sleeping with her in the bed was going to be torture. He really didn't know if he had it in him. Probably the best thing to do was sleep on the couch in the living room and set an alarm for something ridiculous like 5:00 a.m. Then he could go for a jog and come back like he'd slept in Viv's bed all night long. Of course he'd never jogged in his life…but he could start. Might burn off some of the awareness he couldn't shake.

That was the best plan. He headed back to the bedroom they shared to tell her.

But when he eased open the door and slipped inside, she was still in the bathroom. He settled onto the bed to wait, next to her open suitcase. There was literally no reason for him to glance inside other than it was right there. Open. With a frothy bunch of racy lingerie laid out across the other clothes.

Holy crap. Jonas's eyes burned the longer he stared at the thin straps and drapes of lace. Was that the *top*? Viv's breasts were supposed to be covered by that? Something that skimpy should be illegal. And red. But the lace was lemon yellow, the color of the frosting Viv slathered all over the cupcakes she always brought him when they had lunch. His mouth watered at the thought of tasting Viv through all that lace. It would be easy. The pattern would show 90 percent of her skin.

The little panties lay innocuously to the side as if

an afterthought. Probably because there wasn't enough lace making up the bottom half of the outfit to rightfully call them panties. He could picture them perfectly on his wife's body and he could envision slowly stripping them off even more vividly.

Wait. What was Viv doing with such smoking-hot lingerie?

Was she planning to wear it for *him*? His brain had no ability to make sense of this revelation. She'd brought lingerie. To wear. Of course the only man in the vicinity was Jonas. Who else would she be wearing it for?

That was totally against the rules.

And totally against what he was capable of giving her in this marriage. She might as well drape herself in hearts and flowers. Viv clearly thought love was a recipe for marriage. Stir well and live happily ever after. He wasn't the right ingredient for that mix.

The sound of running water being shut off rattled through the walls. Viv had just emerged from the shower. He should get the hell out of that bedroom right now. But before he could stand, she walked out of the bathroom holding a towel loosely around her body. Her *naked* body. She was still wet. His gaze traced the line of one drop as it slid down her shoulder and disappeared behind the towel.

"Oh. I didn't know you'd come back," she announced unnecessarily as he was reasonably certain she wouldn't have waltzed into the room mostly naked if she'd known he was sitting on the bed.

"Sorry," he muttered, and meant to avert his eyes but the towel had slipped a little, which she'd done nothing to correct.

Maybe she wanted him to catch a glimpse of her perfect breasts. Not that he knew for sure that they were perfect. But the little half-moon slices peeking above the towel flashed at him more brightly than a neon sign, and his whole body went up in flames.

Anything that powerful at only a quarter strength had to be perfect in its entirety.

"Did you want to take a turn in the bathroom?" she asked casually. Still standing there. Wet. In a towel. Naked.

"Uh, sure." He didn't stand. He should cross the room and barricade himself in the bathroom, where it wouldn't matter if she'd used all the hot water because the shower needed to be glacial.

"Okay. Can you give me two minutes? I need to dry my hair." And then she laughed with a little peal that punched him the gut. "Normally I would wrap it up in the towel but there are only two and I didn't want to hog them all."

Then she pulled on the edge of the towel, loosening it from the column it formed around her body and lifted the tail end to the ends of her dripping hair. A long slice of skin peeked through the opening she'd unwittingly created and the answering flash of heat that exploded in his groin would have put him on his knees if he'd been standing. Good thing he hadn't moved.

"You should get dressed," he suggested, but she didn't hear him because his voice wasn't working. Besides, *dressed* could have a lot of different meanings, and the frothy yellow concoction in her suitcase appeared to be the next outfit of choice. If she hadn't been planning to slip it on, it wouldn't be on top, laid out so carefully.

Oh, man. Would she have been wearing it when he got into bed later? No warning, just bam!

He should pretend he hadn't seen the yellow concoction. How else could he find out if that had been her plan? That had to be her plan. Please, God, let it be her plan.

He was so hard, it was a wonder his erection hadn't busted out of his zipper.

Clearing his throat, he tested out speaking again. "I can come back."

That, she heard. "Oh, you don't have to. Really, I've taken way too long already. We're sharing and I'm not used to that. The shower was lovely and I couldn't help standing there under the spray, just letting my mind drift."

Great. Now his mind was drifting—into the shower with her as she stood there. Naked. Letting the water sluice down her body, eyes closed with a small, rapturous smile gracing her face.

He groaned. What was he doing to himself?

"Are you okay?" Her attention honed in on him and she apparently forgot she wasn't wearing anything but a damp towel because she immediately crossed the room to loom over him, her expression laced with concern.

It would take less than a second to reach out and snag her by the waist, pulling her down into his lap. That towel would fall, revealing her perfect breasts, and they'd be right there, ripe and available to taste. No yellow concoction needed. But that would be criminal. She should get to wear her newlywed lingerie if she wanted.

"Oh." Viv blushed all at once, the pink stain spreading across her cheeks, and Jonas could not tear his eyes off her face. But she was staring at the open suitcase. "You didn't see that ridiculous thing Grace gave me, did you?"

She picked up the yellow lacy top and held it up to her body, draping it over the towel one-handed, which had the immediate consequence of smooshing her breasts higher. "Can you imagine me wearing this?"

With absolute, brilliant clarity.

"I don't know what she was thinking," Viv continued as if his entire body wasn't poised to explode. "'Open this with Jonas,' she says with a sly wink. I thought it was going to be a joke, like a gravy boat, and besides, this isn't a real marriage, so I didn't think you'd actually want to help open gifts. Sorry I didn't wait for you."

She rolled her eyes with another laugh that did not help things down below.

"That's okay. Next time." What was he saying? *Sure, I'll help open future gifts full of shockingly transparent clothing that would make a porn star blush?* "Your sister meant well. She doesn't know we're not sleeping together."

Or rather they weren't yet. In a scant few minutes, they'd be in the bed. Together. Maybe some sleeping would occur but it wasn't looking too likely unless he got his body cooled down to something well below its current thermonuclear state.

"Well, true. But obviously she expects us to be hot and heavy, right? I mean, this is the kind of stuff a woman wears for a man who can't keep his hands off her." Suddenly, she swept him with a glance that held a glittery sort of challenge. "We should probably practice that, don't you think?"

"What?" he squawked. "You want me to practice not being able to keep my hands off you?"

Actually, he needed to practice self-control, not the other way around. Restraint was the name of the game. Perfect. He could focus on that instead of the fact that the lingerie had been a gift, not a carefully crafted plan to drive him over the brink.

It was a testament to how messed up he was that he couldn't squelch his disappointment.

She nodded. "My sister just got married not too long ago and she's pretty open with me about how hot the sex is. I think she envisions all newlyweds being like that."

"That doesn't mean she expects us to strip down in your parents' foyer," he countered a little too forcefully. Mostly because he was envisioning how hot *this* newlywed couple could be. They could give Grace and her husband a run for her money, all right.

No. No, they could not.

Viv was not wearing the yellow lacy gateway to heaven for him tonight or any night. She wasn't challenging him to out-sex her sister's marriage. There was no sex at all in their future because Viv had a career she cared about and really didn't have time for a man's inconvenient attraction. Even if the man was her husband. Especially if the man was her husband who had promised to keep things platonic.

Of course he'd done that largely for himself. He'd never experienced such a strong physical pull before and he wasn't giving in to it no matter how badly he wanted to. There was a slippery edge between keeping himself out of trouble so he could honor his promise to his late friend and maintaining his integrity with Viv and his family about the nature of his marriage.

On that note, he needed to change the subject really fast. And get his rampant need under control before he lost everything.

Viv couldn't quite catch her breath. Her lungs ached to expand but the towel was in a precarious spot. If she breathed any deeper, it would slip completely from her nerveless fingers.

Though based on how long it was taking Jonas to clue in that this was a seduction scene, maybe throwing her boobs in his face would get the point across.

God, she sucked at this. Obviously. The girls on TV made it look so simple. She'd bet a million dollars that if this scene had happened on *Scandal*, the seductress would already be in the middle of her third orgasm.

Maybe she *should* have opened the wedding gift with Jonas instead of laying it out so he could find it. For some reason, she'd thought it would give him ideas. That he'd maybe take the lead and they could get something going while they had the perfect setup to indulge in the sparks that only burned hotter the longer they didn't consummate their marriage.

How was she supposed to prove she could be the opposite of clingy with a man she wanted more than oxygen if he wouldn't take her up on the invitation she'd been dangling in his face?

"Instead of practicing anything physical," Jonas said, "we should get our stories straight. We're not going to be hanging out with your family anytime soon but mine is just on the other side of the door. I don't want any missteps like the one at dinner where we didn't plan our responses ahead of time and somehow ended up promising to go to Korea."

"I don't mind going to Korea, Jonas. I would love to see it."

He shook his head with bemusement. "It's a sixteen-hour trip and that's only if there's a not a horribly long line in customs, which even a Kim cannot cut through. Trust me, I'm doing you a favor by not taking you."

How had they shifted from talking about hot sex to visiting his grandfather? That was not how this was supposed to go.

"Well, we have plenty of time to talk about our stories, too," she said brightly. "And the good news is that my hair is almost dry so the bathroom is yours. I like to read before going to sleep so I'll just be here whenever you're ready."

"Oh. Um…" Jonas glanced at the bed and back at her. "Okay. I was thinking about sleeping on the couch and setting an alarm—"

"You can't do that," she cut him off in a rush. That would ruin everything. "What if someone gets up for a midnight snack? Also, the couch would be so uncomfortable. Sleep here. I insist."

She shooed him toward the bathroom and the moment he shut the door, she dragged air into her lungs in deep gulps as she dropped the towel and twisted her hair into a modified updo at her crown, spilling tendrils down her cheeks. Then she slithered into the shameless yellow teddy and panties set that she'd picked out with Grace yesterday. Strictly so she could rub it in that she had a hot husband to wear it for, of course. And then she'd had Grace gift wrap it. The sly wink had been all her sister's idea, so she really hadn't fibbed much when she'd related the story to Jonas.

The lace chafed at her bare nipples, sending ripples

of heat through her core. The panties rode high and tight, the strings threading between her cheeks. Not a place she was used to having pressure and friction, but it was oddly exciting.

No wonder women wore this stuff. She felt sexy and more than a little turned on just by virtue of getting dressed. Who knew?

The sound of running water drifted through the walls as Jonas went through his nightly routine. She dove into bed and pulled up the covers until they were tight around her shoulders. Wait. That wasn't going to work. Experimentally, she draped the sheet across her chest like a toga, and threw her shoulders back. Huh. The one breast looked spectacular in the low-cut lace teddy, but the other one was covered up, which didn't seem like the point. Inching the sheet down, she settled into place against the pillow until she was happy with how she looked.

That was a lot of skin on *display*. Much more than she was used to. The lace left little to the imagination.

Surely this would be enough to entice Jonas into making the most of this opportunity to share a bedroom.

Light. She leaped up and slammed down the switch, leaving only the bedside lamp illuminated and leaped back under the covers. The doorknob to the bathroom rattled and she lost her nerve, yanking the sheet back up to cover the yellow lace until X-ray vision would be the only way Jonas could tell what she was wearing. He strode into the room.

Oh, God. Was a more delicious man ever created in the history of time? He'd untucked his button-down and the tail hung casually below his waist. Plenty of access for a woman to slide her hands underneath. There was a gaping hole where his tie had been. A V framed a slice of his chest and he'd rolled his sleeves up to midforearm. It was the most undressed she'd ever seen him and her pulse quickened the closer he came.

This gorgeous creature was about to strip all that off and *get into bed*. With her. This was such a bad idea. Alluring and aloof was not in her wheelhouse and at that moment, she wanted Jonas with a full body ache that felt completely foreign and completely right at the same time.

"I thought you were going to be reading," he said, and stopped in the middle of the room as if he'd hit an invisible wall.

So close. And yet so far.

She shook her head, scrambling for a plausible excuse when she'd just said that was what she planned to do. Couldn't hold an e-reader and pretend you weren't wearing sexy lingerie that screamed *put your hands on me* at the same time.

In retrospect, that might have been a nice scene. She could have been reading with the tablet propped up on her stomach, which would have left her torso completely bare without making it look like she'd set up the scene that way. Dang it. Too late now.

"I couldn't find anything that held my attention."

"Oh. Okay."

And then the entire world fell away along with most of her senses as Jonas started unbuttoning his shirt. It was a slow, torturous event as he slipped the buttons free and each one revealed more of his beautiful body.

Thank God she hadn't stuck a book in front of her face. Otherwise she'd have missed the Jonas Striptease.

She glanced up to see his dark eyes on hers. Their

gazes connected and she had the distinct impression he hadn't expected her to be watching him undress. But he didn't seem terribly unhappy about the audience, since he kept going. She didn't look away either.

He let the shirt fall, revealing first one shoulder, then the other. It shouldn't have been such a shock to see the indentations of muscles in his biceps as his arms worked off the shirt. She knew he hit the gym on a regular basis. They'd been friends for a year and talked about all manner of subjects. Sometimes he told her about his workout routine or mentioned that he'd switched it up and his arms were sore. Little had she realized what a visual panorama had been in store for her as a result.

"I feel like I should be wearing something sparkly underneath my pants," Jonas said with wry amusement. "Would it be possible for you to not watch me?"

"Oh. Um…sure." Cheeks on fire, she flipped over and faced the wall, careful to keep the sheet up around her neck. With the motion, it stretched tight. More mummy than Marilyn Monroe, but this was her first seduction. Surely even a woman like Marilyn had a few practice runs before she got it right. This one was Viv's.

And she needed a lot of practice, clearly, since she'd been caught staring and made Jonas uncomfortable at the same time. The whisper of fabric hitting the carpet made her doubly sorry she hadn't been facedown in a book when he came out of the bathroom because she could easily have pretended to be reading while watching the slow reveal out of the corner of her eye.

The bed creaked and the mattress shifted with Jonas's weight. "Still think this is a good idea?"

"I never said it was a good idea," she shot back over her shoulder. "I said our friendship could take it."

Which wasn't a given now that he was so close and so male and so much the subject of her fantasies that started and ended in a bed very much like this one. And she'd been forced to miss half of it due to Jonas's inconvenient sense of propriety. Well, he was done undressing now, right? This was her seduction and she wanted to face him. Except just as she rolled, he snapped off the bedside lamp, plunging the room into darkness.

"Good night," Jonas said, his voice sinfully rich in the dark.

The covers pulled a little as he turned over and settled into position. To go to sleep.

As mood killers went, that was a big one. She'd totally botched this.

Okay. Not totally. This was just a minor setback, most likely because she was trying to play hard to get, which was not as easy as it sounded, and frankly, not her typical method of operation. Plus? This was not a typical relationship. Jonas needed to keep her around, so by default this wasn't going to go like it had with her ex-boyfriends.

She had to approach this like a new recipe that hadn't quite turned out because she'd gone against her instincts and added an ingredient that she didn't like. And if she didn't like it, what was the point?

This was her cupcake to bake. Being the opposite of clingy and needy had only gotten her a disinterested husband—and rightfully so. How was he even supposed to know she wished he'd roll back over and explore the lingerie-clad body she'd hidden under the covers like a blushing virgin bride? Viv wasn't the kind of woman to inspire a man to slavish passion or it would have happened already.

She had to be smart if she couldn't be a femme fatale.

She blinked against the dark and tried not to focus on how the sound of Jonas breathing fluttered against her skin in a very distracting way. Somehow she was going to have to announce her interest in taking things to the next level in big bold letters without also giving him the impression she couldn't live without him. Though perhaps that last part wouldn't be too difficult; after all, she'd already been pretending for a year.

Six

After the weekend of torture, Jonas went to work on Monday with renewed determination to get his grandfather moving on the Park Industries merger. The sooner the ink was dry on that deal, the better. Then Jonas could get over his irritation that his marriage to Viv was what had tipped the scales toward his grandfather's decision to retire.

Grandfather recognized Jonas's accomplishments with Kim Electronics. Deep down, he knew that. But it rankled that the conversation about naming Jonas as the next CEO had come about *after* Grandfather had met Viv.

Didn't matter. The subject had come up. That was enough. And Jonas intended to make sure the subject didn't get dropped, because if he was forced to stay married to Viv, he should get something out of it. An Academy Award wouldn't be out of line after the stellar performance he'd turned in at his parents' house. How he'd acted like he'd been sleeping all night while lying next to his wife was still a mystery to him and he was the one who'd pulled it off.

Her scent still haunted him at odd moments. Like now. This conference call he'd supposedly been participating in had gotten maybe a quarter of his attention. Which was not a good way to prove he deserved the position of CEO.

But it was a perfect way to indulge in the memory of the sweet way she'd curled up next to him, her even breathing oddly arousing and lulling at the same time. He'd expected it to be weird the next morning, like maybe they wouldn't look each other in the eye, but Viv had awoken refreshed and beautiful, as if she'd gotten a great night's sleep. He pretended the same and they settled into an easy camaraderie around his parents that hadn't raised a single brow.

At least that part was over. Viv's mom and dad had invited them for dinner on Friday and he was plenty nervous about that experience. It would probably be fine. As long as he didn't have to act like he couldn't keep his hands off Viv. Or act like he didn't want to touch her. Actually, he'd lost track of *what* he was supposed to be doing. Hence the reason he hated lying. The truth was so much easier.

But when he got home that evening after a long day that had included a two-hour debrief with Legal regarding the merger proposal, Viv was sitting on the couch with two glasses of wine. She smiled at him and he felt entirely incapable of faking anything. Especially if it came down to pretending he didn't want to be with her.

His answering smile broadened hers and that set off

all sorts of fireworks inside that should have been a big fat warning to back off, but he was tired and there was absolutely nothing wrong with having a glass of wine with his friend Viv after work. That was his story and he was sticking to it.

"Are we celebrating something?" he asked as he hung his work bag on the hook near the refrigerator.

"Yes, that I can in fact open a bottle of wine all by myself." She laughed with that little peal he'd never noticed before he'd married her, but seemed to be a common occurrence lately. Or had she always laughed like that and he'd been too stuck in his own head to notice how warm it was?

"Was that in question?" He took the long-stemmed glass from her outstretched fingers and eased onto the couch next to her. Instantly, that turned into a big mistake as her scent wrapped around him. It slammed through his gut and his arm jerked, nearly spilling the wine.

For God's sake. This ridiculousness had to stop, especially before Friday or the second family trial by fire would end in a blaze.

"I'm just not talented in the cork-pulling arena," she answered casually as if she hadn't noticed his idiocy. "My skills start and end with baking."

Yes. Baking. They could talk about cupcakes while he got back on track. "Speaking of which, I wasn't expecting you home. Doesn't the shop stay open until seven on Mondays?"

She smiled. "You've been memorizing my work schedule? That's sweet. Josie is closing up for me. I wanted to be here when you got home."

"You did? Why?"

Because I couldn't stay away, Jonas. You're so much more interesting to me than cupcakes, Jonas. I want to strip you naked and have my wicked way with you, Jonas.

There came her gorgeous laugh again. He couldn't hear it enough, especially when he was in the middle of being such a doofus. If she was laughing, that was a good thing. Otherwise, he'd owe her an apology. Not that she could read his thoughts, thank God.

"I wanted to see you. We're still friends, right?"

Oh, yeah. "Right."

"Also, I wasn't kidding when I said my sisters are going to have an eagle eye on our relationship this Friday." Viv sipped her wine, her gaze on his over the rim. "We're still a little jumpy around each other. I'm not sure why, but sharing a bed didn't seem to help."

Huge mystery there. Maybe because his awareness level had shot up into the stratosphere since he'd woken up with a woman whom he hadn't touched one single time. Or it could be because he'd been kicking himself over his regret ever since. He shouldn't regret not touching her. It was the right move.

"No, it didn't help," he muttered. "That wasn't ever going to be the result of sleeping together platonically."

She nodded sagely. "Yes, I realized that sometime between then and now. Don't worry. I have a new plan."

"I wasn't worried. What is it?"

"We're trying too hard. We need to dial it back and spend time as friends. We were comfortable around each other then. It can totally be that way again."

That sounded really great to him. And also like there was a catch he couldn't quite see. Cautiously he eyed her. "What, like I take you to lunch and we just talk about stuff?"

"Sure." She shrugged and reached out to lace her fingers through his free hand. "See, we can hold hands and it doesn't mean anything. I'm just hanging out with my friend Jonas, whom I like. Hey, Jonas, guess what?"

He had to grin. This was not the worst plan he'd ever heard. In fact, it was pretty great. He'd missed their easy camaraderie and the lack of pretension. Never had she made him feel like he should be anything other than himself when they hung out. "Hey, Viv. What?"

"I made reservations at this new restaurant in Cary that sounds fab. It's Thai."

"That's my favorite." Which she well knew. It was hers, too. He took the first deep breath in what seemed like hours. They were friends. He could dang well act like one and stop nosing around Viv like a hormonal teenager.

"Drink your wine and then we'll go. My treat."

"No way. You opened the bottle of wine. The least I can do is spring for dinner."

"Well, it was a major accomplishment," she allowed, and clinked her glass to his as he held out the stemware. "I'm thrilled to have it recognized as such."

And the evening only got better from there. Jonas drove Viv to the restaurant and they chattered all the way about everything and nothing, which he'd have called a major accomplishment, too, since he managed to concentrate on the conversation and not on the expanse of Viv's bare leg mere inches from his hand resting on the gearshift. The food was good and the service exceptional.

As they walked in the door of the condo later, Jonas paused and helped Viv take off her jacket, then turned to hang it up for her in the foyer coat closet.

"I have to say," he called over his shoulder as he slid the hanger into place. "Dinner was a great idea."

He shut the door and Viv was still standing there in the foyer with a small smile.

"It's the best date I've been on in a long time," she said. "And seems like the plan worked. Neither of us is acting weird or jumpy."

"True." He'd relaxed a while back and didn't miss the edginess that had plagued him since the wedding ceremony. He and Viv were friends and that was never going to change. That was the whole reason he'd come up with this idea in the first place. "We may not set off the fire alarms when we visit with your family on Friday, but we can certainly pull off the fact that we like each other, which is not something all married couples can say."

That was fine with him. Better that way anyway. His reaction to the pull between him and Viv was ridiculous. So unlike him. He had little experience with something so strong that it dug under his skin, and he'd handled it badly.

Fortunately, he hadn't done anything irreversible that would have ruined their friendship. Though there'd been more than a handful of moments in that bed at his parents' that he'd been really afraid it was going to go the other way.

But then she stepped a little closer to him in the foyer, waltzing into his space without hesitation. The foyer was just a small area at the entrance of the condo with a coat closet and nothing more to recommend it. So there was little else to take his attention off the woman who'd suddenly filled it with her presence.

"We've been friends a long time," she said, and it was such a strange, unnecessary comment, but he nodded anyway because something had shifted in the atmosphere.

He couldn't put his finger on it. The relaxed, easy vibe from the restaurant had morphed into something else—a quickened sense of anticipation that he couldn't explain, but didn't hate. As if this really was a date and they'd moved on to the second part of the evening's activities.

"We've done a lot of firsts in the last little while," she continued, also unnecessarily because he was well aware that he'd shifted the dynamic of their relationship by marrying her.

"Yeah. Tonight went a long way toward getting us back to normal. To being friends without all the weirdness that sprang up when I kissed you."

That was probably the dumbest thing he could have said. He'd thrown that down between them and it was like opening the electrical panel of a television, where all the live components were exposed, and all it would take was one wrong move to fry the delicate circuitry.

Better to keep the thing covered.

But it was too late. Her gaze landed square on his mouth as if she was reliving the kiss, too. Not the nice and unexpectedly sweet kiss at the wedding ceremony. But the hot, tongue-on-tongue kiss outside her bedroom when they'd been practicing being a couple. The necessity of that practice had waned since his family had bought the marriage hook, line and sinker. Sure, they still had to get through her family, but he wasn't worried about it, racy lingerie gifts aside.

Now the only reason to ever kiss Viv again would be because he couldn't stop himself.

Which was the worst reason he could think of. And keep thinking about, over and over again.

"I don't think it was weirdness, Jonas," she murmured.

Instantly, he wished there was still some circumstance that required her to call him Mr. Kim. Why that was such a turn-on remained a mystery to him. But really, everything about Viv was a turn-on. Her laugh. Her cupcakes. The way her hair lay so shiny and soft against her shoulders.

"Trust me, it was weird," he muttered. "I gave myself entirely too many inappropriate thoughts with that kiss."

And that was the danger of being lulled back into a false sense of security with the sociable, uneventful dinner. He'd fallen into friendship mode, where he could say anything on his mind without consequence.

The admission that had just come out of his mouth was going to have consequences.

Her smile went from zero to sixty in less than a second and all at once, he wasn't sure the consequences were going to be anything close to what he'd envisioned. She waltzed even closer and reached up to adjust his tie in a provocative move that shouldn't have been as affecting as it was.

The tie hadn't needed adjusting. The knot was precisely where he'd placed it hours ago when he'd gotten dressed for work. It slid down a few centimeters and then a few more as she loosened it.

Loosened it. As if she intended to take it off.

But she stopped short of committing, which was good. Really…good. He swallowed as she speared him with her contemplative gaze, her hands still at his collar in an intimate touch. She was so close he could pull her into his arms if he wanted to.

He wanted to. Always.

Dinner hadn't changed that.

"The thing is, Jonas," she said. "I've had some thoughts, too. And if yours are the same as mine, I'm trying to figure out why they're inappropriate."

She flattened her hands on his lapels. The pressure sang through him and it would feel even better if he didn't have a whole suit jacket and two shirts between her palms and his skin.

The direction of this conversation floored him. And if she kept it up, the floor was exactly where they were going to end up.

"What are you saying, Viv?" he asked hoarsely, scrambling to understand. "That you lie awake at night and think about that kiss, aching to do it again?"

She nodded and something so powerful swept through his body that he could hardly breathe. This was the opposite of what should be happening. She should be backing off and citing her inability to focus on a man and her career at the same time. She was too busy, too involved in her business to date. This was the absolute he'd banked on for long agonizing hours, the thing that was keeping him from indulging in the forbidden draw between them.

Because if he gave in, he'd have no control over what happened next. That certainty had already been proven with what little they'd experimented so far. More would be catastrophic.

And so, so fantastically amazing.

"After tonight, I'm convinced we're missing an opportunity here," she said, her voice dripping with something sensual that he'd never have expected from his sunny friend Viviana Dawson. *Kim.*

Viv wasn't his friend. She was his wife. He'd been ignoring that fact for an entire day, but it roared back to the forefront with an implication he couldn't ignore. Except he didn't know what it meant to him, not really. Not just a means to an end, though it was an inescapable fact that she'd married him as a favor.

And he wanted to exploit that favor to get her naked and under him? It was improper, ridiculous. So very illicit that his body tightened with thick anticipation.

"What opportunity is that?" he murmured, letting his gaze flick over her face, searching for some sign that the answer about to come out of her mouth *was not* a green light to get naked.

Because he'd have a very difficult time saying no. In fact, he couldn't quite remember why he should say no. He shouldn't say no. If nothing else, taking this next step meant he wasn't lying to anyone about their marriage.

Her limpid brown eyes locked on to his. "We're both too busy to date. And even if we weren't, I have a feeling that 'oh, by the way, I'm married' isn't a great pickup line. You said it yourself. We spark. If our friendship can take a kiss, maybe it can take more. We should find out."

More. He liked the word *more* a lot. Especially if her dictionary defined it as lots and lots of sex while maintaining their friendship. If things got too intense, he could back off with no harm, no foul. It was like the absolute best of all worlds.

Unless that wasn't what she meant.

Clarification would be in order, just to be sure they were speaking the same language. "More?"

"Come on, Jonas." She laughed a little breathlessly and it trilled through him. "Are you going to make me spell it out?"

"Yes, I absolutely am," he growled, because the whole concept of Viv talking dirty to him was doing things to his insides that he was enjoying the hell out of. If he'd known dinner was *this* kind of date, he'd have skipped dessert. "I want to be crystal clear about what's on the table here."

Instead of suggesting things Jonas could do to her—all of which he'd immediately commit to memory so he didn't miss a single one—she watched him as she hooked the neckline of her dress and pulled it to the side. A flash of yellow seared his vision as his entire body tensed in recognition.

"I'm wearing my sister's gift," she murmured, and that admission was as much of a turn-on as any dirty talk. Maybe more so because he'd been fantasizing about that scrap of yellow lace for a million years.

"I bet it looks amazing on you."

"Only one way to find out," she shot back and curled her fingers around his lapels to yank him forward.

He met her mouth in a searing kiss without hesitation. All of his reservations melted in an instant as he sank into her, shaping her lips with his as he consumed her heat, letting it spread deep inside.

Why had he resisted this? Viv didn't want anything from him, didn't expect an emotional outpouring or even anything permanent. This was all going to end at some point and thus didn't count. No chance for

romantic nonsense. No declarati~~~~~~~~
be forthcoming—on either side. ~~~~~~~~
would be intact, as would his sw~~~~~~~~
and Hendrix.

Instead of two friends pretendin~~~~~~~~
couple having sex, they were going~~~~~~~~
friends who *were* having sex. Living th~~~~~~~~ppealed
to him enormously. Desire swept through him as he got
great handfuls of Viv's skin under his palms and everything but his wife drained from his mind.

Viv would have sworn on a truckload of Bibles that
the kiss outside her bedroom last week had been the
hottest one she'd ever participate in.

She'd have been wrong.

That kiss had been startling in its perfection. Unexpected in its heat. It had gotten her motor humming
pretty fast. She'd been angling for another one just like
that. Thank God she hadn't gotten her wish.

This kiss exploded in her core like a cannon. Desire
crackled through the air as Jonas backed her up against
the wall, crowding her against it with his hard body,
demanding that her every curve conform to him. Her
flesh rapidly obeyed. She nearly wept with the glory
of Jonas pressed against her exactly as she'd fantasized
hundreds of times.

He angled her jaw with his strong fingers until he
got her situated the way he apparently wanted and then
plunged in with the wickedest of caresses. His tongue
slicked across hers so sensuously that she moaned
against it, would have sagged if he hadn't had her
pinned to the wall.

His hands nipped at her waist, skimmed upward and

both sides of the neckline. The fabric tore at seams as he separated it from her shoulders, and she gasped.

"I need to see you," he murmured fiercely. "I'll buy you two to make up for this one."

And with that, the dress came apart in his hands. He peeled it from between them, following the line of the reveal with his hot mouth, laving at her exposed flesh until he caught the silk strap of the yellow teddy in his teeth, scraping the sensitive hollow of her shoulder.

The sensation shot through her center with tight, heated pulls. *Oh, my.* His fingers tangled in the strap, binding his palm to her shoulder as he explored the skin beneath the yellow lace with his tongue, dipping and diving into the holes of the pattern. Then his lips closed around her nipple through the fabric and her whole body jerked. Hot, wet heat dampened the scrap between her legs. The awareness that Jonas had drenched her panties so quickly only excited her more.

What had happened to the kind, generous man she'd been so intent on seducing? He'd become a hungry, untamed creature who wanted to devour her. She loved every second. His tongue flicked out to tease her nipple, wetting the lace, and it was wickedly effective. Moans poured from her throat as her head thunked back against the wall.

All at once, he sank to his knees and trailed his lips across the gap between the top and the bottom of her sexy lingerie set, murmuring her full name. *Viviana.* The sound of it rang in her ears as he worshipped her stomach with his mouth, and it was poetry.

Her thighs pressed together, seeking relief from the ache his touch had created, and she arched into his lips, his hands, crying out as his fingers worked under the hem of her soaked panties. The gorgeous man she'd married glanced up at her from his supine position, his gaze so wickedly hot that she experienced a small quake at that alone, but then he slid one finger along her crease, teasing her core until she opened wider, begging him to fill her.

He did. Oh, how he did, one quick motion, then back out again. The exquisite friction burned through her core a second time and she cried out.

"Please, Jonas" dripped from her mouth with little gasping sighs and she whimpered as she pleaded with him for whatever he planned to give her next.

She didn't know she could be this wanton, that the man she'd married could drive her to neediness so easily. It was so hot that she felt the gathering of her release before she was ready for the exquisite torture to end. No way to hold back. She crested the peak and came with hard ripples against Jonas's fingers. The orgasm drained her of everything but him.

Falling apart at his hands was better than what she'd dreamed of, hoped for, imagined—and then some. And it still wasn't over.

He nipped at her lace-covered sex and swept her up in his arms, still quaking, to carry her to his bedroom. Blindly, she tried to clear her senses long enough to gain some semblance of control. Why, she wasn't sure, but being wound up in Jonas's arms wearing nothing but wet lace while he was still fully dressed felt a lot like she'd surrendered more than she'd intended to.

But he wasn't finished with the revelations.

He laid her out on the comforter and watched her as he stripped out of his suit jacket and tie. She shivered long and hard as he began unbuttoning his shirt, but she didn't dare blink for fear of missing the greatest show on earth—the sight of her husband shedding his clothes. For her. Because she'd finally gotten him to see reason.

They were friends. What better foundation was there to get naked with someone than because you liked each other? It was sheer brilliance, if she did say so herself. The fact that she'd been racking her brain over how to best get to this place when the answer had been staring her in the face for a year? She'd rather not dwell on that.

Good thing she had plenty else to occupy her mind. That beautiful torso of his came into sight, still covered by a white undershirt that clung to his biceps and lean waist, and she wanted to touch him so badly her fingers tingled. But then his hands moved to his belt and she didn't move. Couldn't. Her lungs rattled with the need to expand. Slowly, the belt loosened and he pulled it from the loops. After an eternity, it dropped to the floor, followed shortly by the pants, and then came the pièce de résistance. Jonas stripped off his undershirt and worked off his boxers in the most spectacular reveal of all. Better than Christmas, her birthday and flipping the sign in Cupcaked's window to Open for the first time.

Her husband's body was gorgeous, long, lean. Vibrating with need that hungrily sniffed out hers as he crawled onto the bed and onto her, easily knocking her back to the mattress, covering her body with his.

And then she wasn't so coherent after that. His arms encircled her as easily as his dominant presence did. His kiss claimed her lips irrevocably, imprinting them with his particular brand of possession, the likes of which she'd never known. Never understood could exist.

The sensuous haze he dropped her into was delicious

and she soaked it in, content to let him take his time as he explored her body with his hands more thoroughly than she'd have imagined possible when she still wore the yellow lace. She was so lost in him that it took her a minute to remember that she could indulge herself, too, if she wished.

Viv flattened her palms to his chest, memorizing the peaks and valleys of his body, reveling in the heat under her fingertips. She slid downward to cup his buttocks, shifting to align their hips because the ache at her core had only been awakened, not sated, and he had precisely what she needed.

He groaned deep in his throat as she circled against his thick, gorgeous erection, grinding her hips for maximum impact. The answering tilt of his hips enflamed her. As did the quickening of his breath.

"I need to be inside you," he murmured. "Before I lose my mind."

Rolling with her in his arms, he reached one hand out to sling open the bedside table and extracted a box of condoms with ruthless precision. In seconds, he'd sheathed himself and rolled back into place against her.

His thumb slid into the indentation in her chin, levering her head up to lock his hot-eyed gaze onto her as he notched himself at her entrance.

The tip of his shaft tormented her, sensitizing everything it touched as he paused in the worst sort of tease.

"Jonas," she gasped.

"Right here, sweetheart. Tell me what you want."

"Everything." And she couldn't take it back, no matter how much of a mistake it was to admit that she wasn't the kind of woman who could be in the midst of such passion and hold back.

Except she wasn't entirely sure he meant for her to as he gripped her hip with his strong fingers, lifted and pushed in with a groan, spreading her wide as he filled her. The luscious solid length of him stretched her tight, and before she could question it, one tear slipped from the corner of her eye. It was a testament to the perfection of how he felt moving inside her, how wholly encompassing the sensations were that washed over her as Jonas made love to her.

And she was ten kinds of a fool if she thought she could keep pretending this was practice for her next relationship.

"Amazing. Beautiful. Mine." Words rained down on her from Jonas's mouth as he increased the tempo. "I can't believe how this feels…you're so wet, so silky. I can't stop. Can't hold back."

For a woman who had never incited much more than mild interest in a man, to be treated to this kind of evidence that she was more than he could take—it was everything. "Give it all to me."

Unbelievably, there *was* more and he gave it to her, driving her to a soaring crescendo that made her feel more alive than anything in her memory. No longer was this bed a proving ground to show she could be with a man and not pour all of herself into him. He demanded her participation, wrung every drop of her essence out of her body.

She gladly surrendered it. Jonas was it for her, the man she'd married, the man she'd wanted for so very long.

As they both roared toward a climax, she had half a second to capture his face in her palms and kiss him with all the passion she could muster before they both shattered. She swallowed his groan and took the shudders of his body, absorbing them into hers even as she rippled through her own release. Everything was so much bigger, stronger, crisper than she'd have ever imagined and his mouth under hers curved into a blissful smile that her soul echoed.

And as he nestled her into his arms for a few badly needed moments of recovery time, she bit her lip against the wash of emotions that threatened to spill out all over their friendship.

She'd told him their relationship could take this. Now she had to stick to her promise. How in the world she was going to keep him from figuring out that she was in love with him?

Seven

For the second day in a row, Jonas struggled to maintain his composure at work. It was for an entirely different reason today than it had been yesterday. But still. His wife swirled at the center of it and he wasn't sure what to do with that.

Last night had been legendary. Off the charts. Far more explosive than he would have ever guessed—and he'd spent a lot of time contemplating exactly how hot things with Viv could be.

She'd surpassed everything he'd ever experienced. Even here in his somewhat sterile office that had all the hallmarks of a CEO who ran a billion-dollar global company, his loins tightened the second he let his thoughts stray. She'd made him thoroughly question what he knew about how it could be between a man and a woman. How it could be between Jonas and Viv, more importantly, because he had a feeling they weren't done.

How could they be done? He'd barely peeled back the first layer of possibilities, and he was nothing if not ravenous to get started on the second and third layers. Hot Viv. Sensual Viv. The list could be endless.

Instead of drooling like an idiot over the woman he'd married, Jonas squared his shoulders and pushed the erotic images from his mind. The merger with Park was still just a nebulous concept and no one had signed anything. This was the deal of the century, and Jonas had to get it done before anyone thought twice about marriage alliances. Sun Park's grandfather could still pull the plug if he'd had his heart set on a much more intimate merger. Thus far, Jonas had done little but meet with Legal on it.

Four hours later, he had sketched out a proposed hierarchy for the business entities, worked through the human resources tangle of potential duplicate positions and then run the numbers on whether the Kim Building could support the influx of new people. His grandfather would be coming by soon to take a tour and this was exactly the data Jonas needed at his fingertips. Data that would solidify his place as the rightful CEO of Kim Electronics, with or without an *impulse of the heart* on his résumé.

So that was still a sore spot apparently. Jonas tried to shrug it off and prepare for his grandfather's arrival, but wasn't at all surprised that Jung-Su showed up twenty minutes early. Probably a deliberate move to see if Jonas was prepared.

He was nothing if not ready, willing and able to prove

that he was the right choice. He'd been preparing to be his grandfather's successor since college.

He strolled to the reception area, where his admin had made Grandfather comfortable. Technically Jung-Su was the boss of everyone in this building, but he hadn't visited America in several years. Jonas held the helm here and he appreciated that Grandfather didn't throw his weight around. They had professional, mutual respect for each other, which Jonas had to believe would ultimately hold sway.

Jung-Su glanced up as Jonas came forward, his weathered face breaking into a polite smile. Grandfather stood and they shook hands.

"Please follow me," Jonas said, and indicated the direction. "I'd like to show you the executive offices."

Jung-Su nodded and inclined his head, but instead of following Jonas, he drew abreast and walked in lockstep toward the elevator. Over the weekend, they'd done a lot of sitting down and Jonas hadn't noticed how much his grandfather had shrunk. Jonas had always been taller and more slender to his grandfather's stocky build, but more so now, and it was a visual cue that his grandfather had aged. As much as Jonas had focused on getting his grandfather comfortable with passing the mantel, he'd given little thought to the idea that becoming the next CEO of the global company meant his mentorship with Jung-Su would be over.

"Tell me," Grandfather said as they reached the elevator. "How is your lovely wife?"

"She's…" *A vixen in disguise.* Not the kind of information his grandfather was looking for with the innocuous question. "Great. Her shop is constantly busy."

And Viv had ducked out early to take him on the ride

of his life last night. For the first time, he wondered if she'd planned the evening to end as it had or if it had been as spontaneous on her part as it had been on his. Maybe she'd been thinking about getting naked since the weekend of torture, too. If so, he liked that she'd been similarly affected.

They rode two floors up to the executive level. As they exited, Jonas and Jung-Su nodded to the various employees going about the business of electronics in a beehive of activity.

"You've mentioned your wife's business frequently," his grandfather commented just outside the boardroom where Jonas conducted the majority of his virtual meetings. "Doesn't she have other interests?"

The disapproval in his grandfather's voice was faint. "You don't understand. Her bakery is much more than just a business. It's an extension of her."

Cupcakes had been a mechanism to fit in among her older, more accomplished sisters, as she'd told him on numerous occasions. But it had morphed from there into a business that she could be proud of. Hell, it was a venture *he* was proud of.

"Anyone can pull a package of cupcake mix off the shelf at the grocery store," Jonas continued, infusing as much sincerity into his speech as he could. His grandfather had no call to be throwing shade at his wife's profession. "That's easy. Viv spends hours in her kitchen doing something special to hers that customers can't get enough of."

"It seems as if you are smitten by her cupcakes, as well," Grandfather commented with a tinge of amusement.

Jonas forced a return smile that hopefully didn't look

as pained as he suspected it did. *Smitten*. He wasn't smitten with Viv and it rankled that he'd managed to convince his grandfather that he was. Cupcakes, on the other hand—no pretending needed there. "Of course I am. That's what first drew me to her."

Like it was yesterday, he recalled how many times he'd found excuses to drop by Cupcaked to get a glimpse of Viv in those first few weeks after meeting her. Often she was in the back but if she saw him, she popped out for a quick hi, ready with a smile no matter what she had going on in the kitchen. That alone had kept him coming back. There was always someone in the office with a birthday or anniversary, and cupcakes always made an occasion more festive.

"Ah, yes, I recall that conversation at dinner where she mentioned you pretended to go there for her cupcakes but were really there to see her."

"It was both," he corrected easily since it was true. He could own that he liked Viv. They were friends.

Who'd seen each other naked.

Before he could stop it, images of Viv spilled through his mind.

The rush of heat to his body smacked him, sizzling across his skin so fast he had little chance of reeling it back. But he had to. This was the most inappropriate time to be thinking about his wife wearing that see-through yellow lacy concoction strictly for his benefit.

"Pardon me for a moment," Jonas croaked, and ducked into the executive washroom to get himself under control. Or as close to it as he could with an enormous erection that showed no signed of abating.

And while he stood in front of the mirror concentrating on his breathing and doing absolutely nothing constructive, he pulled out his phone to set a reminder to drop by the jewelry store on the way home. Viv had expressly asked for jewels as compensation for the favor she was doing him. She needed something pretty and ridiculously expensive.

Thinking of her draped in jewelry he'd bought wasn't helping.

After the longest five minutes of his life, Jonas finally got the tenting mostly under control. No one had noticed. Or at least that's what he tried to tell himself. His staff didn't walk around with their eyes on his crotch.

The biggest hit was to Jonas's psyche. How had he let Viv get under his skin like that? It was unacceptable. If nothing else, he needed to maintain his professionalism during this period when his grandfather's support meant everything. There were other contenders for Jung-Su's job, such as vice presidents who lived in Korea and had worked alongside the CEO for thirty years. Some of Mr. Park's staff could rise to the top as worthy heads of a global company, and those under the Park umbrella arguably had more experience running the factories that would come into play with the merger.

Jonas had to reel it back with Viv. Way back. There was no excuse for falling prey to baser urges and he definitely didn't want to find out what happened next if he kept going down this path. That was one absolute he trusted—the less he let a woman get tangled up in his emotions, the better.

Resolute, Jonas returned to find his grandfather in deep discussion with Jonas's chief financial officer, a man without whom Kim Electronics would suffer in the American market.

Perfect. This was an opportunity to guide the discussion to Jonas's accomplishments as well as those of his staff, who were a reflection of his ability to run the Americas branch. Back on track, Jonas smiled at the two men and jumped into the conversation as if he hadn't just had a minor freak-out over an incontrollable urge to drive straight home and bury himself in his wife.

That wasn't happening. Boundaries needed to happen. Jonas didn't have the luxury of letting his wife dig further under his skin. But when he got home later that night, it was to an empty house, and boundaries didn't seem like such a fun plan.

More disappointed than he had a right to be, Jonas prowled around the enormous condo to be sure Viv hadn't tucked herself away in a corner to read or watch TV. *Nada.* He glanced at his watch. It was well after seven. She must have gotten caught up at the shop. Totally her right to work late. They didn't answer to each other.

For a half second, he contemplated walking the four blocks to Cupcaked. Strictly so he could give Viv her gift, of course. But that smacked of eagerness to see her that he had no intention of admitting to. So instead, he flopped on the couch and scrolled through his never-ending inbox on his phone, desperate for something to take his mind off the resounding silence in the condo. Wow, was it quiet. Why had he never noticed that before? The high ceilings and exposed beams usually created an echo that reminded him of a museum, but he'd have to be making noise for that echo to happen.

Viv had made a lot of noise last night, but he hadn't been paying a whole lot of attention to whether the sounds of her gasps and sighs had filled the cavernous part of the loft. And now he was back to thinking about his wife, her gorgeous body and why she wasn't currently naked in his lap.

He scowled. They'd done zero to establish how their relationship would progress after last night. They should have. *He* should have. Probably the smartest thing would have been to establish that last night was a onetime thing. He couldn't keep having meltdowns at work or moon around over whether Viv planned to hang out with him at night.

He should find something else to do. Like... He glanced around the condo, suddenly at a loss. Prior to getting married, what had he done on a random Tuesday when he was bored?

Nothing. Because he was rarely bored. Usually he had work and other stuff to occupy him. *Friends.* Of course the answer was to ping his friends. But Warren didn't respond to his text message and Hendrix was in New York on a business trip.

Viv's key rattled in the lock. Finally. He vaulted off the couch to greet her, totally not okay with how his pulse quickened at the prospect of seeing her and completely unsure how to stop it.

As she came through the door, her smile widened as she spied Jonas standing in the hall, arms crossed, hip casually cocked out against the wall.

"Hi," she said, halting just short of invading his space. "Were you waiting for me?"

No sprang to his lips before he thought better of it. Well, he couldn't really deny that, now, could he? If he'd stayed sprawled on the couch and given her a casual "what's up?" as she strolled through the door, he might have had a leg to stand on. Too late.

"Yeah," he admitted, and held up the shiny blue foil bag clutched in his fingers. "I have something for you."

Her eyes widened as she held out her hand to accept the bag. The most delicious smell wafted between them, a vanilla and Viv combo that made him think of frosting and sex and about a million other things that shouldn't go together but did—like marriage and friendship.

Why couldn't he greet his wife at the door if he felt like it? It wasn't a crime. It didn't mean anything.

The anticipation that graced her smile shouldn't have pleased him so much. But he couldn't deny that it whacked him inside in a wholly different way than the sultry smile she'd laid on him last night, right before she informed him that she had on yellow lingerie under her clothes.

Which was not up for a repeat tonight. Boundaries should be the first order of business. Viv had sucked him down a rabbit hole that he didn't like. Well, he *liked* it. It just didn't sit well with how unbelievably tempting she was. If she could tempt him into letting go of his professionalism, what other barriers could she knock down? The risk was not worth it.

But then she opened the box, and her startled gasp put heat in places that he should be able to control a hell of lot better.

"Jonas, this is too much," she protested with a laugh and held out the box like she expected him to take it back or something.

"Not hardly. It's exactly right." Before she got ideas in her head about refusing the gift that had taken him thirty minutes to pick out, he plucked the diamond necklace from its velvet housing and undid the clasp so he could draw it around her neck. "Hush, and turn around."

She did and that put him entirely too close to her sweet flesh. That curve where her shoulder flared out called to him. Except it was covered by her dress. That was a shame.

Dragging her hair out of the way, she waited for him to position the chain. He let the catch of the necklace go and the ten-carat diamond dropped to rest against her chest, just above the swell of her breasts. Which were also covered, but he knew precisely where they began.

His lips ached to taste that swell again. Among other things. Palms flat across her back, he smoothed the chain into place, but that was really just an excuse to touch her.

"If you're sure," she murmured, and she relaxed, letting her body sink backward until it met his and heat flared between them.

"Oh, I'm sure." She'd meant about the diamond. Probably. But his mouth had already hit the bare spot she'd revealed when she'd swept her long brown hair aside and the taste of Viv exploded under his tongue.

Groaning, he let his hands skim down her waist until he found purchase and pulled until their bodies nested together tighter than spoons in a drawer. The soft flesh of her rear cradled the iron shaft in his pants, thickening his erection to the point of pain. He needed a repeat of last night. Now.

He licked the hollow of her collarbone, loving the texture under his tongue. More Viv needed. Her answering gasp encouraged him to keep going.

Gathering handfuls of her dress, he yanked it from between them and bunched it at her waist, pressing harder into the heat of her backside the moment he

bared it. His clothes and a pair of thin panties lay between him and paradise, and he wanted all that extra-
neous fabric gone.

She arched against him as his fingers cruised along
the hem of her drenched underwear and he took that as
agreement, stripping them off in one motion. Then he
nudged her legs wider, opening her sex, and indulged
them both by running a fingertip down the length of her
crease. Her hands flew out and smacked the wall and
she used it to brace as she ground her pelvis into his.

Fire tore through his center and he needed to be inside her with an uncontrollable urge, but the condoms
were clear across the cavernous living area in his bedside table. He couldn't wait. Viv cried out his name as
he plunged one then two fingers into her center, groaning at the slick, damp heat that greeted him. She was
so wet, so perfect.

As he fingered her, she shuddered, circling her hips
in a frenzied, friction-induced madness that pushed him
to the brink. Her hot channel squeezed his fingers and
that was nearly all she wrote. Did she have a clue how
much he wanted to yank his zipper down, impale her
and empty himself? Every muscle in his body fought
him and his will crumbled away rapidly. Reaching between them, he eased open his belt.

But then she came apart in his arms, huffing out little noises that drove him insane as she climaxed. His
own release roared to the forefront and all it would take
was one tiny push to put him over the edge. Hell, he
might not even need a push. Shutting his eyes against
the strain, he drew out her release with long strokes that
made her whimper.

She collapsed in his arms as she finished and he

held her upright, murmuring nonsense to her as she caught her breath.

"Let me take you to bed," he said, and she nodded, but it was more of a nuzzle as she turned her cheek into his.

To hell with boundaries.

He hustled her to his room, shed his clothes and hers without ripping anything this time—because he was in control—and finally she was naked. Sultry smile in place, she crawled onto the bed and rolled into a provocative position that begged him to get between her legs immediately and hammer after his own release. But despite being positive the only thing he could possibly do next was get inside her as fast as humanly possible, he paused, struck immobile all at once.

That was *his wife* decked out on the bed.

The sight bled through him, warming up places inside dangerously fast. Places that weren't what he'd call normal erogenous zones. And that's when he realized his gaze was on her smile. Not her body.

What was wrong with him? A naked woman was on display for his viewing pleasure. He forced his gaze to her breasts, gratified when the pert tips pebbled under his watchfulness. That was more like it. This was about sex and how good two people could make each other feel.

With a growl, he knelt on the bed and kissed his way up her thigh. He could absolutely keep his hands off her if he wanted to. He had total control over his desires, his emotions. There was nothing this woman could do to drive him to the point of desperation, not in bed and certainly not out of it. To prove it, he pushed her thighs open and buried his face between them.

She parted for him easily, her throaty cry washing over him as he plunged his tongue into her slickness. That wet heat was *his*. He'd done that to her and he lapped at it, groaning as her musky scent flooded his senses. The ache in his groin intensified into something so strong it was otherworldly. He needed to feel her tight, slick walls close around him, to watch her face as it happened. He needed it, but denied himself because she didn't own his pleasure. He owned hers.

Her hips rolled and bucked. He shoved his mouth deeper into her center as she silently sought more, and he gave it to her. Over and over he worked his lips and tongue against her swollen flesh until she bowed up with a release that tensed her whole body. And then she collapsed against the mattress, spilling breathy, satisfied sighs all over him. Only then did he permit his own needs to surge to the surface.

Fingering on a condom that he'd retrieved from the drawer, he settled over her and indulged his intense desire to kiss her. She eagerly took his tongue, sucking it into her hot mouth, and he groaned as he transferred her own taste back to her. Their hips came together, legs tangling, and before he could fully register her intent, she gathered him up in her tight fist and guided him into the paradise at her core.

A strong urge to fill her swelled. But he held on by the scrabbly edge of his fingertips, refusing to slam into her as he ached to do. Slowly, so slowly that he nearly came apart, he pushed. Her slickness accepted him easily, wringing the most amazing bliss from a place he scarcely recognized. The deeper he sank, the better it felt.

Her gaze captured his and he fell into her depths.

She filled him, not the other way around. How was that physically possible? He couldn't fathom it, but neither could he deny it. Or halt the rush of Viviana through his veins as she streamed straight to his heart in a kill shot that flooded all four chambers at once.

And then there was nothing but her and the unbelievable feel of her skin against his, her desire soaking through his pores in an overwhelming deluge. He meant to hold back, determined to prove something that escaped him as she changed the angle. Somehow that allowed him to go deeper, push harder. Her cries spurred him on, and unbelievably, she took it higher, sucking him under into a maelstrom of sensation and heightened pleasure.

When her hips began pistoning in countermeasure to his, it nearly tore him in two. Delirious with the need to come, he grabbed one of her legs and pushed at the knee, opening her wider so he had plenty of room to finger her at the source of her pleasure. Two circular strokes and she climaxed, squeezing him so tight that it tripped the wire on his own release.

Bright pinpoints of light streamed behind his eyes as he came so hard that he would have easily believed he'd crossed over into an alternate dimension. In this new dimension, he could let all the things crowding through his chest spill out of his mouth. But those things shouldn't exist in any universe.

If he didn't acknowledge them, they didn't exist. Then he wouldn't be breaking his word.

As his vision cleared and his muscles relaxed, rendering him boneless, he collapsed to the mattress, rolling Viv into his arms.

The heavy diamond swung down from the chain he'd

latched around her neck, whacking him on the shoulder. He fingered it back into place silently, weighing out whether he could actually speak or if that spectacular orgasm had in fact stolen his voice.

"I get the sense you've been saving up," Viv commented huskily, her lips moving against his chest, where her face had landed after he'd nestled her close. Probably he shouldn't have done that, but he liked coming down from a post-lovemaking high with her in his arms.

"It's been a while," he allowed. "I mean, other than last night, obviously."

Her mouth curved up in a smile. "Both times were amazing. I could get used to this."

He could, too. That was enough to get the panic really rolling. "We should probably talk about that."

To soften the blow, he threaded some of her pretty, silky hair through his fingers. That felt so nice, he kept going, running all the way down her head to her neck and back again.

"Mmm," she purred, pressing into his fingers, which were somehow massaging her with little strokes that she clearly liked. "I'm listening."

"We're still friends, right?" Pathetic. That hadn't been what he'd intended to say at all, but now that it was out there…it was exactly what he wanted to know. He wanted to hear her say that having an amazing encounter that he'd felt to his soul hadn't really affected her all that much. Then he could keep lying to himself about it and have zero qualms.

"Sure."

She kissed his chest right above his nipple and then flicked her tongue across the flat disk. Flames erupted under his skin, fanning outward to engulf his whole body, including his brain, because he suddenly couldn't recall what he'd been so convinced he needed to establish.

Then she slung a leg over his, nestling her thigh against the semi-erection that grew a lot less semi much faster than he would have credited, considering how empty he'd have sworn he was already.

"Geez, Viv." He bit back the curse word that had sprung to his lips. "You're insatiable."

Not that he was complaining. Though he should be saying something that sounded a lot like "Let's dial it back about one hundred and eighty degrees."

"You make me that way," she said throatily. "I've been celibate for like a billion years and that was totally okay, but all of a sudden, you kiss me and I can't think. I just want to be naked with you 24/7."

"Yeah?" he growled. That pretty much mirrored his thoughts perfectly. "That can be arranged."

No. No, it could not.

He had a merger to manage. Reins to pick up from his grandfather. What was he talking about, letting Viv coerce him into a day-and-night screw fest? That sounded like a recipe for disaster, especially given how strong his reactions to her were. They needed to cool it off.

"We can't." She sighed. "I've got a mountain of paperwork and Josie requested the rest of the week off so she can study for final exams. As nice as this is, we should probably back off for a while. Don't you think?"

"Absolutely not." Wrong answer. *Open your mouth and take it back.* "We're doing fine winging it. Aren't we? There's no pressure. If you come home from work hot and needy and want to strip down in the foyer to let me take care of you, I'm perfectly fine with that."

In fact, he'd gladly etch that date on his planner with a diamond drill bit. Mental note: buy Viv more jewelry and more racy lingerie. If he really tried, he could space out the gifts, one a night for oh, at least two weeks.

She arched a brow. "Really? This isn't feeling a little too real?"

His mood deflated. And now he was caught in a trap of his own making. He couldn't lie to Viv, but neither could he admit that it had been feeling too real since the ceremony. The same one he'd tried to sell to Warren and Hendrix as a fake wedding when Warren had clued in immediately that there was nothing fake about any of this.

This was what he got for not nodding his head the second the words *back off* came out of her mouth.

"See, the thing is," he began and would have sworn he'd been about to say that being friends with no benefits worked better for him. But that's not what happened. "I need this to be real. I don't have to pretend that I'm hot for you, because I am. We don't have to sell that we're burning up the sheets when we have dinner with your family on Friday. Why not keep going? The reasons we started this are still true. Unless I've dissatisfied you in some way?"

"Oh, God. No!" Her hand flew to her mouth. "Not in the slightest. You're the hottest lover I've ever had, bar none."

That pleased him enormously. "Then stop talking about easing off. We can be casual about it. Sometimes you sleep in my bed. Sometimes you don't. No rules. We're just friends who're having really great sex."

"That sounds like a plan."

She shrugged like she could take it or leave it, which raked across his spine with a sharpness that he didn't like. She obviously wasn't feeling any of the same things he was. She'd been a half second from calling it quits. Would have if he hadn't stopped her.

"Great." And somehow he'd managed to appease his sense of honor while agreeing to continue sleeping with his wife in what was shaping up to be the hottest affair he'd ever had.

It was madness. And he couldn't wipe the grin off his face.

Eight

If there was a way to quit Jonas, Viv didn't want to know about it.

She should be looking for the exit, not congratulating herself on the finest plea for remaining in a man's bed that had ever been created in the history of time. She couldn't help it. The scene after the most explosive sexual encounter of her life had been almost as epic. Jonas had no idea how much it had killed her to act so nonchalant about ending things. He'd been shocked she'd suggested backing off. It had been written all over his face.

That kept her feeling smug well into the dawn hours the next morning. She rolled toward the middle of the bed, hoping to get a few minutes of snuggle time before work. Cold sheets met her questing fingers. Blinking an eye open, she sought the man she'd gone to sleep with.

Empty. Jonas had gotten out of bed already. The

condo was quiet. Even when she was in her bedroom, she could hear the shower running through the pipes in the ceiling—a treat she normally enjoyed, as she envisioned the man taking a shower in all his naked glory.

Today, she didn't get that luxury, as Jonas was clearly already gone. Profoundly disappointed that he hadn't kissed her goodbye, said goodbye or thought about her at all, she climbed out from under the sheets and gathered up her clothes for the return trek to her bedroom.

It was fine. They'd established last night that there were no rules. No pressure. When he'd gotten on board with convincing her that they could keep sleeping together—which she still couldn't quite believe she'd orchestrated so well—she'd thought that meant they were going to spend a lot of time together. Be goofy and flirty with each other. Grow closer and closer until he looked up one day and realized that friendship plus marriage plus sex equaled something wonderful, lasting and permanent. Obviously she'd thought wrong.

The whole point had been to give him the impression she wasn't clingy. That Independence was her middle name and she breezed through life just fine, thanks, whether she had a man or not. Apparently he'd bought it. *Go me.*

The sour taste wouldn't quite wash from her mouth no matter how much mouthwash she used. After a long shower to care for her well-used muscles, Viv wandered to the kitchen barefoot to fight with Jonas's espresso machine. She had a machine at Cupcaked but Jonas's was a futuristic prototype that he'd brought home from work to test. There were more buttons and gizmos than on a spaceship. Plus, it hated her. He'd used it a couple of times and made it seem so easy, but he had a natural affinity with things that plugged in, and the machine had his name on it, after all. Finally, she got a passably decent latte out of the monstrosity.

She stood at the granite countertop to drink it, staring at the small, discreet Kim Electronics logo in the lower right-hand corner of the espresso machine. Jonas's name had been emblazoned on her, too, and not just via the marriage license and subsequent trip to the DMV to get a new driver's license. He'd etched his name across her soul well before they'd started sleeping together. Maybe about the third or fourth time they'd had lunch.

Strange then that she could be so successful with snowing him about her feelings. It had never worked with any man before. Of course, she'd never tried so hard to be cool about it. Because it had never mattered so much.

But now she wasn't sure what her goal here really was. Or what it should be. Jonas had "talked" her into keeping sex on the menu of their relationship. She'd convinced him their friendship could withstand it. Really, the path was pretty clear. They were married friends with benefits. If she didn't like that, too bad.

She didn't like it.

This wasn't practice for another relationship and neither was it fake, not for her. Which left her without a lot of options, since it was fake to Jonas.

Of course, she always had the choice to end things. But why in the world would she want to do that? Her husband was the most amazing lover on the planet, whose beautiful body she could not get enough of. He bought her diamonds and complimented her cupcakes. To top it all off, Viv was *married*. She'd been after that holy grail for ages and it had felt really nice to flash her ring at her sisters when they'd come to the shop last week. It was the best possible outcome of agreeing to do this favor for Jonas.

Convinced that she should be happy with that, she walked the four blocks to Cupcaked and buried herself in the kitchen, determined to find a new cupcake flavor to commemorate her marriage. That was how she'd always done things. When something eventful occurred, she baked. It was a way of celebrating in cake form, because wasn't that the whole point of cake? And then she had a cupcake flavor that reminded her of a wonderful event.

The watermelon recipe she'd been dying to try didn't turn out. The red food coloring was supposed to be tasteless but she couldn't help thinking that it had added something to the flavor that made the cupcake taste vaguely like oil. But without it, the batter wasn't the color of watermelon.

Frustrated, she trashed the whole batch and went in search of a different food coloring vendor. Fruitless. All her regular suppliers required an industrial sized order and she couldn't commit to a new brand without testing it first.

She ended up walking to the market and buying three different kinds off the shelf. For no reason, apparently, as all three new batches she made didn't turn out either. Maybe watermelon wasn't a good cupcake flavor. More to the point, maybe she shouldn't be commemorating a fake marriage that was real to her but still not going to last. That was the problem. She was trying to capture something fleeting that shouldn't be immortalized.

After the cupcake failure, her mood slid into the dumps. She threw her apron on the counter and stayed out of the kitchen until lunch, when she opened for business to the public. On the plus side, every display case had been cleaned and polished, and the plate-glass window between Cupcaked and the world had not one smudge on it. Camilla wouldn't be in until after school, so Viv was by herself for the lunch rush, which ended up being a blessing in disguise.

Wednesday wasn't normally a busy day, but the line stretched nearly out the door for over an hour. Which was good. Kept her mind off the man she'd married. Josie had the rest of the week off, and Viv had approved it thinking she and Camilla could handle things, but if this kind of crowd was even close to a new normal, she might have to see about adding another part-time employee. That was a huge decision, but a good sign. If she couldn't have Jonas, she could have her cupcakes. Just like she'd always told him.

After locking the bakery's door, tired but happy with the day's profits, she headed home. On the way, she sternly lectured herself about her expectations. Jonas might be waiting in the hall for her to come in the door like he had been last night. Or he might not. Her stomach fluttered the entire four blocks regardless. Her husband had just been so sexy standing there against the wall with a hot expression on his face as if he planned to devour her whole before she completely shut the door.

And then he pretty much had, going down on her in the most erotic of encounters. She shuddered clear to her core as she recalled the feel of that first hot lick of his tongue.

Oh, who was she kidding? She couldn't stop hoping he'd be waiting for her again tonight. Her steps quickened as she let herself anticipate seeing Jonas in a few minutes.

But he wasn't in the hall. Or at home. That sucked.

Instead of moping, she fished out her phone and called Grace. It took ten minutes, but eventually her sister agreed to have dinner with Viv.

They met at an Italian place on Glenwood that had great outdoor seating that allowed for people watching. The maître d' showed them to a table and Grace gave Viv a whole three seconds before she folded her hands and rested her chin on them.

"Okay, spill," she instructed. "I wasn't expecting to see you before Friday. Is Jonas in the doghouse already?"

"What? No." Viv scowled. Why did something have to be wrong for her to ask her sister to dinner? Besides, that was none of Grace's business anyway. Viv pounced on the flash of green fire on her sister's wrist in a desperate subject change. "Ooooh, new bracelet? Let me see."

The distraction worked. Grace extended her arm dutifully, her smile widening as she twisted her wrist to let the emeralds twinkle in the outdoor lighting. "Alan gave it to me. It's an anniversary present."

"You got married in April," Viv said.

"Not a wedding anniversary. It's a…different kind of anniversary."

Judging by the dreamy smile that accompanied that admission, she meant the first time she and Alan had slept together, and clearly the act had been worthy of commemorating.

Viv could hardly hide her glee. It was going to be one of *those* discussions and she *finally* got to participate. "Turns out Jonas is big on memorializing spectacular sex, too."

"Well, don't hold back. Show and tell." Grace waggled her brows.

Because she wanted to and she could, Viv fished the diamond drop necklace from beneath her dress and let it hang from her fingers. Not to put too fine a point on it, but hers was a flawless white diamond in a simple, elegant setting. Extremely appropriate for the wife of a billionaire. And he'd put it around her neck and then given her the orgasm of her life.

The baubles she could do without and had only mentioned jewelry in the car on the way to Jonas's parents' house because he'd pushed her to name something he could do for her. She hadn't really been serious. But all at once, she loved that Jonas had unwittingly allowed her to stand shoulder to shoulder with her sister when it came to talking about whose marriage was hotter.

"Your husband is giving you jewelry already?" Grace asked, and her tone was colored with something that sounded a lot like she was impressed. "Things must be going awfully well."

"Oh, yeah, of course," Viv commented airily and waved her hand like she imagined a true lady of the manor would. "We didn't even make it out of the foyer where he gave it to me before his hands were all over me."

Shameless. This was the raciest conversation she'd ever had with anyone except maybe Jonas, but that didn't count. She should be blushing. Or something. Instead she was downright giddy.

"That's the best." Grace's dreamy smile curved back into place. "When you have a man who loves you so much that he can't wait. I'm thrilled you finally have that."

Yeah, not so much. Her mood crashed and burned as reality surfaced. Viv nodded with a frozen expression that she hoped passed for agreement.

Obviously Grace knew what it felt like to have a man dote on her and give her jewelry because he cared, not because they were faking a relationship. Grace could let all her feelings hang out as much as she wanted and Alan would eat it up. Because they were in love.

Something that felt a lot like jealousy reared its ugly head in the pit of Viv's stomach. Which was unfair and petty, but recognizing it as such didn't make it go away.

"Jonas was worth waiting for," she said truthfully, though it rankled that the statement was the best she could do. While Viv's husband might rival her sister's in the attentive lover department, when it came to matters of the heart, Grace and Alan had Viv and Jonas beat, hands down.

"I'm glad. You had a rough patch for a while. I started to worry that you weren't going to figure out how stop putting a man's emotional needs ahead of yours. It's good to see that you found a relationship that's on equal footing."

Somehow, Viv managed to keep the surprise off her face, but how, she'd never know. "I never did that. What does that even mean?"

"Hon, you're so bad at putting yourself first." Grace waved the waiter over as he breezed by and waited until he refilled both their wineglasses before continuing. "You let everyone else dictate how the relationship is going to go. That last guy you dated? Mark? He wanted to keep things casual, see other people, and even though that's not what you wanted, you agreed. Why did you do that?"

Eyebrows hunched together, Viv gulped from her newly filled wineglass to wet her suddenly parched throat. "Because when I told him that I wanted to be exclusive, he said I was being too possessive. What was I supposed to do, demand that he give me what I want?"

"Uh, *yeah*." Grace clucked. "You should have told him to take a hike instead of waiting around for him to do it for you."

"It really didn't take that long," she muttered, but not very loud, because Grace was still off on her tangent.

Her sister was right. Viv should have broken up with Mark during that exact conversation. But on the heels of being told she was "clingy," "controlling" and "moving too fast" by Zachary, Gary and Judd respectively, she hadn't wanted to rock the boat.

Why was it such a big deal to want to spend time with a man she was dating? It wasn't clingy. Maybe it was the wine talking, but Grace's point wasn't lost on Viv—she shouldn't be practicing her independence but finding a different kind of man. One who couldn't stand being apart from her. One who texted her hearts and smiley faces just to let her know he was thinking of her. One who was in love with her.

In other words—not Jonas.

The thought pushed her mood way out of the realm of fit for company. Dinner with Grace was a mistake. Marrying Jonas had been a mistake. Viv had no idea what she was doing with her life or how she was going to survive a fake marriage she wished was real.

"I just remembered," she mumbled. "I have to…do a thing."

Pushing back from the table, Viv stood so fast that her head spun. She'd planned to walk home but maybe a cab would be a better idea.

"What?" Grace scowled. "You called me. I canceled drinks with the ladies from my auxiliary group. How could you forget that you had something else?"

Because Viv wasn't perfect like Grace with the perfect husband who loved her, and frankly, she was sick of not getting what she wanted. "Jonas has scrambled my wits."

Let her sister make what she would out of that. Viv apologized and exited the restaurant as quickly as she could before she started crying. After not seeing Jonas this morning and the watermelon-slash-red-food-coloring disaster and the incredibly busy day at the store and then realizing that she had not in fact gotten to join the club her sisters were in, crying was definitely imminent.

The icing on the cake happened when she got home and Jonas was sprawled on the couch watching TV, wearing jeans with a faded Duke T-shirt that clung to his torso like a second skin.

His smile as he glanced up at her was instant and brilliant and that was all it took to unleash the waterworks.

With tears streaming down her face, Viv stood in the foyer of the condo she shared with Jonas until whatever point in the future he decided to pull the plug on their marriage and it was all suddenly not okay.

"Hey, now. None of that." Jonas flicked off the TV and vaulted to his feet, crossing the ocean of open space between the living room and the foyer in about four strides.

He didn't hesitate to gather Viv in his strong arms, cradling her against his chest, and dang it, that T-shirt was really soft against her face. It was a testament to how mixed-up she was that she let him guide her to the leather couch and tuck her in against his side as he held her while softly crooning in his baritone that she'd heard in her sleep for aeons.

What was wrong with her that she was exactly where she wanted to be—in his arms? She should be pushing away and disappearing into her bedroom. No pressure, no love, no nothing.

"What's wrong, sweetheart?" he asked softly into her hair. "Bad day at work?"

"I wasn't at work," she shot back inanely, sniffling oh so attractively against his shoulder.

"Oh. Well, I wondered where you were when you weren't here."

"You weren't here either," she reminded him crossly. "So I went to dinner with Grace."

He pulled back, the expression on his face both confused and slightly alarmed. "Did we have plans that I forgot about or something? Because if so, I'm sorry. I didn't have anything on my calendar and my grandfather asked me to take him to the airport. I texted you."

He had? And how desperate would it appear to pull out her phone to check? Which was totally dumb anyway. It was obvious he was telling her the truth, which he didn't even have to do. God, she was such a mess. But after he'd disappeared this morning and then she'd come home to an empty house and…so what? He was here now, wasn't he? She was making a mountain out of a molehill.

"It's okay, we didn't have plans. You called it. Bad

day at work," she said a bit more brightly as she latched on to his excuse that wasn't even a lie. Sales had been good, sure, but Cupcaked meant more to her than just profits. "I tried out a new recipe and it was a complete failure."

All smiles again, Jonas stroked her hair and then laid a sweet kiss on her temple. "I hate days like that. What can I do to fix it?"

About a hundred suggestions sprang to her mind all at once, and every last one could easily be considered X-rated. But she couldn't bear to shift the current vibe into something more physical when Jonas was meeting a different kind of need, one she'd only nebulously identified at dinner. This was it in a nutshell—she wanted someone to be there for her, hold her and support her through the trials of life.

Why had she gotten so upset? Because Jonas hadn't fallen prostrate at her feet with declarations of undying love? They were essentially still in the early stages of their relationship, regardless of the label on it. Being married didn't automatically mean they were where Grace and her husband were. Maybe Viv and Jonas were taking a different route to get to the same destination and she was trying too hard.

Also known as the reason her last few relationships hadn't worked out.

"You're already fixing it," she murmured as his fingers drifted to her neck and lightly massaged.

Oh, God, that was a gloriously unfulfilled need, too. After a long day on her feet, just sitting here with Jonas as he worked her tired muscles counted as one of the highest points of pleasure she'd experienced at his hands. Her eyelids drifted closed and she floated.

"Did I wake you up this morning?" he asked after a few minutes of bliss.

"No. I was actually surprised to find that you were gone." Thank God he'd lulled her into a near coma. That admission had actually sounded a lot more casual than she would have expected, given how his absence had been lodged under skin like a saddle burr all day.

"That's good." He seemed a lot more relieved than the question warranted. "I'm not used to sleeping with someone and I was really worried that I'd mess with your schedule."

What schedule? "We slept in the same bed at your parents' house."

"Yeah, but that was over the weekend when no one had to get up and go to work. This is different. It's real life and I'm nothing if not conscious that you're here solely because I asked you to be. You deserve to sleep well."

Warmth gushed through her heart and made her feel entirely too sappy. What a thoroughly unexpected man she had married. "I did sleep well. Thank you for being concerned. But I think I slept so well because of how you treated me before I went to sleep. Not because you tiptoed well while getting dressed."

He did treat her like a queen. That was the thing she'd apparently forgotten. They were friends who cared about each other. Maybe he might eventually fall in love with her, but he certainly wouldn't if she kept being obsessive and reading into his every move.

Jonas chuckled. "Last night was pretty amazing. I wasn't sure you thought so. I have to be honest and tell you that I was concerned I'd done something to make you angry and that's why you weren't here when I got home after taking my grandfather to the airport. I could have called him a car."

"No!" Horrified, she swiveled around to face him, even though it meant his wonderful hands slipped from her shoulders. "We just talked about no pressure and I was—well, I just thought because you weren't here…"

Ugh. How in the world was she supposed to explain that she'd gone out to dinner with Grace because of a hissy fit over something so ridiculous as Jonas not being here because he'd taken his grandfather to the airport? Maybe instead of using the excuse that she'd missed his text messages, she should tell him how she felt. Just flat out say, *Jonas, I'm in love with you.*

"We did talk about no pressure," Jonas threw out in a rush. "And I'm definitely not trying to add any. I like our relationship where it is. I like *you.* It's what makes the extra stuff so much better."

Extra stuff. She absorbed that for a second. Extra stuff like deeper feelings he didn't know he was going to uncover? Extra stuff like being there for each other?

"I value our friendship," she said cautiously, weighing out how honest she could be. How honest she wanted to be given how she managed to screw up even the simplest of relationship interactions.

And just as she was about to open her mouth and confess that she appreciated the extra stuff, too, maybe even tell him that she had a plethora of extra stuff that she could hardly hold inside, he smoothed a hand over her hair and grinned. "I know. I'm being all touchy-feely and that's not what we signed up for. Instead, let's talk about Cupcaked."

"Um…okay?" He'd literally switched gears so fast, she could scarcely keep up.

That was him being touchy-feely? Jonas wasn't one to be gushy about his feelings and usually erred on the side of being reserved; she knew that from the year of lunches and coffee. Clearly, he was uncomfortable with the direction of the discussion. She definitely should not add a level of weirdness, not on top of her storming in here and having a minor meltdown.

This was her relationship to make or break. All at once, it became so obvious what she should be focusing on here.

No, this wasn't practice for the next man she dated. She was practicing for *this* one. If she hoped to get to a point where they were both comfortable with declarations of love, she had to tread carefully. While she didn't think Jonas was going to divorce her if she moved too fast, neither did she have a good handle on how to be less intense.

She needed to back off. Way off. Otherwise, she was going to freak him out. And suddenly she could not fathom giving up this marriage under any circumstances.

"I'd love to talk about Cupcaked," she said with a smile. "Seems like you owe me some advice."

"Yes, exactly." His return smile bordered on relieved. "You've been so patient and I'm a selfish jerk for not focusing on your career when that's the one thing you're getting out of this deal."

"The sex is nice, too," she teased. Look at that. She could be cool.

Jonas shot her a wicked once-over. "That's what makes you so perfect. We can hang out as friends, but if I wanted to, say, slip my hand under your dress, you'd gladly climb in my lap for a little one-on-one time. It's the best."

She shrugged to cover how his compliment had thrilled her to the marrow. "I promised it wouldn't make things weird."

Now she'd stick to that. At the end of the day, Cupcaked *was* important to her. She'd just have to make sure that eventually Jonas realized that he was important to her, as well.

Jonas ducked out of a meeting on Friday with a guilty conscience. While he knew Viv would understand if he put off a thorough analysis of her business plan, he wasn't okay with ignoring his promise. Unfortunately, Park had come through with some amendments to the merger agreement Jonas had drafted, which had taken his time and attention for the whole of the week.

The moment he stepped outside the Kim Building, the sunshine raised his spirits. He was on his way to see his wife at Cupcaked, which oddly would mark the first time he'd graced the store since they'd gotten married. Before the wedding, he found excuses to drop by on a frequent basis. But now he didn't have to. The cupcake baker slept in his bed and if he wanted to see her, all he had to do was turn his head.

It was pretty great. Or at least that's what he'd been telling himself. In reality, the look on Viv's face when she'd told him she valued their friendship had been like a big fat wake-up call. Basically, she was telling him no pressure worked for her regardless of how hot he could get her with nothing more than a well-placed caress.

Well, that *was* great. He didn't have any desire to pressure her into anything. But he couldn't deny that he might like to put more structure around things. Would she think it was weird if he expected her to be his plus-one for events? His admin was planning a big party for the whole company to commemorate the anniversary of opening the Kim Americas branch. He wanted Viv by his side. But it was yet another favor. If they were dating instead of married he wouldn't think twice about asking her.

Everything was backward and weird and had been since that no-pressure discussion, which he'd initiated because he needed the boundaries. For no reason apparently. Viv so clearly wasn't charging over the imaginary lines he'd drawn in the sand. In fact, she'd drawn a few lines of her own. Yet how could he change those lines when Viv had gotten so prickly about the subject? In fact, she'd already tried to call off the intimate aspects of their relationship once. He needed to tread very carefully with her before he got in too deep for them both.

When he got to Cupcaked, the door was locked. Not open yet. He texted Viv that he was outside and within thirty seconds, she'd popped out of the kitchen and hurried to the plate-glass door with a cute smile.

"I didn't know you were coming by," she commented unnecessarily since he was well aware it was a surprise. After she let him in, she locked the door and turned, her brown hair shining in the sunlight that streamed through the glass.

Something was wrong with his lungs. He couldn't breathe. Or think. All he could do was soak in the most beautiful woman he'd ever seen in his life. And all of his good intentions designed to help her with her business flew out the window in a snap.

Without hesitation, he pulled her into his arms and kissed her. She softened instantly and the scent of vanilla and Viv wound through his senses, robbing him of the ability to reason, because the only thing he could think about was getting more of her against him.

Almost as if she'd read his mind, she opened under his mouth, eagerly deepening the kiss, welcoming the broad stroke of his tongue with her own brand of heat. Slowly she licked into his mouth in kind, teasing him with little flutters of her fingers against his back.

That was not going to work. He wanted to feel her fingers against his flesh, not through the forty-seven layers of clothing between them.

Walking her backward, he half kissed, half maneuvered her until they reached the kitchen, and then he spun her through the swinging door to the more private area, where the entire city of Raleigh couldn't see them.

Her mouth was back on his without missing a beat, and he pushed her up against the metal counter, trapping her body with his. Her sweet little curves nestled into the planes of his body and he wasn't sure if he could stand how long it was taking to get her naked.

The zipper of her dress took three tries to find and then slid down easily, allowing him to actually push the fabric from her shoulders instead of ripping it, a near miracle. There was something about her that drove him to a place he didn't recognize, and it bothered him to be this crazy over her. But then her dress slipped off, puddling to the floor, and he forgot about everything but her as she unhooked her bra, throwing it to the ground on top of her dress.

Groaning, he looked his fill of her gorgeous breasts, scarcely able to believe how hard and pointy they were from nothing other than his gaze. Bending to capture one, he swirled his tongue around the perfection of her nipple and the sound she made shot through his erection like an arrow of heat.

"Hurry," she gasped. "I'm about to come apart."

Oh, well, that was something he'd very much like to witness. In a flash, he pushed her panties to her ankles and boosted her up on the counter. Spreading her legs wide, he brushed a thumb through her crease and, yes, she was so ready for him.

She bucked and rolled against his fingers, her eyes darkening with the pleasure he was giving her, and he wanted her more than anything he could recall. As much as he'd like to do any number of things to bring her to climax, there was one clear winner. Ripping out of his own clothes in record time, he stepped back between her thighs and hissed as she nipped at his shoulder.

"Tell me you have a condom," she commanded, and then smiled as he held it up between his fingers.

He'd stashed a couple in his wallet and he really didn't want to examine that particular foresight right now. Instead, he wanted to examine the wonders of Viv and sheathed himself as fast as humanly possible, notching himself at the slick entrance to her channel. Her wet heat welcomed him, begged him to come inside, but he paused to kiss her because that was one of his favorite parts.

Their tongues tangled and he got a little lost in the kiss. She didn't. She wrapped her legs around him, heels firm against his butt, and pushed him forward, gasping as he slammed into her. So that's how she wanted it. Two could play that game.

He engulfed her in his arms and braced her for a demanding rhythm, then gave it to her. She took each and every thrust eagerly, her mouth working the flesh at his throat, his ear, nipping sensuously. *He* was the one about to come apart.

Viv flew through his soul, winging her essence into every diameter of his body. Wiggling a hand between their slick bodies, he fingered her at the source of her pleasure, gratified when she cried out. Her release crashed against his, shocking him with both the speed and intensity.

She slumped against him, still quaking as she held on. He was busy losing the entire contents of his body as everything inside rushed out in a flash to fill her. Fanciful to be sure since there was a barrier preventing anything of the sort. But she'd wrung him out, taken everything and more, and he couldn't have stopped the train as it barreled down the track, even if he wanted to. Why would he want to?

He turned his head, seeking her lips, and there they were, molding to his instantly. Viv was amazing, a woman he liked, cared for deeply even, and they had the most spectacular chemistry. He could hardly fathom how much he still wanted her four seconds after having her. It was everything he said he wanted.

Except the warmth in his chest that had nothing to do with sex wasn't supposed to be there. He wasn't an idiot. He knew what was happening. He'd let her in, pretending that being friends gave him a measure of protection against falling for her. Instead, he'd managed to do the one thing he'd sworn he'd never do—develop feelings for someone who didn't return them.

This was a huge problem, one he didn't have a good solution for. One he could never let her know he was facing because he'd promised not to pressure her.

Best thing would be to ignore it. It wasn't happening if he didn't acknowledge it. And then he wouldn't be lying to her or dishonoring the pact he'd made with his friends, neither of which could ever happen. If he didn't nurture these fledging tendrils of disaster that wound through his chest, he could kill them before they ruined everything.

Actually, the best thing would be to stop being around Viv so much. *Without* letting on to her that he was deliberately creating distance.

The thought hurt. But it was necessary for his sanity.

Nine

Jonas helped Viv off the metal countertop that she'd have to bleach within an inch of its life and pray the fourteen different health-code violations never came to light.

It had been worth it. Whenever Jonas got like that, so into her and excited and feverish as if he'd die if he didn't have her that instant…that was the best part of this fake marriage. Men were never that gaga over her. Except this one. And she secretly loved it. She couldn't tell him. What would she say?

Slow and steady wins the race, she reminded herself. Not-Clingy was her new middle name and she was going to own it. Even if it killed her not to blubber all over him about how it was so beautiful it hurt when he was inside her.

They spent a few minutes setting their clothes back

to rights, no small feat without a mirror. She gladly helped Jonas locate his missing tie and then buttoned his suit jacket for him when he forgot.

"Gorgeous," she commented after slipping the last button into its slot and perusing the final product of her husband in his power suit that she immediately wanted to strip him out of again.

He grinned. "Yes, you are."

Great, now she was blushing, judging by the prickles in her cheeks. Dead giveaway about the things going on inside that she'd rather keep a secret.

"Now, stop distracting me," he continued. "I'm here to get started on my promise to review your books. Lead me to them."

Oh. For some reason, she'd thought he'd come by strictly to have an explosive sexual encounter in her bakery. But in reality, he was here for business reasons. That took a little of the wind from her sails though it shouldn't have. Of course he'd honor his promise to help her, despite absolutely no prompting on her part. "Sure, my office is in the back. We can squeeze in there."

She led him to the tiny hole in the wall where she paid bills and ordered inventory. It wasn't much, not like the Kim Building, where Jonas had an entire office suite expressly designed for the CEO. But she wasn't running a billion-dollar electronics company here, and they both knew that.

He didn't complain about the lack of comfort and space, easily sliding into the folding chair she pulled from behind the door and focusing on her with his dark eyes. "Let me see your balance sheet."

Dutifully, she keyed up her accounting software and ran the report, then pushed the monitor of her ancient computer toward him so he could see it. His gaze slid down the columns and back up again. Within a moment, he'd reviewed the entire thing and then launched into a dizzying speech about how her asset column was blah blah and her inventory was blah blah something else. After five minutes of nodding and understanding almost nothing of what he said, she held up a hand.

"Jonas, while I appreciate your attention on this, you lost me back around 'leveraging your cash.' Can we take a step back and focus on the goal of this?"

She knew what her goal was. Spend time with Jonas. But clearly he'd taken the idea of helping her seriously.

"Sure, sorry." He looked chagrined and adorable as he ran a hand through his hair. "I shouldn't have gone so deep into financial strategy that quickly. Maybe I should ask you what *your* goal is since your career is the most important thing to you. What do you want to see happen with Cupcaked?"

Oh, yeah, right. Her career. The thing she'd sold to him as the reason she didn't date. "I haven't really thought about it."

Should she be thinking about it? She wasn't rich by any stretch, but she made enough and got to bake cupcakes for a living. What else was there?

"Okay." His smile broadened. "I hear you saying that you need help coming up with a five-year plan. Part of that should include a robust marketing strategy and expansion."

Expansion? Her eyebrows lifted almost by themselves. "Are you suggesting I could become a chain?"

The idea seemed so far-fetched. She just made cupcakes and had no ambitions beyond being able to recognize regular customers. But she didn't hate the idea of seeing more Cupcaked signs around Raleigh. Maybe even in Chapel Hill or by the university. The thought of owning a mini-cupcake empire made her smile. Poor substitute for Jonas. But not a terrible one.

"I'm not suggesting it. I'm flat out saying if that's what you want, I will make it happen for you. Sky's the limit, Mrs. Kim." He waggled his brows. "You should take as much advantage of me as you possibly can. Ask for anything."

Mrs. Kim. What if she told him that she'd like to ask him to call her that for the rest of her life? What would he say?

Before she could open her mouth, he launched into another long litany of things to consider for her shop and his gleeful tone told her he was having fun helping her think through the items that might appear on her five-year plan. They talked about any number of ideas from branded cupcake mix to be sold in grocery stores to licensing her flavors to other cupcake bakeries.

Frankly, the discussion was fun for her, too. Partially because she was having it with Jonas and she loved watching his mind churn through the possibilities. But she couldn't deny a certain anticipation regarding the leaps and bounds Cupcaked could take through the doors her husband might open for her.

Camilla popped in to say hi and make sure Viv was okay with her opening the bakery to customers. Viv nodded her assent and dove back into the fascinating concept of franchising, of which Jonas admitted having only a rudimentary knowledge, but he knew way more than she did. She wanted to know more.

His phone rang and he lifted a finger in the universal "one minute" gesture, jabbering away to the caller with a bunch of terms that sounded vaguely legal. Eventually, he ended the call and stood.

"I'm so sorry, but I have to get back to the world of electronics."

She waved off his apology. "You've been here for two hours. I know you're busy. I should give Camilla a hand anyway. If today is anything like the rest of the week, she'll need the help."

Jonas laid a scorching kiss on her and left. Dazed and more than a little hot and bothered, she lost herself in cupcakes until the day got away from her. As planned, she and Jonas went to dinner at her parents' house that night. Given that he shot her smoking-hot glances when he thought no one was watching, and her sisters were nothing if not eagle-eyed when it came to potential gossip, she didn't think they had anything to worry about when it came to revelations about the nature of their marriage.

Or rather, the revelations weren't going to be publicized to the rest of the world. Just to Jonas. As soon as she figured out when she could start clueing him in to the idea that friendship wasn't the only thing happening between them, of course. This was the problem with playing it cool. She wasn't sure when to bring up concepts like *love*, *forever* and *no divorce*.

She bided her time and didn't utter a peep when Jonas carried her to his bed after the successful dinner with her parents. He spent extra time pleasuring her, claiming that tomorrow was Saturday so she had plenty of opportunity to sleep later. Not that she was complaining about his attention. Or anything else, for that matter. Her life was almost perfect.

On Monday, she learned exactly how many people in

the business world jumped when her husband said jump. By nine o'clock, she had appointments lined up every day for the entire week with accounting people, retail space experts and a pastry chef who had ties with the Food Network. A marketing consultant arrived shortly thereafter and introduced herself as Franca, then parked herself in Viv's office, apparently now a permanent part of her staff, as she'd informed Mrs. Kim, courtesy of Mr. Kim.

Franca lived to talk, as best Viv could work out between marathon strategy sessions that filled nearly every waking hour of the day. And some of the hours Viv would have normally said were for sleeping. At midnight, Franca sent a detailed list of the short-term and long-term goals that they'd discussed and asked Viv to vet it thoroughly because once she approved, the list would form the basis of Cupcaked's new five-year plan. Which would apparently be carved in stone.

By Friday, Viv hadn't spent more than five minutes with Jonas. They slept in the same bed, but sometimes he climbed into it well after she had, which was quite a feat since she hadn't hit the sheets until 1:00 a.m. most nights. He'd claimed her busyness came at a great time for him because he was able to focus on the merger with Park Industries without feeling guilty for ignoring her. The hours bled into days and she'd never been so exhausted in her life.

It sucked. Except for the part where sometimes Jonas texted her funny memes about ships passing in the night or had a dozen tulips delivered to the shop to commemorate their one-month anniversary. Once he popped up with Chinese takeout for dinner as a "forced" break for them both. He gave her his fortune cookie and told

her a story about how one of the ladies in his procure-
ment department had gone into labor during a meeting.
Those stolen moments meant the world to her because
she could almost believe that he missed her as much as
she missed him.

The pièce de résistance came when the pastry chef
she'd met with a couple of weeks ago contacted her via
Franca to let her know that he'd loved her cupcakes and
gotten her a spot on one of the cupcake shows on the
Food Network. Agape, Viv stared at Franca as the tire-
less woman reeled off the travel plans she'd made for
Viv to fly to Los Angeles.

"I can't go to Los Angeles," Viv insisted with a head
shake. "I have a business to run."

Franca tapped her phone on Viv's new desk. "Which
will become nationally known once you appear on the
show."

She'd had Viv's office completely redone and expanded at Jonas's expense and the top-of-the-line
computer that had replaced the old one now recessed
underneath the surface of the desk with the click of a
button. It was very slick and gave them a lot more working space, which Franca used frequently, as she spread
brochures and promo items galore across the top of it
at least twice a week.

"How long would I be gone?" Viv asked. Josie and
Camilla had never run the bakery by themselves for a
whole day, let alone several. They needed her. Or did
they? She was often in the back strategizing with Franca
anyway. They had four or five irons in the fire at any
given time and the woman was indefatigable when it
came to details. There was literally nothing she couldn't

organize or plan and often took on more of a personal assistant role for Viv.

"Depends on whether you make the first cut." Franca shrugged and flipped her ponytail behind her back, a move she made when she was about to get serious. "It's a competition. You lose the first round, you come home. You win, you stay. I would advise you to win."

Viv made a face. "You're talking days."

"Sure. I hope so anyway. We're going to launch the new website with online ordering at the same time. It'll be an amazing kick start to the virtual storefront."

Sagging a little, Viv gave herself about four seconds to pretend she was going to refuse when in reality, she couldn't pass up the opportunity. It really didn't matter if she won or not because it was free advertising and all it would cost her was some time away from Jonas. Whom she rarely saw awake anyway.

"When do I leave?"

Franca grinned like she'd known the direction Viv would end up going the whole time. "I'll get the rest of the arrangements settled and let you know."

With a nod, Viv texted the news to Jonas, who instantly responded with at least four exclamation marks and a *congrats* in all caps. Funny, they were basically back to being friends with no benefits, thanks to her stupid career. She had all the success she'd lied to Jonas about wanting and none of the happiness that she'd pretended would come along with it.

Worse, if she hadn't been so busy, she'd be sitting around the condo by herself as Jonas worked his own fingers to the bone. This was really, really not the marriage she'd signed up for.

Or rather it was absolutely the one she'd agreed to but not the one she wanted.

The day before she was supposed to fly to Los Angeles for the taping, Viv came home early to pack. Shockingly, Jonas was sitting on the couch still decked out in his gorgeous suit but on the phone, as he nearly always was anytime she'd been in the same room with him lately.

For half a second, she watched him, soaking in his pretty mouth as it formed words. Shuddered as she recalled what that mouth could do to her when he put his mind to it. God, she missed him. In the short amount of time they'd been married, they'd gone from zero to sixty to zero again. She'd prefer a hundred and twenty.

She waved, loath to interrupt him, but before she could skirt past him to her bedroom, where her clothes still were since she'd never really "moved in" to Jonas's room, he snagged her by the hips and settled her on the couch near him as he wrapped up his phone call.

Tossing his phone on the glass-and-steel conglomeration that he called a coffee table, he contemplated her with the sort of attention she hadn't experienced in a long while. It was delicious.

"You're going to LA in the morning?" he said by way of greeting, and picked up her hand to hold it in his, brushing his thumb across her knuckles.

"Yeah. I don't know for how long. Franca left the plane ticket open-ended." The little strokes of his thumb stirred something inside that had been dormant for a million years. He'd been so distant lately. Dare she hope that they might be coming back together?

No reason she had to let him be the instigator. She lifted his hand to her mouth and kissed it, but he pulled away and sat back on the couch. "That sounds like fun. I hope you have a good time."

Cautiously, she eyed him. Why had he caught her before she left the room if he hadn't been after spending time with her? "Is everything okay? I wasn't expecting you to be here."

"I...came home on purpose. To see you," he admitted. "Before you left."

Her heart did a funny a little dance. But then why all the weird hot and cold? He obviously cared about her—but how much? Enough? She had no idea because they never talked about what was really going on here.

It was high time they had it out. She was leaving for LA in the morning and they rarely saw each other. She had to make this small opportunity work.

"I'm glad. I missed you." There. It was out in the open.

But he just smiled without a hint of anything. "I miss hanging out with you, too. We haven't had coffee in ages."

Or sex. The distinction between the two was legion and she didn't think for a minute that he'd misspoken or forgotten that they'd been intimate. It was a deliberate choice of words. "We haven't had a coffee relationship in ages."

His expression didn't change. "I know. It's been crazy. We're both so busy."

"By design, feels like."

That got a reaction, but why, she couldn't fathom. She watched as unease filtered through his gaze and he shifted positions on the couch, casually folding one leg over the other but also moving away from her. "We're both workaholics, that's for sure."

"I'm not," she corrected. "Not normally. But I've been dropped into an alternate reality where Franca drives me fourteen hours a day to reach these lofty goals that don't represent what I really want out of life."

Jonas frowned, his gaze sweeping over her in assessment. "You're finally getting your career off the ground. She's been keeping me apprised and I've been pleased with the direction she's taking you. But if you're not, we should discuss it. I can hire a different marketing expert, one that's more in line—"

"It's not the direction of the marketing," she broke in before he called in yet another career savant who would be brilliant at taking her away from her husband. "It's that I was happier when Cupcaked was a little bakery on Jones Street and we had sex in the foyer."

Something flitted through his gaze that she wished felt more like an invitation. Because she would have stripped down right here, right now if that had gotten the reaction she'd hoped for. Instead, his expression had a huge heaping dose of caution. "We agreed that we'd take that part as it came. No pressure. You're focusing on your career, just like I am. If Franca's not guiding you toward the right next level, then what do you want her to do?"

"I want her to go away!" Viv burst out. "She's exhausting and so chipper and can do more from 10:00 p.m. to midnight than a general, two single moms and the president combined. I want to have dinner with you, and lie in bed on a Saturday morning and watch cartoons with my head on your shoulder. I want you to rip my dress at the seams because you're so eager to get me naked. Most of all, I don't want to think about cupcakes."

But he was shaking his head. "That's not me. I'm not the kind of guy who rips a woman's dress off."

"But you are. You did," she argued inanely because what a stupid thing to say. He was totally that man and she loved it when he was like that. "I don't understand why we were so hot and heavy and then you backed off."

There came another shadow through his gaze that darkened his whole demeanor. "Because we're friends and I'm nothing if not interested in preserving that relationship."

"I am, too," she shot back a little desperately. This conversation was sliding away from her at an alarming pace, turning into something it shouldn't be, and she wasn't sure how that had happened. Or how to fix it. "But I'm also not happy just being friends. I love the text messages and I'm thrilled with what you've done for my business. But it's not enough."

"What are you saying?" he asked cautiously, his expression blank.

"That I want a real marriage. A family. I want more than just cupcakes."

Jonas let the phrase soak through him. Everything inside shifted, rolling over. In six words, Viv had reshaped the entire dynamic between them, and the effects might be more destructive than a nuclear bomb.

His chest certainly felt like one had gone off inside. While he'd been fighting to keep from treating Viv to a repeat of the dress-ripping incident, she'd been quietly planning to cut him off at the knees. Apparently he'd been creating distance for no reason.

Viv's gorgeous face froze when he didn't immediately respond. But what was he supposed to say?

Oh, that's right. *What the hell?*

"Viv, I've known you for over a year. We've been married for almost five weeks. For pretty much the entire length of our acquaintance, you've told me how important your career is to you. I have never once heard you mention that you wanted a family. Can you possibly expand on that statement?"

The weird vibe went even more haywire and he had the impression she regretted what she'd said. Then, she dropped her head into her hands, covering her eyes for a long beat. The longer she hid from him, the more alarmed he got. What was she afraid he'd see?

"Not much to expand on," she mumbled to her palms. "I like cupcakes, but I want a husband and a family, too."

Which was pretty much what she'd just said, only rephrased in such a way as to still not make any sense. "Let me ask this a different way. Why have you never told me this? I thought we were friends."

Yeah, that was a little bitterness fighting to get free.

How well did he really know the woman he'd married if this was just now coming out after all this time? After all the intimacies that they'd shared?

The lick of temper uncurling inside was completely foreign. He'd asked her to marry him strictly because he'd been sure—*positive* even—that she wasn't the slightest bit interested in having a long-term relationship.

Otherwise, he never would have asked her to do this favor. Never would have let himself start to care more than he should have.

His anger fizzled. He could have been more forthcoming with his own truths but hadn't for reasons that he didn't feel that self-righteous about all at once.

"I never told you because it…never came up." Guilt flickered in her tone and when she lifted her face from her hands, it was there in her expression, too. "I'm only telling you now because you asked."

Actually, he hadn't. He'd been sorting through her comments about the marketing consultant he'd hired, desperately trying to figure out if Viv and Franca just didn't get along or if the references he'd received regarding the consultant's brilliance had been embellished. Instead, she'd dropped a whole different issue in his lap. One that was knifing through his chest like a dull machete.

Viv wanted a real husband. A family. This fake marriage was in her way. *Jonas* was in her way. It was shattering. Far more than he would have said.

He didn't want to lose her. But neither could he keep her, not at the expense of giving her what she really wanted. Obviously he should have given more weight to the conversation they'd had at his parents' house about love being a good basis for marriage. Clearly that was what she wanted from a husband.

And he couldn't give her that, nor was she asking him to. He'd made a promise that he'd never let a woman have enough sway to affect his emotions. Judging by the swirl of confusion beneath his breastbone, it was already too late for that.

If she just hadn't said anything. He could have kept pretending that the solution to all his problems was to keep her busy until he figured out how to make all his inappropriate feelings go away.

But this…he couldn't ignore what he knew was the right thing to do.

"Viv." Vising his forehead between his fingers, he tried like hell to figure out how they'd gotten so off track. "You've been telling me for over a year that your career sucked up all your time and that's why you didn't date. How were you planning to meet said husband?"

"I don't know," she shot back defensively. "And cupcakes are important to me. It's just not the only thing, and this marathon of business-plan goals kind of solidified that fact for me. I love the idea of sharing my recipes with a bigger block of customers. But not at the expense of the kind of marriage I think would make me happy. I want—need—to back off."

Back off. From him, she meant. Jonas blinked as something wrenched loose in his chest, and it felt an awful lot like she'd gripped his heart in her fingers, then twisted until it fell out. "I understand. You deserve to have the kind of marriage you want and I can't give that to you."

Her face froze, going so glacial all at once he scarcely recognized her.

"You've never thought about having a real marriage?" she asked in a whisper.

Not once. Until now. And now it was all he could think about. What was a real marriage to her? Love, honor and cherish for the rest of her days? He could do two out of three. Would she accept that? Then he could keep her friendship, keep this marriage and… how crappy was that, to even contemplate how far he could take this without breaking his word to anyone? It was ridiculous. They should have hashed out this stuff long ago. Like before they got married. And he would have if she'd told him that she harbored secret dreams of hearts and googly eyes. Too bad that kind of stuff led to emotional evisceration when everything went south.

Like now.

"Viv." She shifted to look at him, apparently clueing in that he had something serious to say. "I married you specifically because I have no intention of having a real marriage. It was deliberate."

Something that looked a lot like pain flashed through her gaze. "Because I'm not real marriage material?"

A sound gurgled in his throat as he got caught between a vehement denial and an explanation that hopefully didn't make him sound like an ass.

"Not because you're unlovable or something." God, what was wrong with him? He was hurting her with his thoughtlessness. She'd spilled her guts to him, obviously because she trusted him with the truth, and the best he could do was smash her dreams? "I care about you. That's why we're having this conversation, which we should have had a long time ago. I never told you about Marcus."

Eyes wide, she shook her head but stayed silent as he spit out the tale of his friend who had loved and lost and then never recovered. When he wound it up with the tragedy and subsequent pact, she blinked away a sheen of tears that he had no idea what to do with.

"So you, Warren and Hendrix are all part of this... club?" she asked. "The Never Going to Fall in Love club?"

It sounded silly when she said it like that. "It's not a club. We swore solemn vows and I take that seriously."

She nodded once, but confusion completely screwed up her beautiful face. "I see. Instead of having something wonderful with a life partner, you intend to stick to a promise you made under duress a decade ago."

"No," he countered quietly. "I intend to stand by a promise I made, period. Because that's who I am. It's a measure of my ethical standards. A testament to the kind of man I want to be."

"Alone? That's the kind of man you want to be?"

"That's not fair." Why was she so concerned about his emotional state all at once? "I don't want to be alone. That's why I like being married to you so much. We have fun together. Eat dinner. Watch TV."

"Not lately," she said pointedly, and it was an arrow through his heart. If he was going to throw around his ethics like a blunt instrument, then he couldn't very well pretend he didn't know what she meant.

"Not lately," he agreed. "I'd like to say it's because we've both been busy. But that's not the whole truth. I…started to get a little too attached to you. Distance was necessary."

The sheen was back over her eyes. "Because of the pact. You've been pulling back on purpose."

He nodded. The look on her face was killing him, and he'd like nothing more than to yank her into his arms and tell her to forget that nonsense. Because he wanted his friend back. His lover. His everything.

But he couldn't. In the most unfair turnabout, he'd told her about the pact and instead of her running in the other direction like a lot of women, *he* was the one shutting down. "It was the only way I could keep you as my wife and honor the promises I made to myself and to my friends. And to you. I said no pressure. I meant to keep it that way. Which still stands, by the way."

She laughed, but he didn't think it was because she

found any of this funny. "I think this is about the lowest-pressure marriage on the planet."

"You misunderstand. I'm saying no pressure to stay married."

Her gaze cut to him and he took the quick, hard punch to the gut in stride without letting on to her how difficult it had been to utter those words.

Take them back. Right now.

But he couldn't.

"Jonas, we can't get divorced. You'd lose your grandfather's support to take over his role."

The fact that she'd even consider that put the whole conversation in perspective. They were friends who cared about each other. Which meant he had to let her go, no matter how hard it was. "I know. But it's not fair to you to stay in this marriage given that you want something different."

"I do want something different," she agreed quietly. "I have to go to LA. I can't think about any of this right now."

He let her fingers slip from his, and when she shut herself in her bedroom, the quiet click of the door burst through his chest like a gunshot to the heart. He wished he felt like congratulating himself on his fine upstanding character, but all he felt like doing was crawling into bed and throwing a blanket over his head. The absence of Viv left a cold, dark place inside that even a million blankets couldn't warm.

Ten

The trip to LA was a disaster. Oh, the cooking show was fine. She won the first round. But Viv hated having to fake smile, hated pretending her marriage wasn't fake, hated the fakeness of baking on camera with a script full of fake dialogue.

There was nothing real about her, apparently. And it had been slowly sapping her happiness away until she couldn't stand it if one more person called her Mrs. Kim. Why had she changed her name? Even that was temporary until some ambiguous point in the future.

Well, there was one thing that was real. The way she felt about Jonas, as evidenced by the numbness inside that she carried 24/7. Finally, she had someone to care about and *he* cared about *her*. Yay. He cared so much that he was willing to let her out of the favor of being married to him so she could *find someone else*.

How ironic that she'd ended up exactly where she'd intended to be. All practiced up for her next relationship, except she didn't want to move on. She wanted Jonas, just like she had for over a year, and she wanted him to feel the same about her.

The cooking show, or rather the more correctly labeled entertainment venue disguised as a cupcake battle, wrapped up the next day. Viv won the final round and Franca cheered from the sidelines, pointing to her phone, where she was presumably checking out the stats on Cupcaked's new digital storefront. Every time the show's camera zoomed in on Viv's face, they put a graphic overlay on the screen with her name and the name of her cupcake bakery. Whatever results that had produced made Franca giddy, apparently.

It was all too overwhelming. None of this was what she wanted. Instead of cooking shows, Viv should have been spending fourteen hours a day working on her marriage. The what-ifs were all she could think about.

On the plane ride home, Franca jabbered about things like click-through rates, branding and production schedules. They'd already decided to outsource the baking for the digital storefront because Viv's current setup couldn't handle the anticipated volume. Judging by the numbers Franca was throwing out, it had been a good decision.

Except for the part where none of this was what Viv wanted. And it was high time she fixed that.

When she got home, she drafted a letter to Franca thanking her for all of her hard work on Viv's behalf but explaining that her career was not in fact the most important thing in her life, so Franca's services were no longer needed. The improvements to Cupcaked were great and Viv intended to use the strategies that they'd both developed. But she couldn't continue to invest so much energy into her business, not if she hoped to fix whatever was broken in Jonas's head that made him think that saying a few words a decade ago could ever compare with the joy of having the kind of marriage she'd watched her sisters experience. Viv had been shuffled to the side once again and she wasn't okay with that.

Jonas came home late. No surprise there. That seemed to be the norm. But she was not prepared to see the lines of fatigue around his eyes. Or the slight shock flickering through his expression when he caught sight of her sitting on the couch.

"Hey," he called. "Didn't know you were back."

"Surprise." Served him right. "Sit down so we can talk."

Caution drenched his demeanor and he took his time slinging his leather bag over the back of a chair. "Can it wait? I have a presentation to the board tomorrow and I'd like to go over—"

"You're prepared," she told him and patted the cushion next to her. "I've known you for a long time and I would bet every last cupcake pan I own that you've been working on that PowerPoint every spare second for days. You're going to kill it. Sit."

It was a huge kick that he obeyed, and she nearly swooned when the masculine scent of her husband washed over her. He was too far away to touch, but she could rectify that easily. When it was time. She was flying a little blind here, but she did know one thing—she was starting over from scratch. No familiar ingredients. No beloved pan. The oven wasn't even heated up yet.

But she had her apron on and the battle lines drawn. Somehow, she needed to bake a marriage until it came out the way she liked.

"What's up? How was the show?" he asked conversationally, but strictly to change the subject, she was pretty sure.

"Fine. I won. It was fabulous. I fired Franca."

That got his attention. "What? Why would you do that?"

"Because she's too good for me. She needs to go help someone run an empire." She smiled as she gave Jonas a once-over. "You should hire her, in fact."

"Maybe I will." His dark eyes had a flat, guarded quality that she didn't like. While she knew academically that she had to take a whole different track with him, it was another thing entirely to be this close but yet so far.

"Jonas, we have to finish our conversation. The one from the other day."

"I wasn't confused about which one you meant." A brief lift of his lips encouraged her to continue, but then the shield between them snapped back into place. "You've decided to go."

"No. I'm not going anywhere." Crossing her arms so she couldn't reach out to him ranked as one of the hardest things she'd done. But it was necessary to be clear about this without adding a bunch of other stuff into the mix. "I said I was going to do you this favor and as strongly as you believe in keeping your word, it inspires me to do the same. I'm here for the duration."

Confusion replaced the guardedness and she wasn't sure which one she liked less. "You're staying? As my wife?"

"And your friend." She shrugged. "Nothing you said changed anything for me. I still want the marriage I envision and I definitely won't get that if I divorce you."

Jonas flinched and a million different things sprang into the atmosphere between them. "You're not thinking clearly. You'll never meet someone who can give you what you want if you stay married to me."

"For a smart man, you're being slow to catch on." The little noise of disgust sounded in her chest before she could check it. But *men*. So dense. "I want a real marriage with *you*, not some random guy off the street. What do you think we've been doing here but building this into something amazing? I know you want to honor your word to your friends—"

"Viv." The quiet reverberation of her name stopped her cold and she glanced at him. He'd gone so still that her pulse tumbled. "It's not just a promise I made to my friends. I have no room in my life for a real marriage. The pact was easy for me to make. It's not that I swore to never fall in love. It's that I refuse to. It's a destructive emotion that leads to more destruction. That's not something I'm willing to chance."

Her mouth unhinged and she literally couldn't make a sound to save her life. Something cold swept along her skin as she absorbed his sincerity.

"Am I making sense?" he asked after a long pause.

That she could answer easily. "None. Absolutely no sense."

His mouth firmed into a long line and he nodded. "It's a hard concept for someone like you who wants to put your faith and trust in someone else. I don't. I can't. I've built something from nothing, expanded Kim Electronics into a billion-dollar enterprise in the American market, and I'm poised to take that to the next level. I cannot let a woman nor the emotions one might introduce ruin everything."

She'd only thought nothing could make her colder than his opening statement. But the ice forming from this last round of crazy made her shiver. "You're lumping *me* in that category? *I'm* this nebulous entity known as 'woman' who might go Helen of Troy on your business? I don't even know what to say to that."

Grimly, he shook his head. "There's nothing to say. Consider this from my perspective. I didn't even know you wanted anything beyond your career until a couple of days ago. What else don't I know? I can't take that risk. Not with you."

"What?" Her voice cracked. "You're saying you don't trust me because I didn't blather on about hearts and flowers from the first moment I met you?"

Pathetic. Not-clingy hadn't worked. In fact, it might have backfired. If she'd just told him how she felt from the beginning, she could have used the last five weeks to combat his stupid pact.

Something white-hot and angry rose up in her throat. Seriously, this was so unfair. She couldn't be herself with *anyone*. Instead there were all these rules and games and potholes and loopholes, none of which she understood or cared about.

"Viv." He reached out and then jerked his hand back before touching her, as if he'd only just realized that they weren't in a place where that was okay. "It's not a matter of trust. It's…me. I can't manage how insane you make me."

She eyed him, sniffling back a tsunami of tears. "So

now I make you crazy? Listen, buster, I'm not the one talking crazy here—"

A strangled sound stopped her rant. Jonas shook his head, clearly bemused. "Not crazy. Give me a break. I was expecting you to walk out the door, not grill me on things I don't know how to explain. Just stop for a second."

His head dropped into his hands and he massaged his temples.

"Insane and crazy are the same thing."

"I mean how much I want you!" he burst out. "All the time. You make me insane with wanting to touch you, and roll into you in the middle of the night to hold you. Kiss you until you can't breathe. So, yeah, I'll give you that. It makes me crazy. In this case, it does mean the same thing."

Reeling, she stared at him, dumbstruck, numb, so off balance she couldn't figure out how to make her brain work. What in the world was wrong with *any* of that?

"I don't understand what you're telling me, Jonas."

"It's already way too much." He threw up his hands. "How much worse will it get? I refuse to let my emotions control me like that."

This was awful. He was consciously rejecting the concept of allowing anything deeper to grow between them. Period. No questions asked. She let that reality seep into her soul as her nails dug into her palms with little pinpricks of pain that somehow centered her. If this was his decision, she had to find a way to live with it.

"So, what happens next?" she whispered. "I don't want a divorce. Do you?"

At that, he visibly crumpled, folding in on himself as if everything hurt. She knew the feeling.

"I can't even answer that." His voice dipped so low that she could scarcely make it out. "My grandfather asked me to come to Korea as soon as possible. He got some bad news from his doctor and he's retiring earlier than expected."

"Oh, no." Viv's hand flew to her mouth as she took in the devastation flitting through Jonas's expression. "Is he going to be okay?"

"I don't know. He wants you to come. How can I ask that of you?" His gaze held a world of pain and indecision and a million other things that her own expression probably mirrored. "It's not fair to you."

This was where the rubber met the road. He wasn't asking her to go, nor would he. He was simply stating facts and giving the choice to her. If she wanted to claim a real marriage for herself, she had to stand by her husband through thick and thin, sickness and health, vows of honor and family emergencies.

This was the ultimate test. Did she love Jonas enough to ignore her own needs in order to fulfill his? If nothing else, it was her sole opportunity to do and be whatever she wanted in a relationship. Her marriage, her rules. If she had a mind to cling like Saran Wrap to Jonas, it was her right.

In what was probably the easiest move of the entire conversation, she reached out to lace her fingers with his and held on tight. "If you strip everything else away, I'm still your wife. Your grandfather could still pass his support to someone else if he suspects something isn't right between us. If you want me to go, I'll go."

Clearly equal parts shocked and grateful, he stared at her. "Why would you do that for me?"

She squared her shoulders. "Because I said I would."
No matter how hard it would be.

Jonas kept sneaking glances at Viv as she slept in the reclined leather seat opposite his. She'd smiled for nearly ten minutes after claiming a spot aboard the Kim private jet that Grandfather had sent to Raleigh to fetch them. It was fun to watch her navigate the spacious fuselage and interact with the attentive staff, who treated her like royalty. Obviously his grandfather had prepped them in advance.

But after the initial round of post-takeoff champagne, Viv had slipped back into the morose silence that cloaked them both since their conversation. He'd done everything in his power to drive her away so he didn't hurt her and what had she done? Repacked the suitcase that she'd just pulled off a conveyor belt at the airport hours before and announced she was coming with him to Korea. No hesitation.

What was he going to do with her?

Not much, apparently. The distance between them was nearly palpable. Viv normally had this vibe of openness about her as if she'd never met a stranger and he could talk to her about anything. Which he had, many times. Since he'd laid down the law about what kind of marriage they could have in that desperate bid to stop the inevitable, there might as well have been an impenetrable steel wall between them.

Good. That was perfect. Exactly what he'd hoped for.

He hated it.

This purgatory was exactly what he deserved, though. If Viv wasn't being her beautiful, kind, amazing self, there was no chance of his emotions engaging.

Or rather, engaging further. He was pretty sure there was a little something already stirring around inside. Okay a lot of something, but if he could hold on to that last 50 percent, he could still look Warren and Hendrix in the eye next time they were in the same room.

If he could just cast aside his honor, all of this would be so much easier.

Seoul's Incheon Airport spread out beneath them in all its dazzling silvery glory, welcoming him back to Korea. He appreciated the birthplace of his father and the homeland of his grandfather. Seoul was a vibrant city rich in history with friendly people who chattered in the streets as they passed. It was cosmopolitan in a way that Raleigh could never be, but Jonas preferred the more laid-back feel of his own homeland.

"It's beautiful," Viv commented quietly as the limo Grandfather had sent wound through the streets thronged with people and vehicles.

"I'll take you a few places while we're here," he offered. "You shouldn't miss Gyeongbokgung Palace."

They could walk through Insa-dong, the historic neighborhood that sold art and food, then maybe breeze by the Seoul Tower. He could perfectly envision the delighted smile on her face as she discovered the treasures of the Eastern world that comprised a portion of his lineage. Maybe he'd even find an opportunity to take her hand as they strolled, and he could pretend everything was fine between them.

But Viv was already shaking her head. "You don't have to do that. I don't need souvenirs. You're here for your grandfather and I'm here for you."

That made him feel like crap. But it was an inescapable fact that she'd come because he needed her.

Warmth crowded into his chest as he gazed at her, the beauty of Seoul rushing past the limousine window beyond the glass.

"Why?" he asked simply, too overcome to be more articulate.

Her gaze sought his, and for a brief moment, her normal expressiveness spilled onto her face. Just as quickly, she whisked it away. "No matter what, you're still my friend."

The sentiment caught in his throat. Her sacrifice and the unbelievable willingness to be there for him would have put him on his knees if he wasn't already sitting down. Still might. It didn't make any sense for her to be so unselfish with her time, her body, her cupcakes even without some gain other than the righteous promise of *friendship*. "I don't believe that's the whole reason."

A tiny frown marred her gorgeous mouth and he wished he could kiss it away. But he didn't move. This was something he should have questioned before they got on the plane.

"Is this another conversation about how you don't trust me?" she asked in a small voice.

Deserved that. He shook his head. "This is not a trust issue. It's that I don't understand what you're getting out of all of this. I've always wondered. I promised you that I would help you with your business since you claimed that as your passion. Then you politely declined all the success my efforts have produced. I give you the option to leave and you don't take it. Friendship doesn't seem like enough of a motivator."

Guilt crowded through her gaze. What was that all about? But she looked away before he got confirmation that it was indeed guilt, and he had a burning need to understand all at once.

The vows he'd taken with Warren and Hendrix after Marcus's death seemed like a pinky swear on the playground in comparison to Viv's friendship standards, yet he'd based his adult life on that vow. If there was something to learn from her about the bonds of friendship, he'd be an instant student.

Hooking her chin with his finger, he guided her face back toward his, feathering a thumb across her cheek before he'd barely gotten purchase. God, she felt so good. It was all he could do to keep from spreading his entire palm across her cheek, lifting her lips into a kiss that would resolve nothing other than the constant ache under his skin.

He'd enjoy every minute of the forbidden, though.

Since she still hadn't answered, he prompted her. "What's your real reason, Viv? Tell me why you'd do this for me after all I've said and done."

She blinked. "I agreed to this deal. You of all people should know that keeping your word is a choice. Anyone can break a promise but mine to you means something."

That wasn't it, or rather it wasn't the full extent. He could tell. While he appreciated her conviction, she was hedging. He hadn't expanded Kim Electronics into the American market and grown profits into the ten-figure range by missing signs that the person on the other side of the table wasn't being entirely forthcoming. But she wasn't a factory owner looking to make an extra million or two or a parts distributor with shady sources.

She was his wife. Why couldn't he take what she said at face value and leave it at that?

Because she hadn't told him about wanting a real

marriage, that was why. It stuck under his rib cage, begging him to do something with that knowledge, and the answer wasn't pulling her into his arms like he wanted to. He should be cutting her free by his choice, not hers.

Yet Viv was quietly showing him how to be a real friend regardless of the cost. It was humbling, and as the limo snaked through the crowded streets of Seoul toward his grandfather's house, his chest got so tight and full of that constant ache he got whenever he looked at Viv that he could hardly breathe.

Caught in the trap of his own making, he let his hand drop away from her face. He had a wife he couldn't let himself love and two friends he couldn't let himself disappoint. At what point did Jonas get what he wanted? And when had his desire for something more shifted so far away from what he had?

There was no good answer to that. The limo paused by his grandfather's gates as they opened and then the driver pulled onto the hushed property draped with trees and beautiful gardens. The ancestral home that Grandfather had given Jonas and Viv lay a kilometer down the road up on a hill. Both properties were palatial, befitting a businessman who entertained people from all over the world, as Jung-Su did. As Jonas would be expected to do when he stepped into Grandfather's shoes. He'd need a wife to help navigate the social aspects of being the CEO of a global company.

But the painful truth was that he couldn't imagine anyone other than Viv by his side. He needed *her*, not a wife, and for far more reasons than because it might or might not secure the promotion he'd been working toward. At the same time, as much as he'd denied that his questions were about trust, he was caught in a horrible catch-22. Trust *was* at the root of it.

Also a trap of his own making. He was predisposed to believe that a woman would string him along until she got tired of him and then she'd break his heart. So he looked for signs of that and pounced the moment he found evidence, when in reality, he'd have to actually give his heart to a woman before it could be broken. And that was what he was struggling to avoid.

Grandfather's *jibsa* ushered them into the house and showed them to their rooms. A different member of the staff discreetly saw to their needs and eventually guided Jonas and Viv to where his grandfather sat in the garden outside, enjoying the sunshine. The garden had been started by Jonas's grandmother, lovingly overseen until her death several years ago. Her essence still flitted among the mugunghwa blooms and bellflowers, and he liked remembering her out here.

His grandfather looked well, considering he'd recently been diagnosed with some precursors to heart disease and had begun rounds of medication to reverse the potential for a heart attack.

"Jonas. Miss Viviana." Grandfather smiled at them each in turn and Viv bent to kiss his cheek, which made the old man positively beam. "I'm pleased to see you looking well after your flight. It is not an easy one."

Viv waved that off and took a seat next to Jung-Su on the long stone bench. His grandfather sat on a cushion that was easier on his bones but Viv didn't seem to notice that she was seated directly on the cold rock ledge. Discreetly, Jonas flicked his fingers at one of the many uniformed servants in his grandfather's employ, and true to form, the man returned quickly with another cushion for her.

She took it with a smile and resituated herself, still chatting with Grandfather about the flight and her impressions of Korea thus far. Grandfather's gaze never left her face and Jonas didn't blame him. She was mesmerizing. Surrounded by the lush tropical beauty of the garden and animated by a subject that clearly intrigued her, she was downright breathtaking. Of course, Jonas was biased. Especially since he hadn't been able to take a deep breath pretty much since the moment he'd said *I do* to this woman.

"Jonas. Don't hover." Grandfather's brows came together as he shot a scowl over the head of his new granddaughter-in-law. "Sit with us. Your lovely wife was just telling me about baking cupcakes on the American television show."

"Yes, she was brilliant," Jonas acknowledged. But he didn't sit on the bench. The only open spot was next to Viv and it was entirely too much temptation for his starving body to be that near her.

"Jonas is too kind." Viv's nose wrinkled as she shook her head. "The show hasn't even aired yet."

"So? I don't have to see it to know that you killed it." Plus, she'd told him she'd won, like it was no big deal, when in fact, it was. Though the result was hardly shocking. "*Brilliant* is an understatement."

Viv ducked her head but not before he caught the pleased gleam in her eye. He should have told her that already and more than once. Instead, he'd been caught up in his own misery. She deserved to hear how wonderful she was on a continual basis.

"It's true," he continued. "She does something special with her recipes. No one else can touch her talent when it comes to baking."

Grandfather watched them both, his gaze traveling back and forth between them as if taking in a fascinating tennis match. "It's very telling that you are your wife's biggest fan."

Well, maybe so. But what it told, Jonas had no idea. He shrugged. "That's not a secret."

"It's a sign of maturity that I appreciate," his grandfather said. "For years I have watched you do nothing but work and I worried that you would never have a personal life. Now I see you are truly committed to your wife and I like seeing you happy. It only solidifies my decision to retire early."

Yeah. *Committed* described Jonas to a T. Committed to honor. Committed to making himself insane. Committed to the asylum might well be next, especially since his grandfather was so off the mark with his observation. But what was he supposed to do, correct him?

"It's only fair," Viv murmured before Jonas could formulate a response. "I'm his biggest fan, as well."

"Yes, I can see that, too," Jung-Su said with a laugh.

He could? Jonas glanced at Viv out of the corner of his eye in case there was some kind of sign emanating from her that he'd managed to miss. Except she had her sights firmly fixed on him and caught him eyeing her. Their gazes locked and he couldn't look away.

"You're a fan of workaholic, absentee husbands?" he asked with a wry smile of his own. Might as well own his faults in front of God and everyone.

"I'm a fan of your commitment, just like your grandfather said. You do everything with your heart. It's what I first noticed about you. You came into the shop to get cupcakes for your staff, and every time, I'd ask you 'What's the occasion today?' and you always knew the smallest details. 'It's Mrs. Nguyen's fiftieth birthday' or 'Today marks my admin's fourth anniversary working for me.' None of my other customers pay attention to stuff like that."

He shifted uncomfortably. Of course he knew those things. They'd been carefully researched excuses to buy cupcakes so he could see Viv without admitting he was there to see her. Granted, she'd already figured that out and blathered on about it to his parents during their first official married-couple dinner. Why bring that up again now?

"That's why he'll make the best CEO of Kim Global," she said to his grandfather as an aside. "Because he cares about people and cares about doing the right thing. He always keeps his word. His character is above reproach and honestly, that's why I fell for him."

That was laying it on a bit thick, but his grandfather just nodded. "Jonas is an honorable man. I'm pleased he's found a woman who loves him for the right reasons."

Except it was all fake. Jonas did a double take as Viv nodded, her eyes bright with something that looked a lot like unshed tears. "He's an easy man to love. My feelings for him have only grown now that we're married."

Jonas started to interrupt because…come on. There was playacting and there was outright lying to his grandfather for the sake of supporting Jonas's bid to become the next CEO. But as one tear slipped from her left eye, she glanced at him and whatever he'd been about to say vanished from his vocabulary. She wasn't lying.

He swallowed. Viv was in love with him? A band

tightened around his lungs as he stared at her, soaking in the admission. It shouldn't be such a shock. She looked at him like that all the time. But not seconds after saying something so shocking, so provocative *out loud*. She couldn't take it back. It was out there, pinging around inside him like an arrow looking for a target.

A servant interrupted them, capturing Grandfather's attention, and everything fell apart as it became apparent that they were being called for dinner. Jonas took Viv's hand to help her to her feet as he'd done a hundred times before but her hand in his felt different, heavier somehow as if weighted with implications. She squeezed his hand as if she knew he needed her calming touch.

It was anything but calming. She was in love with him. The revelation bled through him. It was yet another thing that she'd held back from him that changed everything. He worked it over in his mind during dinner, longing to grab her and carry her out of this public room so he could ask her a few pointed questions. But Grandfather talked and talked and talked, and he'd invited a few business associates over as well, men Jonas couldn't ignore, given that the whole reason he was in Korea was to work through the transition as his grandfather stepped down.

Finally all the obstacles were out of the way and he cornered his wife in their room. She glanced up as he shut the door, leaning against it as he zeroed in on the woman sitting on the bed.

"That went well," she commented, her gaze cutting away from his. "Your grandfather seems like he's in good spirits after his diagnosis."

"I don't want to talk about that." He loved his grandfather, but they'd talked about his illness at length before Jonas had left the States, and he was satisfied he knew everything necessary about Jung-Su's health. Jonas's wife, on the other hand, needed to do a whole lot more talking and he needed a whole lot more understanding. "Why did you tell my grandfather that you're in love with me?"

"It just kind of...came out," she said. "But don't worry, I'm pretty sure he bought it."

"I bought it," he bit out. "It wasn't just something you said. You meant it. How long have you been in love with me?"

She shrugged. "It's not a big deal."

"It is a big deal!" Frustrated with the lack of headway, he crossed the room and stopped short of lifting her face so he could read for himself what she was feeling. But he didn't touch her, because he wanted her to own up to what was really going on inside. For once. "That's why you married me. Why you came to Korea. Why you're still here even though I told you about the pact."

That's when she met his gaze, steady and true. "Yes."

Something wonderful and beautiful and strong burst through his heart. It all made a lot more sense now. What he'd been calling friendship was something else entirely.

Now would be a *really* good time to sit down. So he did. "Why didn't you tell me? That's information that I should have had a long time ago."

"No, Jonas, it's not." She jammed her hands on her hips. "What does it change? Nothing. You're determined to keep your vow to your friends and I can't stop being in love with you. So we're both stuck."

Yes. *Stuck.* He'd been between a rock and a hard place for an eternity because he couldn't stop being in love with her either.

He'd tried. He'd pretended that he wasn't, called it friendship, pushed her away, stayed away himself, thrown his honor down between them. But none of it had worked because he'd been falling for her since the first cupcake.

Maybe it was time to try something else.

"Viv." He stood and waited until he had her full attention. But then when she locked gazes with him, her expressive eyes held a world of possibilities. Not pain. Not destruction. None of the things that he'd tried to guard against.

That was the reason she should leave. Instead of feeling stuck, she should divorce him simply because he was a moron. The character she'd spoken of to his grandfather didn't include being courageous. He was a coward, refusing to acknowledge that avoiding love hadn't saved him any heartache. In fact, it had caused him a lot more than he'd credited. Had caused Viv a lot, too.

Worse, he'd avoided the wonderful parts, and ensured that he'd be lonely to boot. And what had he robbed himself of thus far? Lots of sex with his wife, a chance to have a real marriage and many, many moments where she looked at him like she was looking at him right now. As if he really was worthy of her devotion, despite his stupidity.

He'd had plenty of pain already. Avoiding the truth hadn't stopped that. The lesson here? No more pretending.

"Tell me," he commanded. "No more hiding how you really feel. I want to hear it from you, no holds barred."

"Why are you doing this?" Another tear slipped down her face and she brushed it away before he could, which seemed to be a common theme. She had things inside that she didn't trust him with and he didn't blame her.

"Because we haven't been honest with each other. In fact, I'd say my behavior thus far in our marriage hasn't been anything close to honorable, and it's time to end that. You know what? I should go first then." He captured her hand and held it between his. "Viv. You're my friend, my lover, my wife, my everything. When I made a vow to never fall in love, it was from a place of ignorance. Because I thought love was a bad thing. Something to be avoided. You taught me differently. And I ignored the fact that I took vows with you. Vows that totally overshadow the promise I made to Warren and Hendrix before I fully understood what I was agreeing to give up. I'm not okay with that anymore. Not okay with pretending. What I'm trying to say, and not doing a very good job at, is that I love you, too."

Like magic, all of his fear vanished simply by virtue of saying it out loud. At last, he could breathe. The clearest sense of happiness radiated from somewhere deep inside and he truly couldn't fathom why it had taken him so long to get to this place.

Viv eyed him suspiciously instead of falling into his waiting arms. "What?"

He laughed but it didn't change her expression. "I love you. I wouldn't blame you if you needed to hear it a hundred more times to believe me."

Her lips quirked. "I was actually questioning the part where you said you weren't doing a good job explaining. Because it seemed pretty adequate to me."

That seemed like as good an invitation as any to sweep her into his arms. In a tangle, they fell back against the mattress, and before he could blink, she was kissing him, her mouth shaping his with demanding little pulls, as if she wanted everything inside him. He didn't mind. It all belonged to her anyway.

Just as he finally got his hands under her dress, nearly groaning at the hot expanse of skin that he couldn't wait to taste, she broke the kiss and rolled him under her.

That totally worked for him. But she didn't dive back in like his body screamed for her to. Instead, she let him drown in her warm brown eyes as she smiled. "What's going to happen when we get home and you have to explain to Warren and Hendrix that you broke your word to them?"

"Nothing. Because that's not what I'm going to say." He smoothed back a lock of her hair that had fallen into her face, and shifted until her body fell into the grooves of his perfectly. This position was his new favorite. "We made that pact because we didn't want to lose each other. Our friendship isn't threatened because I finally figured out that I'm in love with you. I'll help them realize that."

"Good. I don't want to be the woman who came between you and your friends."

"You couldn't possibly. Because you're the woman who *is* my friend. I never want that to change."

And then there was no more talking as Viv made short work of getting them both undressed, which was only fair since she was on top. He liked Take Charge Viv almost as much as he liked In Love with Him Viv.

She was everything he never expected when he fell in love with his best friend.

Epilogue

Jonas walked into the bar where he'd asked Warren and Hendrix to meet him. He'd tried to get Viv to come with him, but she'd declined with a laugh, arguing that the last person who should be present at the discussion of how Jonas had broken the pact was the woman he'd fallen in love with.

While he agreed, he still wasn't looking forward to it. Despite what he'd told Viv, he didn't think Warren and Hendrix were going to take his admission lightly.

His friends were already seated in a high-backed booth, which Jonas appreciated given the private nature of what he intended to discuss. They'd already taken the liberty of ordering, and three beers sat on the table. But when he slid into the booth across from Warren, Hendrix cleared his throat.

"I'm glad you called," Hendrix threw out before

Jonas could open his mouth. "I have something really important to ask you both."

Thrilled to have an out, Jonas folded his hands and toyed with his wedding band, which he did anytime he thought about Viv. He did it so often, the metal had worn a raw place on his finger. "I'm all ears, man."

Warren set his phone down, but no less than five notifications blinked from the screen. "Talk fast. I have a crisis at work."

Hendrix rolled his eyes. "You always have a crisis. It's usually that you're not there. Whatever it is can wait five minutes." He let out a breath with a very un-Hendrix-like moan. "I need you guys to do me a favor and I need you to promise not to give me any grief over it."

"That's pretty much a guarantee that we will," Warren advised him with cocked eyebrow. "So spill before I drag it out of you."

"I'm getting married."

Jonas nearly spit out the beer he'd just sipped. "To one woman?"

"Yes, to one woman." Hendrix shot him a withering glare. "It's not that shocking."

"The hell you say." Warren hit the side of his head with the flat of his palm. Twice. "I think my brain is scrambled. Because I'd swear you just said you were getting married."

"I did, jerkoff." Hendrix shifted his scowl to Warren. "It's going to be very good for me."

"Did you steal that speech from your mom?" Warren jeered, his phone completely forgotten in favor of the real-life drama happening in their booth. "Because it sounds like you're talking about eating your veggies, not holy matrimony."

"You didn't give Jonas this much crap when he got married," Hendrix reminded him as Warren grinned.

"Um, whatever." Jonas held up a finger as he zeroed in on the small downturn of Hendrix's mouth. "That is completely false, first of all. You have a short memory. And second, if this is like my marriage, you're doing it for a reason, one you're not entirely happy about. What's this really about?"

Hendrix shrugged, wiping his expression clear. "I'm marrying Rosalind Carpenter. That should pretty much answer all of your questions."

It *so* did not. Warren and Jonas stared at him, but Warren beat him to the punch. "Whoa, dude. That's epic. Is she as much a knockout in person as she is in all those men's magazines?"

He got an elbow in his ribs for his trouble, but it wasn't Warren's fault that there were so many sexy pictures of Rosalind Carpenter to consider.

"Shut up. That's my fiancée you're talking about."

Jonas pounded on the table to get their attention. "On that note…if the question is will we be in the wedding party, of course we will." They had plenty of time to get the full story. After Jonas steered them back to the reason why he'd called them with an invitation for drinks. "Get back to us when you've made plans. Now chill out while we talk about my thing."

"Which is?" Warren gave him the side-eye while checking his messages.

"I broke the pact."

The phone slipped out of Warren's hand and thunked against the leather seat. "You did what? With Viv?"

Jonas nodded and kept his mouth shut as his friends lambasted him with their best shots at his character, the depths of his betrayal and the shallowness of his definition of the word *vow*. He took it all with grace because he didn't blame them for their anger. They just needed to experience the wonders of the right woman for themselves and then they'd get it.

When they were mostly done maligning him, Jonas put his palms flat on the table and leaned forward. "No one is more surprised by this than me. But it's the truth. I love her and I broke the pact. But it's not like it was with Marcus. She loves me back and we're happy. I hope you can be happy for us, too. Because we're going to be married and in love for a long time."

At least that was his plan. And by some miracle, it was Viv's, too.

"I can't believe you're doing this to us," Warren shot back as if he hadn't heard a word Jonas said. "Does keeping your word mean nothing to you?"

"Integrity is important to me," he told them without blinking. "That's why I'm telling you the truth. Lying about it would dishonor my relationship with Viv. And I can't stop loving her just to stick to a pact we made. I tried and it made us both miserable."

"Seems appropriate for a guy who turns on his buddies," Hendrix grumbled.

"Yeah, we'll see how you feel after you get married," Jonas told him mildly. Hendrix would come around. They both would eventually. They'd been friends for too long to let something like a lifetime of happiness come between them, strictly over principle.

Warren griped about the pact for another solid five minutes and then blew out a breath. "I've said my piece and now I have to go deal with a distribution nightmare. This is not over."

With that ominous threat, Warren shoved out of the booth and stormed from the restaurant.

Hendrix, on the other hand, just grinned. "I know you didn't mean to break the pact. It's cool. Things happen. Thank God that'll never be me, but I'm happy that you're happy."

"Thanks, man." They shook on it and drank to a decade of friendship.

When Jonas got home, Viv was waiting in the foyer. His favorite. He flashed her the thumbs-up so she would know everything was okay between him and his friends—which it would be once Warren calmed down—then wrapped Viv in his arms and let her warmth infuse him. "I have another favor to ask."

"Anything."

No hesitation. That might be his favorite quality of hers. She was all in no matter what he asked of her—because she loved him. How had he gotten so lucky? "You're not even going to ask what it is?"

She shrugged. "If it's anything like the last favor, which landed me the hottest husband on the planet, by the way, why would I say no? Your favors are really a huge win for me so…"

Laughing, he kissed her and that made her giggle, too. His heart was so full, he worried for a moment that it might burst. "Well, I'm not sure this qualifies as a win. I was just going to ask you to never stop loving me."

"Oh, you're right. I get nothing out of that," she

teased. "It's torture. You make me happier than I would have ever dreamed. Guess I can find a way to put up with that for the rest of my life."

"Good answer," he murmured, and kissed his wife, his lover, his friend. His everything.

* * * * *

If you loved this story,
pick up these other sexy and emotional reads
from USA TODAY *bestselling author*
Kat Cantrell!

TRIPLETS UNDER THE TREE
A PREGNANCY SCANDAL
THE PREGNANCY PROJECT
FROM ENEMIES TO EXPECTING
THE MARRIAGE CONTRACT

Available now from Mills & Boon Desire!

* * *

"Who knows when I might be in your bed again?"

Kaden stopped to consider Pippa's words. Oh yeah, there were all sorts of buts and second thoughts. She didn't seem like a one-night-stand kind of girl but maybe he'd read her wrong. It was just sex after all. A way to forget.

He studied her expression, thought about what he knew of her. Pippa Duncan was a sweet woman who wanted to make the world a better place. She wanted to help people. And this was her way of helping him. Somehow, in spilling his guts about the day's revelations, he'd become one of her charity cases.

The more he thought about it, the more Kade understood what Pippa was trying to do. What would it hurt to accept what she was offering?

He gave in to the need.

His lips skimmed her jaw, seeking her mouth. Then he took their kiss deeper, yet kept it quiet and dreamy, hovering just on the edge of desire.

He eased back to look at her and asked, "Are you sure?"

* * *

Best Friend Bride
is part of the Red Dirt Royalty series:
These Oklahoma millionaires
work hard and play harder.

CLAIMING THE
COWGIRL'S BABY

BY
SILVER JAMES

First Published in Great Britain 2017
By Mills & Boon, an imprint of HarperCollins*Publishers*
1 London Bridge Street, London, SE1 9GF

© 2017 Silver James

ISBN: 978-0-263-92828-0

51-0717

Our policy is to use papers that are natural, renewable and recyclable products and made from wood grown in sustainable forests. The logging and manufacturing processes conform to the legal environmental regulations of the country of origin.

Printed and bound in Spain
by CPI, Barcelona

Silver James likes walks on the wild side and coffee. Okay. She LOVES coffee. A cowgirl at heart, she's been an army officer's wife and mum and worked in the legal field, fire service and law enforcement. Now retired from the real world, she lives in Oklahoma, spending her days writing with the assistance of two Newfoundlands, the cat who rules them all and the characters living in her imagination.

To every person who has ever
created a family of the heart.

And with special thanks to my great
Harlequin team: Charles Greimsman,
Stacy Boyd, Tahra Seplowin, Keyren Gerlach,
Erin Crum and the magicians in the art department.
Y'all keep me on the straight and narrow.
looks shifty-eyed Mostly.

One

Kaden Waite was a simple man. Standing on the street staring up at the massive glass-and-steel tower that housed the offices of Barron Enterprises, he wondered why he'd been summoned here. Kade managed the Crown B Ranch for the Barron family. He belonged in the country, not here in downtown Oklahoma City.

Two women, chattering like blue jays, brushed past him, then slowed to glance back over their shoulders. Their appraisal embarrassed him.

Other people, men and women in suits moving at a hectic pace, pushed in and out of the building's entrance intent on their business. The city was full of rush and commotion. Kade liked to take his time. Especially today when he was out of his element. Bells from a church near the Oklahoma City National Memorial chimed, reminding him the hour for his appointment was rapidly approaching.

Removing his cowboy hat, he reached for the bandanna in his hip pocket, only to discover he didn't have one. Instead, his fingers encountered the crumpled envelope containing a certified letter requesting his presence today. And he had no freaking idea why. Cyrus Barron had hired him straight out of Oklahoma State University to run the Crown B Ranch, putting him in charge rather than one of Mr. Barron's five sons. Now that Mr. Barron was dead, was that about to change? Was that why Kade had been summoned?

He was dressed up—at least by his standards. Starched jeans with a knife-edged crease, buttoned-up shirt, polished boots. No bandanna to wipe the sweat from his forehead, no spurs jangling as he walked. Kade used an index finger to ease the pressure of his collar against his throat. Hat in hand, he entered the building.

Kade stayed pressed into a back corner of the elevator as it stopped on lower floors. People got on and off. A few women smiled. Several men did double takes before their expressions turned speculative. This wasn't the first time his presence caused that reaction. He wondered what people saw in him that created this response. Was it his Chickasaw heritage? His mother was a full-blood. He knew nothing about his father.

By the time the elevator doors opened on the thirty-sixth floor, Kade was the sole occupant. He stepped into an impressive reception area defined by dark wood and leather. Both receptionists—one male, one female—glanced up. The young man frowned, the slightly older woman smiled.

Hat still in his hands, Kade approached the desk. "Ah… good morning? I think I have an appoint—"

Smile still in place, the woman interrupted him. "Good morning, Mr. Waite. Heidi, Mr. Barron's assistant, will be here momentarily."

He eyed the plush leather couches and the tall-backed chairs in the waiting area wondering if he should sit down. The tall mahogany doors leading to the inner sanctum of Barron & Associates, the law firm headed up by Cyrus Barron's middle son, Chance, opened, making a decision unnecessary. A petite dark-haired woman bustled toward him.

"Good morning, Kaden." She extended her hand and he automatically shook it.

He remembered her. Chance's longtime legal assistant looked refined in her stylish business suit and low heels. Kade was careful not to squeeze her hand too tightly despite his nervous inclination to do so. Ever since Cyrus Barron's funeral, he'd fought down a sense of unease. Then a week ago, he'd gotten the certified letter.

Heidi ushered him down a long hallway. Her heels clicked on the hardwood floor only to be silenced when she stepped onto one of the expensive rugs lining the corridor. Stopping at a wide door, she knocked sharply and waited a count of five before opening it. Kade got the impression this was all stage dressing but he couldn't figure out why it would be necessary.

He made three strides into the room before the door closed at his back with a quiet snick. Kade gazed at the people seated around the massive conference table, then glanced to the windows lining one wall. He could see for miles across the rolling countryside beyond the metropolitan environs of Oklahoma City. He refocused on the people in the room and didn't miss the looks they exchanged.

"Thanks for coming, Kaden. We'll get started as soon as Mr. Shepherd gets here." Chance's voice cut through the heavy silence.

Kade noticed the plates and coffee mugs on the table in front of the Barron brothers, and then located the long cherrywood credenza loaded with food and coffee decanters. Full of nervous energy, he took his time pouring a cup of dark roast coffee and choosing something to eat from the array of muffins, doughnuts and pastries.

Black coffee, a buttermilk spice muffin and the chair

at the far end of the polished wood table. This worked. He had his back to the windows but faced the Barrons and the door. Except for the occasional sidelong look, the brothers ignored him—not that they paid much attention to each other either. He didn't want to think about his predicament. With the old man's death, he figured he was here to be fired, and if that was the case, he wished they'd just get on with it.

When Cyrus first hired him, Kade had been young and full of ideas. It wasn't until later, after years of watching the interactions of the Barron family from the outside, that he started wondering why the brothers didn't resent him. The ranch was their birthright. They'd grown up there and even though each had made his own mark in the world, the Crown B was still their home, still the heart of their family. To have its management turned over so completely to a stranger must have chapped their butts. It would have chapped his.

He'd poured his heart into the ranch for eight years. It was more than just a job; the Crown B had become his home too. And his passion. Their prime beef herds were the envy of cattlemen's associations in ten states and the horses he bred? They were coveted by horsemen the world over. His personal project had been to breed a "super stallion"—a stud to rival the American Quarter Horse Association's foundation studs. He now had a yearling colt that was the culmination of all his work.

If he had to leave the ranch, it would break his heart.

A sharp rap on the door jerked him out of his thoughts. When the door opened, an older man in a three-piece pin-striped suit marched in, set a briefcase on the conference table, looked around then fixed his unwavering gaze on Kade.

"Kaden Waite, I presume?"

* * *

Pippa Duncan pressed the pillow over her head. Jagged lightning danced behind her closed eyelids. The last thing she needed this morning was a massive migraine. She had too much to do plus a lunch date with Kade. No, not a date, she reminded herself. A lunch meeting. She needed to finish writing a grant and she had some notes she wanted to share with the Barrons' ranch manager to get his opinion.

She'd gone to high school with Chase and Cash Barron, had gone to parties and hayrides at the Crown B Ranch. Her father and Cyrus Barron had shared the same country club, poker games and social set. Her mother had done everything possible to pair her off with one of the Barron brothers, and had never been particular about which one. She'd endured her mother's disappointed sighs at four weddings. Her parents hadn't been invited to the fifth so Pippa pretty much invited herself to Cash's wedding because she'd needed to get reacquainted with Kade. She needed his expertise and horse sense to build a string of horses for Camp Courage, her riding therapy program. That was her only reason. Okay, she'd crushed on the Barrons' ranch manager when they'd both been students at Oklahoma State, but she'd outgrown those feelings. Really she had.

It was all about business now because getting Camp Courage financed and running was her priority. Since Cash's wedding, she'd spent time with Kade at the ranch and he'd come to town for lunch or dinner a few times, all so she could pick his brain. Kade had volunteered with the Oklahoma State Outreach Riders, a group of students working with disabled kids and horses. When he called last night to ask her to meet him in Bricktown for lunch, she'd ignored the zing of excitement that coursed through her. Because…business. And she was too old for crushes. Even if there was a whole lot about Kade Waite for a woman to crush on. Beyond the obvious—tall, handsome, employed—he ticked off several items on her Perfect Man list. He was a cowboy—and that was the biggest priority. Yes, she was shallow like that.

If her head hadn't been pounding, Pippa would have laughed. She was such a cliché—the rich debutante falling for a common cowboy. Except there was nothing common about Kade Waite. She'd known that from the first time she saw him at OSU when she was hanging out on the corral fence watching the rodeo team work. She wasn't too proud to admit fantasizing about the tall cowboy in the faded jeans with work-roughened hands, and some of those fantasies had gone straight to all things sexy. Because Kade starred in every erotic dream she'd ever had.

The prescription medication she'd taken for the migraine was finally having an effect and she could unsquint her eyes. She wasn't ready to remove the pillow yet, afraid her room would be too bright to bear. The migraines had begun to manifest more frequently, a worry that nagged at the back of her mind. She didn't have time to be incapacitated. She had grant proposals to write, stable and arena space to rent, horses to buy. Camp Courage was so close to becoming a reality.

Eyes scrunched closed, she lifted the edge of the pillow and peeked. When no blinding pain lanced through her head, she opened both eyes. The medications had fully kicked in. She still had tunnel vision but managed to focus on the clock next to the bed. She had time to make her lunch with Kade—if she hurried.

After showering and getting dressed, she was ready to head out when her mother met her at the front door. Pippa had been so close to escaping, but she knew she was stuck. She plastered a smile on her face. "What brings you out here, Mother?"

"I thought we might have lunch together, discuss your current activities."

"Sorry. I have a lunch date."

Her mother perked up. "Someone I know?" Then her eyes narrowed. "Why are you wearing those awful jeans and boots?"

"They're comfortable, and no, you probably don't know him. I'm meeting Kaden Waite, the Barrons' ranch manager. He's consulting on my foundation."

Millicent Duncan shook her index finger in Pippa's face. "I don't understand you at all. There are days I can't believe you are my daughter." Her mother closed her eyes in an obvious effort to control her temper. The bitter edge had smoothed from her voice when she continued. "I wanted to send you to ballet school. You wanted riding lessons. You have always had this obsession with horses. And helping unfortunate people."

Fighting her own temper, Pippa made her face blank. This was not a new argument. "It's my money, Mother."

"No. Technically, it was your grandmother Ruth's. Your father and I both tried to dissuade her from setting up that trust fund. We knew you would just fritter it away on—"

"Enough." She cut her mother off as lights started flickering in her peripheral vision again. Pippa needed to get away before the migraine precursors bloomed into crashing pain and roiling nausea. She squeezed her eyes shut and rubbed her temple in an unconscious motion.

"That man is not someone you should be seeing, Pippa." Millicent's voice grated on her nerves as the headache gained strength. "You need to stop all this nonsense."

"It's not nonsense, Mother. Now, if you will excuse me, I'm going to be late." Pippa slipped past her mother, shutting the door to the guesthouse behind her.

* * *

Pippa still managed to arrive a few minutes early. The patio of Cadie B's Southern Kitchen was one of her favorite spots—especially in late spring. Overlooking the Bricktown Canal, the restaurant catered to locals and tourists alike with a menu of southern cooking favorites. Her usual table hugged the outer railing but today, she opted for one closer to the brick warehouse building that housed the restaurant. The secluded table she chose was squarely in the shade and would remain so during lunch. She kept on her sunglasses just to be on the safe side. The perky waitress set a sweating glass of sweet tea in front of Pippa and she settled in to wait.

Thirty minutes later, she checked her watch, then her smartphone. Kade was officially late and he hadn't called or texted. Which was unusual. The guy really was a gentleman. She called him and when her call rolled to voice mail, she left a rushed message.

"Hey, Kaden. I'm at Cadie B's. Did I mess up and get the day or time wrong? Give me a call, please. Talk to you soon."

She wouldn't panic. But she reflected on her mother's pursed lips and condescension when Pippa mentioned she was meeting Kade. Even though she'd assured her mother this was a working lunch, Millicent Duncan seemed to have the idea that Pippa was dating him. Ha. She wished.

After no return call and repeated texts to Kade, three refills of tea and a waitress morphing from perky to pitying, Pippa lost her own easygoing demeanor. Her thumbs flew over the virtual keyboard on her phone as she typed an angry message.

CALLED YOU AND TEXTED. NO REPLY. IF STANDING ME UP IS YOUR WAY OF BLOWING ME OFF, YOU SUCK!

* * *

Kade's phone blew up with calls and texts starting about ten minutes after he walked out of Barron Tower. Numb, he'd climbed into his truck and started driving. Now he was northbound on I-35 headed home. Only it wasn't his home. Not any longer. A highway exit loomed and he jerked the steering wheel, taking the ramp at twice the posted speed. He didn't care.

Turning into the parking lot of a truck stop, he parked in the farthest corner. Stiff-armed, fingers bloodless as he gripped the steering wheel, he pressed back against the seat.

"Shut up!" he yelled at the cell phone. He wanted to turn it off. He wanted to slam it against the concrete and drive over it with his pickup. He wanted his life back. The damn phone pinged again. Another text. Wait…from Pippa?

Breathing like he'd just run a forty-yard dash, he opened her text. Standing her up? Blowing her off? He clicked over to voice mail. He had multiple missed calls from…what did he call them now? The Barrons. He'd refer to them as he always had. He couldn't wrap his head around what else they were at this point in time. Kade listened to Pippa's voice mail and winced. He'd blanked out about meeting her for lunch. Completely.

He hated texting. His thumbs were broad, unwieldy when it came to hitting the virtual letters but he didn't trust his voice. Thank goodness for autocorrect.

I totally messed up. Bad morning. I'm sorry. Really really sorry.

The big diesel engine of his truck rumbled as he stared out the windshield trying to marshal his emotions. Kade ignored the phone when it rang. It stopped after three rings. His text program dinged almost immediately, and he glanced at the message.

Will you please answer the phone so we can talk? What happened? I'd like to help if I can.

Pippa couldn't. How could anyone? He slammed his fists against the steering wheel. His mother had known. The whole damn time. She'd known who his father was. Had known the people he worked for were his half brothers. The sense of betrayal clawed at him, gnawed on his bones with teeth-jarring viciousness.

His phone rang again. He stared at the caller ID. Pippa. Accepting the call, he didn't say anything. Had nothing to say.

"Kade? Are you there?" When he didn't respond, she continued. "What happened? I know you were supposed to meet with Chance this morning." Her voice trailed off but he remained silent. With a quick intake of breath, she gasped out, "Oh, no! Did he fire you? That's… They… That's despicable. After everything you've done at the ranch, after all the improvements, after…after…" She stopped and inhaled. "I'm so sorry, Kade. I can try to talk to them."

And she could talk to them. She was part of their social class. He knew she'd gone to school with the twins, Chase and Cash. Grew up knowing all of the brothers. His brothers. Half brothers, he amended. And wasn't that a kick in the ass. He closed his eyes, leaning back against the headrest.

Feeling exhausted, he huffed out a breath. He didn't need Pippa to fight his battles. He didn't need or want anyone involved in this very personal decision. He hadn't been fired, not outright. In fact, the Crown B could be his, lock, stock and barrel. "You don't understand, Pippa. It's not really like that. This is something—"

He stopped speaking. This really wasn't something he wanted to talk about. Not to her. Not to anyone. Not yet. It was too personal and he couldn't talk about it until he figured out what he was going to do. "Never mind, Pippa. Look, I'm sorry about lunch. You can't help, but thanks. Just leave it be. Please." So far, so good. He could finish this conversation without losing it. "I need to go. I'll… just…ah, later, Pippa. Bye."

Clicking off his phone, he leaned back against the head-rest. He could get everything he'd ever wanted. All he had to do was accept the callous edict of a dead man.

Two

Pippa stared at her phone. Kade had very politely hung up on her without her getting another word in. What was going on? Before she could contemplate the situation, the waitress appeared again. If she didn't eat something, Pippa would pay for it later. She ordered then headed to the ladies' room. There was a line, and when she returned, her salad was waiting for her.

Still trying to decide what to do about Kade, Pippa ate and people-watched. That's when she recognized the five men occupying a nearby table. The last time she'd seen all five Barron brothers together had been at Cash's wedding. They were all incredibly successful. Clay was a US senator. Cord ran the family's oil company. Chance headed up a huge law firm. Chase normally lived in Las Vegas, Hollywood or Nashville as head of the family's entertainment empire. She seldom saw Cash, though he lived in Oklahoma City. He was president of the security company in charge of safeguarding all the rest of the family's enterprises.

"So what are we going to do?" Chance sounded glum and Pippa stilled. It was rude to eavesdrop but instinct had her skulking behind the arrangement of plants between her table and theirs to remain unnoticed.

"We can't make him accept." Clay shrugged and Pippa wished she could see his face. Who were they talking about?

"It's not like we hadn't figured it out," Chase added. "We've all hinted to Kade that we knew."

Wait…what? She was beyond confused now and waved away the waitress who was approaching with the iced water pitcher in her hand.

Cord glanced around the restaurant and Pippa ducked down as he spoke. "Leave it to the old man to screw up things all the way from the grave."

A waitress arrived to take their orders and no one spoke for a few minutes after her departure. It was Cash who reopened the conversation. "How did you expect him to react? Jump up and down for joy? The guy works for us. For the old man. Never once did Dad treat him as anything but an employee. Put yourselves in Kade's boots. He's told he's a bastard son and that the only way he can keep his job—keep everything he's worked for the last eight years—is to change his name. If he doesn't become a Barron, he's out on his butt." He met the gaze of each of his brothers and added in a sarcastic voice, "Yeah, I'd be thrilled to death with that ultimatum."

Pippa didn't want to hear anything else. Her first thought was to get to Kade. No wonder he'd stood her up. Maybe she was too softhearted, as her mother so often complained, but she wanted to find him, try to make things better. If she jumped up and dashed from the restaurant, the Barrons would see her. She had to wait. That meant dessert. And coffee. And more stalling.

She finally paid out and was just waiting for her chance to sneak away when a waitress and busboy began to clear the table between her and the Barrons. With a surreptitious glance toward their table, she slipped out of the chair and scuttled toward the door leading to the restaurant's interior. She now had one goal in mind—find Kade.

Walking to the parking garage, she considered what she'd overheard. Was Kade really a Barron? He'd never really talked about his family. Granted, she hadn't exactly been forthcoming about her own. She and Kade were friends but not particularly close. Not that she didn't want to know him better. She did because part of her remembered how she'd been that starry-eyed coed mooning over the handsome cowboy.

Cash said that Kade had to change his name or he was out. What exactly did that mean? Obviously, they wanted him to be a Barron, but did they mean to kick him off the ranch if he didn't? Her sense of justice surged again. Kade had told her she couldn't help, but she was determined to do something. Besides, what was the worst that could happen? He'd get mad, tell her to go away and that would be that. He'd still help out with the therapy program. Probably.

Before she could second-guess her motives, she headed toward the ranch, figuring that's where Kade would go. He'd lived there since graduating from OSU. She knew he was from somewhere down south—Sulphur or Davis or somewhere. Surely he wouldn't head that direction.

There was only one way to find out. She kept driving north. Her foot might have been a little heavy on the accelerator because she made the drive in record time. She followed the long, sweeping trip to the big house. No vehicles were parked there.

Pippa took a secondary road and headed toward the building that housed the ranch office. Kade's truck wasn't parked there either. She kept driving until she found the pickup in front of his house. She parked her Highlander next to his truck, worked up her courage and got out. After knocking on the door for several minutes and listening intently, she decided he must not be home. She stood on the porch and looked around. What would she do if she lived out here and was upset?

The open door of the main horse barn caught her attention. Had he gone riding? After picking Kade's brain about horse breeding and ranching, she understood enough about the Crown B operation to know that when the ranch hands rode horseback, they used the stock horses kept in the smaller barn. Kade worked and rode the blood stock stabled in the main building.

She headed to the barn and found Kade there. He stood in front of a stall, arms folded across the top of the stall door, chin resting on his fisted hands.

He looked…forlorn. Deflated. Utterly defeated. Pippa wanted to run to him, throw her arms around his waist and hug him until the stuffing came out, as her grandmother used to say. But her feet remained encased in emotional concrete.

"Go away, Pippa."

He hadn't looked up, but of course he'd know she was here. He always seemed attuned to his surroundings. There was no heat in his voice so she didn't move.

"Do you want to talk about…" She couldn't tell him she knew. He'd have to share that on his own. "About whatever has you upset?"

"No." He swiped his ball cap off his head and tunneled fingers through his thick, black hair but refused to look in her direction. "Just…leave me the hell alone."

"Don't curse at me. And I'm not leaving. You owe me lunch." She made a show of looking at her watch before glancing up at him, a smug expression firmly in place before she winked. "Though at this point, it is closer to suppertime."

Kade turned his head and her heart broke a little at the utter devastation etched on his face. His brown eyes were shadowed by a soul-deep pain. She moved then, walking toward him like she would a skittish horse. She stopped short of touching him, choosing instead to lean on the stall door in a mirror image of his posture when she'd arrived.

The yearling colt inside the stall whickered. Barron's Imperial Pride, Imp for short. "He's growing fast." Imp was Kade's crowning accomplishment and a safe topic.

"Yeah. Too bad I won't watch him grow up."

Or not. Pippa had to get Kade to tell her everything because this dancing around what she knew without tripping up was hard. She leaned a little closer to him, *accidentally* brushing her arm against his. "You can talk to me, Kade. Always. You know that, right?" He didn't say anything so she tried again. "We're friends, Kade. Friends help friends. I can see you're upset. Won't you tell me what happened today?"

He shook his head and the next words out of his mouth stabbed her heart.

"What makes you think we're friends?" Kade jammed the cap back on his head and glowered at her.

She flashed him what she hoped was a sweet smile before nudging his biceps with her shoulder. "I did drive all the way up here after you blew me off for lunch. Only a friend would do that." She considered her next words carefully. "Even if you don't want to tell me what's got you upset, I still think you need a friend right now, and I just happen to be here all handy and stuff."

She tilted her head to look up at him. "Besides, you're a growing boy," she said. "You need to eat. I'll even cook, provided you have something in the fridge."

* * *

Pippa wasn't going to leave him be, and part of him didn't want to be alone. "I'm not fit for company, Pippa."

"Yeah, and?" She grinned at him, totally unrepentant for intruding on his solitude.

Kade settled at her words and that surprised him. He didn't want company of any sort, but if he had to have some, Pippa would do. Seeing her at Cash's wedding, he'd remembered her from college, from when he'd catch her sitting on the fence mooning over him. He hadn't wanted a girlfriend then. He didn't want one now, especially not someone like Pippa. She should be with someone rich, like a Barron— He cut off that thought. Technically, he was a Barron, or could be.

He started to decline her offer but she was smiling all cute and sunny at him. Her long blond hair was caught up in a ponytail and the sprinkling of freckles across her nose went perfectly with her blue eyes. The quintessential girl next door.

It was just an early dinner. Between friends. And she was right. He needed to eat.

"C'mon, then." His voice was gruff as he ushered her out.

They exited the barn and Dusty, the ranch mutt, galloped toward them. He leaped up on Pippa and would have taken her to the ground had Kade not braced her with his body, one arm automatically going around her waist. He stiffened, fending off the dog with a terse command, then tensed more as Pippa pressed back against him. She shouldn't feel this good in his arms.

After releasing her, he kept his hands jammed in his pockets as they walked up the road to the house he'd called home since the day he'd arrived as the newly hired ranch manager. The place reminded him of the houses found on cattle and sheep stations in Australia. A wide porch wrapped around all four sides and the metal roof gleamed dully beneath the bright afternoon sun.

Pippa stumbled and he automatically caught her arm to steady her. "Pip? You okay?"

Her face had paled and she was squinting against the sun. Lips pressed together, she shook her head. "Migraine coming. Been fighting it all day."

He scooped her up into his arms without thinking. His mother suffered debilitating migraines and he knew what to do. "Keep your eyes closed until I can get you inside."

Lengthening his stride, Kade quickly got her into his dim living room. He set her on the couch and hunkered down on his heels. "What can I do to help?"

She reached blindly for him so he snagged her hand with his own. "I have meds in my purse. In the Highlander."

He pulled his hand away from hers reluctantly. "Keys?"

"Not locked."

"Be right back." Kade resisted the sudden urge to brush his knuckles over her cheek as he rose and headed outside. He returned moments later, her purse in hand. He didn't like the wince on her face as light spilled in from the open door.

"Sorry about not fixing dinner for you."

He brushed her apology away. "Not a problem. It's more important for you to lie down. I'm going to carry you into my bedroom, okay? It's darker in there."

She nodded so he lifted and cradled her. After she was settled, had taken her medication along with a long drink of water, she held his hand as he sat on the edge of the bed with her.

"I'll go away so you can rest."

"Don't. Please. I like the sound of your voice." A little

smile teased the corners of her mouth and she patted the bed beside her. "And a girl likes to be fussed over. I'll be okay in a little while. I caught this migraine early." She offered him a tentative smile and a scrunched-up nose. "Besides, it feels a little weird being in your bedroom all by myself."

Concerned about her, Kade acquiesced. He stretched out beside her and moments later, she'd curled into him, her head on his chest. Was it wrong that lying here with her felt so right? Even so, he didn't want to talk about his situation, especially not to Pippa. He liked her more than he should, and liked her idea for a horse therapy program. He'd considered asking her out but figured she wouldn't be interested. Still, she was easy to be around. Too easy.

"Are you going to talk to me?" She asked the question without opening her eyes.

The feelings of bewilderment and resentment hadn't gone away. He didn't want to talk about his day and the choice that had been forced on him.

As a kid, he'd lain in bed next to his mom when her headaches put her down for the count. He'd read stories to her, and it always seemed to help. Since there was no reading material nearby, he began to talk.

Kade started out talking about the ranch, about Imp. He spoke of his grandparents and growing up on their small ranch outside of Davis, Oklahoma. He talked about OSU. About getting hired by Cyrus Barron. About making the Crown B his home. Without a conscious decision, he opened up to Pippa. He voiced his bewilderment at going from the only child of a single mother to having five brothers who'd grown up with their shared father, and expressed his concern over how they viewed him. Eventually, he got around to the feelings of betrayal engendered by his mother's deceit—a deceit he wasn't ready to confront her with yet.

He spoke until he was hoarse, hoping that Pippa had fallen asleep so she didn't hear the catch in his voice when he said, "Then the lawyer dropped Cyrus's ultimatum on the table. If I want to stay here, keep my home here, keep the Crown B..." He had to breathe before he could continue. "And it would mean keeping the ranch as CEO of the Barron Land and Cattle Company, it would mean owning Imp." And having more money than he could wrap his brain around.

Her hand pressed against his chest. "What do you have to do, Kade?"

"Turn my back on the only family I've ever known."

"I don't understand." Pippa's voice was soft as she craned her head to see his expression.

"To keep my place here on the ranch—to have absolute control over it, I have to change my name. I can't be a Waite. I have to be a Barron."

"Is that so bad?"

Kade almost shoved her away, remembered the pain she'd been in and forced his muscles to relax. Still, he needed distance so he eased out from under her and stood. What did she know about anything like this? Pippa was the beloved daughter of the Duncan family. They were rich, like the Barrons, while he'd worked for everything he had—all of which could be ripped away at the whim of the man who'd donated his sperm to create Kade.

He paced away from the bed then whirled to face her. "What would you say to someone who came to you and told you that you weren't a Duncan, could no longer be a Duncan? That you were someone totally different."

"But you wouldn't be somebody totally different. You'd

still be Kaden. The name doesn't make a person. It's just a label."

He stalked to the edge of the bed and glowered at her. "Being a Waite shaped who I am, Pippa. My grandparents. My…" Anger surged again. He'd always been close to his mother. He'd adored her as a boy, respected her as a teen and admired her as a man. He'd never questioned their love for each other. Until that damn attorney read Cyrus Barron's will.

Pippa sat up on the edge of the bed, watching. After a moment, she spoke. "I'm going to repeat myself. The man you are is the man you've always been. Your family—the one that raised you—had a profound effect on who you are. You could change your name to John Doe, and you would still be the same man who is standing in this room. Understand?"

Her stomach picked that moment to grumble. "You need to eat," he said, relieved at the interruption. "Me, too. Do you feel up to food?" At her nod, he added, "I'll go see what's in the fridge."

"Okay," she replied. As he started to turn, Pippa slanted twinkling eyes at him. "But I need something else first."

He wrinkled his brow, not quite trusting her expression. "What?"

She crooked her finger, beckoning him, and when he stood before her, she crooked it again. As he leaned over, she laid her hands on his cheeks. Urging him to come closer still, she stretched up and pressed her lips to his. "You're good medicine. Thank you."

He enjoyed the kiss, brief though it was. Pippa was an attractive woman. Lying there in the darkened room with her, just talking, was intimate in unexpected—and not entirely undesirable—ways. "Okay. But I'm going to feed you now. Food is better medicine."

Kade slipped away from her. When she started to get up, he shook his head. "No. Stay put. I'll serve you dinner in bed." Which sounded far sexier than he'd intended.

In the kitchen, he made soup and sandwiches on autopilot while thinking about Pippa and what he knew about her. She was a sweet woman who wanted to make the world a better place. She needed to help people, and this was her way of helping him, he decided. Somehow, in spilling his guts, he'd become one of her charity cases. Just like he'd been for Cyrus Barron. His father. The word twisted in his gut. Bitterness welled up, but Kade reined it in. That wasn't fair to Pippa. She wasn't part of this mess. And while Cyrus might have been despicable, his sons had never really jerked Kade around. He needed to get a grip on his emotions.

The microwave dinged and he reached in to retrieve two bowls of homemade chicken noodle soup.

"Can I help?" He almost dropped the bowls at the sound of Pippa's voice.

Concentrating, Kade set the dishes on the counter without burning his hands or spilling the contents. He turned to gaze at her. She leaned against the door jamb, her eyes still looking a little bruised from the pain but her lips—and he knew what they tasted like now—curved up.

"No, I've got it." He glanced around. "I guess since you're vertical now, we can eat at the table."

Pippa laughed, a deep, throaty purr that caused Kade's brain, and other parts of his body, to go places far beyond the gentle kiss they'd shared. "And forfeit the opportunity to eat in bed? Not on your life!" She whirled and was gone.

Gathering up bottled water, utensils and napkins, Kade set up the tray and followed her. She was sitting cross-legged on the bed, her back against the headboard. He handed her the tray to steady, then settled opposite her, doing his best to hide his body's reaction.

"This is nice," she said after finishing her soup. "Sitting here with you like this."

"Yeah."

"Want to know something?"

"Sure."

"I had a big crush on you in college."

"Uh-huh." Was she blushing? Kade swallowed hard, feeling a little more Neanderthal than he was comfortable with. "I kinda figured that out." She didn't reply and he fumbled for something else to say. "You were cute, sitting on that fence mooning over me."

Tilting her head, she studied him, a half smile on her lips and mischief twinkling in her eyes. "I had lots of dirty thoughts about you while sitting there."

Kade opened his mouth but no words came out. Dirty thoughts? His libido overrode his brain. "How dirty?"

Laughing now, Pippa shoved the tray away. "Really dirty. Sexy dirty. Cowgirl-style dirty." She pressed her hand against her mouth. "I can't believe I'm telling you this. I blame the chicken soup."

"What's going on, Pippa?"

She glanced down at her hands clasped in her lap and her cheeks pinkened. "Probably nothing. I just…" She raised her chin and met his gaze directly. "I like you, Kade. A lot."

"The feeling's mutual."

"Is it?" She licked her lips and his eyes tracked her tongue.

Kade rolled off the bed, putting distance between them and easing the building pressure behind the buttons of his fly. What was Pippa saying? What did she want? For that matter, what did he want? "Are you done?"

"Yeah, I guess so."

Was that disappointment in her voice? Kade reached for the tray, hesitated, staring. "What's happening here, Pippa?"

Her eyes bored into his, as though she was searching for something. "I don't know." She breathed deeply. "A connection maybe."

Connection? Kade liked that idea probably more than he should.

"It felt good—my head on your shoulder. And the kiss. Maybe we could just lie here. Talk. Or kiss. If you want to."

If he wanted to? She was a beautiful woman. Sweet. And too good for him. But he definitely wanted to. Kade grabbed the tray, shifted it to the top of his dresser. When he returned to stand beside the bed, he felt awkward. Pippa slid down until she was prone and patted the bed. He stretched out next to her and she rolled into him as if it was the most natural thing in the world. Maybe it was. Maybe he was overthinking things.

Yet, the more he thought about it, the more Kade understood what Pippa was trying to do, what she sought from him and sought to give back. She was kind and caring, and it dawned on him. She wanted to grant him tenderness, and if he gave in to the need for her, he would give her the same in return. This moment of...*belonging* was a gift. Aftershocks from the day's revelations continued to rock him, but Pippa could vanquish them. For a while at least.

His lips skimmed her jaw, seeking her mouth. Then he took their kiss deeper, yet kept it quiet and dreamy. And Pippa, this generous, concerned woman, opened for him. He held her as the kiss continued and they hovered just beyond the edge of desire. He discovered a sense of peace with her in his arms, mouth-to-mouth, body-to-body.

He eased back to look at her and asked, "Are you sure?"

She smiled, nodded and sat up. Neither broke eye contact as they unbuttoned each other's shirts. He felt her fingertips skim across his abs, his chest, and his breathing turned ragged. Working for control, finally steady again, he slid her shirt off her shoulders so he could touch her. His fingers glided over her surprisingly delicate skin. She was a cowgirl, with a cowgirl's strength. He was astounded when he discovered that fact, especially now as she sat on his bed, all but naked. A low hum thrummed in her, a sound of pleasure as she spread her hands over his chest while he skimmed his hands down her arms.

He gathered her close, eased her to the mattress and followed her down. They faced one another, touching, exploring, learning each other for the first time. He stripped the rest of her clothes off, kissing, licking, touching every part of her. He wasn't in a hurry when he kicked off his own boots and jeans, and he was male enough to enjoy the way Pippa's eyes widened and her mouth formed a perfect O at the sight of his naked body.

He wanted to spoil her so he offered lazy caresses that teased then soothed. His mouth found her breast, his hand cupping it for easy access. He wanted to tantalize, stoking her passion in a slow burn. Pippa arched and sighed beneath him, her fingers tangling in his hair. He swirled his tongue around her other breast, making her gasp.

Using his mouth and his hands, Kade ensured she had a long, slow climb to her peak. Her sighs tripped over into moans, and she quivered in anticipation, waiting, wanting, needing the pleasure. When he brought her to climax, she drew his head up, begged him with her eyes.

"Inside me." Her command rushed out on a hiss of breath. "Now."

Kade recognized her desire and slipped into her. She surrounded him, welcomed him with drenched heat, her inner muscles holding him in a fierce grip. They moved together, an intimate dance of retreat and advance so unconditional his heart pounded. She clenched around him.

"Kade."

When she spoke his name, the tenderness shattered him.

Three

Pippa considered the empty space beside her on the bed. The spot was cold so Kade had likely been gone for some time. She couldn't decide which was more awkward—waking up to the man she'd made love to for the first time, or waking up to his absence. Their relationship had changed—obviously—but for better or worse?

She listened but caught no sounds. Pushing off the covers, she rolled out of bed and stood, waiting to see if her head was going to cooperate this morning. For the first time in over a week, she had no vestiges of a headache lurking. Excellent. She grabbed her clothes and scuttled into the bathroom. She freshened up, using her finger for a toothbrush, dressed and headed toward the main part of the house. Which was empty. There was no sign of Kade but for a pot of hot coffee and a tented piece of paper propped up in front of it.

Opening cabinet doors until she found a mug, she poured a cup, rummaged for milk and sugar, fixed her coffee just the way she liked it and settled at the breakfast bar with Kade's note in front of her. Pippa swallowed a few sips while working up her nerve to read it.

"You're a big chicken," she chided herself out loud. And she was. The fact that he hadn't stuck around to face her the morning after—and they were in *his* house—didn't bode well for their relationship to continue. If he was blowing her off, she'd have to figure out a way to salvage things. She still needed his expertise to get Camp Courage up and running.

Pippa stalled another couple of minutes while she fixed a second cup. Finally unable to put off the inevitable any longer, she opened the note.

Morning, Pip. You were sleeping sound so I didn't wake you. I have some work this morning and need the early start. I left coffee. Hope it's not too strong by the time you get up. Talk to you soon. KW

Well, alrighty then. Pippa had no idea what to think. It wasn't a Dear Jane letter. Not exactly. But it wasn't a declaration of undying love, either. Not that she really expected such a thing. She just wanted a chance to explore their relationship—especially after last night. Her whole body heated just thinking about it. He was… Her brain short-circuited and she puffed out a deeply feminine sigh of appreciation. He had real muscles and his hands were work-roughened. And his…oh yeah, *his* was something to behold. And enjoy. She thought about splashing cold water in her face then glanced at the paper on the breakfast bar.

She reread the note. He'd called her Pip. Which is what her best friend called her. Plus, it sounded like what a guy might call his best friend's little sister. While Pippa might be an only child, her best friend, Carrie Longford, had two older brothers. Carrie had bemoaned the guy code loudly and often. Guys didn't date their friend's sisters. Nor did they date their sister's friend. Good thing Pippa had never been attracted to Carrie's brothers. But where did that leave her with Kade? She wasn't in the sister zone. Was his reticence due to her friendship with Chase and Cash? He'd also written that he'd talk to her soon. What did that mean? She obviously needed her BFF's advice.

She finished her coffee, rinsed out the mug and put it in the dishwasher. Her stomach rumbled from hunger. She also hadn't mentioned she was on birth control in the heat of the moment, nor had he brought up the subject. Wondering if she should wait until he came back so they could talk, she stared out the window. Movement at the ranch office building drew her attention. Uh-oh. A black SUV was disgorging tall, handsome men. Four of them. The only Barron missing was Clay.

Yikes! She had to get out of here. She could avoid driving by the office, though it involved a circuitous route. Kade's truck was still parked in front of the house and she figured the brothers would be headed here next. She located her purse and keys, glanced around to make sure no other evidence of her presence remained and boogied outside. She twisted the lock on the door handle, hoping it would secure the door, and pulled it shut behind her.

Skulking to her car, she scrunched down behind the wheel, started the engine and eased away from Kade's house. Taking the back road toward the houses where other ranch hands lived, she eventually circled around toward the big house, gained the driveway and rocketed down it. Pippa didn't take a deep breath until she'd hit the section line road headed toward I-35. Then she started laughing. She was so ridiculous sometimes.

Kade sat on his horse. The small hill gave him a good view of the ranch buildings on the left and the grass range where a herd of Black Angus cattle grazed. He'd ridden out before dawn looking for some peace. He hadn't found it. He took off his Stetson and turned his face toward the sun. Wind teased his hair, loosening a few strands from the cord he used to tie it back.

He loved this land. Every scrap of it—the river to the south, the scrubby trees and rocky hills, the sweeping grasslands. He could admit to himself that he'd once wanted his own spread but after all the years here at the Crown B, this was home and he was satisfied. Until now.

Cyrus Barron. The man had been a master manipulator and he'd led Kade like a lamb to slaughter. Land management? *You're the expert, Kade.* Cattle breeding program for high-yield, Grade A beef on the hoof? *I trust you, Kade.* Want a "super horse" stud? *Do whatever you need, Kade.* And he'd fallen right into the old man's nasty web. Everything Kade worked for had been done to further the Barrons' brand. And he'd been proud of what he'd achieved.

Then the truth came out.

Shoving the hat back on his head, he judged the time by the height of the sun on the eastern horizon. Was Pippa awake yet? And man, wasn't that another can of worms he needed to sort out. He shoved that problem to the back of his mind. At the moment, he didn't have the time or energy to sort out his feelings for Pippa. But he worried last night had been a mistake. A big mistake.

Kade shifted in the saddle to ease the pressure in his jeans. Physically, last night had been amazing. Emotionally? He wasn't ready to go there. He liked Pippa. She was funny and cute and smart and sexy and sweet. Very sweet. She came from money—lots of it—and was the type of woman a Barron would date. Which brought him right back into that mental box he'd been trying to escape. He *was* a Barron. According to Cyrus's will. But he wasn't. He was Kaden Waite, half Chickasaw son of Rose Waite, grandson of William and Ramona Waite. He was a cattle-man. He worked with his hands. He did *not* wear an expensive suit and tie.

But he'd put down roots in this place and it could all be his. His horse nickered and pawed the ground with a front foot. Kade loosened his grip on the reins. He'd freaked and stormed out of Barron Tower—and wasn't that one of his finest moments. *Not.* He shook his head, feeling rueful. His half brothers had risen to their feet, all of them talking to him at once as he'd lost his cool. Chance had blocked the door, tried to manage the situation. Kade scrubbed at his face as he remembered the scene. He'd threatened to coldcock Chance if he didn't get out of the way.

Chance held him in that conference room just long enough to say a few things—things he didn't want to hear. Take some time, Chance had said. Think things over. Kade heard the murmurs of agreement coming from the rest of the Barron brothers. Yeah, easy for them to say. They'd grown up as Barrons, knew who and what they were.

Since coming to work at the ranch, he'd walked a fine line between employee and friend with the five brothers. Looking back, he recalled the sideways glances and the hints. They'd suspected all along and he'd been… What? An idiot? Stupid? Clueless? Pretty much. He'd definitely been blind. He was still too angry to call his mother and too unsure to call his grandparents.

How could she not tell him? And why hadn't she gone after the sonavagun for child support? She'd worked hard all his life, sometimes two and three jobs until her paintings started to sell. His grandparents had all but raised him. All that time his *father*—Kade spit on the ground. Cyrus Barron had money. Lots of it. And he'd known of the bastard son living in Davis, Oklahoma.

The cell phone in his shirt pocket pinged. Jerking it

out, he read the text from Selena Diaz, the ranch secretary. The Barron brothers had descended like locusts on the office. When was he coming back? He hated texting and she knew it. Stewing over whether to text back or call, and what to say, he chose to just ignore it.

He urged his horse off the hill and pointed him toward the far northwest side of the ranch. Selena's husband Pedro and several other hands were moving cattle today. They needed supervision, he decided. There was something soothing about pushing cattle, even with the dirt and grit. Kade was good at this job. It settled him. He was desperate for that right now.

Six hours later, Selena caught him in the barn as he unsaddled his horse. She was full of sass as she stomped toward him, face twisted into her version of a snarl—mostly crinkled nose, pursed lips and narrowed eyes. She stopped several feet from him, planted her fists on her hips.

"Did you lose your phone?"

Kade didn't look up. "No." He carried the saddle and pad he'd just stripped off into the tack room and returned with a curry brush.

She opened her mouth to start again, but Kade beat her to the punch. "Don't want to hear it, Leenie."

"Seriously? Then don't listen. Just stand there and don't pay any attention to me while I talk." When he continued brushing the horse, she launched into a speech. "Dude, you do not want to be jacking the brothers around. I know things have been really weird since Mr. Barron died. I mean the Crown B has always been sort of a…a sideline. Oh, sure, Cord was nominally in charge as president of Barron Land and Cattle but that was just a thing on a line of a corporate tax return because we all know he's into all that oil and gas stuff. You have no idea how excited Pop was when old Mr. B hired you."

Her father, Manuel Sanchez, was his ranch foreman now. Leenie and her sister, Rosalie, grew up on the Crown B. He tuned out her voice while he curried the horse. Then he turned his mount out in a big stall and set about watering and feeding the animal. Selena dogged him every step. He finally paid attention again when she grabbed his arm and jerked him around to face her.

"You could have at least replied to my text so I could tell them what was what so they'd get the heck out of my office. There was so dang much testosterone in the air even Dusty was hiding under my desk. What the heck is going on between you and them?"

Head lowered, he studied the tips of his boots. "Long story, Leenie."

She ducked and twisted so she could look into his face. "They didn't threaten to fire you or something, did they?"

How was he supposed to answer that? "Not your business."

Leenie straightened and glowered. "Seriously? I work for you, dude. If you get fired, it is most definitely my business. And FYI, they'd be stupid if they did. I grew up on this ranch. I know what it was before. And what you've done with it? Absolutely no comparison, boss man."

Kade removed his hat and scrubbed his fingers across the top of his head, loosening long strands of his hair. "It's not my work ethic being questioned."

"Then what the heck is going on?"

"Again, not your—"

"Business. Yeah, yeah. I call BS. I grew up with those five. Granted, I'm closer to the twins, but Cord and Chance spent a lot of time here too. You can talk to me, Kade. And if I can help, I will."

Shaking his head, he stepped around her, though he wasn't surprised when she pivoted and matched him stride for stride. He halted at the barn door, staring at the demarcation line in the dirt. Where he stood remained in shadow. One step and he'd be in sunlight. Was that a metaphor for something? He didn't have the energy to be philosophical and he was tired of the emotions bottled up so tightly inside that his whole body hurt.

"I'm Cyrus Barron's illegitimate son."

Four

Selena stared at him, her eyes almost as wide as her gaping mouth. "Holy cow. Talk about dropping a bombshell! Do the boys know?" She grimaced and rolled her eyes. "Of course they know. Hence the rugby scrum in the office today. Dang, boss. Talk about a tangled web. When did you find out?"

"Yesterday."

"Wow. Just…wow." She pushed his arm aside and moved close, her arms snaking around him. "Welcome to the family."

That startled him—both her action and her declaration. Leenie laughed and hugged him tighter as he tried to disengage. "I meant that in the figurative sense, not literally. Rosalie and I are sort of…" She smirked before finishing. "Kissing cousins." Laughing, she added, "Big John caught us in the barn with the twins when we were kids."

She turned him loose and stepped into the late afternoon sunshine. "When you're ready to talk, I've got big ears and a closed mouth." She offered a jaunty wave as she headed back to the office. He started to follow her. He probably had work piled up on his desk but he didn't want to think about the ranch, the will, the Barrons or anything having to do with his predicament. He turned toward home. And stopped. That was the heart of the matter.

"It's just a house," he muttered, walking forward again. "Just a place where I sleep at night."

Not surprisingly, Pippa's Highlander was gone when he got there. That was a good thing, right? He didn't want to deal with her, with the inevitable questions she would ask for which he had no answers. He stomped up the stone steps and across the wide porch to his front door. Kade pushed through and stopped. The place was empty—as it was every time he returned. Why it bothered him now, he couldn't say. He hung his Stetson on the rack next to the door and headed to the kitchen. He'd missed lunch—his own fault. His stomach growled and he felt a little stupid for avoiding the Barrons. He still hadn't listened to their voice mails on his phone.

He grabbed a TV dinner and tossed it in the microwave, then popped the top on a long-neck beer. Retrieving his phone, he stared at the number of missed messages. He'd finished the beer by the time the oven dinged. He snagged another beer, peeled the plastic off his dinner and prepared to listen to what the Barrons had to say. He clicked on the speaker icon and opened voice mail.

"This is Chance. I wish you'd stayed to talk with us, Kade. I know this is a shock. Let's discuss things."

"Clay here. Welcome to the family, Kade. Talk to Chance."

"Dude, don't be stupid, says your big brother Cord. We're here when you're ready."

"Don't make me hunt you down." There was laughter and somebody said Cash's name. "Seriously, let's go get a beer, talk about this."

"Kade, this is Chase. Bad news, bud. You realize the

wives are gonna be all over this. Fair warning. You know where to find me when you're ready."

Huh. Nothing at all like what he'd expected. He knew what the Crown B was worth. Millions. Why wouldn't they be upset at losing control of that kind of money? Wouldn't he, if he was in their shoes?

The messages from the Barrons continued in a round robin, before clicking over to the angry then conciliatory messages from Pippa. A stab of guilt burned in his chest and he glanced at the coffee maker. The note he'd left for her was gone. Yeah. He'd definitely taken the chicken way out of that deal. He didn't know why he'd kissed her...and more. He swallowed a gulp of beer. He was a guy and Pippa was gorgeous. He'd thought about getting her into bed—and the experience had been everything he could have hoped for. Well, almost everything. He still had a fantasy about her mouth that hadn't been fulfilled.

He didn't bother listening to the rest of the messages. He switched to the number pad and tapped in Pippa's phone number.

Pippa leaned her head back against the pool lounger and sipped her wine cooler through a straw. "Was I stupid?"

Her best friend occupied the next lounger, a frozen margarita in her hand. Carrie slurped from her glass. "Are you attracted to him?"

Tipping her sunglasses to the end of her nose, Pippa glowered over the top of them. "Is this where I say d'uh?"

"Then no. You weren't stupid. You saw what you wanted and you went for it. Rock on!" Carrie held up her empty hand, index and pinky fingers stabbing into the air while her thumb held down her two middle fingers.

"Seriously? You're flashing the Hook'em Horns sign at me?"

"That wasn't the University of Texas Longhorn salute—state college football rivalries aside." Carrie carefully set down her drink, sat up, extended her arms and waved both hands in the same gesture. "Rock and roll, babe! It's all about the rock and roll."

"Uh-huh." Pippa wasn't convinced but then again, Carrie had always been the wild child.

Carrie settled back on the lounger. "Look, Pip, you've always been uptight." She waggled her brows in mock apology. "You know I'm right. And Kade is hot. I mean *really* hot. Frankly, I'm confused about why he hasn't put the moves on you before now. I mean, seriously. Most guys get grabby on the first date. Not that you two have been on a real date. But, dudette, all those working lunches and dinners? Less work, more play." She rolled her eyes. "Leave it to you to find the last true gentleman in the state."

"There is nothing wrong with being with a gentleman." Pippa was slightly affronted.

"True that. I'm just saying they're few and far between. And I admit, I'm a little jealous. Look, did he have a good time?"

Pippa blushed to the roots of her hair. "I don't even know how to answer that."

"Well, he didn't kick you out after the big climax, right?"

"Carrie!"

"You two had some spectacular sex—at least I'm assuming it was because, girlfriend, I've seen that man in tight jeans."

Her face flaming, Pippa sucked down the rest of her cooler and pushed up out of the lounger. "I am not going to sit here while you embarrass the socks off me."

"You aren't wearing any. Just nod yes or no, okay? Was he good?"

Pippa chewed on her lips but jerked her chin to her

chest in a brief nod. Carrie pumped her fist and uttered a breathless, "Yes!" before continuing. "And the man is a rancher. They're up before the chickens. I think it's sweet he let you sleep in. Frankly, I don't know many guys who would leave a girl in their bed the morning after their first time. Most dudes are too insecure or private or weird or something. Just doesn't happen."

"So…you think he'll call me? Ask me out on a real date? Or is this just one of those friends with benefits things?"

"Hmm…" Carrie pursed her lips and stroked her chin in an exaggerated gesture. "Yes."

Huffing out a breath, Pippa resisted the urge to throw up her hands in frustration. "Yes what? Yes, he'll—" Her phone rang.

Carrie let out a whoop at the ringtone. "Pip! Jason Aldean's 'Burnin' It Down'? That's gotta be Kade." She flicked imaginary tears from her eyes. "You make me so proud."

Scrambling, Pippa found her phone and winced at her breathless "Hello?" She made a face at Carrie while shushing her.

"Hey, Pippa. Uh…are you busy?" Kade's voice sounded uncertain.

She glowered at Carrie and made a shut-it motion with her hand. "No. Not busy. I'm just sitting out by the pool."

"Oh."

And didn't that word just drop into a void of uncertain meaning. Pippa suddenly felt the need to defend herself. Or make excuses. She wasn't sure which. She lived at home because her parents' Heritage Hills mansion was huge, and also had a separate guesthouse. While she had a trust fund that would pay her expenses, she was putting all her money, time and effort into setting up her riding therapy foundation.

"It's a nice evening so I thought I'd sit out here and enjoy the weather." Okay, that was totally inane.

"Are you wearing a bikini?" His voice had gone husky.

She glanced down her body and considered lying. "Um, no. Capris and a camisole."

"Oh."

And this time, there was a whole different tone and meaning to that syllable. A giggle bubbled out before she could stop it. "Okay. Guilty. Only it's not really a bikini. Just a two-piece."

"Mmm uh."

Pippa wasn't sure how to translate that and without thinking, she blurted, "Would you like to come over? We could swim. Maybe grill some burgers or something?"

Carrie gave her big eyes while covering her mouth with both hands as Pippa waited. Kade's answer finally came.

"Yeah. That'd be cool. Thanks. I'll be there in about an hour. Okay?"

Her heart was pounding so hard in her chest she was afraid Kade might be able to hear it. She nodded, realized she needed to speak. "That's great. Yes. Perfect."

"'Kay. See you then."

Dead air hummed between them and she panicked. "Oh, crud, Carrie! What am I going to do? I'm not prepared for a cookout."

"Breathe, babe. I got this. I'll run to Whole Foods, grab stuff. You go fix your hair and get out of that granny suit and into the hot bikini you bought for our trip to Aruba. The one with the sexy little wrap. And put on makeup."

"My parents."

Carrie was already at the door leading into the house. "What about them? They won't care." And then she was gone.

Would her parents care? She might live in close proximity but they most often went their own ways, very seldom crossing paths. Her mother always had some event or party and her dad was a workaholic. Pippa glanced at the Cartier watch on her wrist. She didn't have time to procrastinate.

Kade smoothed back his hair, feeling a little naked without a hat on his head. Despite being invited to a "pool party," he wore jeans and boots, and a crisp Western-style shirt over a clean white T-shirt. Pippa's parents had always seemed staid and traditional whenever he ran into them. While one of the Barrons might have gotten away with showing up in board shorts, he just wasn't comfortable. Again, he wondered what it would have been like growing up with the kind of money that guaranteed entrance and acceptance no matter where.

Not that he'd trade. Growing up on his grandfather's homestead outside of Davis had been perfect for a wild kid. He'd had horses to ride, ponds to swim in, trees to climb. He'd learned to hunt and fish and be a good steward of the land. Bill Waite had taught him to take responsibility, to work hard, to be an honorable man. Those lessons were priceless and there wasn't enough money in the world to get him to change. And that was the core of his dilemma.

The door opened, catching him off guard. Mrs. Duncan stared at him for a moment before saying in an icy voice, "May I help you?"

Offering a smile, he introduced himself. Again. "Evening, Mrs. Duncan. I'm Kaden Waite. Pippa invited me over."

"I see."

"Mom! Is that Kade?"

He heard pattering footsteps and then the door opened wider to reveal Pippa wearing... He blinked and tried to work up enough spit in his mouth to swallow. She wore a scrap of a bikini top with some sort of swirly see-through scarf thing tied around her waist. If it was meant to cover her up, it totally failed.

"Mom, you remember Kade." Pippa reached out and snagged his hand. "I invited him over for a swim and burgers on the grill."

"I see." The woman's tone hadn't warmed any.

"You and Daddy have that deal tonight at the art museum. You're gonna be late." Pippa was all bouncy and sweet as she maneuvered her mother out of the doorway so she could draw Kade into the house.

He wondered, briefly, if his reception would have been so chilly if he'd been introduced as Kaden Barron. The news hadn't hit the media yet, for which he was grateful and also curious. He wondered how the Barrons were keeping the story quiet.

He watched Mrs. Duncan leave. The woman didn't walk so much as glide and when she climbed the sweeping curve of stairs, he'd take bets that she could balance a book on her head, her posture was so stiff.

"C'mon out back." Pippa tugged his hand and glanced down at his clothing. "You did bring a swimsuit, right?"

He nodded, and indicated the small backpack slung over one shoulder. "I figured you had somewhere to change?"

"Of course! You can change at my place." She continued to hold his hand as she drew him through the house to a set of glass-paned doors leading to a terrace and pool. He caught glimpses of fancy furniture, antiques and artwork that probably cost as much as he made in a year. "What would you like to drink? I have that beer you like in the ice chest."

"That'd be great, thanks."

While the big house on the Crown B was expensively furnished with Pendleton rugs, leather furniture and West-

ern art, it was comfortable—looking and feeling lived-in
and homey. This house reminded him of a show home—
each room decorated in a different style and looking pris-
tine. No self-respecting speck of dust would dare land on
any of the furniture.

Out on the patio near the pool, Pippa pointed him toward a second building—which had probably been either
a carriage house or servants' quarters when the mansion
was built at the turn of the last century. Two stories tall,
it was made of the same yellow-and-buff bricks and stone
with matching red tile roof.

"Technically, it's the guesthouse, but it's where I live."
She offered a crooked grin. "Just so you know? You don't
have to go to the front door. You can come straight back
here and knock." She opened the door and he found himself
standing in a combined living area and dining room. He
glimpsed a full kitchen beyond the stairs. "You can change
in here." She opened a door to a bathroom with a shower.

Quickly changing, he emerged and set his folded clothes
on the couch. Pippa had disappeared but the outside door
was open. He headed out and found her waving at him
from the door to the main house.

"Beer's in the ice chest over there in the outdoor kitchen.
I'll be back in just a sec. Mom needs something."

The outdoor kitchen was every bit as impressive as the
one at the ranch, but for the life of him, he couldn't find an
ice chest. Kade finally resorted to opening cabinet doors
because he *really* needed a beer. After searching the entire
kitchen, he discovered the built-in ice chest, with its own
ice maker. This is how rich people lived—people like his
half brothers. That's when he knew. Half his DNA might
be Barron, but he'd never be one of them.

Five

Pippa knew her mother was watching from the windows in the kitchen—not that her mother spent much time *in* the kitchen. The woman's disapproval was almost palpable. She glanced at her watch, willing her mother to leave for the cocktail reception for some charity or another. Just her mother's cup of tea. There were times her parents' snobbery embarrassed her, and this was definitely one of them.

Yes, she'd insisted, when questioned by her mother a few minutes ago, the only relationship she had with Kade was of a business nature. And it had been—but for a few late-night fantasies with her battery-operated friend and a lot of what-if scenarios. Until last night. Pippa still didn't completely understand why she'd all but seduced him. She sipped her wine cooler and admitted that she wasn't sorry. Still, she needed to bring up the subject so she could let him know they were covered on the no-baby front. They hadn't discussed it. And she was a little bothered by that. True, she wasn't the most experienced, but it was a conversation she always insisted on—and not just because of pregnancy.

"You're thinking too hard."

She startled at Kade's voice. "Sorry."

"Nothing to apologize for, Pippa." His gaze shifted from her to the kitchen window. *Crud.* He knew they were being watched.

"I'm sorry. About my mother. She's…" How did she explain her mother's actions? "Well…she is who she is." His dry chuckle helped her relax. "She and Dad will be leaving soon." Hopefully. "Would you like to swim before we fire up the grill?"

Twilight was slow to fall this time of year but photosensitive lights were beginning to glow around the pool and landscaped garden. The air was also cooling and a light shimmer of steam rose above the heated pool.

"Or we could sit in the hot—" Car doors slamming cut off her words. At last! "—tub," she finished.

Kade waited until the sound of the car motor faded. "A swim sounds good. You don't have to get wet unless you want to."

She tilted her head, puzzled. "Why wouldn't I want to get wet?"

He waved a hand toward her hair. "A lot of girls don't like to get their hair messed up."

Pippa laughed and before he could react, she'd jumped out of her chair, ripped off her sarong and was sprinting for the edge of the pool. He was bigger and faster but she still hit the water in a sleek dive before he caught up. She was halfway to the far end when arms snaked around her waist and he halted her forward momentum. Kade turned her to face him and their legs tangled gently as they both treaded water to keep their heads above the surface.

"About last night—"

His lips pressed against hers, cutting off speech. One of his strong arms stayed around her waist while his other hand cupped the back of her head, angling her so he could deepen the kiss. This was good. Very, very good. Her arms circled his neck and she clung to him, mouth-to-mouth, their hearts beating almost in sync. The water lapped around them as his legs moved, treading to keep them afloat. Then he was standing, strong and sure, on the bottom of the pool.

She tasted the malty richness of the beer he'd been drinking. Warm steam rose from the water around them, kissing her skin. This was dreamy, she thought. Like a romantic scene in a movie. Pippa wanted to get lost in his kisses, in the feel of his hard body pressed against hers. They fit, and they shouldn't have. Still, they needed to discuss what had happened the previous night. That hard reality was a shadow on an otherwise shining moment.

Pippa shouldn't have been surprised to discover that she wanted him as much now as she had then. As the evidence that he felt the same pressed against her core, she knew she couldn't stall any longer.

"You're still thinking too hard," Kade murmured against her lips as he broke the kiss.

"Last night. I wanted to explain."

He loosened his hold on her as he reared his head back. "What about last night?" He sounded defensive and it distressed her that she'd been responsible for putting that tone in his voice.

"First, I'm on the pill. And as far as I know I don't have any STDs."

Kade's expression morphed into shock. "Wow. That was blunt. Okay. True. My turn to apologize. I didn't stop to think about a condom. That said, I'm clean."

She held back the sigh of relief. "Okay then. Now that that's out of the way, I—" She paused to breathe deeply. She only realized she was rolling her lips between her teeth when Kade's gaze dropped to her mouth and she felt his erection throb. It was all she could do to keep her hands on his shoulders because she wanted to fan her suddenly heated face. Luckily, with the falling darkness, she doubted he could see her blush.

"First." She laughed. "Or I guess second, I normally don't throw myself at guys."

His head tilted and his brows drew closer together as he watched her. "As gorgeous as you are, why would you have to?"

Okay, he could probably see her blush now, and she fought the smile forming because she was pretty sure if it got loose, she'd be beaming. "You think I'm gorgeous?"

"Absolutely."

"Oh." She was inordinately pleased. "That goes both ways, you know."

"Really? You think you're gorgeous?"

A laugh burst out and she covered her mouth. "No, silly. I think *you* are gorgeous."

"Ah," he said dryly. Still, Pippa could tell Kade was pleased with her admission.

"Ahem. Where were we?" She let her hands explore his shoulders, palms rubbing over warm skin and the muscles that came from tough work, not a gym.

"Right about here," he murmured, tightening his embrace and angling his head to kiss her again.

This kiss was slow, almost soothing, and obviously meant to distract her. He was working her into an easy arousal that felt natural and right. Her heart beat fast and steady and when he nudged the shoestring straps of her bikini top down her arms, she didn't care. When he held her, his mouth taking hers in a long kiss, she could forget where she was, forget her mother's snobbery, forget everything but the way he made her feel. Beautiful. Wanted. Being in his arms was beyond her ability to describe.

* * *

Pippa, in this moment, was his. She was all soft curves tucked against his hard planes. Pliant and eager as he kissed her again, she tasted sweeter than any woman he'd been with. He trailed kisses over the gentle slopes of her shoulders. He found the soft spot under her chin where her pulse beat and he pressed his lips there.

"Is this something special?"

He froze for a minute, her question taking him by surprise. Was it? He didn't want it to be. Or did he? He liked Pippa. Liked her smile, the sound of her laughter, the way she asked questions and chattered and the way she smelled. Did that make what they were doing special? Did it make her special? He owed her honesty so he said, "I don't know."

Kade swam them to the edge of the pool and braced her back against the smooth side. "This is new, Pippa. Whatever this is. I like you. I can say that and mean it. Do you think it's something special?"

Pippa pursed her lips as she studied him. He could almost see her mind working. "I don't know either. But it might be. Someday. Maybe." She blinked rapidly and looked like she wanted to take the words back before her expression showed resolve. "Does that freak you out?"

"Naw. Not really. I'm a guy. I don't like to play games. I want to know what you like. What you don't."

She wiped her forehead with the back of her hand and blew out an exaggerated "Whew! That's good to know."

Kade laughed. Doing so brought him in closer contact with her very feminine curves and he liked the way it felt. A lot. He was male enough that he just wanted to go with the here-and-now, but was that fair? He'd been in a bad head space last night. She'd been convenient. And willing. Was she more? And, being a guy, shouldn't he be a little freaked out by that thought? He didn't want to think. In fact, what he wanted was a repeat of last night.

"Will you trust me?" And wasn't that typically male too?

"I always trust you."

Her quick response stunned him. A warm glow spread in his chest as a result. "I want to give you this. To give it to both of us."

At her nod, he clutched her waist and lifted. She unwrapped her legs so he could boost her to the edge of the pool. Spreading her knees, he moved between them. Kade tugged her bikini top all the way off and smiled. "I like the way you look, sitting here all wet and waiting." He flicked his tongue over her breasts, tasting and teasing each one.

She arched her back, her arms around his head, urging him to continue. He wanted her to float ever higher until he could send her flying. Desire rammed through him as she moaned softly, the sound and taste of her as rich as a sip of wine. He caught the sound of traffic in the distance, the slap of tires on pavement, but for all intents and purposes they were locked in a private hideaway. He caught a musical sound—a mockingbird. The thing evidently intended to serenade them.

Pippa chuckled; it was little more than a puff of air. "Persistent thing, isn't he?"

Kade captured her breast again and her moan drowned out the irritating bird calls.

The moon topped the trees around the yard and its light turned her skin luminescent. His hands found her hips, discovered the ties on the sides of her bikini and jerked. The material fell away. Now he could see all of her. Steam rose from the water. Kade was the least romantic man he knew, but Pippa was like some nymph in a book or movie.

"Beautiful," he murmured. Then he swept his tongue between her legs.

The act had her fingers digging into his shoulders. Her nails would leave marks but he didn't care.

"Ohhh," she sighed.

He teased her with his mouth but then he wanted to watch her so he switched to his hand. She was braced on her arms now, body arched, throat exposed, hair trailing over her shoulders. Pleasure was obvious in her expression and she seemed almost shocked. There was something endearingly innocent about her. The odd combination of Pippa's wide-eyed pleasure and wanton need turned him on like crazy.

His body throbbing, he pushed her higher, watched her eyes close as her breath caught in her chest right as her shuddering climax claimed her. Before she'd stopped, Kade had shed his swim trunks and had Pippa back in the water. He slid into her slick heat with a groan and found her mouth.

Bracing her against the side of the pool, he drove into her. Kade's body tingled, as if his nerves were raw-edged and exposed. Breaking the kiss, he closed his mouth over her breast, teeth nipping lightly. She cried out and dug her nails into his shoulders as her thighs tightened around his waist. Kade switched to the other breast, licking, playing with her until she was rocking, hard and frantic as she ground her hips against him.

Her body tensed, clamped down on him.

Kade lost his mind. His brain shut down, bombarded by sensations. Her body surrounded him. Their pounding hearts echoed each other. It was impossible to think around the intense pleasure. His body pulsed, plunging into Pippa over and over until he came, throbbing deep inside her.

"When I'm inside you…" His voice was rough and his vision foggy. "When I'm in you, I can't think. I can't… you kill me, Pippa." Words failed him so he lowered his mouth, crushed hers, his tongue sweeping in to claim her for his own. "Do you feel it?" he growled. "Do you feel what you do to me?"

She bucked against him, riding him hard, milking every last bit of his climax from him. She gripped his hair, dragged his mouth back to hers. "Kiss me."

He did. He devoured her mouth, nipping and sucking on her lips, her tongue until they were both breathless. Then he eased from her, slowly, so slowly his body shuddered and he had to hold himself rigid to keep both their heads above water.

"Whew," Pippa breathed once he broke the kiss. "Are we still alive?"

Kade laughed. She looked so smugly satisfied he couldn't help it. "I'm not sure." He didn't know how they could have survived. Even now, sensations pounded him, leaving his vision blurred around the edges and his ears ringing. "I'd ask if it was good for you—"

"Honey, that could almost make me start smoking," Pippa interrupted. "Because it feels like I need a cigarette. Or a drink."

This time, his kiss was playful and he was about to find her breasts again when the clearing of a throat froze them both.

"What do you think you're doing, Pippa? Have you no shame?"

Six

Pippa cringed and hid her head against Kade's shoulder. "She's going to go ballistic. I'm sooo sorry," she murmured against his skin.

Kade's arms tightened around her and he shifted his body so that he blocked her mother's view of her.

"Get out of that pool right now, Pippa Duncan." Her mother's demanding tone left no room for argument. "David! David, come out here. Come see what your daughter is doing."

Her father appeared at the back door. "Leave her be, Millie. Come inside and have a drink. Pippa is a big girl and if she wants to entertain a man—"

"Entertain?" Millicent tossed her hands into the air and stormed toward the rear of the house. "That's not what she was doing, David. They were… She… That man…" She was so incensed she couldn't speak in coherent sentences. As her mother marched up the stone steps to the door, Pippa's father handed her a crystal glass filled with amber liquid.

"Come inside, dear."

Her face flaming, Pippa watched the door close behind her parents. As soon as she was alone with Kade, she pushed away and struggled to hoist herself out of the pool. He gripped her hips in his warm hands and boosted her up. She scrambled to the nearest lounger, grabbed one of the large beach towels folded on the end and wrapped it around herself.

Kade joined her a moment later but she couldn't meet his eyes. "I'm sorry," she whispered. "You should probably leave now."

His thumb and fingers caught her chin. With gentle pressure, he lifted her head. "Look at me, Pip." When she kept her gaze lowered, he ducked down to her height. "Please?"

She sighed, complying with his request. "I'm sorry," she repeated.

"For what?" He looked amused but she got the feeling it wasn't due to her embarrassment.

"For...well..." She spread her arms. "For this."

While her arms were wide, Kade undid the tuck she'd made in the towel. Before she could react, he'd rewrapped it around her so she was completely covered and then he tied the two ends together for a more secure fastening. Finished, he winked, a grin creasing his face. "I think that's the first time I've ever been caught by a parent."

His wry smile was infectious and Pippa rolled her lips between her teeth to keep her own from matching it. "Seriously! I wanted to die." Then a giggle burbled out and she slapped her hand over her mouth to contain the sound.

"You still owe me dinner. I vote we order in pizza."

"Ooh. Good idea. I don't want to be within range of my parents just now." She leaned around his broad body and checked the windows overlooking the patio and pool. "But all the beer is in the ice chest."

"I'll grab what's left and meet you at the door to your place."

"And can you grab my stuff off the table?"

"You bet. Now scoot."

She scooted, and dashed upstairs just long enough to pull on a pair of shorts and a T-shirt. Then she rushed back to the door, hovering just in case her mother put in another appearance. Now that she was dressed—mostly—she could rush out to defend Kade from her mother's acerbic presence.

Pippa watched him move around the patio, a shadowy figure. But he wasn't skulking at all. He walked with purpose, like he had every right to be there as her guest. She smiled to herself. Since he'd dealt with Cyrus Barron, her mother—while not necessarily a pushover—probably wouldn't bother Kade at all. Straightening, she felt as though a weight had been lifted from her shoulders. Boys she'd previously been interested in had run for the hills whenever her mother got started.

As Kade approached, his hands and arms full of beer bottles and all her paraphernalia, she opened the glass storm door. Kade stopped in front of her and bent to give her a kiss before sliding on past. And that, she decided, was the difference between Kade and all the others. They'd been boys. He was most definitely a man.

"What kind of pizza do you like?" she asked, shutting and locking the door. She wouldn't put it past her mother to come charging into the house hoping to catch them in another compromising position.

"Anything with meat," he called over his shoulder as he headed toward the kitchen. She trailed after him. "Are you one of those veggie types?"

"Yes." She smirked as he rolled his eyes. "I like veggies with my meat, especially jalapenos."

That earned her an arched brow. "Well then, I think we can work something out. As long as those veggies are onions and peppers."

"Mushrooms and olives too. What kind of meat?"

"All of it."

She laughed at that. "Okay. I'll call it in." She did and surprised both Kade and the clerk on the other end of the phone when she read off the list of ingredients. "Yes, that's right," she said. "Onions, mushrooms, black olives, green peppers, jalapenos, and every kind of meat you have. Extra large, thick crust." She listened then glanced at Kade. "Do you want chicken, Canadian bacon and ham too?"

Laughing, he nodded. "Those are meat, so yeah."

She muttered something about clogged arteries, confirmed her address and that the driver needed to come to the rear house and hung up. She looked around, unsure what to do next.

After Pippa called in the order, Kade considered inviting her to share a shower. Two things stopped him—the tense lines around her eyes and the growling in his stomach. They only had a maximum of thirty minutes before the pizza arrived, and frankly, he wasn't ready for a case of "pizza interruptus."

Instead, he excused himself to grab a quick rinse off in the downstairs bath. After changing back into his jeans and shirt, he stepped out five minutes later. Pippa was nowhere to be seen. Then he heard water running upstairs.

Kade grabbed a fresh beer and settled on the couch. Surprised that the furniture was far more comfortable than it appeared, he found the TV remote and turned on the flat-screen hanging above the fireplace. Zipping through the channels, he found the Cardinals baseball game and sat back to watch.

Pippa was coming down the stairs when a knock sounded at the door. She sucked in a breath and tried to beat him there. He was closer, had longer legs and was faster. She slid to a stop at his side but she wasn't quick enough to keep him from opening the door. A bored teenage boy wearing a T-shirt advertising the local pizza place held a cardboard box. Pippa huffed out a breath. Kade glanced at her and wondered why she looked relieved.

"That'll be twenty-three sixty-four," the kid announced.

Passing the box to Pippa, Kade dug money out of his pocket and peeled off two twenties. He handed the cash to the delivery driver and said, "Keep the change."

"Thanks, man," the teen said with a little more enthusiasm as he spun around and jogged back to the beat-up compact car parked in the driveway.

Kade shut the door and Pippa called out. "Be sure to lock it."

She stood in the kitchen, her back turned to him so he took the opportunity to study her. Something was up. She was tense, uncomfortable. Maybe sticking around hadn't been such a good idea. He'd been serious when he said he didn't like to play games so he asked straight out, "Is something wrong, Pip?"

A plate clattered on the granite counter as she whirled to look at him. Guilt suffused her face. "No. Not at all. Why—"

"Don't pretend with me, Pip. What's going on?"

Pippa gave him her back and scooped the spilled piece of pizza back onto the plate. "Do you want Parmesan cheese? I have some fresh-grated in the fridge."

"Sure." He gave her time to duck into the stainless steel refrigerator before he pressed her again. "I'd appreciate an answer to my question, Pippa."

She braced both hands on the center island. "Nothing."

Everything about her—from the defensive hunch of her shoulders to the carefully blank expression on her face—screamed *leave me alone.*

"Really?" Sarcasm leaked into his tone and her eyes flicked up to meet his gaze.

"Fine," she huffed. "I'm worried that Dad won't be able to contain Mother. I keep waiting for her to march out here and confront us for our *lapse of decorum* in the pool. I've never quite seemed to live up to her expectations and tonight was just another glaring example of my lack."

"I don't find you lacking. Not in any way." Her startled gaze found his steady one. "You're smart, dedicated, responsible. And gorgeous. But I like you anyway." That startled a little giggle out of her. Good. He held out his hand and was gratified when she walked over to take it. He pulled her into a hug. "Families are weird. Trust me." And wasn't that the truth. Everything he'd discovered about his own turned his world upside down.

She giggled again and when her arms slipped around his waist, he felt her relax. "I've heard that. Mine are ultratraditional, which is why I'm a disappointment. Mother expected me to make my debut, go to an Ivy League school, marry some scion of a rich and respectable family and become the perfect society wife."

"Oops," He said dryly.

That got an outright laugh from her.

"You can't live your life worrying about what she wants, Pip. You are your own woman. Live your life the way that lets you face yourself in the mirror every morning, knowing that you're the person you're meant to be."

She pushed back to look up at him. "Wow...that's rather profound."

Kade pasted a wry smile on his face. "You sound surprised. I can be a deep thinker when necessary."

"No, not surprised at all. Those things you said about me? Yeah, right back at'cha, buddy!"

He considered her challenge, remembering what she'd

said last night about his identity. She fought to be herself, not who her parents wanted her to be. Wasn't he trying to do the same? Except she would always have her name, her identity. He felt like he was losing his. And it hurt—enough that he didn't want to think about it anymore tonight.

He served up pizza and they retreated to the couch.

"Hope you don't mind me turning on the game."

Pippa favored him with a brilliant smile. "The only thing better than Saint Louis Cardinals baseball is Oklahoma State baseball. Well, and Cowboy football too."

"A woman after my own heart."

"It's important to be compatible sportswise."

Her dry tone got a laugh from him. "Truth!"

The rest of their evening was spent cheering on the Cards in friendly companionship. As the game was on the West Coast and went into extra innings, Pippa was asleep on Kade's shoulder when the Cards pulled it out in the thirteenth inning with a walk-off home run. Kade didn't want to enjoy having Pippa curled up next to him.

He'd asked her to trust him but he didn't trust himself. Not where this thing with Pippa was concerned. He was just selfish enough to drag her into his mess and she didn't belong there. She didn't belong with him. Not until he figured things out.

Then there was Mrs. Duncan. The woman had decided he wasn't worthy of her daughter, sentiments not too far from his own. Kade had no desire to put Pippa in a bad spot and he'd bet dollars to doughnuts that if his truck remained parked in front of the Duncans' house all night, her mother would give Pippa hell.

He needed to go, but should he leave Pippa napping on the couch or carry her upstairs to her bedroom. He glanced at the stairs. No problem getting her up there. Not joining her in bed? Yeah, that would be a problem. He needed to leave her right where she was or he wouldn't leave at all.

In slow motion, he slipped away and eased her down on a pillow. A soft throw was draped over the back of the couch and he took a moment to spread it over her. He gathered up his belongings and crept to the door. Kade paused halfway there, then returned to the couch. He bent over and kissed Pippa's forehead.

"I'll call," he whispered.

"Okay," she mumbled and snuggled deeper into the pillow.

Kade locked the door behind him and strode down the driveway. As he climbed into his truck, movement in an upstairs window of the mansion caught his attention. He paused, staring. A shadowed figure, too small to be a man, watched. Pippa's mother was something else. And that put him in mind of his own.

He drove away and pointed his truck toward the ranch. Once he was out of Oklahoma City, the only lights came from sporadic traffic and the occasional lighted billboard along the side of the interstate. Kade had about forty-five minutes to do nothing but think.

He should hash out things with his mom. She seemed as intent on avoiding him as he was her. After the reading of Cyrus's will, he'd left one angry voice mail for her. She hadn't returned his call nor had he made any further attempt to contact her. It felt weird, this gulf between them. Rose Waite had always been there for him—his biggest fan, staunchest champion and well…his mom.

But soon, he realized, he'd have to confront her.

Seven

Kade pulled into his mom's place a few minutes before noon. She didn't know he was coming. After a series of restless nights, partly due to some pretty lurid dreams involving Pippa but also the unresolved tension with his mom, he decided to confront her face-to-face rather than over the phone. Today, he'd done his morning chores on autopilot, then headed for Davis.

As he parked his truck, she appeared on the front porch, wiping her hands on a dish towel. She stood stiffly, waiting, probably guessing why he'd come. Hands jammed in his hip pockets, he stopped with one booted foot on the bottom step.

"Mom."

"Kaden." They stared at each other, neither of them moving. Rose was the one who broke the tension. "Well, come inside. I have iced tea made, and brownies. I can fix you lunch if you're hungry."

He climbed the four steps to reach her. On a normal day—before Cyrus died, before Kade discovered his lineage—he would have bounded onto the porch, swept his mom into a bear hug and swung her around until she was breathless and laughing. He didn't like this stiffness and distance between them. Resigned, he followed her word-lessly into his childhood home.

In her sunny kitchen, she pointed to the table set in the bay nook that overlooked the sweeping backyard. "Sit."

He did as she ordered and watched her putter around the kitchen filling tall plastic glasses with ice and pouring tea from a large glass jar. She'd made sun tea—leaving tea bags in the water-filled jar sitting under the hot sun. His mother drank iced tea year-round and only resorted to brewing it on the stove when the weather was too cold. She mixed a packet of sweetener in hers but handed his over plain.

"So," she said, settling heavily onto the chair across from him.

That was as much of an opening as she would give him. There was no sense beating around the bush. "You should have told me."

Rose crossed her arms over her chest and pursed her lips, studying him. He knew this look. He'd certainly been on the receiving end of it enough growing up. This time, he wasn't in trouble, though.

Kade pushed her. "I had a right."

"Did you?" She arched her brow and managed to look down her nose at him even though he was taller.

"Yeah, Mom, I did."

"Why didn't you ask me when you were growing up?"

"Why didn't you tell me?"

"It's not proper to answer a question by asking one."

"Sometimes, that's the only way I get an answer. What are you afraid of?"

That got him a bitter laugh. "You think I kept your par-entage a secret because I was afraid? Of what?"

"Not what, who." He was watching her closely. Had he

not been, he would have missed the tiny tick in the corner of her eye.

"I was never afraid of your father, Kaden."

"Then why keep it...keep *me* a secret?"

"You weren't a secret, son. Cyrus knew about you. There were...complications. If we'd met at a different time, or maybe in a different place." Her eyes turned dreamy as her gaze strayed to the scene outside the window. "I think he loved me in his own way. But he had demands on his time. He had to make a choice and it wasn't us." One shoulder lifted and fell in a negligent shrug. "It all turned out for the best."

Kade watched her as she had him earlier. "It almost sounds like you're defending him, Mom. Why? He left you. Left us."

"That's not exactly true, Kaden."

"Then tell me."

She pushed out of her chair and marched to the sink where she dumped out her glass of tea and fixed a fresh one. "Too sweet," she said without looking at him. "He paid my medical bills. Made sure I saw one of the best ob-gyns in Oklahoma City." She pivoted and braced her backside against the counter. She morphed her face into a scowl and mimicked Cyrus's voice. "'No child of mine will ever be born in an Indian clinic.'"

Rose almost smiled, her thoughts obviously far away. "He was all bluster, your father, but he did pay the medical bills. When you were born, he came to the hospital to see you. He..."

She turned away from Kade to stare out the window and he rose to go to her. She glanced up as he stopped beside her.

In a soft voice, Rose continued with her story. "He said you looked just like his other sons. Chance was just a toddler, the others slightly older. I think he was surprised, as if he'd been wondering if you were truly his, despite the blood tests and all. He refused to hold you. He just stood there looking. Then he offered to pay me a large sum of money to sign over your custody to him and walk away. I refused to accept anything else from him."

Kade tensed every muscle in his body to stay upright. "Why didn't you tell me this when he offered me the job at the Crown B?"

Rose continued staring out the window. "I thought about it. But…" She sighed heavily and faced him. She raised her hand as if to cup his cheek then dropped it to her side. "You have brothers, Kade. I wanted you to have the chance to meet them, get to know them. Maybe even be friends with them."

"Did you know about his will?"

She looked perplexed so he told her, his explanation spilling out in angry tones.

Her bewilderment morphed into regret. "I had no idea your father would do this. That he would saddle you with this decision, but I can't say I'm surprised."

She walked into the living room and went to the mantel above the native stone fireplace. He followed her. That fireplace held a lot of memories—hanging his Christmas stocking, being curled up in a sleeping bag "camping out" in front of it in the wintertime. Roasting marshmallows for s'mores. The heavy wooden mantel held a variety of knick-knacks. Photos. A couple of trophies from high school sports. A belt buckle he won at the College Finals Rodeo. His mom took down a picture, one of him when he was about twelve.

"Were you ever going to tell me?" He tucked his chin and rubbed at the tense muscles on the back of his neck.

"If he hadn't named me in the will, would you have ever told me?"

That question seemed to stump her, or maybe she just chose to ignore him. She walked back into the kitchen, with Kade trailing along, and she placed the photo face-down on the counter. Digging in a drawer, she came up with a screwdriver and started taking the back of the picture frame off.

"Mom?"

She stared through the window over the sink again. He moved up beside her to check what was out there, saw what she was looking at—a doe and her half-grown fawn nibbling grass near the tree line and an image much closer—his reflection standing next to hers in the window glass.

Families. As Pippa had said, they were complicated.

Rose handed him the piece of paper she'd retrieved from inside the frame. He took it, wordlessly, and unfolded it. It was an old newspaper clipping with a picture of Clay, Cord and Chance standing with their father at the opening of some building. His mother had cut this out of the Oklahoma City paper. He glanced at the photo of himself, lying faceup on the counter. For the first time, he recognized the family resemblance and wondered why he hadn't before.

His mother leaned against his arm and he automatically shifted to hug her shoulders. "I'm sorry. I've made a mess of things."

She shifted, and now she cupped his cheeks, holding him still so she could look at him. "I should have told you, but…I was afraid I'd lose you. I was afraid his name, his money and power…" Her voice trailed off and her hands dropped to her sides. "In the end, he still got his way."

"Maybe." Kade shrugged. "We'll figure it out."

"I love you. I always have, from the very first moment they handed you to me. Your father could have offered me a million dollars. Ten million. It didn't matter. You were my own sweet baby. And look at you now."

He felt his skin flush but he dropped a kiss on her hair. "Now his will makes sense. He wanted me to take the Barron name one way or another. He set it up so I'd have to or lose everything."

"It's a terrible position to be in, but have you considered this?" She faced him and tugged nervously at the plackets of his shirt. "What if I had given you up?" He stiffened but she tugged to get his attention and continued. "What if he'd been single and we'd married? And one last what-if. What if I'd simply added his name to your birth certificate?"

His brow knit into furrows as he thought about her questions. The answer to each of her questions was the same. As if she recognized the moment he came to that conclusion, Rose added, "You would have been named Kaden Barron."

It was hard to argue or refute that.

Pippa woke up disoriented. Why had she slept on the couch? Then she remembered. Kade had come for dinner again. She glanced around but he was gone. She focused bleary eyes on the LED clock on the cable box and yawned. Gray light filtered in through the windows. Since it was only 6:34, that shouldn't have surprised her. Yawning again, she stretched and wondered when Kade had left. With that thought came panic.

Tangled in the light cotton afghan, she almost fell on the floor until she got her legs free. Since the night her mother caught them in the pool, she'd insisted he leave by midnight.

She surged off the couch. They'd been watching a movie and she'd fallen asleep leaning against Kade's side with his arm around her.

She grabbed her phone, thinking to text him. If he'd stayed all night, she had to leave now before her mother arrived at the door. Yes, Pippa was an adult. Yes, she technically lived on her own. Yes, she should be able to do whatever she wanted. But. Millicent Duncan was a force to be reckoned with when she went on one of her crusades. And for some reason, whom Pippa dated and what she did with them was akin to a holy war for her mother.

An unread text caught her eye. It was from Kade with a 1:30 a.m. time stamp.

Hey sleepyhead. I'm home but wanted to thank you again for a great night. I enjoyed the burgers and chick flick. I'll call you soon.

Whew! He hadn't fallen asleep, too. Pippa knew her mother. She would have stayed awake as long as Kade's truck was parked out front. Pippa poured a glass of orange juice and slid onto a barstool at the center island. She needed to work on some grant requests today, and she should check with Kade about leads on horses to buy. That would be a good excuse to call him. That was her story and she was sticking to it. Her thoughts, as they often did, returned to that *swim* she and Kade had shared. She'd felt wicked and risqué making love to him outdoors like that, even if the yard was secluded, with a tall privacy fence and a screen of landscaped trees and foliage.

Her parents hadn't been home that night. Their charity event should have kept them occupied until midnight. Her mother was a society maven who lived for such glittering affairs. Had Pippa daring to entertain a man brought them home early? At least she and Kade had finished, even though they'd been caught—Pippa laughed as a term she'd first read in a historical romance came to mind.

Déshabille. Oh, yes indeedy. She and Kade had definitely been undressed when her mother caught them.

She saluted the empty room with her orange juice. "Here's to striking a blow for freedom."

Thirty minutes later, she eased her Highlander out of the garage and down the driveway. If she stayed home, her mother would come to harangue her about Kade's presence. With her laptop, Pippa could work anywhere. She considered going to the neighborhood coffee shop. They made a killer white chocolate blended iced coffee and had fresh-baked pastries, but it would be one of the first places her mother would look, should the woman decide to stalk her.

Inspiration hit. She'd head to the downtown library. She could park in the Barron Tower garage, her vehicle out of sight, and then walk up the street to the library. The place was huge, with free Wi-Fi and lots of out-of-the-way places where she could set up to work without interruption. She doubted her mother would think to look for her there. Even if she did, the chances of being found were slim to none.

A few minutes later, when she pulled into the parking garage and found a space, she realized the library wouldn't be open yet. Her stomach grumbled and she really wanted coffee too. The Colcord was a block away. The hotel restaurant opened early—and had free Wi-Fi. She grinned. Perfect. She could get a real breakfast and lots of coffee while getting some work done. Then she could walk off breakfast going to the library. She loved it when a plan came together.

Shouldering her laptop bag and her purse, she locked her car and headed for the ground level. When she reached the restaurant, only a few tables were occupied. The hostess, noting her messenger bag, led Pippa to a table tucked back in a corner and showed her where the electrical plug was located.

Firing up her computer, Pippa surfed through some sites with lists of available grants. She made notes while eating, then savored one last cup of coffee. At the library, she worked diligently, forcing her mind away from Kade. They were friends. With benefits. Weren't they? She wasn't sure and she didn't want to ask him.

She emailed requests for more information. Wrote proposals and forwarded them to Carrie for editing and proofreading. She caught herself doodling Kade's name so when an email from Carrie popped up, she needed a break. After reading Carrie's invitation, she was ready to call it a day. She packed up and headed back to the garage to retrieve her car.

Pippa didn't even have to go home. Her best friend had suggested a movie, complete with appetizers and cocktails followed by dinner. The theater down in Moore had balconies and director suites with reclining chairs, VIP service and drinks. She didn't even care what movie—anything to keep her mind off Kade.

If she was lucky, Carrie would suggest a sleepover. Pippa laughed. Who was she kidding? All she had to do was mention her mother and Carrie would insist she spend the night. Yes, distractions were good things to have. So was a best friend.

Eight

Pippa settled into her chair and took a sip of her white wine. She'd nibble, have the one drink then switch to a Diet Coke for the duration of the movie. Her cell phone vibrated. She let it go to voice mail, thinking it was most likely her mother. When it vibrated again, indicating she had a voice mail, she scrambled to get it out of her back pocket without spilling her drink. Her mother refused to leave messages and the only other person who might be calling her on a Saturday evening was Kade. Scrolling through the missed calls, she saw his name. She couldn't listen to the message fast enough.

"Hey, Pip. I'm on my way back from Davis and just hit Norman. I know it's late notice but I wondered if you might like to get together tonight. Call me."

With wide eyes, and her heart pounding way too fast, she remembered to breathe. "Kade," she whispered to Carrie. "He's in Norman headed north and he wants to do something tonight."

"Call him!" Carrie commanded. "There's an empty seat next to you. While you're talking to him, I'll go reserve it. Hurry."

"You don't mind?"

Laughing, Carrie stood. "I'm sticking around for the movie but we came in separate cars. You're a big girl. You can go do whatever."

Fifteen minutes later, Kade had a Coke and a bucket of popcorn and was sitting next to Pippa as the credits began to roll. Moments after that, his hand curled around hers and he gave it a little squeeze. He leaned over and whispered in her ear.

"I know I'm horning in on your girl time. Thanks for letting me. After the movie, I'd like to take you and Carrie to dinner."

Pippa turned to whisper back and he caught her chin in his other hand. His lips descended on hers. His tongue traced the seam of her lips, teasing them apart until she opened for him and he could deepen the kiss. She kissed him back and when the movie started, they were both a little breathless.

"Are you sure?" she asked softly, waggling her eyebrows in what she hoped was a suggestively teasing way.

"Yeah. S'long as it's a short dinner."

A laugh burst out and she clapped her hand over her mouth to the hissing sounds of disapproval from other theater patrons. Pippa slunk low in her seat but eventually straightened and found herself enjoying the movie despite her awareness of the very attractive man sitting next to her. At the end, she held his hand and was a little teary-eyed in a that-was-so-romantic way.

Out in the parking lot, the three of them debated where to go for dinner. Carrie stared pointedly at Pippa. "Where is the last place your mother would stalk you?"

The question got a narrow look from Kade, but Pippa wasn't ready to discuss that situation with him. A sudden thought struck. "Cattlemen's."

"Ooh! I haven't eaten there in years," Carrie admitted. She glanced at her watch. "It's Saturday night. How long do you think the line will be?"

"There aren't any events in town," Kade said. "Probably not too bad by the time we get there."

"Let's go!" Carrie was off and running toward her car.

Kade's prediction proved to be right. They didn't have to wait long and after giving their orders to the waiter, Carrie didn't waste any time getting straight to her intentions to embarrass Pippa.

"Did you know Pip had *the* biggest crush on you in college?" she asked with a sly glance at Pippa.

She blushed and glowered. "Carrie," she warned.

"No. Really?" Kade squeezed Pippa's thigh gently and cut his eyes in her direction. Did he just wink at her? She settled back against the booth, leaving the discussion in his hands.

Carrie nodded like a bobblehead doll. "Really and truly. Why do you think she was hanging around the barns all the time? She was a sociology major, for goodness' sake."

Kade leaned away so he could turn to face Pippa. "Sociology? Yeah, I knew that. All the guys on the rodeo team just figured she was studying the flirting habits of the American Cowboy."

Carrie snorted iced tea out her nose. "Dude. Don't make me laugh when I'm taking a drink. That's so rude."

He handed her the bandanna perpetually tucked in his back pocket. Carrie blew her nose into it and announced, "I am so keeping this now."

Pippa used her napkin to hide her smile. She was right—Kade had been letting her know he planned to tease Carrie. That was wonderful as far as she was concerned. Carrie was her oldest and best friend and there was no way Pippa would let a man come between them. The fact that Kade wanted to include her bestie was one more reason she was attracted to him.

Carrie leaned across the table and said in a stage whisper, "I like him."

Laughing, Pippa said, "Of course you do."

"No, you don't understand. I *really* like him." Carrie settled back on her side of the booth and turned her attention to Kade. "Are there any more like you at home?"

Kade went still. Once upon a time, he would have laughed at Carrie's question and said something along the lines that no, he was an original. He would then most likely follow up with the information that he was an only child. But he wasn't. Not anymore. He had five brothers now. Not that any of them were available.

"No," he said eventually, and left it at that.

"Shoot," Carrie groused. "That's too bad." She flashed an impish smile. "Maybe I'll just wait until Pip gets tired of you…" She didn't finish the statement, blowing him a kiss with a suggestive wink instead.

Finding Pippa's hand, Kade squeezed it to pull her attention to him. "Will you, Pippa?"

"Will I what?"

He liked that she sounded breathless. "Get rid of me?"

His gaze remained glued on Pippa. The pulse point on her neck throbbed and she wasn't breathing. When she did inhale, her breasts rose and fell, drawing his gaze for a brief moment. He returned to her face, watching for telltale clues about her thoughts. Her lips parted and her tongue curled over the bottom one, drawing it into her mouth. Kade took that for an invitation.

Dipping his head, he zeroed in on her lips. He intentionally kept the kiss gentle—almost chaste, in fact. When he released her mouth, he whispered, "Glad you want to keep me around."

Their food arrived, disrupting the romantic interlude. Carrie kept the conversation light as they ate. While contemplating dessert, Pippa swiveled on the bench seat to face him. "We need to talk," she said, voice solemn and expression serious.

Was there a hint of worry as well? More curious than concerned, Kade asked, "Okay?"

"I need your help."

"Okay."

She startled at his quick agreement. "You don't even know what I'm asking of you."

He lifted a brow and waited.

"Okay, then. Well, two things. First, I need a date."

"Sure."

She straightened her shoulders as if she was about to say something unpleasant. "Do you own a tux?"

He didn't. The last time he'd worn one, he'd rented it. If he and Pippa had a future, maybe he should consider buying one, but he had the distinct feeling something else was up. "Why?"

"Because Chase is cosponsor of the fund-raiser for my foundation—a big gala at the Barron Hotel. It's black tie and all the movers and shakers will be there." Her words tumbled out in a rush, like a confession, and she wouldn't meet his gaze.

Ah. There were tricky undercurrents in her statement. The easy one was that she was concerned he'd feel out of place. He was a working cowboy, not upper class like her. Still, he knew which fork to use and standing on the periphery of the Barron family for the past several years had exposed him to the real and the fake in local society. It was kinda cute that Pippa didn't want him to feel uncomfortable. At one time, he might have taken offense, but he wasn't that Indian kid wearing worn boots and patched jeans anymore.

That left the other aspect of her admission. She'd been working closely with Chase, and given the current situation where he and the Barrons were concerned, how difficult would it be for him? Could he stand up to the scrutiny and the innuendos? He could, but why would he put himself in that situation?

He made a snap decision, one he might come to regret but the hopeful look on Pippa's face was too much to resist.

"I'll get one."

Pippa's eyes widened and her mouth gaped open for a few seconds. Then she beamed. "You'll come with me?"

"Yeah."

"Well...okay then." She sounded so relieved, as though she knew she'd put him on the spot.

She'd mentioned two items on her agenda. "What's the second thing?"

"Oh! Yes...well." She inhaled and squared her shoulders again. "I want to hold a second fund-raiser. This one more about the people Camp Courage will be working with. I want the big-money sponsors to have the chance to meet our clients."

"Seems like a good idea."

"Do I have your permission to hold it at the Crown B?" The request came in a rush of words and she bulled ahead. "I mean, it makes sense. We could show them how the riding therapy works. The sponsors would have the chance to meet and interact with some of the kids, the veterans, all types of people we want to help, and do it in a casual setting."

Surprised, he stared at her. "Isn't that a question you should ask the Barrons?"

"But you're the ranch man—" She snapped her mouth closed as a look of panic washed over her face.

It seemed as though she'd just figured out the situation. Kade stuffed away his anger. If he walked away from the Barrons, he'd be leaving the Crown B behind. And if he didn't make a decision soon, one would be made for him, according to the terms of the will.

"Oh, Kade...I...I didn't stop to think." Pippa glanced at Carrie, who was intently studying them both. After a not-so-covert exchange of looks, Carrie excused herself with a lame excuse, leaving him alone with Pippa.

Her hand hovered over his arm before she jerked it back. "I'm so sorry, Kade. I... Things...I forgot." She hung her head, looking miserable.

He didn't want Pippa to feel bad. The situation between him and the Barrons... He persisted in labeling them that, refusing to call them what they were—brothers, even if only half. That didn't stop the three older ones from accepting the twins. They'd all made overtures, reaching out to him. He was the one resisting. Pulling Pippa into the middle of this wasn't fair.

"You should ask them," he finally said.

She dropped her gaze. "It was sort of Chase's idea. He's been incredibly helpful. He even offered to recruit Deacon for an appearance. Having Deacon Tate, country music's hottest star, there would be a real draw, and Chase said he wasn't afraid to play the cousin card." She kept her eyes on the hands she'd clasped in her lap beneath the table as she continued. "Chase said the hotel is donating everything for the gala. I'm pretty sure Chase is picking up the tab on the sly but it's just so wonderful because all the donations will go to the foundation."

Kade gritted his teeth. Why was Chase so involved in Pippa's stuff? Was it a way to get to Kade? Was Pippa in on the Barrons' machinations? A flash of anger constricted his breathing.

Pippa stopped speaking and the tension between them ratcheted up a notch in the ensuing silence. "I'm sorry," she whispered, voice catching. Her hand landed lightly on his forearm where he'd braced it on the table. "I'm incredibly insensitive."

He had to know. "Did they put you up to this?" He asked the question between gritted teeth. Her sharp inhalation and the tremor in her fingers before she jerked her hand back told him what he needed to know before he even turned his head to look at her. He'd hurt her—and he regretted it.

Scrubbing a hand through his hair, Kade examined his emotions, something he usually avoided. Lashing out at Pippa wasn't the answer to his dilemma. He closed his eyes, saw his grandfather's disapproving face. Instead of facing the situation like a man, he was running away like a kid with a case of the "Don't wannas." He should apologize but the simmering anger clogged his throat. Instead, he skirted everything by asking, "So when is this fancy deal requiring a tux?"

Pippa winced, her gaze flicking up to his before sliding away. "Next month?"

The month flashed by. While Kade spent time with Pippa, the easy camaraderie they'd previously shared was strained. Kade admitted the disconnect was his fault, but he didn't know how to fix things. He also avoided interacting with any of the Barrons, including Chase's wife, Savannah. Savvie was like Kade's little sister, but she was a Barron now. Since none of the wives—known for their meddling—had gotten involved, he suspected their husbands hadn't told them about the terms of the will.

Kade hoped he could put things to rights by escorting Pippa to her gala. He bought a Western cut tuxedo and, like a teenage boy taking the prom queen to the dance, he went to work on the rest of the evening. Carrie, as if she sensed what he was doing, informed him that Pippa's gown was *pewter and Oklahoma blue*—whatever that meant. He finally gave up and asked. She informed him, "Gray and a blue the color of the state flag."

Why couldn't Carrie have just said that? She went on to explain that he should coordinate his tux accessories to match and no, this wasn't prom, so no flowers.

He hated shopping but found a formal vest with silver threads running through it and snatched it without even looking at the price tag. He wasn't about to mess with a bow tie so he added a black bolo tie with pewter tips and a large turquoise slide in lieu of the bow. He also made arrangements for very special transportation.

When the big night finally arrived, just as he was about to walk out the door, Pippa called him in a panic.

"I don't know what to do," she all but wailed.

"Breathe, Pip. Tell me what's wrong."

"Mother. I'm so mad I could spit. I just got back from the hairdresser and she met me at the door. *I expect you to do your duty*, she says. *Everyone is gathering here pre-function for cocktails and you will be here to act as hostess.*" Kade was impressed at how well Pippa imitated her mother. "She hates my foundation and she's hijacking my party just to be contrary. I don't have time for this command performance of hers. I have so much left to finish with the event itself and she must have set this up weeks ago but she chose *now* to drop this little bombshell on me? *Argh!*"

"So what you're saying is that your mother planned this

party for two hundred of her closest friends and she expects you to play hostess?"

"Yes."

"Are these people also invited to the deal at the hotel?"

"Yes."

"Okay."

"Okay? Okay? That's all you have to say?" Her voice rose in pitch.

"You aren't breathing, Pip. What time does your mother's thing start?"

"Six."

"What time does the other thing start?"

"Eight."

"What can Carrie and I do at the hotel so you can relax for a bit?"

"I can't…you… Carrie…" He could almost hear her jaw snap closed through the phone. "Let me think. Carrie has a copy of my list. If she's dressed early, she can deal with the hotel on the final room setup and menu."

"Can I handle that for you if she can't?"

"You'd do that for me?"

"Sure. I was just on my way out the door anyway. I'll be there early just hanging around. If I pick you up at seven, you'll have an hour to make nice with your mother's friends, who are your potential donors. When I get there, I'll whisk you away, giving you enough time to regroup and be ready to make your entrance at the hotel."

Pippa didn't speak for a long moment. Then she said, "Kade?"

"Yeah?"

"I *love* you."

He went very still, like prey sensing danger. Except he knew she didn't mean what she'd just said. It was a throwaway line meant to show her relief and appreciation. But a part of him kind of liked the idea of her saying it for real. Which was crazy.

"Anything to help, hon. Email me the list. I'll make sure everything is good and then I'll pick you up at your parents' at seven."

Kade drove into Oklahoma City and parked near the Barron Hotel. He'd arranged for the horse-drawn carriage to meet him there. The round-trip to the Duncan's home and back to the hotel was about three miles on mostly quiet streets. The carriage was for her grand entrance. After the event, he planned to drive her home in his truck. He checked his watch and had more than enough time to deal with arrangements before the ride to Pippa's.

Tonight was the culmination of so many of Pippa's plans and he wanted everything to be perfect for her despite the last-minute wrench her mother had thrown into things. The hotel event director was an efficient woman who eyed him speculatively. He was saved when Chase and his wife, Savannah, arrived. Chase took over the preparations, leaving him alone with the woman who knew Kade well.

"So…anything you want to tell me?" Savannah went straight for his jugular.

"About what?"

Her brows lowered over squinted eyes. "The brothers have been really closed-mouthed about you of late, despite all of us wives bugging them."

"You should take it up with your husband, Savvie."

"Is it true?" Her gaze was both speculative and knowing.

"What?"

"Don't go all…*man* on me, Kade."

"I am a man."

"Argh!" Savvie threw her arms up and almost clipped Chase on the chin as he walked up behind her.

"Whoa, kitten. I'm the only one who gets to frustrate you like that." He kissed the back of her neck before looking at Kade. "You look good. What time are you picking up our hostess with the mostest?"

"Seven. Her mother did this thing."

Chase grimaced. "Ah yes. The inestimable Millicent. I dodged that bullet for us, Savvie. You can thank me later. When we're alone."

"So," Savvie continued, ignoring her husband. "Are you going to tell me or what?"

"Tell her what?" Chase asked.

"That's what I asked," Kade said.

"You guys! Stop it. I want to know."

Kade exchanged a look with Chase, one he hoped the other man understood.

"So, you serious about Pippa?"

And that was not the direction he expected Chase to take, but Kade could run with this diversion. "I'm just helping her out with foundation stuff. She's picking my brain since I did all that research about therapy riding when Cord was hurt."

"Uh-huh." Chase sounded totally unconvinced. "Will you offer the use of the ranch for her next event?"

Kade wasn't sure what Chase meant. Keeping his expression carefully blank, he said, "It's not up to me to give permission about how the Crown B is used."

"Uh-huh."

Now Chase sounded…what? Skeptical? Smug? Whatever it was in his voice, Kade wasn't going to play this game. "Since you seem to have things well in hand here, I'm going to pick up Pippa before her mother drives her completely nuts."

He walked out of the ballroom, well aware that both Chase and Savvie were staring holes in his back. One thing at a time. And here and now, his one thing—his only thing—was Pippa Duncan.

Nine

Cars clogged the street but the horse-drawn carriage stopped in the one available spot at the end of the Duncans' driveway. The coachman set the brake on the carriage wheel and let the reins go slack. The dappled gray draft horse patiently flicked an ear as his driver glanced back at Kade. "Big party."

"Yeah. Sorry. I'll have to extract her from this mess."

The man chuckled. "No worries, sir. Dozer and I will be here."

When he got to the front porch, Kade tugged his jacket into place and rang the doorbell. And waited. After several minutes, he knocked. When he still didn't get an answer, he tried the knob. The door wasn't locked. As he started to push, the door was jerked open and he faced the haughty Millicent.

"May I help you?" She arched one perfectly plucked and dyed brow and frowned.

"I'm Pippa's escort tonight. I'm here to pick her up."

"She's not ready to leave yet." Millicent did her best to shut the door on him.

Kade wasn't having any of that. He shouldered his way

inside. Politely, despite Millicent's arrogant attempts to stop him. His frustration boiled to the surface so he leaned down to whisper in her ear, "I don't give a damn about appearances so making a scene is no skin off my nose."

The woman huffed out a breath, but stepped out of his way. He pasted a smile on his face and worked very hard to keep his cool. Pippa's mother really was a piece of work. Luckily, he was tall enough to see over most of the crowd milling around. He pushed through the throng until he found Pippa pinned in a corner of the dining room. Millicent dogged his footsteps like she was afraid he might steal something.

He caught Pippa's eye and almost smiled at her relieved expression. He edged through the four women surrounding her and used his most charming smile as he addressed them. "Excuse me, ladies, but Pippa has a gala to attend."

Pippa snatched the hand he held out and he extracted her smoothly. He caught a few whispered comments as they threaded their way back to the front door.

"Who's that?"

"Handsome, isn't he?"

"I didn't realize Pippa was seeing someone."

"I think that's one of those Barron boys, but I don't recall which one he is."

Speculation, snideness and honest curiosity coated the expressions and remarks of those who uttered them. Pippa looked pale and her eyes showed a tightness Kade was all too familiar with. She had a migraine coming on. Part of him wanted to sweep her into his arms and get the hell out of there. He hoped that once he got her away from these people and out in the open air of the carriage, she'd be able to relax.

"Do you have whatever you want to take with you?" he asked, keeping her tucked close to his side.

"I need my evening bag. It's in Dad's office. Here."

She tugged on his hand, veering to the left. She opened French doors and slipped inside. The room was wood paneled, dark and furnished with antiques. Pippa grabbed the small beaded bag on her father's desk and they headed back into the crush.

Kade bulled his way through. He'd been kidding about two hundred of Millicent's closest friends. But there were probably close to that many crammed into the Duncan home. He and Pippa made it to the door, but stalled as more people arrived. She had to acknowledge the newcomers for a few minutes and then they finally escaped.

He led her to the sidewalk. That's when she realized there was a white carriage waiting for them. Kade had arranged to have blue ribbons and silver roses for decorations and he was glad he'd gone to the extra trouble and expense. Pippa stopped in the middle of the sidewalk, her hand pressed over her heart, eyes wide and glistening.

"Oh, Kade," she sighed. "You did this for me?" She bounced up on her toes and kissed him. "This is the most romantic thing ever," she whispered in his ear.

"Your carriage awaits, princess."

Pippa insisted on being introduced to Dozer. The coachman was happy to oblige. By the time Kade lifted her into the backseat, she was smiling and the tightness around her eyes had disappeared.

"This is just…I'm…" Pippa laughed and the sound went straight to his chest.

Kade *liked* it when she laughed and he really liked it when he was the one putting a smile on her face. But he shouldn't. He wasn't in the position to get involved. Not until he figured out his own messed-up life. Dozer took off at a rousing walk, his big hooves clopping rhythmically on the pavement. The bells on the draft horse's harness jangled a merry counterpoint.

SILVER JAMES

"I can't believe you did this, Kade."

Slightly embarrassed now, he sought to change the subject. "You look beautiful, Pippa." Color flooded her cheeks, which seemed to make her eyes bluer. Her long, wavy blond hair had been twisted up in some fancy style that his fingers itched to undo. And her dress...*wow*. It was the color of storm clouds, the skirt swirling around her legs. The top was covered in beading and sparkles the color of the Oklahoma sky on a perfect autumn day. She wore little makeup, her freckles vibrant against her flush. Small and colorful and delicate, she reminded him of a ladybug.

As if on impulse, she leaned closer and kissed his cheek. "Thank you for making the rest of my night perfect."

"You're welcome, ladybug." Riding in the back of the carriage, with Pippa snuggled up next to him, holding her hand, he realized, yeah, she was right. The night was perfect.

When Kade had walked into the room, Pippa had never been so glad—and relieved—to see anyone in her life. And bless him, he'd taken one look, figured out what was going on and gotten her out of there with minimal fuss and bother. And he'd even hired a horse-drawn carriage for a quiet ride through Heritage Hills and then downtown to the Barron Hotel. She would be arriving at her fundraising gala in style.

While slowly unwinding from the stress of her mother's cocktail party, she was still nervous about the event. "Did you—"

"Chase was there with Savannah. I left everything in his far more capable hands."

She laughed again, and the tenseness in her muscles dissipated. With it went the last vestiges of her headache. She wouldn't have to medicate tonight. That meant she could have a glass of wine and eat some of the wonderful refreshments prepared by the Barron Hotel's five-star kitchen staff.

Kade gently squeezed her hand, then raised it and kissed its back. "You are an amazing, talented, caring, beautiful woman, Pippa. Tonight will be everything you hope because you're the one who put it together. You'll make lots of money for Camp Courage and we'll get started with looking for a location and for horses."

"You're really good for my ego, Kade Waite."

"I try, ma'am." He winked then kissed her—carefully—so he didn't mess up her lipstick.

For the next ten minutes, they simply sat close together, holding hands, enjoying the sounds of the horse and carriage. As they passed landscaped yards, she caught the scents of honeysuckle and mimosa, both sweet but just different enough to distinguish. New-mown grass added a note of green that hid the scent of hot motors and car exhaust.

Kids ran out to wave at them like they were a parade consisting of one float. Pippa practiced her princess wave, much to Kade's amusement. She didn't care. She felt like a princess tonight and had her very own Prince Charming by her side. In the distance, the sound of traffic intruded. They were close to downtown now and they'd be arriving at the hotel soon.

"What time is it?"

"A little after eight. You are arriving fashionably late."

She blanched. "Oh, no! I should have been there to greet—"

"Shh, Pippa. You have others there to greet the early arrivals. I was informed that you need to make an entrance so that's what we're going to do."

She made a disgusted face and rolled her eyes. "Carrie."

"And Chase."

"They're in cahoots." She thought about her best friend and the Barron twins. "Did you know that she and Chase dated in high school?"

He gave her a look that said volumes, like *How would I know that? I didn't go to your private high school.* She wanted to bite her tongue. "Everyone figured they'd end up with each other eventually. Carrie told us we were nuts. Turned out we were. Still, those two together are far too devious for their own good!"

She very carefully laid her cheek on Kade's shoulder. She didn't want to smear her makeup on his black tux jacket. "You see, Carrie was a female version of Chase. They were all about the opposite sex and never settling down." She raised her head so she could look at him. "And do you know how crazy happy he is with Savannah? I never thought he'd fall so deeply in love with anyone."

"Yeah, weirdly enough, I think Savannah feels the same way about him."

Pippa realized she was wearing a soft smile when she saw it reflected in Kade's dark eyes. Street lamps were glowing and stars were twinkling in the sky. A crescent moon peeked over the top of the downtown skyline. She sat up straighter as they stopped at the light at the intersection of Park Avenue and Broadway. When it changed, Dozer trotted into the circular drive in front of the Barron and joined the queue of cars lined up for the hotel's valet parking.

Looking around, Pippa was amazed. Lots of people had self-parked and were walking into the hotel. "So many people…" She couldn't have hidden the wonder in her voice even if she'd wanted to.

"Why wouldn't there be? This is a good cause, Pippa. An amazing cause. You've tapped into lots of people's soft spots. Even those without deep pockets."

While she'd worried Kade might feel out of place at a black-tie affair, the man sitting beside her looked nothing but proud—of her and to be with her. And she thought she might have fallen just a little bit in love with him.

Kade watched her work the room—not from afar but at her side. Once they arrived and he'd handed her down from the carriage, she'd been all but swallowed by the crowd. Somehow, they'd remained together, most likely due to the fact that she clung to his hand like it was her lifeline. He'd anticipated finding a place on the periphery from which to watch. Now he stood next to her while she visited with guests, her face animated and all but glowing with the passion she held for her cause.

He believed in her cause. He'd first looked into therapy riding programs after Cord Barron had been injured in an accident on an oil rig. Active in the OSU Outreach Riders, Kade had worked with disadvantaged kids but had no clue there was so much more to a therapy program. Physically and emotionally challenged children and adults, military veterans, even recovering drug addicts and felons had all benefited from association with horses. Kade would do everything he could to help Pippa see her dream come true.

Currently, she was talking to a neurosurgeon and his wife. Kade stood slightly behind her and schooled his face so he didn't smile whenever she rocked back to lean against him. He'd figured out that she touched him when she was feeling anxious or needed support.

"What do you think, Mr. Waite?" the doctor's wife asked. "Will this program have an impact on autistic children?"

Kade scrambled to catch up with the conversation he'd mostly tuned out. "I can't say for sure, ma'am. The research I've done indicates that kids can and do connect with the horses. I know when I was at OSU and we brought in foster kids for field trips, they really got into it. I'm just sort of the horse consultant in this deal."

The woman looked thoughtful, then interrupted her husband as he was about to reply. "Get the checkbook out, Oscar. And add a zero to the amount we discussed earlier." She turned a megawatt smile on Pippa. "I think this is a wonderful idea and I wish you much success. Please let me know as soon as you open. I'd like to sign up my grandson."

Pippa looked startled then regrouped. "Of course! I'll be in touch with you, Mrs. Amadi, just as soon as we're up and running. Thank you."

Dr. Amadi had done as his wife requested and when Pippa looked at the check, she almost choked. Kade was afraid he'd have to slap her on the back to get her breathing again. She sucked in a breath and added, "This is beyond generous. Thank you both so very, very much!" She shook the doctor's hand and when she offered her hand to Mrs. Amadi, the woman hugged Pippa.

"No, my dear, thank you. I hope you can reach my grandson."

"We'll do our very best, Mrs. Amadi!"

The couple moved away and Pippa sagged against Kade. She waved the check in front of him. "Look," she gushed.

He did a double take. Twenty thousand dollars was a lot of zeros. "Carrie's working the donation table, right?" Pippa nodded, still stunned by what she held in her hand. "Let's take her the check and then I want to dance with my date."

Carrie had a running total for them and Pippa was all but floating as he took her into his arms on the dance floor. The band was playing something soft and romantic and he liked having her head on his shoulder as they swayed in time to the music. The gala had garnered well into six figures and Kade regretted his paltry thousand dollar donation. It had seemed like a lot when he signed the check—especially when comparing his bank account to others' in the room.

The people attending this gala were the movers and shakers of Oklahoma society. He noted the knot of men at the end of the bar—Cord Barron, his father-in-law, J. Rand Davis, and three other energy tycoons. Their conversation was intense. The governor held court at a table on the edge of the dance floor. The OU football coach occupied one table, the OSU coach another. A couple of professional basketball players and their dates shared the floor with Pippa and him.

Kade didn't fit in with these people. He was just a rancher—on a spread that wasn't even his. But it could be. The back of his neck prickled and as he turned Pippa in a slow circle, he searched for the cause. He found the Barron table. All of them but Cord sat there with their wives. Jolie, Cord's wife, was taking a turn at the donation table with Carrie. Clay, Chance, Chase and Cash all watched him.

His brothers. With the Barron name, he could be sitting at that table. He could add zeroes onto the end of a number as he wrote a check for charity. Kade missed a step and caught the hem of Pippa's dress with his boot.

"Sorry," he murmured.

She gazed up at him with worried eyes. "Are you okay? You look like you've just seen a ghost or something."

Yeah, or something all right. He smiled, turning his back on the men with the same eyes as his own. "Naw. Just clumsy."

Her grin was full of mischief as she looked at him. "Thank goodness I'm not the only one."

When the song ended, Carrie grabbed Pippa and insisted she take a turn at the donor table. At loose ends, Kade headed to the buffet. Cord had joined his brothers and now they all sat there watching him. They'd remained true to their word—for the most part. They hadn't approached him about the terms of the will. They'd given him space, dealing with him only when necessary about the ranch or this deal with Pippa. They weren't like their old man—*his* old man. At least he didn't think so.

A short, stout woman, wearing a black dress with so much beading Kade couldn't figure out how she could move in it, nudged him with her elbow.

"Here, young man. Take this." She shoved a plate laden with a bit of everything on the table at him. He grabbed it out of self-preservation. "I can't possibly navigate with a plate and a libation." She held up a crystal flute full of bubbling champagne.

Like a tugboat chugging through a harbor full of cruise ships, she navigated to a table near the one occupied by the Barrons. When they arrived, he placed the plate next to one full of desserts and just managed to hide his amusement as she leaned her head back to look up at him.

"My goodness, you are a tall one. I never could keep all of you straight. Now which one of the Barron boys are you?"

Ten

After the party wrapped up, with Pippa's announcement that they'd raised $243,211 for Camp Courage, she laughed about Kade's encounter with the elderly matron. He'd dodged the woman's question simply by introducing himself. He'd received a sharp-eyed assessment in return, and by the time he escaped, the woman had been distracted by something else.

"Mrs. Mayweather is notorious for picking out one handsome man and making him dance attendance on her. She'll be talking about you for days with her garden club cronies." Pippa leaned back against the leather seat of his pickup. She rubbed at her temple and Kade wondered if she was aware of the action. "My parents didn't come."

That she felt hurt was evident in her voice. He reached over, took her hand and gave it a little squeeze. "Less drama."

That startled a little snort from her. "True, that." She tilted her head to look at him as the truck rolled to a stop at a red light. "Mother is something of a drama queen. Sadly, she managed to keep some potential donors away too."

That made him angry but he held his tongue. Instead,

he offered encouragement as he continued driving toward the Heritage Hills neighborhood. "You'll figure a way to reach out and touch them."

"I hope so. I'm only about halfway to my goal."

"You've been applying for grants."

"Yes, but those can take a year or more and none of them are huge. I'm looking at them for an infusion of operating funds after the first glow wears off. This is a long-term program. I need to find a steady source of revenue."

As they approached the street where her parents' house was located, Pippa sat forward, pulling against the seat belt. "Looks like the party is still in full swing."

The disappointment in her voice was as strong as her previous hurt. "How 'bout you sneak in, pack a bag and come back to the ranch with me. You can sleep late. I'll fix you breakfast and then we'll take a ride."

Pippa's expression lightened. "Perfect! Go up a block and park. I have the code to the back gate."

Kade did as he was told, then helped her out of the truck and escorted her to the gate. She rolled her eyes at him, which he was able to see due to the overhead security light from the neighbor's yard.

"I think I'm safe walking this half block."

"Probably."

"You could have waited in the truck."

"Yup."

"Kade…"

"Pippa…"

She laughed then and smothered it against his chest. "We need to be quiet. If Mother catches us, we'll never get away." After she keyed in the security code for the gate used by the yard care crew, they tiptoed across the pool area and slipped into the guesthouse.

Pippa left him in the living room. One lamp lit the area.

She dashed upstairs without switching on additional lighting. When she returned, she wore jeans, flip-flops and an OSU T-shirt, and pulled a little wheeled suitcase behind her. She paused near the door and grabbed a pair of Western boots from the shelf of an antique hall tree and passed them to Kade.

She peeked out from behind the curtains. "The coast is clear. Let's go."

When they were safely back in his truck, Pippa was giggling like a kindergartner and he couldn't stop the grin spreading across his face.

"Thank you," Pippa said, her voice fervent as he put the truck in gear and pulled away from the curb.

"For what?"

"For…this. For tonight. For making me laugh. For having faith in me."

He glanced at her as he turned the corner at the end of the block. "You're doing a good thing, ladybug."

"I know. And I want all the money possible to go to the program itself. I'll keep doing the administrative side with volunteers for as long as possible. I won't take a salary. I can live on part of the interest from my grandmother's trust. The rest of it will be used for day-to-day expenses. With enough donations, I won't have to touch the principle."

"Is that why you live in the guesthouse?" He'd wondered, given the frequent animosity between Pippa and Millicent.

She stretched out her legs and leaned back against the seat with a yawn. "That's a big part of it. I don't have to pay rent or utilities and it's convenient. I have budgeted for things, should I move out." She turned her head and smiled in his direction. "And the perks are pretty good." She waggled her brows.

By the time he hit the north side of the city, Pippa had dozed off. He thought about what she'd said, about living off the interest of a trust fund, about setting up a charity foundation that didn't have administrative expenses so all the money could go for good.

Kade had worked his whole life. He'd joined baling crews in junior high, and in high school, he'd traveled with harvesting crews. In between, he'd trained horses and competed in rodeos. Even with scholarships, he'd worked his way through college and had graduated debt-free. He compared his life to the Barrons and other rich kids he'd gone to school with. All things considered, the Barrons had turned out fairly normal.

He thought about the ranch and the money that would come with it. He thought about what he could contribute to Camp Courage. And he thought about Pippa. She hadn't given any indication that she wanted to take their relationship beyond what it was—basically friends with occasional benefits. He liked her. A lot. And he enjoyed spending time with her, in or out of the bedroom. Did he want to take whatever they had to the next step? Did she?

Kade already had way too much weighing on his mind. Given his situation, starting a serious relationship with a woman like Pippa was foolish. She belonged with someone like one of the Barrons. Not him, despite his DNA. She was a princess, he was…a simple cowboy. Pippa deserved someone with more class, someone brought up the way she'd been. That sure wasn't him. Money didn't make the man, but having it smoothed out the rough edges. If he accepted the Barron name, he'd have more than enough to give him a veneer. But that wasn't him, and never would be. He was comfortable being Kaden Waite. Kaden Barron? Not so much.

He glanced over at the sleeping woman. She'd never

shown a snobby bone in her body but would she consider something more with him—with the ranch manager and not the ranch owner? Would he be able to give her all the things she was accustomed to on his salary? If he walked away from Cyrus's deal, he'd have to find another job, another place to live. She wouldn't want to give up her dream of the therapy program. He wouldn't expect her to go with him.

Sudden money did bad things to people. He'd watched it happen to members of his tribe who'd come into oil money. He'd been raised to work with his hands. With the kind of wealth the Barrons had, they didn't need to work. But they did. All of them. He hadn't considered that until now.

"You're thinking so hard you're giving me a headache, Kade."

"Sorry. Thought you were asleep."

She chuckled and made a face at him. "What'd I say about thinking?"

"Oh, right. Sorry." But he wasn't, especially when she reached across the center console to touch his arm. He dropped his right hand from the steering wheel and twined his fingers with hers.

"No, you aren't." She squeezed his hand. "Thank you again. For tonight. For…this. It's weird, because there's absolutely no reason I should feel this way, but it's like a weight's been lifted from my shoulders." She gazed out through the windshield. "I love coming out here. I mean, I enjoy living in the city but coming out here where I can really see the stars and it's so quiet… It's peaceful, y'know?"

A wry grin tugged at the corner of his mouth and he let it blossom. "Yeah, I know. But I'm a small-town boy and grew up on a farm. Even Stillwater, while I was there for college, was a big city to me."

"I like that you're a country boy, Kade."

She squeezed his hand again and something eased in his mind. A warmth he didn't want to examine too closely filled him. "Well, this country boy likes the city cowgirl sitting beside him."

Pippa remembered to breathe. Tingles danced across her skin as she gazed at his handsome profile. She knew he didn't like to dress up, yet he had. For her. And that caused more tingles. Kade was a real country boy. He worked hard for a living and didn't she just love the way his rough hands felt against her skin? She shivered and Kade glanced at her.

"Cold? I can turn the AC down." He reached for the controls, still holding her hand. She tugged it back.

"No, I'm good."

He flashed her a wicked grin and her breath caught in her chest. "Yeah, you are."

Blushing furiously, she ducked her head and did her best to hide the very pleased smile spreading across her face. "Not as good as you," she mumbled under her breath.

She settled back in her seat and watched Kade from the corner of her eye. The glow from the dashboard instruments bathed his skin in gold. She'd only pretended to doze on the drive partly because she was exhausted from talking all night and craved some silence. Not that Kade was all that talkative. Her other reason had been so she could simply sink into the pleasure of watching him without his knowing. Pippa got such a kick out of it, she decided to do it at every opportunity.

It was only after his expression had sobered and then he'd looked…not forlorn but deeply saddened. That's when she spoke up. She'd had a wonderful—if tiring—night and having him by her side had been the boost she needed. When he'd appeared at her parents' house, she'd felt such relief and she'd been struck by how handsome he looked—rugged and sexy and very, *very* male.

The carriage waiting outside had been the perfect touch, and was beyond romantic. She'd worried, briefly, when they entered the hotel ballroom, but he'd stuck with her, supporting her and aiding where he could. He stood back and let her shine, and that was such a rare trait in most of the men she knew that she viewed it as a precious gift.

"Have I mentioned how wonderful it was to have you beside me tonight?"

Kade laughed and nodded. "Yeah, once or twice. Trust me, I'll figure out a way for you to pay me back."

He slowed the truck and turned onto the road leading to the ranch. They passed between the fieldstone pillars that supported the metal sign—Crown B Ranch Established 1889—arching over the drive.

The interior of the big house was dark as they drove past. Security lights left soft pools of fake moonlight scattered around the exterior. Pippa caught the crunch of gravel under the truck's tires as the vehicle left the brick-paved drive for the utility road leading to the ranch office, barns and the houses occupied by other ranch workers. As Kade pulled up in front of his house, a light activated by a motion detector went on.

Kade came around to open her door and help her down before grabbing her bag and boots from the backseat of the king cab pickup. They hadn't really talked about the circumstances of his birth since his original confession and without thinking, Pippa blurted, "If you decide to stay, will you take over the big house?"

Her blunt question was a testament to her exhaustion. Appalled by what she'd said, she turned to him, eyes wide. "I'm sorry. That…I… Not my business!"

His expression was inscrutable as he turned away from

her and climbed the steps to the porch. Kade unlocked the front door and held it open for her to precede him. She scuttled past, keeping her face averted. Pippa was positive she'd insulted him somehow.

After locking the door, he headed toward his bedroom. He stopped in the doorway. "No," he said without looking at her. "I'd keep this house. Does that...I don't know. Upset you? Disappoint you?" He passed into the darkened room without waiting for her answer.

Pippa tossed her purse on the boot bench next to the door and hurried after him. In his darkened bedroom, the ceiling fan created a cool breeze to wash over her skin. A lamp occupying one of the bedside tables flicked on with a bluish glow, chasing the dark into the corners. She loved the stained-glass shade that cast those soft colors.

Leaning her shoulder against the doorjamb, she watched Kade place her suitcase on top of his dresser. Her suitcase was heavy but he exerted no effort lifting it. He dropped her boots next to the dresser then started stripping out of his tux. He meticulously hung the jacket on a thick wooden hanger. The turquoise bolo tie went on a rack on the back of the closet door. The fitted vest with its woven threads of silver was placed on a second wooden hanger. Pippa had never truly noticed before but Kade was a precise housekeeper. His home was lived in but everything had a place and was put there.

His fingers tangled with the tiny studs on the tux shirt. She went to him and brushed his hands away as her smaller and more nimble fingers worked the gray pearl and metal studs out of the buttonholes. She saw a plastic box on top of the dresser and dropped the studs into it before going to work on his cuff links.

"Of course not, Kade," she said quietly without looking up. "I don't even know why I asked that stupid question."

He shrugged and the lift of his muscular shoulders parted the plackets of his shirt even more. His sculpted chest had a fine feathering of hair a shade lighter than the black hair on his head. She placed a kiss in the center of his chest before dropping the links in the box with the studs and stepping away. Kade caught her hand.

"It wasn't stupid, Pippa. You live in a mansion."

She snorted and rolled her eyes. Making sure her voice was light and teasing, she said, "I live in the guesthouse of a mansion."

"Okay, fine. You grew up in a mansion. So did the Barrons. Their house in Nichols Hills is every bit as fancy as your parents'. And the big house here could be on one of those home decorating shows. You know them. You know how they live."

He swept one hand wide to encompass the bedroom. The rustic king-size bed was formed from pine logs. The bedside tables and dresser were well worn and carried a patina of age while not being antique. The armchair and matching ottoman were covered in distressed leather and looked comfortably lumpy. The whole place was similarly furnished. "This isn't fancy. *I'm* not fancy, Pippa. I wasn't kidding when I said I was a country boy. At the end of most months, we had more days than money. I've worked— worked hard—for everything I have. I don't know what it's like to have the kind of money they do, that you have."

Kade walked away and sat down on the wooden blanket chest at the foot of the bed. He toed off his polished black boots and held them up. "I bought these at Langston's outlet store. Tonight, the Barrons were wearing custom boots that cost what some people make in a month."

Pippa wasn't sure where he was headed with this so she stayed where she was despite the very visceral need to go to him, to touch him. He pushed off the chest and popped open the fastenings of his slacks. Stepping out of them, he crossed back to the closet, passing so close that had she leaned forward his arm would have brushed her breasts as he walked by. She resisted the urge but dang the man was sexy, even standing there in an open shirt, black knit boxers and black socks.

Emerging from the closet, Kade mirrored her earlier posture by leaning a shoulder against the door. He'd shed both shirt and socks. "My point, Pippa, is this. I've never had anything. My idea of a manicure is using a pocket knife to clean the dirt from under my nails and washing my hands with Lava soap. I'm a working cowboy with a fancy title that doesn't mean crap when the herd needs moving, there's a rough calving or there's a fractious mustang to break to the saddle."

He scrubbed one hand through his hair and breathed hard for several moments. "I don't know what it's like to have that kind of money. I don't *want* that kind of money. And you're the kind of girl who—" Kade chopped off the rest of the sentence, then dipped his chin and stared at his bare feet rather than continuing to look at her.

She blinked, a puzzled look on her face. "I…I'm not following, Kade. Are you breaking up with me?"

Eleven

Pippa's question stung but it also made Kade think. Did they have a relationship serious enough that they'd actually have a breakup? He considered.

They were dating—and sleeping together. She was intent on getting her therapy riding program set up and he was helping her with that. She would come to the ranch and they would ride or they'd laze around the pool at the big house. Being with her made him feel settled, made him want things he hadn't considered before. Knowing she was coming out to the ranch, or he was headed into town to spend time with her made him work a little harder, a little faster, so he could finish that much sooner.

She was important to him but he didn't love her. And he wasn't the kind of man she would ultimately love and marry. He was a man who spoke his mind and he had. He'd been honest with her. And with himself. He was a working man. Pippa was an heiress. She lived on a trust fund and set up foundations to help those in need. She moved in society circles where formal clothing was something hanging in their closet, not rented from the bridal store. Her kind of people lived in mansions and drove expensive cars they paid cash for. That kind of money was foreign, yet as close as his signature on a bunch of legal papers. That kind of money could define a man.

Kade didn't realize he'd been silent too long until Pippa jerked her head around, hiding her face from him as she surreptitiously swiped at her cheek with the back of her hand. "It's too late for you to drive me back to the city. I'll sleep on the couch and you can take me home in the morning."

She thought the answer to her question was yes. His fingers wrapped around her biceps as she stepped away and he tightened his grip until she stopped. "Do we have something to break, Pippa?" Damn but he sounded needy.

She wouldn't look at him but she answered him. "I don't know. I thought we had something special."

Air whooshed out of his lungs as relief washed through him. He was treading dangerous ground but the feel of his heart hammering in his chest made him say, "We do, Pippa. We do have something special."

Then she was in his arms, her tears dampening his chest. He held her close, stroking her back and kissing the top of her head. "I'm sorry, ladybug. I'm sorry. I didn't mean to hurt you. It's just… You deserve a man who's better for you."

"Shut up. Just shut up, Kaden Waite. That's not true. You *are* a better man!"

Her words steadied his pulse rate and he could breathe without the hard hitch in his chest. After a few minutes of just standing there holding each other, her breathing steadied as well. He helped her undress and then they climbed into bed. He wanted to make love to her but the dark circles under Pippa's eyes reminded him of how exhausted she must be. Midnight was a couple of hours past and dawn would arrive all too quickly.

He settled on his back with Pippa curled to his side, her palm warming the spot over his heart, her head on his shoulder. "Sleep, ladybug."

"Are we okay now?"

"Yeah, sweetheart. We're good."

Kade lay awake long after Pippa drifted off. Eventually he fell asleep, but woke up early with Pippa still in his arms. His mind couldn't let go of their conversation. Her question last night had thrown him, and made him wonder if everyone thought he'd take over the big house if he accepted the terms of Cyrus's will. Of course, if he didn't agree, it wouldn't matter. He'd be packing everything he owned into his old truck, because the truck he normally drove belonged to the ranch fleet, and moving away. He had no idea where he'd go. It wasn't like he'd started sending out résumés or anything.

Pippa stirred beside him and he inhaled the ginger orange scent of her long hair. Sleeping with her in his arms brought him more peace than he figured he was entitled to at present. She made him forget, even when they weren't having amazing sex. Just her presence soothed the ache in his chest.

He was leaning over to kiss her good morning when she violently shoved against his chest and jolted upright. Kade jerked his head back just in time to avoid getting clocked on the chin. Pippa's legs got tangled in the sheets and she would have fallen face-first on the floor if he hadn't grabbed her.

"Pippa?"

She had her hand pressed over her mouth and she looked a little green. He got the sheet unwrapped and then she was off the bed and bolting for the bathroom. A few seconds after the door slammed shut, he heard the unmistakable sounds of heaving. Yeah, time to vacate the room and start coffee. He wanted to help but his gut reaction told him Pippa would not appreciate the intrusion.

She hadn't appeared by the time the coffee finished dripping into its carafe. Kade gulped down a cup and when she still hadn't emerged, he tapped softy on the bathroom door.

"You okay, ladybug?"

He heard a muffled yes.

He waited for more, got nothing. "Can I do anything to help?"

"Grab my clothes?"

"I can do that."

He took her suitcase from the top of his dresser and tapped on the door again, which opened just wide enough for him to pass the bag through. Pippa stayed hidden behind the door so he couldn't even get a glimpse of her. The door closed with a soft snick and he heard the lock turn. That didn't bode well.

When she appeared ten minutes later, she'd showered and gathered her wet hair into a ponytail. He fought the urge to kiss the tip of her freckle-sprinkled nose. Shadows bruised her eyes and she was pale beneath the freckles. He preferred her like this—no makeup, hair natural, in faded jeans and a soft shirt, but he could tell just by looking she was sick.

"You okay?"

Pippa lifted one shoulder and huffed out a hitching breath. "Sorry. I don't normally wake up needing to throw up. It must have been something I ate."

"That's not good."

She nodded morosely. "It would be very bad if something was wrong with the food at the gala. I'll have to call Chase and ask if anyone else got sick."

"I'm sorry, bug. Want some coffee or juice?"

She closed her eyes and shook her head. "No. Still queasy. I'm sorry about today. Maybe you should just drive me home."

He shook his head. "Do you really want to deal with your mother feeling like this?"

"Good point."

"You can either go back to bed or I'll set you up on the couch. You rest and I'll take care of some work this morning. Then, if you feel better, we'll ride or something this afternoon. Sound like a plan?"

Her smile was tentative. "Yeah. Thanks." She closed her eyes and swallowed hard. "Do you have any ginger ale or crackers?"

Kade had both. He went to the kitchen and grabbed a box of crackers and a can of soda. While she ate a couple of crackers, he put ice into a glass and poured the liquid into it. He watched as she nibbled and sipped, was glad when color returned to her pallid cheeks.

He did have some work he could do but he was hesitant to leave her after he made her a comfy nest on his couch. He made sure the sleeve of crackers and the glass were within easy reach, along with the TV remote and her phone. Pippa snuggled against the pillows he'd brought from the bedroom and he tossed a light throw over her. Her smile was warm and her eyes had lost their tense look.

"I can stay with you," he offered.

"No, you have things to do. Go take care of them. Maybe I'll feel like lunch and a ride when you get back."

He left, still reluctant. Kade hadn't invited her out to spend the night and following day just so he could work. Still, he recognized that her illness had embarrassed her and she wanted a little time apart as much to regroup emotionally as recuperate physically.

His first stop was the office, which was locked up tight.

Not unusual for a Sunday. He let himself in and went to his desk. A stack of messages awaited his attention. Flipping through them, he decided there was nothing demanding his immediate response.

He grabbed a six-wheeled ATV parked outside and headed toward the barns. He paid a visit to Imp's stall. The yearling nickered and moved toward him. The straw on the floor was fresh; the colt had been fed and given fresh water. Kade grabbed the lead rope and halter hanging next to the stall and slipped them onto the horse. Leading Imp outside, he turned the colt out into the large corral next to the barn.

That done, he checked the other stalls. All was well. Dusty appeared during his inspection and jumped into the ATV's passenger seat, intent on accompanying Kade on the rest of his rounds. He drove out to the nearest pastures to check other horses and then herds of cattle. Sunday was a rest day for the cowboys on the ranch.

When he got back, a lone figure with blond hair blowing in the wind leaned against the corral fence watching Imp play. He parked the ATV and walked toward her as Dusty raced to her side for petting and attention.

When Kade reached her, Pippa favored him with a smile and she reminded him of daisies. "You must be feeling better."

"I am. I'm fine now. What would you like to do?"

Things low in his belly stirred to life but he fought the urge to suggest going back to bed. Instead, he said, "Let's go on a picnic. We'll ride out to the lake, take a swim, eat." Then he couldn't resist. He waggled his brows. "And see what happens."

Pippa laughed and waggled her finger. "I see what you're doing here."

"And?"

"I didn't bring a swimsuit."

Kade's cheeks stretched with his grin. "Good. Then I know what's going to happen!"

"Thank goodness!" Pippa grabbed his hand and pulled him toward his house. "I'm hungry. What are you going to feed me?"

And didn't that just put all sorts of ideas into his head.

No. Just…no. This conversation could not be happening. Pippa stared in horror at her best friend. "Wash your mouth out! I've always been careful. I'm on birth control for goodness' sakes."

After a month of intense meetings in the aftermath of the gala, Pippa'd planned for a day of shopping fun and lunch at Cadie B's with her BFF. They occupied a shady table on the patio. She'd wanted time with Carrie but this conversation had not been on the agenda.

"You might be but there's always the possibility for an oops moment. Let's look at the evidence." Carrie raised her index finger. "You wake up nauseous every morning."

"It's just that stomach bug going around." Of course it was. The virus had even made the nightly news. Except she'd been living on crackers and ginger ale from the time she woke up in the morning until just before noon. Then she felt fine. The first few days had been intense, though. Upon waking every morning, she'd had to run to the bathroom even though she made sure she ate nothing before bed.

Carrie put up another finger, as if counting things off, and stared at Pippa's plate. "When was the last time you ate sauerkraut? I've known you since we were five, Pip, and you have never, ever eaten a Reuben sandwich. You inhaled that one. And you ate kraut on your bratwurst at the baseball game the other night. I sat there and watched you. And then you wanted another one. You don't like hot dogs, much less bratwurst. You get pizza or Frito's Chili Pies when we go to the ballpark. Even Kade noticed."

"He did not!" She scowled at Carrie then blanked her expression to one of unconcern. "What's the big deal? So I had a craving."

"Precisely. Think about why women have cravings." Carrie raised a third finger. "And other than being a little stressed over setting up the foundation, you haven't acted PMS-y in well over a month."

"I don't PMS." She didn't. Much. But Pippa also couldn't remember her last period. Stress. It was just stress. Besides, she'd never been all that regular. That's why she'd first gone on birth control and the whole not-getting-pregnant thing was just a side benefit, especially since she and Kade had been spending so much time together. She hadn't missed a pill since they'd started dating.

Raised eyebrows lost under her bangs, Carrie shook her head, looking for all the world like a disappointed parent, though with a humorous twist to her mouth. Pippa was all too familiar with the real thing. Leveling a look at her, Carrie was insistent. "Of course you do. You forget. We roomed together at OSU. Trust me, you PMS. Not as bad as me, but you get witchy. It pains me to say this, but sweetie, you are in denial."

"No, I'm not. This is ridiculous, Carrie, and I'm not talking about it anymore. Subject closed. I set aside today to shop and spend time with my best friend, not get a lecture." Pippa pushed to her feet and snagged her purse from where it hung on the back of her chair. Fighting a wave of dizziness, she walked, with as much dignity as she could summon, to the door.

She was still wobbly when Carrie caught up to her. "Pip? You okay?"

"Migraine coming on," she muttered. "I don't have my meds with me. I…sorry, Care Bear. I need to get home."

"C'mon. I'll walk you to the parking garage." Luckily, they weren't far and once Pippa made it into the gloomy interior, she felt a little better. She said goodbye to Carrie, climbed into her Highlander and cranked the air-conditioning after punching the ignition. She closed her eyes, waiting for the next wave of precursors, only there were none—no sparkles, no tunnel vision, no pain tuning up to the beat of her pulse. Idling in the shade of the garage, she realized she'd simply misdiagnosed the problem. Her dizziness wasn't a result of the debilitating headache she'd expected, just more symptoms from that erratic stomach flu.

Feeling better, she decided to head toward her favorite coffee shop. Even if this was a very tiny migraine, the infusion of caffeine would help. She had her favorite e-reader in her purse. She'd find a quiet corner, drink an iced coffee and read for a bit. Between her tummy troubles and the stress of meeting with high-powered people regarding grants for Camp Courage, it was no wonder she was queasy.

Pippa was in no hurry to go home. Her parents were in Barbados. They'd embarked on a two-week cruise with friends on their yacht and would be home in a few days. In the meantime, no one would be waiting for her. Honestly, she'd enjoyed her mother's absence. Since the night of the gala, Pippa had received either the cold shoulder or scathing accusations.

Still, she faced eating dinner alone and found the idea unappealing. She considered calling Kade to see if he wanted to come into town and hang out with her. They could watch a movie. Or baseball. She didn't care. She just wanted company—his company. And with her parents away, he could spend the night.

She passed one of the big chain drugstores and a little voice told her to stop. Pippa kept driving. For two blocks. Then she whipped around and returned to the store. She stood in the aisle for almost twenty minutes before making her selection.

And that's when she realized she'd be spending tonight alone—until she figured things out.

Twelve

The next morning, wrapped in nothing but a towel after her shower, Pippa stared at the test stick in her hand. She immediately grabbed the other two brands of pregnancy test and read the instructions. Took them both. And got the same result.

This. Could. Not. Be. Happening.

She sank onto the closed lid of the toilet and cried. How could she be pregnant? She splashed her face with cold water, staring at her reflection in the mirror. She didn't know what to do. Crying hadn't helped. Holding out hope that all three tests were false positives was grasping at straws. Breathing through another wave of panic, she grabbed her cell phone and scrolled through the contacts to find her doctor.

Able to get an emergency appointment, she dressed and headed to the doctor's office. After the nurse ran a series of tests, took her blood pressure and weighed her, Pippa sat on pins and needles for two hours, refusing to leave the waiting room until she had confirmation and an explanation. The nurse finally escorted her into Dr. Long's office. She knew the moment she saw the doctor's face. Sinking into the nearest chair, she fought another onset of tears.

Dr. Long pushed a box of tissues toward her. Pippa pulled a handful and blew her nose. "So, it's true."

"Yes."

She'd always liked Dr. Long. The woman was calm, deliberate and blunt when the situation called for it. Even as her heart sank, she appreciated the doctor's directness. "Two questions." At the doctor's nod, she said, "How did it happen and what do I do now?"

Dr. Long leveled a look at her. "I presume you got pregnant the way most women do."

That called for a glower and she tossed one the doctor's direction. "Okay, d'uh. But I've been on the pill for three years."

"What other drugs are you taking?"

"I…several. You know I have severe migraines. Dr. Nevin is my neurologist." Pippa frowned. "And I've doubled up recently because…well…lots of stress."

"That likely explains how. Some of those drugs affect the efficacy of birth control pills."

"Why didn't you warn me? I would have made Ka— my partner use other precautions."

"Three years, Pippa. And how many sexual relationships have you had in those three years?"

She opened her mouth to answer, then closed it.

Dr. Long's severe expression softened. "This is a recent development, I'm guessing?" Pippa nodded. "The young man I saw you with at the gala?"

"Yes."

"As to your second question, I can't tell you what to do. You have options and you know what they are. The one thing I need to know is whether or not you plan to carry the pregnancy to term. If you do, then we'll need to adjust your medications to prevent…complications."

"Complications? You mean like—" Pippa swallowed down a surge of panic. "Like birth defects?"

"Among other things. We'll need to find alternatives to managing your migraines."

Pippa sat quietly, considering. Options. Keep the baby. Give it up for adoption. Abortion. Part of her wanted to run away and just deal with it all by herself. Maybe tell Carrie for moral support but her parents… Oh, Lord, her parents. They would go ballistic. And Kade. What would Kade do? They'd only been close for a matter of months. She had to tell him. And she knew in her heart of hearts that he had a right to help her make the ultimate decision.

"Pippa?"

"I need to think, Dr. Long."

"I figured you might." The doctor scrolled through her computer records. "You'll need to get with Dr. Nevin to begin a step-down on the migraine medications. He won't want you to quit cold turkey. And you didn't ask, but you're about eleven weeks along. We're looking at a January due date."

"Okay," Pippa said with no emotion. Dr. Long looked concerned. "No. I'm fine. Okay, not so much." The soft laugh that escaped bordered on hysterical. "I'll be fine. I'll get through this."

"I know you will, Pippa."

Sitting in her car in the parking lot, Pippa fought the urge to call Carrie so she had a shoulder to cry on. But she couldn't tell Carrie before she told Kade. Or her parents. She dug her phone out of her purse. Should she call him or text him? Not to tell him but to set up a time to talk. Or maybe she should just drive out to the ranch. Yes, that was the ticket. No sense making him fret while she drove out there, right?

Depending on traffic, the drive could take between forty-five minutes and an hour. Pippa caught herself speeding several times. She didn't normally have a lead foot but it was as though the weight in her chest had sunk all the way into her foot. She didn't *want* to get to the ranch fast. Part of her argued that she should turn around and just go home. But she couldn't do that.

Pippa did her best to concentrate on driving but thoughts tumbled through her mind. What would Kade do? They'd really only just begun their relationship. She cared for him a great deal and she suspected she was in love with him. That didn't necessarily mean that she loved him. To her, being *in love* was the butterflies and silly grins, the yearning, the dreaming, the flash of heat. Loving someone over the long haul meant so much more. Being honest with herself, she could admit she'd dreamed about their relationship becoming more. Friends with benefits, lovers, a couple, and then marriage and babies. Wow, had she messed up that timeline.

Another thought intruded. How would the pregnancy affect the funding of her foundation? Would she be able to participate fully in Camp Courage? She had too much going on. Too many decisions.

And she had no one to blame but herself. Pippa had been so cocky and sure that they were covered in the birth control area. Glancing at the speedometer, she eased off the gas pedal again. She glanced at the sign announcing the next exit and cringed. Two more exits and then she'd almost be at the ranch. She had to tell Kade but she had no idea what to say.

"Um, hi, Kade. You're going to be a father." She grimaced. "Yeah, no." She thought some more. "Hey, Kade, we need to talk. You know when I said I was on the pill? Well, about that…"

She continued talking to herself until she turned off the section line road and drove under the arch announcing the ranch's name. Cattle grazed on both sides of the winding drive. As she neared the big house, she could see the smaller pastures closer to the barns. Horses nibbled the early summer grass. She didn't see Kade's truck at first and relief warred with dread. She didn't think she could maintain her equilibrium if she had to wait much longer.

As she passed the big house, Pippa saw Big John unloading groceries from his Explorer. Dusty was dancing around him until the dog saw her Highlander. He chased her all the way to the ranch office. Kade's truck wasn't parked there or at his house, either. She had to focus on breathing around the knot in her chest. She parked at the office but before she could get out, she caught a flash of white in her rearview mirror. Kade's truck. He was driving along one of the ranch tracks.

Steeling herself, she got out and waited for him. Dusty, as if sensing her mood, leaned against her leg rather than his usual jumping and frolicking to get her attention. Her hand dropped to his head and she rubbed the dog's ears.

Kade pulled up but didn't park. The passenger window glided down and he leaned across the seat to call to her.

"Hey, ladybug, did I forget something?" He looked confused but pleased. Pippa wondered how long that expression would last.

"No. I guess I should have called. I know you have work—"

His expression morphed to one of concern. "Work can wait. What's up?"

"I…we need to talk, okay?"

Now he looked blank. "Yeah, sure. Get in. We'll drive over to the house."

That was probably for the best. He reached across and popped the door open for her. She shooed Dusty away, climbed in and shut the door.

"You okay, Pip?"

She didn't answer. She didn't know what to say. They covered the short distance in silence and she waited in the truck while he got out, came around and opened the door for her. "Pip?"

"Inside, okay?" She couldn't look at him, knew the look on his face would kill her.

In the shady interior, he offered her a cold drink, which she declined. She wouldn't sit, either. She couldn't. There was too much nervous energy zinging through her body to settle. All the words she'd planned to say, the ones she practiced on the drive fled as she looked at him. She opened her mouth and two words came out.

"I'm pregnant."

Kade didn't breathe. Surely he hadn't heard that right. But as he looked at her, he saw the truth. And everything snapped into place. The morning sickness. The odd things she'd eaten on their dates. The way her face had rounded, grown softer.

"Mine?" The question was out before he could stop it and regret followed on its heels at the look on her face. He hurried to add, "Of course it is. How far along are you?"

She frowned even after he answered his own question. "Almost three months. And you know it's yours."

"We'll get married. My child is gonna have my name." He blurted that without thinking too, and in a much harsher voice. It was true though. His child would carry his name, would know who his—or her—father was.

"No." Anger flushed Pippa's cheeks.

What did she have to be mad about? He was offering to make an honest woman of her, to give their child a name. Then he wanted to kick himself. His mother's name had been good enough for him. It still was. He lowered his chin and rubbed the back of his neck.

"That came out wrong, Pippa." He glanced at her. "Will you marry me?"

"No." Again with the quick denial.

He felt his own anger surge. "Why not? Am I not good enough for you? Is my name not good enough for our baby? Would the Barron name be more suitable?"

Pippa blanched and Kade felt like the worst SOB. Maybe he carried more of his father's DNA than he thought. He reached for her. "I didn't mean that, Pip. I…this…"

"Yes," she said and he brightened for a moment. Then she continued. "It is…this. I just found out this morning. Got in to see my doctor. She confirmed things. I'm sorry, Kade. I didn't plan this. I…I'm not one of those women who would trap a man like this."

Kade rocked back, stopped himself and reached for her. She jerked away but he went after her. Being as gentle as he could, he reeled her in until he could wrap his arms around her and she was leaning into his chest. "I know, ladybug. I know that."

"I…" She sniffled. "I didn't know my migraine medication would mess with the birth control. I didn't want this to happen."

Cold dread filled him. Was she thinking of doing something drastic? The idea hadn't even occurred to him. Yeah, having a wife and baby would be a huge change but the idea that she might terminate the pregnancy? He stiffened.

Pippa leaned back and stared up at him. "What?" Her

eyes widened and filled with panic. "No. Don't you dare ask me that. Just don't. I can't. I won't. This baby is mine!"

Relief replaced the dread as an adrenaline rush tingled in his extremities. "Never, sweetheart. I would never ask that. I was just…I was afraid that's what you wanted. When you said you wouldn't marry me, that you planned to—"

Her hand covered his mouth, silencing him. "Don't even say it, Kade. Just don't."

"I won't, Pip. Please, come sit down. Okay? We'll talk."

She nodded so he walked backward, drawing her with him until his calves bumped into the couch and they sat. He kept her in the loose circle of his arms and let her find a bit of emotional balance. He needed to find it too. Damn. He was going to be a father. He started to grin.

"It's not funny," Pippa huffed.

"No," he agreed. "It's not. But it is pretty freaking amazing." His enthusiasm shocked her, if her expression was anything to go by. "Marry me, Pip."

She shook her head. "Still no."

"Why? If you're planning—" His breath seized again. "You aren't giving our baby away, are you?" Oh, hell no. He'd fight her every step of the way if that was her plan.

"No. I hadn't really even considered adoption. It's just… your proposal isn't sincere, Kade. It's a knee-jerk reaction. You don't love me."

She had him there. He cared about her but love? What did he really know about love? Still, she was carrying his child and he had a responsibility to them both. "I won't let you deal with this alone, Pippa. I'm in for the long haul."

Kade placed his hand over hers where they cupped her stomach. He had the feeling she wasn't even aware she was doing that. How long would it take before he could feel his child move there? He chuckled, realizing he knew nothing about human pregnancies. Horses and cows? He was an expert.

"Are you laughing at me?"

"No, ladybug. At myself." He started to ask her about marriage again but she cut him off.

"The answer is still no, Kade."

"Fine." His abrupt reply got a startled blink from her and he used her momentary surprise to pull her into his lap. "I'm not going anywhere. I want to marry you, to give our child my name legally. I want to take care of you both. Fair warning—I'm not backing down on this. My father…wasn't one. Not to me, anyway. I won't follow in his footsteps."

Her gaze narrowed and he braced for her next denial. She surprised him when she said, "We don't know each other well enough to get married. We have no choice when it comes to being parents."

"Then let's get to know each other better. We'll keep dating. We'll see where things go. Will you agree to that?"

Suspicion crept into her expression. "It's not that simple, Kade. What's the catch?"

He kissed her pursed mouth before she could avoid him. "No catch, ladybug."

Not much of one anyway. He was determined to wear her down—which, judging by her dubious reaction, wouldn't be easy. They would be married before his child came into the world or his name wasn't Kaden… And then reality slapped him in the face. Because at the root of everything, he was no longer sure exactly who he was.

Thirteen

When he came to Pippa's house, Kade always parked on the street. Then he'd walk up the drive, avoiding the main house, to the guesthouse where Pippa lived. The whole place reeked of luxury. Living around the Barrons should have insulated him from this kind of wealth. Except the Barron brothers didn't flaunt theirs. Not exactly. They were used to obscene amounts of money yet at the same time, they lived mostly normal lives. They lived with the power and money but they didn't throw it in people's faces. Unlike Pippa's parents.

Kade still smarted over the first time he'd arrived at Pippa's invitation for a pool date. Her mother was something else, and every interaction he'd had with the woman since just reinforced his initial appraisal.

He pushed through the ornamental metal gate and headed to Pippa's door. As he approached, raised voices coming from the pool area caught his attention.

"How could you!" Millicent Duncan's voice was as shrill and grating as a screech owl. "What are we going to do, David?"

He could picture the woman wringing her hands, a gesture Kade had seen often enough since he and Pippa had been together. He didn't want to eavesdrop but depending on where they were sitting, he couldn't approach Pippa's door without drawing her parents' attention. He hesitated, taking cover behind some bushes.

"She can always go to a clinic." Pippa's father had a deep voice that carried in the still evening air. "Or we could send her to Europe and place it for adoption after the birth."

A softer voice vibrated with anger. Pippa's. Kade knew it instinctively. He also knew what her father meant by "going to a clinic." They wanted her to abort the baby. *His* baby. Without conscious thought, he charged toward them. No one noticed him. Tensions were running too high. He halted, a potted tree screening him from the three.

"I'm not doing either of those things," Pippa insisted as she stood. She wasn't shouting but her voice carried clearly now. "This is the twenty-first century. Single women have babies all the time."

"Not our daughter," David Duncan snarled.

"But that's the problem, isn't it?" Millicent turned toward her husband. Kade caught her face in profile and the disgust in her expression halted him in his steps. "She *isn't* our daughter."

Those four words were followed by a stunned silence. Face white, Pippa stared at her mother. "What is that supposed to mean?"

Millicent tossed back the remains of the martini in her glass. "You aren't stupid, Pippa. What do you think it means? I didn't give birth to you. Your father is sterile. Our attorneys arranged a closed adoption and we paid your birth mother for you. Twenty thousand dollars."

Pippa stood there, her face devoid of color and emotion. Kade remained frozen.

"That's why you wouldn't give me a detailed health record." Pippa's voice sounded stunned and hurt as she sank back onto her chair as if her knees could no longer support her. When she faced her mother, her eyes looked bruised.

"You are no better than the woman who gave birth to you. She couldn't keep her legs closed either. I want you out of here, Pippa. You aren't my daughter. You never have been."

"Now, Millicent…" David attempted to soothe his wife. "We can work this out to our satisfaction."

"Don't patronize me, David. It was bad enough that she wouldn't date within our circle of friends, and then she went slumming when she started going out with that… that…" Millicent sputtered, evidently too disgusted to finish her accusation. The woman pushed out of her chair and with posture so rigid she might break from the sheer tension, she returned to the house. Eyes straight ahead, she never noticed Kade standing there.

"Dad?" Pippa said. "I don't understand any of this."

"I don't understand how you could be so careless." Her father's voice was coated in disappointment, and something harder, something colder that Kade couldn't quite pin down.

"I wasn't, Daddy." Pippa stretched her hand across the table reaching for her father's. The man jerked it out of her reach and Kade had to shove his hands in his pockets to keep from striking out at him. Instinct told him to wait. Assaulting her father was not the answer.

"You're pregnant, Pippa. It's rather obvious that you were careless." Mr. Duncan pushed back from the table, the metal chair grating on the terrace stones. "Your mother has a point. It will be best for everyone if you go somewhere else for a while. You can come back once you've resolved this situation."

* * *

Pippa had to snap her mouth shut and take several deep breaths before she could speak. "This *situation*?" Her palms protectively curled over her stomach. "I'm having a baby, Dad. Your grandchild."

Her father shrugged as if what she said was of little consequence. "You're young, Pippa. Take care of it, settle back into your role and your mother will eventually come around. This foundation thing should go on the back burner until Millicent can come to grips that you work with charity cases. While I understand your altruistic tendencies—you always were too soft-hearted for your own good—"

"My own good? Are you serious?" She was horrified. The man she loved, the man in whose lap she'd felt warm and safe, was turning out to be a total stranger. She'd never been close to her mother but her dad? He'd been her rock and now he was... Pippa couldn't breathe for a minute. He *wasn't* her dad. Had he ever loved her?

Her father looked bored. "This discussion is over, Pippa. You know what needs to be done. I'll make a reservation for you at the Barron Hotel. You can stay there until you can get a doctor's appointment to deal with this. Then you can move back into the guesthouse. I'll help you convince your mother—"

"But she's not my mother, is she?" The question was out of her mouth before she could stop and think. Just like he wasn't her father. "She was quite emphatic about that, *David*."

He sighed and blasted her with his "I'm so disappointed in you" look. Pippa didn't crumble the way she would have before this evening. In fact, she wasn't feeling much of anything.

"Don't bother with reservations." The coldly controlled

voice came from the shadows behind the potted tree beside the terrace. Kade. She was out of her chair even as her father whirled to face him.

"Pippa has a place to stay—with people who care about her."

Kade strode over, all tall and strong and self-contained. His face held very little emotion but she knew that look. Inside, he was fuming, anger churning like hot lava. He came to her side rather than confronting her father. That was good. She let out the breath she'd been holding. She wouldn't put it past Kade to punch her father's lights out, and then she'd have to spend the night arranging bail for him.

"I'll help you pack up whatever you want to take, Pippa." His big, warm hand on her shoulder was meant to convey support but now she felt hemmed in between these two determined men.

"She's not going anywhere with you, Waite. You're the problem here. Pippa's infatuation with you and your inability to control your base nature—"

"That's enough!" Pippa shook off Kade's hand. "I don't need this. Any of it." She marched toward the guesthouse without looking back, leaving the two men glaring at each other.

"Stay away from my daughter."

Kade laughed at the order, and the sound was chilling. "I thought you just admitted she wasn't yours. Is she or isn't she? Because if she's not your daughter, you have no right to dictate her life. Can't have it both ways, Mr. Duncan."

The sarcasm in his voice was so thick, Pippa would need a steak knife to cut through it. She sped up to cover the short distance to her front door. She fumbled with the knob and a moment later, warmth covered her back.

"Let me help," Kade said. "He headed inside, which is good. I'd have punched him in another minute."

The back door to the main house slammed, the sharp slap of wood on wood echoing in the deepening shadows. Pippa jumped. Kade didn't.

"I'm sorry." She didn't stutter and was glad for her self-control.

"For what, ladybug?"

"How much did you hear?"

"Enough." His arm curled around her waist and he pulled her back against his broad chest. "Probably not all of it, but enough to know they hurt you."

"Are you angry with me?"

He stepped back and she missed his warmth. But he only moved far enough away so he could spin her around to face him. "Why would I be angry with you?"

"My parents aren't precisely…politically correct."

Kade snorted. "Especially not where I'm concerned." He brushed his knuckles across her cheek and ended with a gentle tap on the end of her nose. "But you should know, Pippa. No one gets to treat you that way. I don't care who they are."

His serious expression and the hard glint in eyes gone the color of frozen coffee belied his tender touch. Without thinking, Pippa reached up to cup his face in her palm. "They treat you awful."

"That doesn't matter. But understand, Pippa, I won't stand by and let anyone hurt you. I care about you."

"Why? Why do you care?"

"Because you're carrying my baby."

And there was the real truth, she thought. She thinned her lips in a disapproving frown and twisted away from him. He cared about her but he didn't love her. And truthfully, all that really mattered was the child in her womb.

There were times when she was convinced that was the only reason he was with her. They had horses and the foundation in common. Was it enough? They really were from two distinct social strata and while that didn't matter to her, she suspected it stuck in Kade's craw. Then she remembered. He was a Barron, despite the way he'd grown up. He was the heir to a fortune in land, horses and cattle. If he wanted to be.

She managed to get her door open this time and almost shut it in Kade's face but he was quicker than she was. Choosing to ignore his presence, she flopped down on the couch and rubbed at her temples. Kade was there in a flash.

"Are you okay?"

What a stupid question. Of course she wasn't. She was pregnant by a man who didn't love her, a man despised by her parents, and oh, wait. She'd just discovered she was adopted and that her birth mother had sold her for twenty thousand dollars.

"Let me rephrase that," Kade continued. "I know you aren't okay, not after what happened out there. I meant your head. Do you have a migraine coming on?"

Elbows braced on her knees, Pippa bent forward and dropped her face into her hands. "No. I don't even have a headache." She peeked up at him. "Yet." She sighed, then flopped back, head against the couch. With her eyes closed, she said, "What a mess."

Kade was smart enough to keep his mouth shut. They sat in silence while she thought. Pippa knew her parents. This would all blow over if she just stayed out of sight and kept her head down. Every other time she'd disappointed them, that's what she'd done. Eventually, they forgave her. They would this time, too, and when her baby came into the world they would love her child as much as she did. They would. They had to. They were her parents.

Except they weren't. At least not genetically. She had questions now. Lots of them. Who had her mother been? And her father? Did they have diseases or genetic defects that could affect her baby's life? She needed to find them. Talk to them. Get the answers to her questions. Except how was she going to do that? *Closed adoption.* She knew what that meant. All the files would be inaccessible until her father agreed to help. Did he draw up the papers or would he have had his partner do it? She'd call Leo in the morning…

"Do you want me to help you pack?"

Kade's voice pulled her out of her reverie. She opened her eyes and blinked rapidly at him. "Pack? Why would I pack?"

"I thought your par—" He cut off the word. "Didn't they tell you to leave and not come back until—" His jaw snapped shut. It seemed that she wasn't the only one having trouble finishing sentences and thoughts.

"No. Well, yes, but they didn't mean it."

He eyed her dubiously. "Sure sounded like they did to me."

"The last time Mother got this angry, she threw me out of the house. Dad moved me out here. I was a junior in college. This is my home. They don't really expect me to pack up and—"

A knock on the door interrupted her. Casting an I-told-you-so look toward Kade, she headed to the door. "See? Already forgiven." She opened the door to find her family's longtime housekeeper standing there, her fingers twisting the material of the starched, white apron she wore.

"Delores? What are you doing here?"

"I'm sorry, Pippa. Your mother sent me out here to…" The older woman's face crumpled and tears welled up in her eyes. "I'm supposed to watch you pack and leave so you don't take anything that isn't yours. I'm to get the keys from you." Delores glanced at Kade. "And I'm to call the police if there is any trouble."

Pippa's vision darkened and sparkles danced across the blackness. This wasn't a migraine, but lack of air. She couldn't breathe. Arms surrounded her, steadied her. Warmth at her back. Someone whispering in her ear.

"Easy, ladybug. You need to breathe. We'll deal with this." Kade murmured something else but she didn't understand—couldn't follow his words. He was speaking to the housekeeper. Then she felt a phone being pressed into her hand. "Call Carrie to come help. We'll get you packed and moved out tonight."

She followed his orders but by the time her best friend arrived, Pippa was too numb to help. Thank goodness for Carrie. For Kade. Even Delores. They found her luggage. Packed her clothes, her personal items.

"Furniture?" Kade asked.

Pippa ran her palms over the suede couch she occupied. She loved this couch. Had enjoyed picking it out on a shopping trip with her mother. Mother and daughter had had a lovely day—shopping, lunch, then more shopping followed by massages and mani-pedis at her mother's favorite day spa.

"I'm sorry," the housekeeper said. "Mrs. Duncan says the furniture belongs to the family, not to Pippa. She can only take her clothes and the personal items Miss Carrie packed."

Pippa felt Kade's anger from where he stood behind her. At least she could feel something instead of the icy numbness that had gripped her since the housekeeper's earlier pronouncement.

"Okay," she murmured.

Kade came around the couch, helped her to her feet. "I'm taking you home, Pippa."

"Home?"

"With me. You're staying with me."

Her gaze found Carrie, who hovered nearby.

"That's a good idea, Pip. Go home with Kade until we get this figured out. I'll drive out to see you tomorrow, 'kay?"

"Okay."

Still in a fog, she allowed Kade to draw her outside, listened while Carrie fumbled with her keys. "Change of plans, Kade. I'll follow you to the ranch. Is it okay if I spend the night? Somebody can bring me back in the morning."

"Yeah, fine. What about your car, Carrie?"

"I didn't drive. I caught a cab. Good thing, since I don't want to leave her Highlander here."

Kade nodded curtly. "Understood."

Pippa was glad someone understood what was going on. She certainly didn't. She wasn't sure she would understand anything ever again.

Fourteen

Pippa stretched before opening her eyes. The bed beside her was cold but she'd come to expect that. Kade worked for a living and ranch chores waited for no one. She focused on her body, felt the wave of nausea. Sitting up slowly, she discovered a sleeve of crackers and a can of ginger ale on the bedside table nearest her. She'd read somewhere that eating a couple of crackers before getting up could help control the morning sickness.

She had three crackers and washed them down with the ginger ale. And almost immediately felt better. Who knew? Well, obviously Kade. The thought made her laugh, then she remembered that Carrie had followed them to the ranch the previous night. Her stomach clenched at the ugly memory. What in the world would she do now?

A soft tap at the door was a welcome distraction to her gloom-and-doom thoughts. Her best friend's face appeared in the doorway. "Hey, you. How do you feel?"

That was a loaded question. Pippa sat up and plumped the pillows behind her so she could lean against the headboard. She decided to answer honestly. "I'm not sure."

"Fair enough." Carrie joined her on the bed, sitting on

the end, her back braced against one of the large pine bed-posts. "Kade filled me in on the scene last night. Your mother is a royal—" She bit off the word. "Well, you know what she is. Any clue about what comes next?"

When Pippa shrugged, Carrie continued. "Kade wants you to move in here. I think that's a good idea. I mean, you can work on the foundation from here. And he'd pre-viously offered to stable any horses you purchase before you get a place leased. Heck, given the way he's catering to you right now, he'd probably let you open Camp Cour-age right here!"

"So…" Pippa arched a brow at the other woman. "Your advice is to move in with the man who is barely my boy-friend."

Carrie stuck out her tongue. "Barely? Girl, that horse is so far out of the barn you'll never catch it. He's your baby daddy."

It was Pippa's turn to make a face. "I hate that term. Yes, he and I made a baby together. That doesn't neces-sarily make us a couple."

"It doesn't?" Kade's voice came from the threshold, startling her.

But she was quick to take up the gauntlet. "We're dat-ing, Kade. That's all. At this point, I'm not even sure if we're doing that anymore." Pippa was determined to stand up to him. She was emotionally bruised and refused to let him run over her.

"We're going to be parents, Pip. You're having my baby. Carrie's right. You should move in here. In fact, we should get married."

"No!" Pippa was absolutely adamant. "We aren't hav-ing this discussion again. We are *not* getting married." She glanced at Carrie and held up her hand in a halting gesture. "And don't you start on me either. I refuse to get married just because I'm pregnant. In fact, I should leave here now. Can I stay with you, Carrie? Just until I can find a place of my own."

Carrie's gaze bounced between Kade and Pippa. "Um… sure. I guess."

Pippa climbed out of bed and grabbed some clothes. "I'm leaving, Kade. Just stay away from me until I figure out what to do."

Kade was a patient man. He would wear Pippa down eventually, would convince her that it was best for their child for them to be married. Except she wouldn't take his calls. When he showed up at Carrie's door, Pip refused to see him. He was about ready to kick that door in. It had been close to a month. He'd done as she asked for the first week. Then he called her. Daily. After two weeks, he tried to see her. Often. Luckily, Carrie was on his side and kept him informed. It didn't make him happy that Pippa was miserable too.

He was halfway home from the latest failed attempt to see her when his phone rang. Thinking it was Pippa and that she'd relented, he hit the Bluetooth button and answered. "Hey, ladybug."

"Excuse me?"

Kade recognized that voice. David Duncan. "Sorry, Mr. Duncan, I'm driving and was expecting a call from your daughter so I didn't check caller ID."

His finger hovered over the disconnect button but he decided to find out why Pippa's father would call him.

"If you want what is best for Pippa, stay away from her. While she might not be our biological daughter, she does carry the Duncan name. Millicent and I refuse to allow her to sully it."

"Sully your name? How is she doing that?"

"An illegitimate child is nothing to be proud of. But you wouldn't understand that."

Kade's fingers squeezed the steering wheel like he wanted to strangle Pippa's father. Approaching an exit, he veered over and took it. Pulling into a gas station, he slammed the transmission into Park and leashed his temper as Mr. Duncan continued.

"We're hoping Pippa comes to her senses. If she won't terminate the pregnancy, I'll arrange a private adoption and she can resume her life. Thankfully, she is keeping a low profile and has put plans for her idiotic foundation on hold."

In a frigid but calm voice, Kade said, "If Pippa decides she doesn't want our baby, custody comes to me."

"Yes, well. That is the problem, isn't it? You don't quite fit into our world, now, do you? It would be best if you stop attempting to contact Pippa. In fact, I will file a restraining order against you if you don't desist. You are not a suitable match. You never will be. Stay out of our lives, Waite. I won't warn you again." Pippa's father hung up without waiting for a response.

Kade's fiery temper was replaced by icy resolve. Duncan had implied that he was calling on Pippa's behalf. Was it true that she would deny him access to their child? Kade was not his father. He would not ignore—

His father. Cyrus Barron. Kade was a Barron. Is that what it would take to win Pippa over? He had one more ace up his sleeve before he went down that road. Actually, he had five of them. He dialed a number.

"Savannah? I have a favor to ask."

Pippa was not a happy camper as Carrie exited the highway headed toward the Crown B. Then she saw all the cars parked at the truck stop, and the people lined up to board a shuttle bus. As they neared the ranch, more cars lined the road and the drive when they pulled in. There was a carnival feel to the place—families everywhere. She recognized a passenger van from a local veteran's group, and one from Children's Hospital.

At the big house, the Barron brothers and their wives were holding court over a host of activities. Pony and horse rides. A tractor pulling a trailer piled high with hay and filled with laughing people. Dusty, the ranch dog, and Harley, the Newfoundland belonging to Cash and his new wife, Roxanne, pranced around wearing Camp Courage T-shirts.

Pippa's gaze found the tall dark-haired man holding a small boy on the saddle in front of him, riding around a small temporary corral. Dr. and Mrs. Amadi leaned on the railing waving. The boy offered a tentative smile in return.

What in the world was going on? She glared at Carrie. "Explain!"

Her best friend grinned. "Kade. He knew you wanted to do another fund-raiser so he put this together. With a little help. Deacon Tate is going to sing this afternoon. His whole band is coming. How awesome is this, Pip?"

She had to blink away the moisture in her eyes. "Kade did all this? For me?"

"Well, d'uh, darlin'. Who else would he do this for?"

Pippa stumbled out of Carrie's car and rushed to the corral. She only had eyes for Kade. He stopped his horse, dismounted and carefully lifted the child down. "Here you go, Tyler."

The boy stared up at the tall cowboy with shining eyes. "Thank you."

The whispered words were almost lost to the wind but Pip heard them, as did the Amadis. Mrs. Amadi grabbed Pip in a fierce hug. "He hasn't spoken in six months. Whatever you need, Pippa. We'll underwrite it."

She all but stumbled when the other woman suddenly released her and turned back to the boy crawling through the bars of the fence panel. Before Pippa could say anything to Kade, she was surrounded by a horde of other people. They led her away, all jabbering at her about this and that. She glanced back. Kade raised his hand to the brim of his cowboy hat and tipped it. How could she stay mad at a man who would do all this for her? How could she block him out of her life?

A young man leaning heavily on a cane, his gait uneven due to a prosthetic leg, approached her. "Somebody said you're the lady in charge?" His voice was soft, almost reverent, as he addressed her.

"In charge?" Her brain still hadn't quite caught up with events.

"Yes'm. Camp Courage?" She nodded and he continued. "My buddies—" He waved toward a group of men with various injuries. "We just want to say thank you. Getting outside, working…it makes us feel…" He ducked his head staring at the ground. "Whole." When he looked up, his smile was so shy, Pippa couldn't help herself. She hugged him, blinking back tears.

This! Camp Courage was all about this man and his friends and the children and everyone who'd been broken by life. "You're welcome."

More people came forward to thank her and when Deacon Tate and the Sons of Nashville started singing, she found herself sitting on a hay bale between the wounded warrior and Tyler Amadi. The little boy slipped his hand into hers and she fought back tears.

Later, as the sun slipped toward the Western hills, after the concert and with the crowd thinning, Pippa looked up from saying goodbye to another group to find Kade walking toward her leading a horse. "Want a ride, little girl?"

She bit down on her lips in a vain effort to hide her smile. "You are a very hard man to ignore."

"Yup."

Pippa spread her arms and turned in a slow circle. "Why did you do this?"

Kade stared at her, forehead furrowed in confusion. "Because it was important to you."

The internal box where she'd kept her emotions locked up burst like it had been hiding fireworks. She was pretty sure she loved this man. And whether he could say the words to her or not didn't seem all that important at the moment. His actions spoke so much louder.

"C'mon. I want to go for a ride."

Before she could react, Kade had lifted her into the saddle. He swung up behind her a moment later and reined the horse away from the lingering crowd. He settled her a little more comfortably across his thighs, one hand resting on her now-rounded tummy. She relaxed back against him, lulled by his touch and the horse's plodding gait.

"Thank you."

He kissed the back of her neck. "For what?"

"For doing all of this. For being you. For giving me the space I need."

"Will you marry me, Pippa?"

She rolled her eyes and swiveled her head around so she could kiss him. "No." Kade stiffened but she kissed him again. "I'm not ready. Not yet." Pippa could toss him that bone.

"I'm going to keep asking."

"I know. Maybe I'll surprise us both one of these days and say yes."

Fifteen

Kade was starting to hate the view from this window. He glared at his reflection in the glass. The door opened and he heard muffled voices. Shoes shuffled softly across the thick carpet. Refreshments had arrived. The waiting was wearing thin.

If he'd thought this out, he would have called Chance to set up an appointment. Instead, when he saw his baby at Pippa's ultrasound that morning, he'd made a snap decision after she declined his proposal yet again. At least they were in agreement about her father and his threats. Pippa had words with him and he hadn't contacted Kade again.

Upon his arrival in the Barron & Associates offices, he'd been ushered into Chance's inner sanctum. Kade had commenced with trying to explain his reason for being there in halting sentences, but Chance stopped him.

"I want to call a family meeting."

Now Kade was second-guessing everything. Cord and Cash arrived simultaneously and both greeted him from across the room. He nodded in silent response then returned his gaze to the vista beyond the window. He breathed through a momentary bout of panic when Clay appeared. He hadn't realized the senator was in town. About ten minutes later, Chase rushed in.

"Sorry. I had to convince Savannah to stay put." He tossed a lopsided grin Kade's direction. "She's really upset with you, dude. She wanted to be here."

Kade couldn't understand why she would, so he asked, "Why?"

Chase finished pouring a cup of coffee and grabbed a doughnut before answering. "For one thing, she's guessed what's going on and wants to officially be your sister. Well…sister-in-law. And you're avoiding her. She was really insistent about coming, though I'm not sure if it was because she wants to chew you out or defend you from us evil Barrons." He said the last with a mischievous grin but quickly sobered. "So…seriously, bro. She's feeling hurt. Why *are* you avoiding her?"

Kade dropped his chin to his chest and stared at the toes of his boots. He didn't want to answer that question—not in front of these men, one of whom was Savannah's husband. Even though Chase and Savannah were polar opposites, they loved each other deeply and Kade was happy for her. Chase continued staring at him, waiting for his answer.

"Yeah, about that. Been sorta busy. I'll call her."

"When?" Kade glanced up to discover amused annoyance on Chase's face. "Because she's gonna want to know. Look, bro. We've been really patient and we—" he swept a hand across the room to encompass his brothers "—have done our best to keep the wives out of the loop. You have no idea what they're like. Well, Savannah maybe, but I'm tellin' ya, we are all under pressure." Chase's grin was unrepentant. "Chance insisted we give you space, especially after that bombshell you dropped about dating Pippa. You have met our wives, right? Trying to hold them back is like trying to stop a flash flood with a bucket of sand."

Chance fixed a withering stare on his younger brother. "Cool it, Chase."

Kade knew Chase was teasing and it made him feel odd. He'd always maintained a friendly aloofness in his dealings with the Barron brothers. With Cyrus Barron, the relationship had most definitely been employer and employee.

When Chance appeared next to him, he concentrated on keeping his emotions in check.

"It doesn't have to be this hard, Kade."

"Did you know?" He studied Chance, then shifted his gaze to the other men seated around the conference table. "Did you know who I am?"

"Not for sure," Chance replied. "We suspected you were related to us, but the old man never let on you were anything more than his ranch manager. That said, when the will named you, we weren't exactly shocked either."

Jamming his hands into his front pockets so Chance wouldn't see the fists he made, Kade turned his head just enough to see his half brother in profile. "It doesn't make you mad? Any of you? I'm…nobody, and your father decreed that y'all had to hand over a major part of your inheritance to me. How does that not make you angry?"

Chance leaned his shoulder against the window. After a long moment of studying Kade, he spoke. "He was your father, too, Kade. That makes you our brother, whether you accept us or not. Does this situation suck? Absolutely." Chance quickly held up his hand to stay the argument forming on Kade's lips. "We already have what we want from this deal. That's not why I say it sucks. We know you. We understand that the ranch means everything to you. Nothing has been done yet. I filed an injunction against the ranch trustees to give you time to decide."

Glancing around at his brothers, Chance returned his

focus to Kade. "If it was up to us, you wouldn't have to do a thing to keep your job. And I want to apologize to you. It never occurred to me that the old man would so totally screw things up. The ranch has always been like home to us, but I think that has more to do with the fact that Big John and Miz Beth live there. Even so, I knew what an SOB Cyrus could be. When I originally set up the family trust that secured what was important to each of us—knowing he would mess with things to get his way—I just didn't believe that our father would be this callous."

Chance inhaled and raised his chin, as if avoiding a blow. "If I had, I would have taken steps to prevent it. The old man outfoxed us. He outmaneuvered me and set up a blind trust that I can't break. Believe me, after seeing your reaction when Stephenson read the will, I looked into it. I'm sorry."

"We're all to blame, Chance," Clay said, walking over. "Each of us had our own little fiefdom picked out. Our father loved to play us against each other, even when we were kids." He tilted his head toward Chase and Cash. "Especially after you two came along." He offered a wry grin to the twins. "Cord, Chance and I didn't buy into his BS. And Kade, we still don't. When he first hired you, I remembered wondering from the moment I saw you. The more we were around you, the more we wondered. But like Chance said, the old man never gave a hint. It's up to you whether you want to change your name." Clay gripped Kade's shoulder. "We'd be proud to call you brother whether your last name is Waite or Barron."

Kade stared at the one brother who'd remained silent. Cash returned his gaze without a flinch. "How do you feel about this?" Kade asked.

Cash continued to watch him and the silence stretched thin—almost to the breaking point—before he spoke. "I did a background check on you when I took over Barron Security."

He wasn't surprised but he waited, figuring Cash had more to say. He wasn't disappointed.

"There was no paper trail, no indication whatsoever that you were one of us. Trust me when I say that the old man, all of us, in fact, have dealt with our share of gold diggers who wanted a piece of our pie. Then there was you. You graduated from OSU with a degree in agricultural science. You came to work here. Dad was adamant about hiring you. I remember him and the head wrangler arguing about it. Manuel was convinced you were too young and inexperienced. Not that he wanted to take on the place. None of us did. Dad stuck Cord in charge—nominally—as CEO of Barron Land and Cattle."

Pausing to sip from his coffee cup, Cash looked at each of his brothers before his gaze settled once more on Kade. "I didn't trust you. I watched, double-checked the books, had my forensic accountant stay on top of things."

Kade stiffened at this admission. This was what he'd been expecting all along—that proverbial other shoe. He knew there was no way it could be all flowers and sunshine with the brothers.

"Imagine my surprise," Cash continued, "when you proved me wrong. Everything you did, you did for the Crown B. The grazing program you initiated. The breeding program where you emphasized quality over quantity. Because of that, you demanded and got top dollar on our stocker calves. And the horses?" He looked to Chance. "That's your area of expertise, Chance. Your assessment?"

Chance barked out a short laugh. "You tryin' to get me in trouble, little brother? The whole reason I met Cassidy was because the old man wanted to get his hands on her quarter horse stud." He cut his eyes to Kade. "Was it you who wanted Doc?"

"Not exactly. I wanted a stud *like* Doc but I thought I could breed him on my own."

Chance nudged Kade's shoulder with his own. "I figured it was the old man's grudge against Cassie's dad. And you were right. You did breed a super horse. Imp is…" He laughed again, humor suffusing the sound. "Amazing. And my wife is totally jealous."

That startled a chuckle out of Kade. "She has a yearling mare I'm keeping my eye on—"

"And that sums it up," Cash interrupted. "Kade, you're like one of those old Louis L'Amour cowboys." He addressed his brothers with his next comment. "Y'all remember all those paperbacks up in the playroom at the ranch? Granddad was always reading them. L'Amour and Zane Grey. One of the main themes in those books was riding for the brand. You do, Kade. You've always done what was right for the Crown B. Not for yourself, but because it was best for the ranch and therefore the family. In fact, you're such a white hat, it's kinda scary."

"Bottom line," Clay said. "You're our brother. To us, your decision should be easy. The ranch would be yours. What's to even think about? But we aren't you. We grew up Barrons. You grew up…not." He winced a little. "Sorry. For a man used to making speeches, that was lame. I need Georgie here. My wife knows exactly what to say. Thankfully, she still writes my speeches." He chuckled, then his expression turned serious. "Thing is, we can't force you to choose one way or the other. But we also can't fix the situation about your job if you don't accept us as family. Our father tied our hands with the trustees he appointed."

We can't force you to accept us as family. That's not precisely what Clay said, but that's what Kade heard. Did he have a choice in this? If he walked away, his unborn child would suffer. If he stayed, he lost who he was. But was that the truth? He didn't want to consider that Pippa might be correct—that names didn't matter when it came down to what made a person. Still, he knew *who* Kaden Waite was. He had no clue about Kaden Barron. If he signed the papers, what would happen when he woke up the day after? Would he recognize the face staring back from the mirror?

Kade mentally shook himself. That was a ludicrous reaction and he knew it. He could walk out of this room. He could find another job on another ranch. But. And that *but* was what kept him standing here. Pippa was having his child. She refused to marry him, and he needed to stay close. He hoped to persuade her because the idea of his child growing up without his father's name—and more importantly—without his father? The whole notion was unthinkable. They fought over this constantly and each time, his heart shredded a little more. Why couldn't she understand his need to provide for her and the baby, and to ensure the baby had his name? Whichever name he chose. He almost laughed at the irony. Here he was insisting their baby carry his name and he didn't even know what it was…or would be.

Without conscious thought, he placed his palm on the back of his neck and rubbed at the tension lodged there. Kade was thankful he'd skipped breakfast. His stomach ached as if he'd eaten bad food and a wave of nausea rolled over him. This shouldn't be such a big deal, but it was. He studied each of his new brothers, considered what he knew of them.

Clay was the oldest. He'd been running for Congress when Kade first went to work at the Crown B. He'd found the older man to be intense, focused and honorable. He'd also been aloof and mostly blind to Cyrus Barron's machinations. Until he'd fallen in love with the woman who'd become his wife. Clay had walked away from his campaign for the presidency because Georgie became ill and needed him. Kade had been surprised.

Of all the Barrons, the next brother in line would most likely identify with Kade's dilemma. Cord had reunited with his first love after discovering she'd had his son—and had hidden the fact. At least Pippa wasn't trying that. Kade would go freaking crazy if she tried. Now Cord, Jolie and CJ were a family.

The youngest of the first set of Barron brothers, Chance had been the first to break away from their father's yoke. He'd stood up to Cyrus—and his brothers—in order to marry the woman who'd roped his heart. Now Chance and Cassidy were building a ranch and breeding program that might rival the Crown B's one day.

That left the twins, born to Cyrus' second wife. For all that Chase and Cash were identical in looks, their personalities were almost exact opposites. Chase was the carefree playboy living the high life in Vegas, Hollywood and Nashville. He'd been roped and tied by a real Oklahoma cowgirl. Kade still hadn't quite wrapped his brain around that development nor completely reconciled the fact that the girl he considered his kid sister had married and fallen in love with Chase—in that order.

Cash was the black sheep of the family, only that wasn't totally fair. From what Kade had observed, the youngest Barron was the one most entrenched—or maybe ensnared was the better description—in the Barron patriarch's schemes. In the end, though, Cash had seen the light. His brothers kept him in the fold and Cash's new wife had brought him lightness and laughter.

Kade had never been one to speak ill of the dead but

looking around the table at the five Barron brothers, they were in a much better place now their father was gone. Kade had always been a student of human nature and none of the Barrons appeared to be lying when they spoke of the ranch and the fact it should be his. All they asked was that it remain their home as well. As if he would really toss Big John and Miz Beth out? He didn't want the big house. It wasn't his home. The manager's house? He'd made the place his and it had a second, smaller bedroom that would work as a nursery.

Since his grandfather's death, Kade hadn't been back to Davis much. His grandmother no longer recognized him and his mother had started a life without him once he left for college. He hadn't liked the reason she kept his parentage from him. These five men and their wives were waiting to welcome him into their family as a full-fledged member. A brother.

Turning away to stare out the window again, Kade considered his options. In the end, the reality of this decision came down to his responsibilities.

"Where do I sign?"

Sixteen

Kade signed slowly, each letter almost painful to put to paper. He wondered how long it would take him to feel comfortable writing his new name. He almost smiled thinking maybe he should practice like the girls in high school used to do, filling up pages of lined notebook paper writing their "married" names whenever they dated a boy more than a couple of times.

Kaden William Waite. Kaden William Barron. His hand was steady, which surprised him a bit. He didn't want to think about this, what he was doing. He didn't want to be angry about getting shoved in this corner. He'd searched for a way out of the conundrum and hadn't found one. All the conversations echoed in his head.

He'd originally told Pippa, "I can't be a Waite. I have to be a Barron."

Her reply had basically been *So what?* and that made him angry. Her exact words were, *Is that so bad?* She went on to explain her thought process, telling him he would be the same man, not someone different. *You'd still be Kaden. The name doesn't make a person. It's just a label.*

But names and labels defined a person, didn't they? He

thought back to the beginning when he first found out. Each of the Barrons—his brothers—had reached out to him. They hadn't written him off, hadn't pushed things. Chance's reaction had been measured. Since he was an attorney, it made sense. He understood the shock, and Chance wanted to talk things out, discuss the situation.

Clay, as the oldest brother, had taken a more pragmatic approach—a simple welcome to the family and a suggestion to talk to Chance. Cord, next oldest, had been blunt. To Cord, walking away was a stupid reaction, but he expressed a willingness to wait for Kade to come to terms. *We're here when you're ready,* he'd said. Cash and Chase had double-teamed him as twins would. Cash had been teasing—talking about hunting Kade down, then offering to meet for a beer and conversation. Chase had mentioned their wives. Since Chance's marriage to Cassie, Kade had seen just how the women worked. And everything they did was for the good of their men.

His chest burned at that thought. He could admit he was jealous of his brothers now. Calling them that still felt strange but it got easier each time. All he had to do was look at them with their wives to know how much love was there. He *wanted* that. And he wanted it with Pippa. Maybe as a Barron, she would find his name suitable for their child.

Names were important, no matter what others said to him. Cyrus Barron thought bestowing his name on his bastard son was so important that he came back from the grave to force the name on Kade.

His mother's voice whispered in his ear. *That's a terrible position to be in, but have you considered this?* He remembered the expression on her face as she'd asked that question—the sadness mixed with concern. *What if I'd given you up?* He could have been in the same position as Pippa. He would have been adopted. And he definitely wouldn't be Kaden Waite. Or Kaden Barron.

Rose had barely given him time to digest that when she'd hit him with her next hypothetical question. *What if he'd been single and we'd married?* In the time since his talk with her, he had contemplated that one. A lot. He wasn't a physicist and the whole idea of parallel dimensions was a little beyond him, but if that had happened, the odds of Chase and Cash being born were probably between slim and none. It was more than he could—or wanted to—wrap his head around.

He hesitated over writing his last name. His mom's last question was the one that he considered now. *What if I'd simply added his name to your birth certificate?* When he looked down at the papers on the conference table in front of him, he saw the answer she'd given him. Kaden William Barron.

"So what happens now?"

Chance's expression was solemn. "I've already made arrangements with Judge Nelligan. We're doing the name change under an emergency order. The judge has waived the publication period and is signing under seal so the news won't be common knowledge until we're ready to go public. He's expecting us as soon as we can walk over."

Once the gears were set in motion, everything happened with lightning-speed. When Kade walked from Barron Tower to the Oklahoma County Courthouse, all five Barrons were with him. It felt strange. In a few minutes, there would be six Barron brothers. They cleared security then shouldered their way through the crowd getting off an elevator. Kade was very conscious of the looks they received, looks the others seemed oblivious to. He wondered if he'd ever get to a point when he wouldn't notice.

The elevator dinged for the third floor and Chance got

off first, the other Barrons following. They passed groups of people and Kade noticed a woman watching the six of them. She looked vaguely familiar but he couldn't place where he might know her from.

When his party stopped in front of the judge's chamber, he glanced back at her. She had her smartphone out and pointed down the hallway toward them. He quickly turned his back.

The judge's chamber was comprised of a waiting room and the judge's office, along with offices for his bailiff and clerk. Kade and Chance entered the inner office, leaving the rest of their brothers in the outer area. Judge Nelligan rose to shake hands with Chance, who introduced Kade.

"I've got the court clerk coming up here with his seal. We'll get this taken care of as soon as he gets here." A quick tap on the door heralded the clerk's arrival.

Kade wasn't sure what he expected to happen. Chance hadn't prepared him and he was glad there wasn't any sort of real ceremony—just more signatures under the watchful eye of the court clerk, who then stamped the legal papers. Just like that, he was Kaden Barron.

His brothers stood as he and Chance exited. Kade expected handshakes. He got hugs.

"Welcome to the family, Kade."

"About freaking time."

"Y'all realize there's an even number now."

Deep voices rimmed with laughter and affection surrounded him. He should have felt overwhelmed. He didn't. He felt…accepted. And the emotion left him reeling. He just hoped he'd have time to get his bearings before his world changed even more.

Furious beyond all reason, Pippa drove straight to the ranch. This was not a conversation to hold over the phone.

She flew past the big house and skidded to a stop in front of the ranch office. Storming inside, she glared at the woman occupying the front desk.

"Where is he, Selena?"

The ranch secretary shrugged. "Haven't seen him this morning."

A moment later, Pippa had both hands on the desk and was leaning forward to glower at the woman. "Don't cover for him."

"I'm not, Pippa. I really haven't seen him. He could be at his house, one of the barns or he could be out on the ranch somewhere. He doesn't always check in with me."

"He's not answering his phone."

That made Selena laugh. "Well, d'uh. All things considered, would you?"

And that was the problem, wasn't it? Her phone had blown up with calls and text messages as soon as the news leaked, along with a cell phone video. "If he comes back, you tell him to keep his butt right here until I've talked to him."

Selena arched a brow and, fighting a grin, snapped a salute. "Yes, ma'am."

Pippa retreated from the office and stood on the porch wondering what to do. A musical whistle made up her mind. She knew that sound—Kade calling Imp. With determination in every step, she headed to the large corral adjacent the horse barn. She stopped as she turned the corner and saw Kade.

His forearms rested on the top rail of the fence. His stance was relaxed, feet shoulder-width apart. Worn jeans fit him in all the right places and the white T-shirt stretched across his broad torso and muscular biceps. He wore a baseball cap, the bill tipped up as he watched Imp, his pride and joy, frolic with two other yearling colts.

"Why didn't you answer your phone?" she demanded as she stomped toward him.

He turned his head slightly to acknowledge her presence before he returned his attention to the corral.

"Well?" she asked again as she reached him.

"I left my phone at the house."

Pippa huffed. "Likely excuse."

That got an angry glance from Kade. "I'm not glued to the thing like most people."

"What's that supposed to mean?"

"Nothing, Pippa. Nothing at all." He sounded worn out but she was too wound up to really notice.

"How could you!" she challenged.

He ignored her.

"Seriously, Kade. This is…it's…not a little thing."

"No. Not by a long shot." His jaw worked as though he was gritting his teeth.

"That's an understatement because I was trying to be nice. This is…it's huge. You've just changed everything. You should have asked me." Pippa was all but quivering from pent-up anger. "This affects me too. And the baby."

Kade gripped the top rail of the fence until his knuckles turned white. "I'm aware of that."

She wanted to hit him, to pound her fists against his chest. She felt hot and cold all at the same time. "Why? Why would you do this without telling me?" Both hands lifted, fists closed, and she fought her urges. "Do you have any idea how I felt waking up to the news? Carrie came running in screaming, and bounced on my bed. She was thrilled beyond reason."

He continued staring into the corral, watching the three horses mill around. "Do you have any idea how I felt signing the papers?" His voice was a rough whisper, barely more than the sound of sandpaper on wood.

"I don't care!" Pippa snapped at him as she jerked her phone out of her pocket and waved it in front of him. "It's already started. My mother. My father. Everyone involved. You've let them win because you are *acceptable* now. You're a freaking Barron. The prodigal son. The lost heir. She's hiring a wedding planner this morning."

He looked at her then and what she saw on his face made her take a step back. "Did you tell her that's a waste of time because you refuse to marry me?"

"I won't marry you just to keep my child from being a bastard."

"It's my child too."

"Not if I have anything to say about it."

Pippa didn't think Kade could appear any more intimidating than when she'd first walked up but looking at him now? His face had turned to chiseled granite and his eyes looked as hard as agate.

"Be very careful what you say next, Pippa."

She didn't speak. She reacted, her hand flying out to slap him. The sound was so sharp it sent the horses galloping to the other side of the corral. Kade didn't move but his face went completely blank; all the life fled from his eyes. Bile rose in Pippa's throat, threatening to choke her, but she'd gone too far to turn back now.

"We're done." She turned on her heel, and barely managing to keep her head and shoulders straight, she walked with great deliberation back the way she'd come. As she turned the corner of the barn, she glanced back. Kade hadn't moved.

Kade stared into the amber liquid in the beer mug. He'd come to Shorty's to get drunk, not share his feelings with his…brothers. The word froze his brain.

Cash occupied the stool on his left while Cord leaned

against the bar on his right. They bracketed him and he fought a wave of claustrophobia.

"How did you find me?"

Cash laughed heartily and slapped him on the back. "You forget what I do for a living, Kade."

"Selena called you."

"No," Cord said. "She called Chance. She saw Pippa's Highlander tearing down the drive and then your truck doing the same a few minutes later."

"And Chance called me. I pinged your cell phone. Then I called Cord."

Kade slowly glanced from one man to the other. "You pinged my phone? How does that work?"

Smirking, Cash said, "If I revealed my methods, I'd have to kill you. Or something." After a dry chuckle, he added, "That was a joke, dude. You're supposed to laugh."

"Not much to laugh about just now," Kade admitted.

Cord took several deep swallows of his beer. "You gonna explain?"

"She's pissed."

"What did you do?"

Killing his beer in one long drink, Kade snarled, "I signed the damn papers."

"Why is she mad about that?" Cash exchanged a look with Cord.

"I didn't tell her I was changing my name."

The brothers exchanged a second look. Kade, staring in the mirror behind the bar, missed nothing. It was Cord's turn to question him. "So…why is that a problem? All things considered, I'd think she'd be thrilled."

Kade didn't respond, defaulting to killing the beer in his mug with long gulps. Silence stretched between them until the jukebox came to life and the voice of Kenny Chesney crooned his song, "There Goes My Life." Kade stilled, listening to the words—the story of a boy and a girl and the baby they made, all set around a refrain that echoed the song's title. He was ready to change his life, to give up who he was so he could become who Pippa and their child needed. He couldn't understand why she was so obstinate. And why she was so mad about what he'd done. He'd done it for her. For their baby.

He didn't realize a tear had escaped until Cord gripped his shoulder. He angrily brushed his shirtsleeve across his cheek when he realized his skin was wet.

"Man, you need to talk to us," Cash encouraged. "There's obviously something more going on here."

"She's pregnant."

Seventeen

Was she being foolish? After her parents' declaration, Pippa had decided to search for her birth family. This was probably a stupid idea, considering how messed up everything was between her and Kade. Still, she needed to find out, needed to know where she came from. Odd how her life now paralleled Kade's. She thought they were moving toward something truly special. Then he'd done the unthinkable and she'd confronted him. Could she fault him for accepting his birth family when she was so desperately searching for her own? Maybe once she knew about her roots she'd understand. Maybe then she would call him and they could talk.

When she first decided to do this, Pippa had gone straight to Chance to get him to file for her original birth certificate. When he'd handed it to her, she'd stared at it—at her birth name and the name of her birth mother. Disappointment had washed over her when no father was listed and for a moment, she understood how Kade might feel, given his situation. Still, she had her original name. Marcia Rae Gore. She'd tasted it on the tip of her tongue like it was a rare vintage of wine as she'd read it the first time.

After adjusting to the idea of being adopted and having been born with another name, she'd gone hunting.

When she found no leads, she'd turned the search over to a professional—Cash Barron. Thirty-two days later, Cash had called and asked for a meeting at his office. Now she was here, sitting across from him at his desk. A large envelope sat on the blotter in front of him.

"Did you find anything?" She hated that her voice quavered. This shouldn't have been so nerve-racking.

Cash watched her for a tense moment. "Are you sure you want to do this?"

Pippa stared at the envelope resting on the desk. Her heart pounded and she kept her hands clutched in her lap so Cash wouldn't see how badly they were trembling. Taking deep breaths to ease her nerves, she eventually nodded.

He held out the envelope without a word though the expression on his face spoke volumes. She reached for it but had to shake the numbness out of her hand before accepting.

Pushing back from his desk, Cash said, "I'll give you some privacy."

"No!" Her demand came out far more forcefully than she'd anticipated. "No," she added in a quieter tone. "Is it bad? I…the way you're acting. It's bad news, isn't it?"

Cash scrutinized her, his expression not giving anything away. "I don't know how to answer that question, Pippa." He drummed the desk with the fingers of his right hand but then stilled as he continued. "I believe Kade should be here when you open it."

Shocked, her mouth dropped open. "Kade? Why on earth would you even think of him?"

Cash's gaze dropped pointedly to her midsection where she'd begun to show more than a baby bump. "Because he has an investment in this too. And…" Cash's voice softened. "Because he cares about you, about your baby."

"Oh, he's all about the baby," she snapped. "He's all about having his name on the birth certificate."

Arching a brow, Cash didn't say anything. When she didn't continue, he spoke. "It's more than that, Pippa, and I think you know it."

"You don't know anything about it, Cash. About us. Kade and me. He's all *Let's get married because my baby needs a father.* That's stupid. We don't have to get married. In fact, I don't want to get married." She glared when Cash snorted in disbelief. "I don't. Kade doesn't love me. Why would I marry someone who is only doing it out of some misguided sense of obligation? What kind of home is that for a baby? Just stay out of it. You aren't involved."

"Kade is my brother, Pip. And that baby will be my niece or nephew. We're all involved."

"Really? You're all about family now, Cash? Heck, you didn't know anything about him being family until a few months ago."

He inhaled as if reaching for patience. When he continued, he used a soft voice and spoke carefully. "I know what's in the envelope, hon. Please, let me call Kade."

Her stomach knotted up and she had to breathe around the clutch in her chest. She'd started this search to find answers to her medical history. She had a deep-seated fear there would be some horrible genetic anomaly or medical issue in her biological family. Cash had never been known for his empathy, but the compassionate look on his face at this moment terrified her. "It's bad. Really bad, isn't it?"

Cash didn't say a word; he just reached for the phone on his desk.

When the phone on Chance's desk beeped, he held up a finger for Kade to wait. Figuring it was business important enough for Chance's assistant to interrupt their meeting, Kade rose and walked to the bookshelf across the office. He expected it to be filled with law books. He was surprised to discover biographies, histories and a whole shelf dedicated to classic science fiction and Westerns. He turned to discover Chance still on the phone but watching him intently.

"No, this can wait. We'll be right down." Chance hung up and stood. "That was Cash. Pippa is in his office. We need to get down there."

Kade couldn't move. Couldn't breathe. Couldn't talk. He could barely put one foot in front of the other for all the thoughts winging through his brain. Why was she with Cash? Was she hurt? What had happened? He blinked, realized Chance was already to the door of the office. He followed hot on the other man's heels as they rushed toward the interior stairwell. Cash's office was located only two floors down. He and Chance could cover the distance faster on the stairs than waiting for the elevator.

No one stopped them as they slammed through the massive doors of Barron Security and headed toward Cash's private office. Cheri, Cash's assistant, waved them toward his door. Chance tapped twice, then opened it. He stepped back to let Kade precede him into the room. Kade stopped when he saw Pippa, looking frightened and lost, sitting in one of the armchairs.

His first instinct was to rush to her and pull her into a hug. His second was to throw a punch at Cash since the other man obviously had something to do with putting that look on Pippa's face. It was, however, his third—and most measured—instinct that prevailed, especially as Pippa's expression clouded over with anger when she realized he was in the room.

Cash stood up behind his desk. "Thanks for coming,

Kade. I suspect Pippa will need you once she reads what's in that envelope. Chance and I will be outside if you two need us."

With that, Cash and Chance exited the office, leaving him alone with Pippa. She was holding a large envelope. He approached her slowly, hands loose at his sides, like he would with a skittish horse. He checked her over. Her stomach had rounded even more than the last time he'd seen her, but she looked tired and the dark circles under her eyes concerned him. "Pippa?"

"Go away, Kade."

Her shoulders slumped and she sounded worn out. He hadn't seen her in more than a month. He had no clue why she was sitting here in Cash's office, but he was starting to wonder if Cash and Chance had set him up. He wouldn't put it past them—or any of the Barrons, their wives included. The whole family seemed intent on getting him hooked up with Pippa.

Kade squatted down on his heels next to her chair, his hand on the wooden arm, ostensibly to maintain his balance. "What's going on, ladybug?"

"None of your business, Kade."

"It is if it's something that concerns you."

She shifted away from him but it appeared to be more so she could twist to look at him than to put distance between them. "Do you really not know?"

"Not a clue. I was up in Chance's office going over some paperwork regarding the transfer of the Crown B. The next thing I know, he's on the phone. He hangs up, tells me we need to get down here and…" He spread his hands. "Here I am."

Pippa huffed out a breath and started to push a lock of her hair back when she seemed to realize she was still holding the envelope. Kade hooked the errant strand with his finger and tucked it behind her ear. "Talk to me, Pip. Please?"

"The fight I had with my parents. It started because I wanted a medical history. That's when Moth… Millicent told me I was adopted. It might be dumb, or insignificant in the long run, but I want to know where I came from. What and who I am. What health problems I might have or could pass on. So, after thinking about it, I hired Chance. He petitioned to get my birth certificate. The original one. And my adoption papers."

Kade did his best not to tense. This was the first he'd heard of her request. "Is that what's in the envelope?"

"No. I got those about two months ago. My birth name was Marcia Rae Gore. My mother was listed but not my father."

He winced. Yeah, he knew all about that kind of birth certificate. He jerked when her hand landed on his arm. He immediately schooled his expression.

"I'm sorry, Kade. I wasn't thinking. I…it's weird. I was disappointed that I didn't have a name to put with my father, but I had my mother's. It was enough." She lifted one shoulder in a delicate shrug. "Or I thought it would be. Since I had her name, I figured it would be easy enough to locate her."

"Did you?"

Pippa shook her head. "No. I thought I had decent computer search skills and Carrie's mother is into genealogy. We couldn't find anything." She looked away and inhaled. "I asked Cash to do a search for her. I mean, that's what he does, right?"

Her gaze flicked to him then, as if asking his…his what? Permission? Acceptance? This was the longest conversation they'd had since she stormed out of the barn. He didn't want to break this fragile truce springing up between them. "Yeah, it's one of the things he does. Background checks, searching for missing persons. Stuff like that. You were smart to come to him."

"You think so?"

The hope on her face almost broke his heart. Cash knew he and Pippa were estranged. For him to arrange for Kade's presence—and there was no doubt in his mind that this was anything *but* a setup—meant that whatever was in that envelope was going to upset Pippa.

"Yeah, he's the best. I'm guessing he found something?"

Glancing at the envelope, she nodded. "Yeah. But I haven't opened it yet." She suddenly thrust it at him. "Will you open it?"

He didn't immediately take the envelope. Instead, he stared into her eyes. He was praying this was a break in their stalemate, that she was giving him an opening so he could come back into her life. But he had to be positive this was the case. "Are you sure you want *me* to do that?"

Pippa stared back, her expression as solemn as his own surely was. She didn't speak for a long moment. Then she pressed her lips together and nodded—a short, jerky motion. "Yes. Please?"

He accepted the envelope. It hadn't been sealed so he slid out the small sheaf of papers inside.

"Read it, Kade. Then tell me what it says." Pippa sounded certain even as her voice quavered slightly.

"Okay." He partially rose and pulled the second guest chair closer so he could sit right next to her. Settling into the padded leather, he scanned the first page. Then the second. By the third, he had to fight to keep any emotion off his face. He had no idea how Pippa would react to this news. He suspected she wouldn't take it well. He wouldn't if their places were reversed.

Just in case he'd misread the information, Kade started

at the beginning, reading slowly this time through. Pippa's hand touched his thigh, squeezed gently. He dropped his hand to take hers, lacing their fingers. He finished the first page and, letting go of Pippa for a brief moment, placed it face down on Cash's desk. He took her hand again and continued reading, repeating his action with each page. He didn't stop until he'd read the last word.

He hadn't been mistaken on his first reading. And he knew Cash would have been extra thorough in this investigation. How was he going to tell her the messy details that were so neatly laid out in print? His chest hurt for Pippa, and he wasn't sure he could speak around the lump in his throat. Her hand trembled in his and he gave it a soft squeeze.

"It's really bad, isn't it?" Pippa shook her head. "No, don't say anything. When I asked Cash the same thing, he told me he didn't know what to say, and he called you to come."

"Yeah, he called me." Kade cut his gaze toward the door. "I'm glad I was close by, ladybug."

"I'm scared, Kade. You should just tell me. You know, like ripping off a bandage."

He wanted to gather her into his lap so he could cradle her. He didn't want to tell her what Cash had uncovered, not while looking into her scared eyes. He'd much prefer whispering it into her hair with the hopes she wouldn't hear. But he couldn't do any of those things. While she might not realize what she was doing, he did. She trusted him enough to take the bad news and give it to her.

He swallowed, hard. The first word he tried to speak got caught and he had to clear his throat. "Your mother. She's still alive. And you have siblings. Two sisters and two brothers."

She squeezed his hand so hard, she all but cut off the

blood flow. Kade did his best to ignore the tears swimming in her eyes.

"That's…it's wonderful, isn't it?"

She sounded so damned hopeful he didn't want to burst her bubble. So how did he answer that? "There's something else, Pippa." Kade inhaled. "There's a real possibility they aren't your half-siblings. You might share the same father."

Pippa stared at him, confusion infiltrating her once hopeful expression. "The same father?"

"Yeah, sweetheart. And that's not all." *Like ripping off a Band-Aid*, he thought. "Your oldest sister. Her name is Marcia Rae."

Eighteen

"Wait. What?" Pippa felt bruised as she jumped out of the chair and lunged for the neat stack of papers Kade had meticulously built on the front edge of Cash's desk. She had a sister with the same name? A *full* sister? She couldn't comprehend any of this.

"Easy, ladybug." Kade intercepted her hands and blocked her from knocking the papers to the floor. He circled her waist with a strong arm and eased her against him.

Pippa collapsed in his arms, forgetting her anger toward him for a moment. He was here. He was warm and strong, and in this moment, she realized he *did* care about her. It wasn't love, but he wasn't just some Neanderthal beating his chest about names.

"Come sit on the couch, sweetheart. I'll bring the papers and you can read them. Okay?"

She allowed herself to be guided to the leather sofa and sank into its buttery softness. Pippa looked up at Kade. She didn't know what to do and that bothered her. She'd never been indecisive, but at present, she was so stunned she couldn't decide anything. Kade cupped her cheek in his palm.

"I'll be right back, ladybug. I want to make sure it's okay for us to stay here for a while."

Oh. She'd forgotten for a moment that she was in Cash's office. He probably had business to attend to and she was in the way. She was embarrassed that she was falling apart. Wrapping her arms around herself to stop her trembling, she nodded. She was in no shape to leave, and she was honest enough to admit that fact.

Kade dropped a soft kiss on her forehead, then strode across the room and disappeared into the outer office. Her shivering grew more pronounced. She had a mother. Sisters. Brothers. She maybe had a father—an unexpected fact given her original birth certificate. But why would her mother give her sister the same name as her? Why would her mother give her away yet have four other children with the man who might have impregnated her the first time?

Was she defective in some way that her mother recognized but that didn't show? Could she be so damaged her mother didn't want to keep her? She buried her face in her hands. She wanted to cry. Needed to cry. But she couldn't. All the tears stayed locked inside her, as did the sobs threatening but never manifesting. Pippa lifted her head and forced it back in a futile attempt to ease the tenseness in her neck and shoulders. She opened her eyes. The papers still waiting on the edge of Cash's desk drew her gaze like a powerful magnet.

She needed to read the words for herself. She should just stand up. Walk over there. Sit in that chair. Read every word in that report. But she didn't move. Couldn't move. She felt drained of all energy. Her initial excitement had deflated, flatlined and been replaced by a sense of dread. Marcia Rae. Her birth name. She'd just learned that's who she was—had been, she mentally corrected. For how long? How old had she been before her parents adopted her? The fact that another girl had her name shouldn't matter. But it did. It mattered a lot. And it hurt, the knowledge ripping through her heart like a dull knife hacking at her emotions.

Where was Kade? She really needed him here. His strength, his calm, she needed those desperately. Had he left the office so he could get away from her? She wouldn't blame him. She was an emotional wreck. What man would want to put up with a hormonal pregnant woman whose world had just dissolved around her? And yes, she could also admit, she was acting the drama queen. All things considered, she had the right to her meltdown.

Kade didn't want to leave Pippa alone for very long. He did want to get her a cup of tea. She needed something… normal, something routine, comforting. If he couldn't hold her, he'd give her something hot to drink because he couldn't think of anything else to do.

He stepped through the door to find not only Cash and Chance, but Cord had joined them as well. Kade pulled up short. He didn't need this whole brother triple-team thing, nor did he have time for their games and pretense at family solidarity.

"Is she okay?" Cord asked in a quiet voice, glancing toward the closed door. That's when Kade realized the other two were on their cell phones. All three men wore concerned expressions.

"Stand by, Chase," Cash said, looking expectantly at Kade.

"He just came out, Clay. I'll find out and call you back." Chance thumbed off his phone.

"Why are you all here?" Kade winced inwardly. He hadn't meant for his tone to sound so accusatory and defensive. Okay, maybe he had, but he was belatedly realizing that the Barrons were truly concerned about Pippa and her situation—and by extension, himself. He closed his eyes and lowered his head. After a few breaths, he straightened and faced them. "Look, I'm sorry. That was uncalled for."

Cord, who was standing the nearest, gripped Kade's shoulder. "S'okay, man. You're worried about your lady. And I'm pretty certain you're still trying to wrap your head around the whole family thing."

"We're here because we care, Kade," Cash cut in. "We may fight like junkyard dogs amongst ourselves, but if you come at one of us, you come at all of us." He lifted his shoulders in an apologetic shrug and added in a rueful tone, "I had to figure that out for myself."

Chance nodded his agreement. "We always have each other's backs, but that doesn't stop us from calling each other out when we've screwed up."

Kade noticed both Cord and Chance were staring at Cash who continued to look sheepish. The three looked so much alike, their family relationship was apparent but it was the real affection they showed that rocked him.

"Look, I just came out to see if I could get Pippa a cup of tea or something." Kade jammed his thumbs in his front pockets. "I don't even know if she likes hot tea. I just…" His voice trailed off.

"You need to do something for her," Chance filled in. "We get that. We've all been there."

"Hot tea coming up." Cash was quick to volunteer. "And there's a blanket—an afghan or something—behind the pillows on the far end of the couch. Roxie gets cold sometimes. Just in case."

"Whatever you need, Kade, whatever Pippa needs, we're here for you." Cord's hand still rested on his shoulder, and his brother gave another squeeze to show support.

It was as though a lightbulb went off in Kade's head. No, not a lightbulb, something more subtle, not as bright but just as warm…and enlightening. Family. Brothers. Love given with no strings attached. It was a revelation.

Kade glanced over his shoulder toward the office door. He wanted this same feeling with Pippa. No, not the same feeling. He wanted something more, something profound. He wanted a soul-deep connection to the woman who carried his child. And not just because of that. He wanted to love her because she was Pippa.

Cash returned with a lidded cup and several packets of sweetener. "I don't remember if she likes her tea hot either, but I do know she likes it sweet."

Kade's hand shook slightly as he reached for the cup. He stopped midgesture. Fisting and unfisting both hands, he took a moment to look at each one of his brothers. Doing so settled something in his chest, and his hand was now steady. "Thank you. All of you. For…everything."

Kade hoped they could hear and understand what he was really saying. Cord's hand tightened more. Chance and Cash both offered quick tucks of their chins and expressions that before this moment he would have found not only inscrutable but suspicious. Yeah, they understood, and wasn't that something?

Cash opened the door to his office but didn't look inside. He simply held it, and as Kade slipped through, he murmured, "We're here if and when you need us, bro. Chase and Clay will be on a plane in a heartbeat. All you have to do is ask."

The door snicked to a close behind him. Kade approached the couch warily. He held out the cup. "I thought maybe some hot tea…?"

Pippa's smile wavered a little and her eyes were moist but she accepted the cup and the sweetener packets. While she fixed the tea to her tastes, Kade located the afghan behind the pillows. It was soft and fluffy, and smelled faintly of dog. Roxanne wasn't the only one to use the blanket. Her dog Harley obviously liked it too. He shook it out and placed it over the back of the couch.

"You're taking care of me again."

He lifted a shoulder in a defensive movement then forced himself to relax. "Yeah, I guess I am. Do you mind?"

She didn't quite meet his eyes. "Feels rather nice at the moment. Thank you."

"You're welcome."

Her gaze skittered to Cash's desk, the cup nestled in her hand forgotten. "Okay. Let's get this over with."

As he crossed the large office, Kade couldn't help but glance at the door. His brothers stood just on the other side. He almost stumbled as that weird sense of acceptance washed over him again. Why had he been fighting them all this time? He needed to do his own soul searching once Pippa's crisis was resolved. But today and the months to come were about her. His issues could wait.

Kade snagged the papers and all but marched back to the couch. He handed them to her and then, without asking, settled next to her and draped an arm around her shoulders. She leaned into him with a little sigh. She held up the first page and started reading.

Unlike when he'd scanned the report, Pippa read each line with deliberation. He watched her closely, squeezing her shoulders when she paled, backing slightly away when she jutted her chin with determination.

"She married two months after I was born," she whispered.

He didn't respond as she kept reading. Kade knew what was coming. Almost one year to the day after Pippa's birth, her sister Marcia Rae was born.

Pippa sucked in a breath and stiffened. Her hand shook so hard the papers she held rattled. When she finally spoke, she sounded broken. "It's like my mother just erased me. Like I never existed." Her eyes sought him, and he cupped her cheek in one hand, using his thumb to brush away the tears that had escaped. "How could she do that?"

Unable to stand it any longer, Kade retrieved the papers and set them on the coffee table. Then he scooped her up and settled her on his lap. She tucked her head against his shoulder and her tears flowed freely. Holding her, he rubbed his chin across the top of her head, dropping occasional kisses on her hair. And he waited until the storm of her hurt ebbed a little.

"I won't ever do that to my baby." Given the tears, her voice was remarkably strong as she made the vow.

"No, ladybug. You would never do that to our baby."

She pushed away so she could look at him. Her eyes still shimmered with unshed tears so he shifted slightly in order to reach his back pocket. He pulled out his bandanna and handed it to her. She wiped her eyes and dabbed at her nose but continued to look at him. She finally said, "I'm sorry, Kade."

Confused, he considered what she could possibly be apologizing for. Unable to figure it out, he asked, "What for?"

"For what I said about names not meaning anything. I was wrong." A little laugh that held a hint of hysteria escaped her. "*So* wrong. You were right. Names do have power. I mean, look at me. I didn't even know what my birth name was until two months ago. But after thinking about it, I knew it was *my* name. For some brief period of time, I was Marcia Rae Gore. I didn't know who that person was, or who she might have been, but I was settling into the idea that she was me at one time."

She paused to blow her nose and made an I'm-sorry-for-being-gross face at him. "And now, I discover there's another me. Who isn't me. She's my sister. It's like I never existed, even for that brief moment between birth and being named and my adoption when I became Pippa."

A tear tipped over her lashes and she brushed at it with the back of her hand. "Anyway, I understand now why you were so upset when you found out that you were a Barron. And I'm sorry for getting mad at you for doing the name change. I had no right."

Kade hugged her gently. "Shh, sweetheart. It's okay."

"No it's not."

He worked to stop the grin tugging at his mouth. "Are we going to fight over that now?"

She shook her head vehemently. "No. It was a stupid thing to fight over. I'd blame it on hormones, but I don't want to be a Pregzilla."

The tight knot in his chest that had started to loosen with his realization about his brothers all but unraveled. He really cared about Pippa and he wanted the chance to make a life with her, to become a real family.

"You? Hormonal?" He smiled and dropped a kiss on her forehead. "Never."

The next thing he knew, she was plastered to his chest, her arms around his neck. "Will you help me, Kade?"

He rubbed her back, gratified that her voice hadn't caught and no sobs shook her body. "Of course I will. Whatever you need. Always."

She pushed back a second time, her expression determined. "I want to see her. Them. I want to see my mother and my sister."

Nineteen

Pippa stared at Kade's profile. Even before she'd walked away, she hadn't told him about her search. Instead of getting angry because she'd shut him out, he'd promised to help. And here he was, strong and sure, and ready to be her…her…whatever she needed him to be. And she definitely needed him, as they drove east toward the town where her mother lived.

She wasn't mad at him any longer. That feeling had quickly faded, overwhelmed by all the other emotions swamping her. At this point, she was no longer sure what she felt—except mostly numb. She'd been in a fog almost a month. Learning her sister, born barely a year after her, had the same name had hurt on a level she never before had experienced. It was as if she'd never existed. Or she'd been thrown away because she was defective. It left her broken with sharp slivers of pain slicing into her heart every time she thought about it.

And Kade had been there. He'd held her in his arms as she wept, even when she didn't know why the hot tears wouldn't stop. He didn't complain. And he'd stopped asking her to marry him. She wasn't sure how she felt about that now. He still hadn't given her the words. Not that she had any reason to complain. She hadn't offered an *I love you* to him either.

Turning away, she watched the mile markers zip past on I-40. Among all the shocks she'd received, the fact her birth family had been in Shawnee the whole time she was growing up was the one she focused on. Forty miles away. Her mother and siblings had been no farther than an hour's drive.

The past month had chafed at her. Cash and Chance had both ganged up on her and counseled caution. She hadn't listened until Carrie weighed in with the advice that Pippa would always wonder if she didn't meet the woman, that the not knowing would eat at her. Her best friend had never steered her wrong.

She'd waited another two weeks before asking Kade to accompany her. Pippa had considered driving herself but she was really showing now and got tired easily. Dr. Long kept telling her it was nothing to worry about but fear always crouched in the back of her mind. Warmth enveloped her hand and she looked down. Kade had wrapped his fingers around hers, his work-roughened skin familiar and soothing. Overloaded hormones or not, she was in love with Kade. He'd stepped up to be the responsible one. He'd been patient. And his actions showed how he felt. He might not have words to give her, but she'd bet there was love in his heart.

"Ask me again," she said. She snapped her mouth shut. What in the world was she thinking? Wasn't she glad he'd stopped badgering her about marriage? She wasn't ready for that step.

Kade ignored her while he flicked on the turn signal and changed lanes for the Shawnee exit. Maybe he hadn't heard. Maybe he didn't understand. Maybe he didn't want to embarrass her by saying he'd changed his mind. They could co-parent without being married. Hadn't she advocated for that very thing? Hadn't she demanded he admit out loud that he loved her? She no longer knew. Just as well he hadn't responded.

Following the directions from the navigation system, Kade drove them toward their destination. He squeezed her hand. "Breathe, ladybug. You got this."

Pippa shook her head. "No. I don't. What am I doing, Kade? How can I walk up to her and introduce myself? What do I say? Hello, I'm the other Marcia Rae. The one you gave away. The one you didn't love enough to keep."

Tears flowed as Kade suddenly veered into a parking lot. He was out of the truck and around to the passenger door in a flash. A moment later, she was in his arms. He smoothed a hand down her back, kissed her temple, made soothing noises.

"Shh, baby. We'll get through this. I'm here. Always. Never gonna leave you."

She knew then. Knew that if he did ask her to marry him again, she would say yes.

Kade should have released Pippa's hand so he could drive with both hands but he didn't. Tension rolled off her in waves and he worried. It couldn't be good for the baby and there was always the chance of her intense emotions triggering a migraine. She'd been so careful with medications during the pregnancy.

He turned onto the street where Pip's birth mother lived and slowly drove toward the address. There were cars parked there and people stood in the front yard. He pulled to the curb where they could watch but not be noticed. Pippa's face drained of color.

"Pip?"

"That…is that woman my mother? She doesn't look anything like me. Neither do those other people. This must be the wrong address."

A teenage boy and girl, probably fourteen and sixteen respectively, looked bored. Another boy and girl appeared to be college age, the girl maybe a bit older. They all had brown hair, as did the woman. The truck wasn't parked close enough that they could discern eye color or the finer nuances of the family's features. A man came out of the house and Pippa gasped. His blond hair, worn long and shaggy, was the exact shade of hers and there was a familiarity to the shape of his face. Kade had no doubt that Pippa's mother had married her birth father and had more children with him. The thought they'd thrown Pippa away burned in his gut.

"Let's go." Pippa's voice was so quiet and small he almost didn't hear her. "This isn't my family."

Turning toward her, worried that she was in denial, Kade was surprised by the fierce determination on her face. He put the truck in Reverse and backed into an empty driveway. Pippa's mother looked up, stared, and he knew the moment the woman recognized her daughter. She extended her hand, took several steps toward the truck, and then Kade pulled into the street and drove away.

Pippa remained silent as they headed west on I-40, leaving Shawnee behind. Kade watched her as much as he could and still pay attention to traffic. Her color hadn't returned and he recognized the signs of pain pinching her features. He glanced down, realized her hands were pressed against her rounded abdomen.

"Ladybug?" He had to work to keep his voice calm.

"Something's not right," she whispered.

Kade—calm, cool, collected Kade—panicked. He was hitting ninety miles per hour when he hit Midwest City on the east side of the metro area. He didn't slow down when an Oklahoma state trooper pulled in behind him with lights and sirens. He dialed *55, connected to the highway patrol dispatch and explained the situation. The trooper pulled around him and led the way to University Hospital's Trauma One. Kade also alerted Savannah. He had her on speed dial.

He stopped at the ER doors and they were met by a gurney and nurses. He made it around to the passenger side just as someone grabbed his arm. He shook off the grip even as his brain registered who had touched him and what she was saying. Jolie. Cord's wife and an ER nurse.

"Breathe, Kade. We've got her." She glanced toward the approaching trooper. "You deal with her then come inside. I'll get the information we need." She squeezed his arm and followed the gurney.

"That was some fancy driving there, slick."

He didn't have time for this. "Just write me the ticket, Trooper—" He glanced at the nameplate on the woman's uniform. "—Kincaid. I need to get inside."

"How far along is she?" The trooper's voice softened and she sounded sincerely concerned.

"Not far enough." His voice echoed the bleakness in his soul.

"Normally, I would lecture you that the smart thing would have been to stop and call an ambulance but while you were driving fast, you were in complete control. No ticket. Get in there with your wife."

The trooper's assumption made his chest hurt. Pippa wasn't his wife. Not yet. But she would be. "Thanks, ma'am."

She smiled. "Quincy. Quincy Kincaid. Ma'am makes me feel old."

Twenty minutes later, the ER was full of Barrons. Clay and Georgie were the only ones missing. They were back in Washington but Clay had called and told Kade they'd come if he asked. Overwhelmed, he didn't resist when Savvie took his phone. His attention was glued to the swinging doors separating the waiting area from the ER exam rooms. Savvie sat next to him, their shoulders brushing. The rest of the clan stood or sat in groups around the room.

When the doctor arrived, everyone surged to their feet but only Savvie walked with Kade to meet Dr. Long and Jolie. Savvie squeezed his hand as the doctor spoke.

"Mom is going to be fine. The baby decided to wait a while longer to make an appearance." Dr. Long looked him up and down. "You're the father."

"Yes." He didn't apologize for growling the word.

"I want to keep her overnight just to be safe. She'll need lots of bed rest between now and January. My office will send you a list of do's and don'ts. C'mon back."

When he followed the doctor into the trauma room, the first thing he noticed was how pale and scared Pippa looked lying against the sheet covering the exam table. He wanted to scoop her into his arms, hug her, kiss her. He settled for sitting next to her and holding her hand. She squeezed his.

"We're gonna be okay. The baby and me."

"I know."

"I didn't mean to scare you."

Kade breathed out, made sure his hand remained gentle while wrapped around hers. "I can't lose you, Pippa. Can't lose our baby. Do you understand that?" She stared up at him but didn't reply. "Marry me. Marry me as soon as we can arrange it. If you hadn't asked for me, I wouldn't be here. I have no rights, not unless I'm your husband. Please, Pippa—" His voice broke. "Please marry me. I love you."

"Yes."

He looked up, unaware that he'd dropped his head

until she spoke. "What did you say?" Had he really heard correctly?

She smiled. "Yes. I'll marry you."

Nurses arrived to get her ready for transfer to a private room and they shooed him out, but not before he kissed her.

When he walked back into the waiting area, he was immediately mobbed. He explained the doctor's orders and then Savvie hugged him tightly before facing the others. "I can tell by that big goofy grin he's wearing Pippa finally said yes."

He was overwhelmed by congratulations, hugs, thumps on his back, and it seemed that everyone was talking at once. Carrie had arrived while he was with Pippa and she whistled sharply. The noise level dropped immediately.

"All right then," Carrie commanded. "Ladies, we have a wedding to plan."

Kade started to object but Carrie cut him off. "I've been her BFF since we were five. I know exactly what kind of wedding she wants. And we're having it at the Crown B." She glowered at everyone. "Any problems with that?" No one dared disagree.

If he'd had his way, they would have been married at the courthouse on the way home from the hospital. His sisters-in-law and Carrie called him blasphemous. Today, as he stood in the backyard of the big house at the Crown B, he was glad the women had overruled him. A glowing and very pregnant Pippa approached him on Big John's arm. Family and friends surrounded them on this perfect November day. Pippa's eyes reflected the brilliant blue sky and her golden hair fell in loose waves around her face. Her gown was simple and appealed to Kade on an elemental level.

His mother, Rose, stood with Miz Beth. Both women

were beaming. He wished his grandparents could have been there. William and Ramona had played a big role in his life. Bill was gone and advance Alzheimer's kept Ramona hospitalized.

The scare over the baby had Pippa cracking open a door for her parents. She'd relented and they were here for the marriage ceremony, though Pippa didn't want David Duncan to walk her down the aisle. She hadn't forgiven them that much yet.

Big John placed Pippa's hand in Kade's and they turned to face Judge Nelligan. Words were said, vows given and accepted. When the judge called for the rings, Kade turned to Clay. He didn't have a best man—he had five. CJ, Cord's son, and now Kade's nephew, acted as ring bearer. The boy handed the ring to Cash, who stood at the end of the line. The ring passed from brother to brother in birth order until Clay handed it to Kade.

Pippa didn't have all that fanfare. Carrie merely took the ring off her thumb and placed it on Pippa's palm. Once the rings were exchanged, the judge pronounced them husband and wife. They kissed to a round of cheers and Kade swept Pippa up in his arms to carry her into the house. He intended for her to sit for the duration of their reception. CJ escorted Carrie, much to the kid's embarrassment, and each of Kade's brothers fell in behind with their wives.

Life was good. He and Pippa would have Thanksgiving, Christmas and the New Year, then they would welcome their baby into the world. Life couldn't get much better than this. Kade had everything he'd ever wanted—and a lot he'd never dared hope for.

"Hello, Mrs. Barron."

"Hi there, Mr. Barron."

And that name didn't sound so unfamiliar after all.

Epilogue

Kade didn't panic. He'd carefully timed Pippa's contractions. They had plenty of time to get to the birthing center in Oklahoma City. The snow from the storm the previous week had melted. The roads were clear. Once the truck hit the interstate, he kept the speed at a steady five miles over the speed limit. As promised, he'd started what Cassie called the Family Phone Tree, a phrase she always placed in air quotes.

"Babies never come at convenient times," Pippa groused.

"Where's the fun in that? Savvie was gloating about waking everyone." He squeezed her hand. "You doing okay?"

She nodded, winced, caught her breath and squeezed his hand. Hard. He nudged the speed up a little. "Almost there, ladybug. And since it's three in the morning, no traffic. That's good."

When he pulled up at the birthing center, the whole group was already gathered. Cash grabbed his keys. Cord grabbed Pippa's bag. Within minutes, Pippa was checked in and settled in a suite. Dr. Long arrived shortly after and while she was examining Pippa, Kade stepped out. He was met in the waiting room by a group of smiling faces and Savvie holding out a cup of hot black coffee.

"Don't even try to tell us to go home. Not happenin', big bro. And I've called your mom. Rose is on her way."

The lump in his throat almost choked him as he looked around at his brothers, his sisters. And he knew. He truly was a Barron. And that was a good thing.

Kade stared at the red-faced baby in Pippa's arms. After eight hours of labor, the birth had been relatively easy. *Relatively* being the operative word. His heart was ready to burst out of his chest. "I am so proud of you, sweetheart."

Pippa beamed at him then gazed at their daughter. "We did good, didn't we?"

"No ladybug, *you* did. I just stood here and got in the way."

She laughed and he breathed easier. Watching their daughter come into the world had been life changing. He'd helped birth foals and calves and always marveled at the miracle of birth and life, but until he cut the umbilical cord on their baby? He'd had no idea how profoundly it would affect him. Nor did he know how deep his capacity to love would become. He loved Pippa and their baby with his whole heart. No, he loved them with his entire being. He claimed both of them then and there. Forever.

One of the nurses appeared on the other side of the bed. "She has a ten Apgar score, which is perfect. What are you going to name her?"

Pippa gazed up at him. "I want to name her Ruth, for my grandmother."

"Whatever you want, ladybug." Kade barely got the words out.

"And Ramona for yours."

Moisture in his eyes blinded him as he slipped his arm beneath her, cradling his wife and their child. "She's beautiful. And perfect, our Ruth Ramona," he murmured against Pippa's temple. "Just like her mother."

Then the horde came, wanting to see baby Ruth, to congratulate. Brothers and sisters-in-law. Cousins. Even Pippa's parents, who were clutching a fuzzy teddy bear and flowers. Clay eventually drew Kade out into the hallway where all his brothers had gathered.

"We need to talk, Kade." Clay looked somber.

"What's wrong?"

"Nothing," Cord answered. "We just want you to know that the ranch truly is yours."

"And that includes the big house," Chance added.

Chase grinned at him. "We want someone living there who loves it like we did. Who will make the big house a home again."

"It's built for kids and family gatherings. Which means you're stuck with Thanksgiving and Christmas from now on," Cash chimed in.

Kade eventually got a word in edgewise. "What about Big John and Miz Beth? They—"

Chase cut him off. "Whose idea do you think this is? They want something small and cozy."

"But where will they go?"

Cord thumped him on the back. "They've already gone. About a quarter of a mile away. We moved your stuff into the big house and their belongings into the manager's. Even trade."

"We're family, Kade. You. Pippa. Baby Ruth. All of us," the brothers said in unison.

Kade was a simple man and he'd discovered what was important. His wife. His baby girl. His brothers. Family. He'd found and claimed his in the most unlikely of places. And he was a happy man because of it.

* * * * *

*Don't miss any of these cowgirl romances
from Silver James*

**COWGIRLS DON'T CRY
THE COWGIRL'S LITTLE SECRET
THE BOSS AND HIS COWGIRL
CONVENIENT COWGIRL BRIDE
REDEEMED BY THE COWGIRL**

Available now from Mills & Boon Desire!

MILLS & BOON®

Desire™

PASSIONATE AND DRAMATIC LOVE STORIES

Just can't wait?
Buy our books online before they hit the shops!
www.millsandboon.co.uk

Also available as eBooks.

MILLS & BOON®

Why shop at millsandboon.co.uk?

Each year, thousands of romance readers
find their perfect read at millsandboon.co.uk.
That's because we're passionate about
bringing you the very best romantic fiction.
Here are some of the advantages of
shopping at www.millsandboon.co.uk:

* **Get new books first**—you'll be able to buy
  your favourite books one month before they
  hit the shops

* **Get exclusive discounts**—you'll also be
  able to buy our specially created monthly
  collections, with up to 50% off the RRP

* **Find your favourite authors**—latest news,
  interviews and new releases for all your
  favourite authors and series on our website,
  plus ideas for what to try next

* **Join in**—once you've bought your favourite
  books, don't forget to register with us to rate,
  review and join in the discussions

Visit **www.millsandboon.co.uk**
for all this and more today!